# The White Queen

*By the same author*

*The Wideacre Trilogy*
Wideacre
The Favoured Child
Meridon

*Historical Novels*
The Wise Woman
Fallen Skies
A Respectable Trade
Earthly Joys
Virgin Earth

*Modern Novels*
Mrs Hartley and the Growth Centre
Perfectly Correct
The Little House
Zelda's Cut

*Short Stories*
Bread and Chocolate

*The Tudor Court Novels*
The Other Queen
The Other Boleyn Girl
The Queen's Fool
The Virgin's Lover
The Constant Princess
The Boleyn Inheritance

*The Cousins' War*

# The White Queen

PHILIPPA GREGORY

SIMON & SCHUSTER

London · New York · Sydney · Toronto

A CBS COMPANY

First published in Great Britain by Simon & Schuster UK Ltd, 2009
A CBS COMPANY



1 3 5 7 9 10 8 6 4 2

Simon & Schuster UK Ltd
1st Floor
222 Gray's Inn Road
London
WC1X 8HB

www.simonandschuster.co.uk

Simon & Schuster Australia
Sydney

A CIP catalogue record for this book
is available from the British Library

ISBN HB 978-184737-455-4
ISBN TPB 978-184737-456-1

Typeset by M Rules
Printed in the UK by CPI Mackays, Chatham ME5 8TD

For Anthony

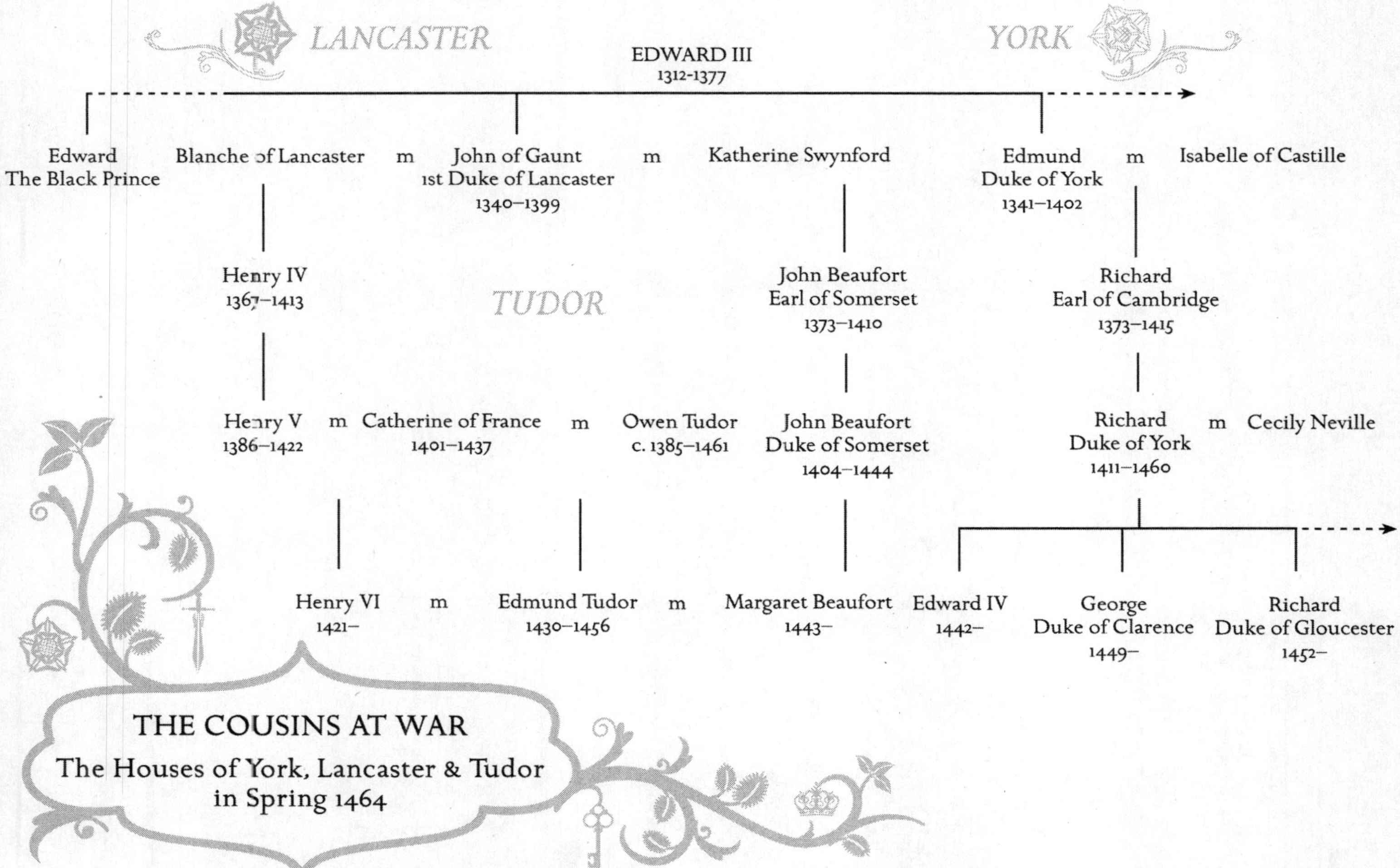
LANCASTER
YORK
EDWARD III
1312-1377
Edward
The Black Prince
Blanche of Lancaster
m
John of Gaunt
1st Duke of Lancaster
1340–1399
m
Katherine Swynford
Edmund
Duke of York
1341–1402
m
Isabelle of Castille
Henry IV
1367–1413
TUDOR
John Beaufort
Earl of Somerset
1373–1410
Richard
Earl of Cambridge
1373–1415
Henry V
1386–1422
m
Catherine of France
1401–1437
m
Owen Tudor
c. 1385–1461
John Beaufort
Duke of Somerset
1404–1444
Richard
Duke of York
1411–1460
m
Cecily Neville
Henry VI
1421–
m
Edmund Tudor
1430–1456
m
Margaret Beaufort
1443–
Edward IV
1442–
George
Duke of Clarence
1449–
Richard
Duke of Gloucester
1452–
THE COUSINS AT WAR
The Houses of York, Lancaster & Tudor
in Spring 1464

*In the darkness of the forest the young knight could hear the splashing of the fountain long before he could see the glimmer of moonlight reflected on the still surface. He was about to step forward, longing to dip his head, drink in the coolness, when he caught his breath at the sight of something dark, moving deep in the water. There was a greenish shadow in the sunken bowl of the fountain, something like a great fish, something like a drowned body. Then it moved and stood upright and he saw, frighteningly naked: a bathing woman. Her skin as she rose up, water coursing down her flanks, was even paler than the white marble bowl, her wet hair dark as a shadow.*

*She is Melusina, the water goddess, and she is found in hidden springs and waterfalls in any forest in Christendom, even in those as far away as Greece. She bathes in the Moorish fountains too. They know her by another name in the northern countries where the lakes are glazed with ice and it crackles when she rises. A man may love her if he keeps her secret and lets her alone when she wants to bathe, and she may love him in return until he breaks his word, as men always do, and she sweeps him into the deeps with her fishy tail, and turns his faithless blood to water.*

*The tragedy of Melusina, whatever language tells it, whatever tune it sings, is that a man will always promise more than he can do to a woman he cannot understand.*

# SPRING 1464

My father is Sir Richard Woodville, Baron Rivers, an English nobleman, a landholder and a supporter of the true kings of England, the Lancastrian line. My mother descends from the Dukes of Burgundy and so carries the watery blood of the goddess Melusina, who founded their royal house with her entranced ducal lover, and can still be met at times of extreme trouble, crying a warning over the castle rooftops when the son and heir is dying and the family doomed. Or so they say, those who believe in such things.

With this contradictory parentage of mine: solid English earth and French water goddess, one could expect anything from me: an enchantress, or an ordinary girl. There are those who will say I am both. But today, as I comb my hair with particular care and arrange it under my tallest headdress, take the hands of my two fatherless boys and lead the way to the road that goes to Northampton, I would give all that I am to be, just this once, simply irresistible.

I have to attract the attention of a young man riding out to yet another battle, against an enemy that cannot be defeated. He may not even see me. He is not likely to be in the mood for beggars or flirts. I have to excite his compassion for my position, inspire his sympathy for my needs, and stay in his memory long enough for him to do something about them both. And this is a man who has beautiful women flinging themselves at him every night of the week, and a hundred claimants for every post in his gift.

He is a usurper and a tyrant, my enemy and the son of my enemy, but I am far beyond loyalty to anyone but my sons and myself. My own father rode out to the battle of Towton against this man who now calls himself King of England, though he is little more than a braggart boy; and I have never seen a man as broken as my father when he came home from Towton, his sword arm bleeding through his jacket, his face white, saying that this boy is a commander such as we have never seen before, and our cause is lost, and we are all without hope while he lives. Twenty thousand men were cut down at Towton at this boy's command: no one had ever seen such death before in England. My father said it was a harvest of Lancastrians, not a battle. The rightful King Henry and his wife, Queen Margaret of Anjou, fled to Scotland, devastated by the deaths.

Those of us left in England did not surrender readily. The battles went on and on to resist the false king, this boy of York. My own husband was killed commanding our cavalry, only three years ago at St Albans. And now I am left a widow and what land and fortune I once called my own has been taken by my mother-in-law with the goodwill of the victor, the master of this boy-king, the great puppeteer who is known as the Kingmaker: Richard Neville, Earl of Warwick, who made a king out of this vain boy, now only twenty-two, and will make a hell out of England for those of us who still defend the House of Lancaster.

There are Yorkists in every great house in the land now, and every profitable business or place or tax is in their gift. Their boy-king is on the throne and his supporters form the new court. We, the defeated, are paupers in our own houses and strangers in our own country, our king an exile, our queen a vengeful alien plotting with our old enemy of France. We have to make terms with the tyrant of York, while praying that God turns against him and our true king sweeps south with an army for yet another battle.

In the meantime, like many a woman with a husband dead and

a father defeated, I have to piece my life together like a patchwork of scraps. I have to regain my fortune somehow, though it seems that neither kinsman nor friend can make any headway for me. We are all known as traitors. We are forgiven but not beloved. We are all powerless. I shall have to be my own advocate, and make my own case to a boy who respects justice so little that he would dare to take an army against his own cousin: a king ordained. What can one say to such a savage that he could understand?

My boys, Thomas, who is nine, and Richard, who is eight, are dressed in their best, their hair wetted and smoothed down, their faces shining from soap. I have tight hold of their hands as they stand on either side of me, for these are true boys and they draw dirt to them as if by magic. If I let them go for a second then one will scuff his shoes and the other rip his hose, and both of them will manage to get leaves in their hair and mud on their faces and Thomas will certainly fall in the stream. As it is, anchored by my grip, they hop from one leg to another in an agony of boredom, and only straighten up when I say, 'Hush, I can hear horses.'

It sounds like the patter of rain at first, and then in a moment a rumble like thunder. The jingle of the harness and the flutter of the standards, the chink of the chain mail and the blowing of the horses, the sound and the smell and the roar of a hundred horses ridden hard is overwhelming and, even though I am determined to stand out and make them stop, I can't help but shrink back. What must it be to face these men riding down in battle with their lances outstretched before them, like a galloping wall of staves? How could any man face it?

Thomas sees the bare blond head in the midst of all the fury and noise and shouts, 'Hurrah!' like the boy he is, and at the shout of his treble voice I see the man's head turn, and he sees me and the boys and his hand snatches the reins and he bellows, 'Halt!' His horse stands up on its rear legs, wrenched to a standstill, and the whole cavalcade wheels and halts and swears at the sudden stop, and then abruptly everything is silent and the dust billows around us.

His horse blows out, shakes its head, but the rider is like a statue on its high back. He is looking at me and I at him, and it is so quiet that I can hear a thrush in the branches of the oak above me. How it sings. My God, it sings like a ripple of glory, like joy made into sound. I have never heard a bird sing like that before, as if it were carolling happiness.

I step forward, still holding my sons' hands, and I open my mouth to plead my case, but at this moment, this crucial moment, I have lost my words. I have practised well enough. I had a little speech all prepared; but now I have nothing. And it is almost as if I need no words. I just look at him and somehow I expect him to understand everything – my fear of the future and my hopes for these my boys, my lack of money and the irritable pity of my father which makes living under his roof so unbearable to me, the coldness of my bed at night, and my longing for another child, my sense that my life is over. Dear God, I am only twenty-seven, my cause is defeated, my husband is dead. Am I to be one of many poor widows who will spend the rest of their days at someone else's fireside trying to be a good guest? Shall I never be kissed again? Shall I never feel joy? Not ever again?

And still the bird sings as if to say that delight is easy, for those who desire it.

He makes a gesture with his hand to the older man at his side and the man barks out a command and the soldiers turn their horses off the road and go into the shade of the trees. But the king jumps down from his great horse, drops the reins and walks towards me and my boys. I am a tall woman but he overtops me by a head; he must be far more than six feet tall. My boys crane their necks up to see him; he is a giant to them. He is blond-haired, grey-eyed, with a tanned, open, smiling face, rich with charm, easy with grace. This is a king as we have never seen before in England: this is a man that the people will love on sight. And his eyes are fixed on my face as if I know a secret that he has to have, as if we have known each other for ever, and I can feel my cheeks are burning but I cannot look away from him.

A modest woman looks down in this world, keeps her eyes on her slippers; a supplicant bows low and stretches out a pleading hand; but I stand tall, I am aghast at myself, staring like an ignorant peasant, and find I cannot take my eyes from his, from his smiling mouth, from his gaze, which is burning on my face.

'Who is this?' he asks, still looking at me.

'Your Grace, this is my mother, Lady Elizabeth Grey,' my son Thomas says politely, and he pulls off his cap and drops to his knee.

Richard on my other side kneels too and mutters, as if he cannot be heard, 'Is this the king? Really? He is the tallest man I have ever seen in my life!'

I sink down into a curtsey but I cannot look away. Instead, I gaze up at him, as a woman might stare with hot eyes at a man she adores.

'Rise up,' he says. His voice is low, for only me to hear. 'Have you come to see me?'

'I need your help,' I say. I can hardly form the words. I feel as if the love potion, which my mother soaked into the scarf billowing from my headdress, is drugging me, not him. 'I cannot obtain my dowry lands, my jointure, now I am widowed.' I stumble in the face of his smiling interest. 'I am a widow now. I have nothing to live on.'

'A widow?'

'My husband was Sir John Grey. He died at St Albans,' I say. It is to confess his treason and the damnation of my sons. The king will recognise the name of the commander of his enemy's cavalry. I nip my lip. 'Their father did his duty as he conceived it to be, Your Grace; he was loyal to the man he thought was king. My boys are innocent of anything.'

'He left you these two sons?' He smiles down at my boys.

'The best part of my fortune,' I say. 'This is Richard and this is Thomas Grey.'

He nods at my boys, who gaze up at him as if he were some kind of high-bred horse, too big for them to pet but a figure for awestruck admiration, and then he looks back to me. 'I am thirsty,' he says. 'Is your home near here?'

'We would be honoured . . .' I glance at the guard who rides with him. There must be more than a hundred of them. He chuckles. 'They can ride on,' he decides. 'Hastings!' The older man turns and waits. 'You go on to Grafton. I will catch you up. Smollett can stay with me, and Forbes. I will come in an hour or so.'

Sir William Hastings looks me up and down as if I am a pretty piece of ribbon for sale. I show him a hard stare in reply, and he takes off his hat and bows to me, throws a salute to the king, shouts to the guard to mount up.

'Where are you going?' he asks the king.

The boy-king looks at me.

'We are going to the house of my father, Baron Rivers, Sir Richard Woodville,' I say proudly, though I know the king will recognise the name of a man who was high in the favour of the Lancaster court, fought for them, and once took hard words from him in person when York and Lancaster were daggers drawn. We all know of each other well enough, but it is a courtesy generally observed to forget that we were all loyal to Henry VI once, until these turned traitor.

Sir William raises his eyebrow at his king's choice for a stopping place. 'Then I doubt that you'll want to stay very long,' he says unpleasantly, and rides on. The ground shakes as they go by, and they leave us in warm quietness as the dust settles.

'My father has been forgiven and his title restored,' I say defensively. 'You forgave him yourself after Towton.'

'I remember your father and your mother,' the king says equably. 'I have known them since I was a boy in good times and bad. I am only surprised that they never introduced me to you.'

I have to stifle a giggle. This is a king notorious for seduction. Nobody with any sense would let their daughter meet him. 'Would you like to come this way?' I ask. 'It is a little walk to my father's house.'

'D'you want a ride, boys?' he asks them. Their heads bob up

like imploring ducklings. 'You can both go up,' he says and lifts Richard and then Thomas into the saddle. 'Now hold tight. You on to your brother and you – Thomas, is it? – you hold on to the pommel.'

He loops the rein over his arm and then offers me his other arm, and so we walk to my home, through the wood, under the shade of the trees. I can feel the warmth of his arm through the slashed fabric of his sleeve. I have to stop myself leaning towards him. I look ahead to the house and to my mother's window and see, from the little movement behind the mullioned panes of glass, that she has been looking out, and willing this very thing to happen.

She is at the front door as we approach, the groom of the household at her side. She curtseys low. 'Your Grace,' she says pleasantly, as if the king comes to visit every day. 'You are very welcome to Grafton Manor.'

A groom comes running and takes the reins of the horse to lead it to the stable yard. My boys cling on for the last few yards, as my mother steps back and bows the king into the hall. 'Will you take a glass of small ale?' she asks. 'Or we have a very good wine from my cousins in Burgundy?'

'I'll take the ale, if you please,' he says agreeably. 'It is thirsty work riding. It is hot for spring. Good day to you, Lady Rivers.'

The high table in the great hall is laid with the best glasses and a jug of ale as well as the wine. 'You are expecting company?' he asks.

She smiles at him. 'There is no man in the world could ride past my daughter,' she says. 'When she told me she wanted to put her own case to you, I had them draw the best of our ale. I guessed you would stop.'

He laughs at her pride, and turns to smile at me, 'Indeed, it would be a blind man who could ride past you,' he says.

I am about to make some little comment but again it happens. Our eyes meet and I can think of nothing to say to him. We just stand, staring at each other for a long moment until my mother passes him a glass and says quietly, 'Good health, Your Grace.'

He shakes his head, as if awakened. 'And is your father here?' he asks.

'Sir Richard has ridden over to see our neighbours,' I say. 'We expect him back for his dinner.'

My mother takes a clean glass and holds it up to the light and tuts as if there is some flaw. 'Excuse me,' she says, and leaves. The king and I are alone in the great hall, the sun pouring through the big window behind the long table, the house in silence, as if everyone is holding their breath and listening.

He goes behind the table and sits down in the master's chair. 'Please sit,' he says and gestures to the chair beside him. I sit as if I am his queen, on his right hand, and I let him pour me a glass of small ale. 'I will look into your claim for your lands,' he says. 'Do you want your own house? Are you not happy living here with your mother and father?'

'They are kind to me,' I say. 'But I am used to my own household, I am accustomed to running my own lands. And my sons will have nothing if I cannot reclaim their father's lands. It is their inheritance. I must defend my sons.'

'These have been hard times,' he says. 'But if I can keep my throne, I will see the law of the land running from one coast of England to another once more, and your boys will grow up without fear of warfare.'

I nod my head.

'Are you loyal to King Henry?' he asks me. 'D'you follow your family as loyal Lancastrians?'

Our history cannot be denied. I know that there was a furious quarrel in Calais between this king, then nothing more than a young York son, and my father, then one of the great Lancastrian lords. My mother was the first lady at the court of Margaret of Anjou; she must have met and patronised the handsome young son of York a dozen times. But who would have known then that the world might turn upside down and that the daughter of Baron Rivers would have to plead to that very boy for her own lands to be restored to her? 'My mother and father were very great at the court of King Henry, but my family and I accept your rule now,' I say quickly.

He smiles. 'Sensible of you all, since I won,' he says. 'I accept your homage.'

I give a little giggle and at once his face warms. 'It must be over soon, please God,' he says. 'Henry has nothing more than a handful of castles in lawless northern country. He can muster brigands like any outlaw; but he cannot raise a decent army. And his queen cannot go on and on bringing in the country's enemies to fight her own people. Those who fight for me will be rewarded, but even those who have fought against me will see that I shall be just in victory. And I will make my rule run, even to the north of England, even through their strongholds, up to the very border of Scotland.'

'Do you go to the north now?' I ask. I take a sip of small ale. It is my mother's best but there is a tang behind it; she will have added some drops of a tincture, a love philtre, something to make desire grow. I need nothing. I am breathless already.

'We need peace,' he says. 'Peace with France, peace with the Scots, and peace from brother to brother, cousin to cousin. Henry must surrender; his wife has to stop bringing in French troops to fight against Englishmen. We should not be divided any more, York against Lancaster: we should all be Englishmen. There is nothing that sickens a country more than its own people fighting against one another. It destroys families, it is killing us daily. This has to end; and I will end it. I will end it this year.'

I feel the sick fear that the people of this country have known for nearly a decade. 'There must be another battle?'

He smiles. 'I shall try to keep it from your door, my lady. But it must be done and it must be done soon. I pardoned the Duke of Somerset and took him into my friendship and now he has run away to Henry once more, a Lancastrian turncoat, faithless like all the Beauforts. The Percys are raising the north against me.

They hate the Nevilles and the Neville family are my greatest allies. It is like a dance now: the dancers are in their place, they have to do their steps. They will have a battle, it cannot be avoided.'

'The queen's army will come this way?' Though my mother loved her and was the first of her ladies, I have to say that her army is a force of absolute terror. Mercenaries, who care nothing for the country, Frenchmen who hate us, and the savage men of the north of England who see our fertile fields and prosperous towns as good for nothing but plunder. Last time she brought in the Scots on the agreement that anything they stole they could keep as their fee. She might as well have hired wolves.

'I shall stop them,' he says simply. 'I shall meet them in the north of England and I shall defeat them.'

'How can you be so sure?' I exclaim.

He flashes a smile at me and I catch my breath. 'Because I have never lost a battle,' he says simply. 'I never will. I am quick on the field, and I am skilled, I am brave and I am lucky. My army moves faster than any other; I make them march fast and I move them fully armed. I outguess and I outpace my enemy. I don't lose battles. I am lucky in war as I am lucky in love. I have never lost in either game. I won't lose against Margaret of Anjou, I will win.'

I laugh at his confidence, as if I am not impressed; but in truth he dazzles me.

He finishes his cup of ale and gets to his feet. 'Thank you for your kindness,' he says.

'You're going? You're going now?' I stammer.

'You will write down for me the details of your claim?'

'Yes. But . . .'

'Names and dates and so on? The land that you say is yours and the details of your ownership?'

I almost clutch his sleeve to keep him with me, like a beggar. 'I will, but . . .'

'Then I will bid you adieu.'

There is nothing I can do to stop him, unless my mother has thought to lame his horse.

'Yes, Your Grace, and thank you. But you are most welcome to stay. We will dine soon . . . or . . .'

'No, I must go. My friend William Hastings will be waiting for me.'

'Of course, of course. I don't wish to delay you . . .'

I walk with him to the door. I am anguished at his leaving so abruptly, and yet I cannot think of anything to make him stay. At the threshold he turns and takes my hand. He bows his fair head low and, deliciously, turns my hand. He presses a kiss into my palm and folds my fingers over the kiss as if to keep it safe. When he comes up smiling I see that he knows perfectly well that this gesture has made me melt and that I will keep my hand clasped until bedtime when I can put it to my mouth.

He looks down at my entranced face, at my hand that stretches, despite myself, to touch his sleeve. Then he relents. 'I shall fetch the paper that you prepare, myself, tomorrow,' he says. 'Of course. Did you think differently? How could you? Did you think I could walk away from you, and not come back? Of course I am coming back. Tomorrow at noon. Will I see you then?'

He must hear my gasp. The colour rushes back into my face so that my cheeks are burning hot. 'Yes,' I stammer. 'T . . . tomorrow.'

'At noon. And I will stay to dinner, if I may.'

'We will be honoured.'

He bows to me and turns and walks down the hall, through the wide-flung double doors and out into the bright sunlight. I put my hands behind me and I hold the great wooden door for support. Truly, my knees are too weak to hold me up.

'He's gone?' my mother asks, coming quietly through the little side door.

'He's coming back tomorrow,' I say. 'He's coming back tomorrow. He's coming back to see me tomorrow.'

When the sun is setting and my boys are saying their evening prayers, blond heads on their clasped hands at the foot of their trestle beds, my mother leads the way out of the front door of the house and down the winding footpath to where the bridge, a couple of wooden planks, spans the River Tove. She walks across, her conical headdress brushing the overhanging trees, and beckons me to follow her. At the other side, she puts her hand on a great ash tree and I see there is a dark thread of silk wound around the rough-grained wood of the thick trunk.

'What is this?'

'Reel it in,' is all she says. 'Reel it in, a foot or so every day.'

I put my hand on the thread and pull it gently. It comes easily; there is something light and small tied onto the far end. I cannot even see what it might be, as the thread loops across the river into the reeds, in deep water on the other side.

'Magic,' I say flatly. My father has banned these practices in his house: the law of the land forbids it. It is death to be proved as a witch, death by drowning in the ducking stool, or strangling by the blacksmith at the village crossroads. Women like my mother are not permitted our skills in England today, we are named as forbidden.

'Magic,' she agrees, untroubled. 'Powerful magic, for a good cause. Well worth the risk. Come every day and reel it in, a foot at a time.'

'What will come in?' I ask her. 'At the end of this fishing line of yours? What great fish will I catch?'

She smiles at me and puts her hand on my cheek. 'Your heart's desire,' she says gently. 'I didn't raise you to be a poor widow.'

She turns and walks back across the footbridge and I pull the thread as she has told me, take in twelve inches of it, tie it fast again, and follow her.

'So what did you raise me for?' I ask her, as we walk side by side to the house. 'What am I to be? In your great scheme of things? In a world at war, where it seems, despite your foreknowledge and magic, we are stuck on the losing side?'

The new moon is rising, a small sickle of a moon. Without a word spoken, we both wish on it; we bob a curtsey, and I hear the chink as we turn over the little coins in our pockets.

'I raised you to be the best that you could be,' she says simply. 'I didn't know what that would be, and I still don't know. But I didn't raise you to be a lonely woman, missing her husband, struggling to keep her boys safe; a woman alone in a cold bed, her beauty wasted on empty lands.'

'Well, Amen,' I say simply, my eyes on the slender sickle. 'Amen to that. And may the new moon bring me something better.'

At noon the next day I am in my ordinary gown, seated in my privy chamber, when the girl comes in a rush to say that the king is riding down the road towards the Hall. I don't let myself run to the window to look for him, I don't allow myself a dash to the hammered-silver looking-glass in my mother's room. I put down my sewing, and I walk down the great wooden stairs, so that when the door opens and he comes into the hall I am serenely descending, looking as if I am called away from my household chores to greet a surprise guest.

I go to him with a smile and he greets me with a courteous kiss on the cheek and I feel the warmth of his skin and see, through my half-closed eyes, the softness of the hair that curls at the nape of his neck. His hair smells faintly of spices, and the skin of his neck smells clean. When he looks at me I recognise desire in his face. He lets go of my hand slowly, and I step back from him with reluctance. I turn and curtsey as my father and my two oldest brothers, Anthony and John, step forwards to make their bows.

The conversation at dinner is stilted, as it must be. My family is deferential to this new King of England; but there is no denying that we threw our lives and our fortune into battle against him, and my husband was not the only one of our household and affinity who did not come home. But this is how it must be in a war that they have called 'the Cousins' War', since brother fights against brother and their sons follow them to death. My father has been forgiven, my brothers too, and now the victor breaks bread with them as if to forget that he crowed over them in Calais, as if to forget that my father turned tail and ran from his army in the bloodstained snow at Towton.

King Edward is easy. He is charming to my mother and amusing to my brothers Anthony and John, and then Richard, Edward, and Lionel when they join us later. Three of my younger sisters are home and they eat their dinner in silence, wide-eyed in admiration, but too afraid to say a word. Anthony's wife, Elizabeth, is quiet and elegant beside my mother. The king is observant of my father and asks him about game and the land, about the price of wheat and the steadiness of labour. By the time they have served the preserved fruit and the sweetmeats he is chatting like a friend of the family, and I can sit back in my chair and watch him.

'And now to business,' he says to my father. 'Lady Elizabeth tells me that she has lost her dower lands.'

My father nods. 'I am sorry to trouble you with it but we have tried to reason with Lady Ferrers and my Lord Warwick without result. They were confiscated after—' He clears his throat. 'After St Albans, you understand. Her husband was killed there. And now she cannot get her dower lands returned. Even if you regard her husband as a traitor, she herself is innocent and she should at least have her widow's jointure.'

The king turns to me. 'You have written down your title and the claim to the land?'

'Yes,' I say. I give him the paper and he glances at it.

'I shall speak to Sir William Hastings and ask him to see that this is done,' he says simply. 'He will be your advocate.'

It seems to be as easy as that. In one stroke I will be freed from poverty and have a property of my own again, my sons will have an inheritance and I will be no longer a burden on my family. If someone asks for me in marriage I will come with property. I am no longer a case for charity. I will not have to be grateful for a proposal. I will not have to thank a man for marrying me.

'You are gracious, Sire,' my father says easily and nods to me.

Obediently I rise from my chair and curtsey low. 'I thank you,' I say. 'This means everything to me.'

'I shall be a just king,' he says, looking at my father. 'I would want no Englishman to suffer for my coming to my throne.'

My father makes a visible effort to silence his reply that some of us have suffered already.

'More wine?' My mother interrupts him swiftly. 'Your Grace? Husband?'

'No, I must go,' the king says. 'We are mustering troops all over Northamptonshire and equipping them.' He pushes back his chair and we all – my father and brothers, my mother and sisters and I – bob up like puppets to stand as he stands. 'Will you show me around the garden before I leave, Lady Elizabeth?'

'I shall be honoured,' I say.

My father opens his mouth to offer his company, but my mother says quickly, 'Yes, do go, Elizabeth,' and the two of us slip from the room without a companion.

It is as warm as summer as we come from the darkness of the hall, and he offers me his arm and we walk down the steps to the garden, arms linked, in silence. I take the path around the little knot garden and we wind our way, looking at the trim hedges and the neat white stones; but I see nothing. He gathers my hand a little closer under his arm and I feel the warmth of his body. The lavender is coming into flower and I can smell the scent, sweet as orange blossom, sharp as lemons.

'I have only a little time,' he says. 'Somerset and Percy are mustering against me. Henry himself will come out of his castle and lead his army if he is in his right mind and can command. Poor soul, they tell me he is in his wits now, but he could lose them again at any moment. The queen must be planning to land an army of Frenchmen in their support and we will have to face the power of France on English soil.'

'I shall pray for you,' I say.

'Death is near us all,' he says seriously. 'But it is a constant companion to a king come to his crown through the battlefield, and now riding out to fight again.'

He pauses, and I stop with him. It is very quiet but for a single bird singing. His face is grave. 'May I send a pageboy to bring you to me tonight?' he asks quietly. 'I have a longing for you, Lady Elizabeth Grey, that I have never felt for any woman before. Will you come to me? I ask it not as a king, and not even as a soldier who might die in battle, but as a simple man to the most beautiful woman he has ever seen. Come to me, I beg you, come to me. It could be my last wish. Will you come to me tonight?'

I shake my head. 'Forgive me, Your Grace, but I am a woman of honour.'

'I may never ask you again. God knows, I may never ask any woman again. There can be no dishonour in this. I could die next week.'

'Even so.'

'Are you not lonely?' he asks. His lips are almost brushing my forehead he is so close to me, I can feel the warmth of his breath on my cheek. 'And do you feel nothing for me? Can you say you don't want me? Just once? Don't you want me now?'

As slowly as I can, I let my eyes rise to his face. My gaze lingers on his mouth, then I look up.

'Dear God, I have to have you,' he breathes.

'I cannot be your mistress,' I say simply. 'I would rather die than dishonour my name. I cannot bring that shame on my family.' I pause. I am anxious not to be too discouraging. 'Whatever I might wish in my heart,' I say very softly.

'But you do want me?' he asks boyishly, and I let him see the warmth in my face.

'Ah,' I say. 'I should not tell you . . .'

He waits.

'I should not tell you how much.'

I see, swiftly hidden, the gleam of triumph. He thinks he will have me.

'Then you will come?'

'No.'

'Then must I go? Must I leave you? May I not . . .' He leans his face towards me and I raise mine. His kiss is as gentle as the brush of a feather on my soft mouth. My lips part slightly and I can feel him tremble like a horse held on a tight rein. 'Lady Elizabeth . . . I swear it . . . I have to . . .'

I take a step back in this delicious dance. 'If only . . .' I say.

'I'll come tomorrow,' he says abruptly. 'In the evening. At sunset. Will you meet me where I first saw you? Under the oak tree? Will you meet me there? I would say goodbye before I go north. I have to see you again, Elizabeth. If nothing more. I have to.'

I nod in silence and watch him turn on his heel and stride back to the house. I see him go round to the stable yard and then moments later his horse thunders down the track with his two pages spurring their horses to keep pace with him. I watch him out of sight and then I cross the little footbridge over the river and find the thread around the ash tree. Thoughtfully, I wind in the thread by another length and I tie it up. Then I walk home.

At dinner the next day there is something of a family conference. The king has sent a letter to say that his friend Sir William Hastings will support my claim to my house and land at Bradgate, and I can be assured that I will be restored to my fortune. My father is pleased; but all my brothers, Anthony, John, Richard, Edward and Lionel, are united in suspicion of the king, with the alert pride of boys.

'He is a notorious lecher. He is bound to demand to meet her, he is bound to summon her to court,' John pronounces.

'He did not return her lands for charity. He will want payment,' Richard agrees.'There is not a woman at court that he has not bedded. Why would he not try for Elizabeth?'

'A Lancastrian,' says Edward, as if that is enough to ensure our enmity, and Lionel nods sagely.

'A hard man to refuse,' Anthony says thoughtfully. He is far more worldly than John; he has travelled all around Christendom and studied with great thinkers, and my parents always listen to him. 'I would think, Elizabeth, that you might feel compromised. I would fear that you would feel under obligation to him.'

I shrug. 'Not at all. I have nothing more but my own again. I asked the king for justice and I received it as I should, as any supplicant should, with right on their side.'

'Nonetheless if he sends, you will not go to court,' my father says. 'This is a man who has worked his way through half the wives of London and is now working his way through the Lancastrian ladies too. This is not a holy man like the blessed King Henry.'

Nor soft in the head like blessed King Henry, I think, but aloud I say, 'Of course, Father, whatever you command.'

He looks sharply at me, suspicious of this easy obedience. 'You don't think you owe him your favour? Your smiles? Worse?'

I shrug. 'I asked him for a king's justice, not for a favour,' I say. 'I am not a manservant whose service can be bought or a peasant who can be sworn to be a liegeman. I am a lady of good family. I have my own loyalties and obligations that I consider and honour. They are not his. They are not at the beck and call of any man.'

My mother drops her head to hide her smile. She is the daughter of Burgundy, the descendant of Melusina the water goddess. She has never thought herself obliged to do anything in her life; she would never think that her daughter was obliged to anything.

My father glances from her to me and shrugs his shoulders as if to concede the inveterate independence of wilful women. He nods to my brother John and says, 'I am riding over to Old

Stratford village. Will you come with me?' And the two of them leave together.

'You want to go to court? Do you admire him? Despite everything?' Anthony asks me quietly as my other brothers scatter from the room.

'He is King of England,' I say. 'Of course I will go if he invites me. What else?'

'Perhaps because Father just said you were not to go, and I advised you against it.'

I shrug. 'So I heard.'

'How else can a poor widow make her way in a wicked world?' he teases me.

'Indeed.'

'You would be a fool to sell yourself cheap,' he warns me.

I look at him from under my eyelashes. 'I don't propose to sell myself at all,' I say. 'I am not a yard of ribbon. I am not a leg of ham. I am not for sale to anyone.'

At sunset I am waiting for him under the oak tree, hidden in the green shadows. I am relieved to hear the sound of only one horse on the road. If he had come with a guard I would have slipped back to my home fearing for my own safety. However tender he may be in the confines of my father's garden, I don't forget that he is the so-called king of the Yorkist army and they rape women and murder their husbands as a matter of course. He will have hardened himself to seeing things that no one should witness, he will have done things himself which are the darkest of sins. I cannot trust him. However heart-stopping his smile and however honest his eyes, however much I think of him as a boy fired to greatness by his own ambition, I cannot trust him. These are not chivalrous times, these are not the times of knights in the dark forest and beautiful ladies in moonlit fountains and promises of love that will be ballads, sung for ever.

But he looks like a knight in a dark forest when he pulls up his horse and jumps down in one easy movement. 'You came!' he says.

'I cannot stay long.'

'I am so glad you came at all.' He laughs at himself almost in bewilderment. 'I have been like a boy today – couldn't sleep last night for thinking of you, and all day I have wondered if you would come at all, and then you came!'

He loops the reins of his horse over a branch of the tree and slides his hand around my waist. 'Sweet lady,' he says into my ear. 'Be kind to me. Will you take off your headdress and let down your hair?'

It is the last thing I thought he would demand of me: and I am shocked into instant consent. My hand goes to my headdress ribbons at once.

'I know. I know. I think you are driving me mad. All I have been able to think about all day is whether you would let me take down your hair.'

In answer I untie the tight bindings of my tall conical headdress and lift it off. I put it carefully on the ground and turn to him. Gently as any maid-in-waiting, he puts his hand to my head and pulls out the ivory pins, tucking each into the pocket of his doublet. I can feel the silky kiss of my thick hair tumbling down as the fair cascade of it falls over my face. I shake my head and toss it back like a thick golden mane, and I hear his groan of desire.

He unties his cloak and swings it on the ground at my feet. 'Sit with me!' he commands, though he means 'Lie with me' and we both know it.

I sit cautiously on the edge of his cape, my knees drawn up, my arms wrapped around them, my fine silk gown draped around me. He strokes my loosened hair and his fingers penetrate deeper and deeper until he is caressing my neck, and then he turns my face towards his for a kiss.

Gently he bears down on me so I am beneath him. Then I feel

his hand pulling at my gown, pulling it up, and I put both hands on his chest and gently push him away.

'Elizabeth,' he breathes.

'I told you no,' I say steadily. 'I meant it.'

'You met me!'

'You asked me. Shall I go now?'

'No! Stay! Stay! Don't run away, I swear I will not . . . just let me kiss you again.'

My own heart is thudding so loud and I am so ready for his touch that I start to think I could lie with him, just once, I could allow myself this pleasure just once . . . but then I move away and say, 'No. No. No.'

'Yes,' he says more strongly. 'No harm shall come to you, I swear it. You shall come to court. Anything you ask. Dear God, Elizabeth, let me have you, I am desperate for you. From the moment I saw you here . . .'

His weight is on me, he is pushing me down, I turn my head away but his mouth is on my neck, my breast, I am panting with desire, and then I feel, unexpectedly, a sudden rush of anger at the realisation that he is no longer embracing me but forcing me, holding me down as if I were some slut behind a haystack. He is pulling up my gown as if I were a whore, he is pushing his knee between my legs as if I have consented, and my temper makes me so furiously strong that I thrust him away again and then, on his thick leather belt, I feel the hilt of his dagger.

He has my gown pulled up, he is fumbling with his jerkin, his hose, in a moment it will be too late for complaints. I draw his dagger out of the scabbard. At the hiss of the metal, he rears back to his knees in shock and I wriggle away from him and spring up, with the dagger unsheathed, the blade bright and wicked in the last rays of the sun.

He is on his feet in a moment, weaving and alert, a fighter. 'Do you draw a blade on your king?' he spits. 'Do you know treason when you do it, Madam?'

'I draw a blade on me, on myself,' I say quickly. I hold the sharp point to my throat and I see his eyes narrow. 'I swear, if you come one step closer, if you come one inch closer, I will cut my throat before you and bleed to death here on the ground where you would have dishonoured me.'

'Play-acting!'

'No. This is not a game to me, Your Grace. I cannot be your mistress. I first came to you for justice, and then I came tonight for love, and I am a fool to do so and I beg your pardon for my folly. But I too can't sleep, and I too can think of nothing but you, and I too could only wonder and wonder if you would come. But even so . . . even so, you should not . . .'

'I could have that knife off you in a moment,' he threatens.

'You forget I have five brothers. I have played with swords and daggers since I was a child. I will cut my throat before you reach me.'

'You never would. You are a woman with no more than a woman's courage.'

'Try me. Try me. You don't know what my courage is. You may regret what happens.'

He hesitates for a second, his own heart hammering in a dangerous mix of temper and lust, and then he masters himself, raises his hands in the gesture of surrender and steps back. 'You win,' he says. 'You win, Madam. And you may keep the dagger as a spoil of victory. Here—' He unbuckles the scabbard and throws it down. 'Take the damned scabbard too, why don't you?'

The precious stones and the enamelled gold sparkle in the twilight. Never taking my eyes from him I kneel and pick it up.

'I shall walk with you to your home,' he says. 'I shall see you safely to your door.'

I shake my head. 'No. I can't be seen with you. No one must know that we have met in secret. I would be shamed.'

For a moment I think he will argue but he bows his head. 'You walk ahead then,' he says. 'And I will follow behind you like a page, like your servant, until I see you safe to your gate. You can revel in your triumph in having me follow you like a dog. Since you treat me like a fool, I shall serve you like a fool; and you can enjoy it.'

There is no speaking against his anger, so I nod and I turn to walk before him, as he said I should. We walk in silence. I can hear the rustle of his cloak behind me. When we get to the end of the wood and we can be seen from the house, I pause and turn to him. 'I will be safe from here,' I say. 'I must beg you to forgive me for my folly.'

'I must beg you to forgive me for my force,' he says stiffly. 'I am, perhaps, too accustomed to getting my own way. But I must say, I have never been refused at the point of a knife before. My own knife at that.'

I turn it round and offer him the hilt. 'Will you have it back, Your Grace?'

He shakes his head. 'Keep it to remember me by. It will be my only gift to you. A farewell gift.'

'Will I not see you again?'

'Never,' he says simply, and bowing slightly walks away.

'Your Grace!' I call and he turns and pauses.

'I would not part with you on bad terms,' I say feebly. 'I hope that you can forgive me.'

'You have made a fool of me,' he says, his voice icy. 'You may congratulate yourself on being the first woman to do that. But you will be the last. And you will never make a fool of me again.'

I sink down into a curtsey, and I hear him turn and the swish of his cape on the bushes on either side of the path. I wait till I cannot hear him at all, and then I rise up to go home.

There is a part of me, young woman that I am, that wants to run inside and fling myself on my bed and cry myself to sleep. But I don't do that. I am not one of my sisters, who laugh easily and cry easily. They are girls to whom things happen; and they take it hard. But I bear myself as more than a silly girl. I am the daughter of a water goddess. I am a woman with water in her veins and power in her breeding. I am a woman who makes things happen: and I am not defeated yet. I am not defeated by a boy with a newly won crown, and no man will ever walk away from me certain that he won't walk back.

So I don't go home just yet. I take the path to the footbridge over the river to where the ash tree is girdled with my mother's thread, and I take another loop in the thread and tie it tightly and only then do I walk home, brooding in the thin moonlight.

Then I wait. Every evening for twenty-two evenings I walk down to the river and pull in the thread like a patient fisherwoman. One day I feel it snag, and the line goes tight as the object on the end, whatever it is, is freed from the reeds at the water's edge. I tug gently, as if I were reeling in a catch, and then I feel the line go slack and there is a little splash as something small but heavy falls deeper, rolls over in the current and then lies still among the pebbles on the stream bed.

I walk home. My mother is waiting for me by the carp lake, gazing down at her own reflection inverted in the water, silver in the greyness of the dusk. Her image looks like a long silver fish rippling in the lake, or a swimming woman. The sky behind her is barred with cloud, like white feathers on pale silk. The moon is rising, a waning moon now. The water is running high tonight, lapping at the little pier. When I stand beside her and look down into the water you would think we were both rising from the water, like the spirits of the lake.

'You do it every evening?' she asks me. 'Pull the line?'

'Yes.'

'Good. That's good. Has he sent you any token? Any word?'

'I don't expect anything. He said he would never see me again.'

She sighs. 'Oh well.'

We walk back towards the house. 'They say he is mustering troops at Northampton,' she says. 'King Henry is gathering his forces in Northumberland and will march south on London. The queen will join him with a French army landed at Hull. If King Henry wins, then it will not matter what Edward says or thinks, for he will be dead, and the true king restored.'

My hand flies out to catch her sleeve in instant contradiction. Swift as a striking viper my mother snatches my fingers. 'What's this? You can't bear to hear of his defeat?'

'Don't say it. Don't say that.'

'Don't say what?'

'I can't bear to think of him defeated. I can't bear to think of him dead. He asked me to lie with him as a soldier facing death.'

She gives a sharp laugh. 'Course he did. What man going off to war has ever resisted the opportunity to make the most of it?'

'Well, I refused. And if he doesn't come back, I shall regret that refusal for the rest of my life. I regret it now. I will regret it for ever.'

'Why regret?' she taunts me. 'You have your land restored either way. Either you get it back by order of King Edward, or he is dead and King Henry is king and he will restore your land to you. He is our king, of the true House of Lancaster. I would have thought we would wish him victory: and death to the usurper Edward.'

'Don't say it,' I repeat. 'Don't ill-wish him.'

'Never mind what I say, you stop and think,' she counsels me harshly. 'You're a girl from the House of Lancaster. You cannot fall in love with the heir to the House of York unless he is king victorious, and there is some profit in love for you. These are hard days we are living in. Death is our companion, our familiar. You need not think you can keep Him at arm's length. You will find He bears you close company. He has taken your husband; hear me: He will take your father and your brothers and your sons.'

I put out both hands to stop her. 'Hush, hush. You sound like Melusina warning her house of the death of the men.'

'I do warn you,' she says grimly. 'You make me a Melusina when you walk about smiling as if life is easy, thinking you can dally with a usurper. You were not born in an untroubled time. You will live your life in a country divided. You will have to make your way through blood, and you will know loss.'

'Nothing good for me?' I demand through gritted teeth. 'Do you, as a loving mother, foresee nothing good at all for your daughter? There is no point cursing me, for I am ready to weep already.'

She stops and the hard face of the seer dissolves into the warmth of the mother that I love. 'I think you will have him, if that is what you want,' she says.

'More than life itself.'

She laughs at me but her face is gentle. 'Ah, don't say that, child. Nothing in the world matters more than life. You have a long road to walk and a lot of lessons to learn if you don't know that.'

I shrug and take her arm and, walking in step, we turn for home.

'When the battle is over, whoever wins, your sisters must go to court,' my mother says. She is always planning. 'They can stay with the Bourchiers, or the Vaughns. They should have gone months ago but I could not bear the thought of them far from home and the country in uproar, and never knowing what might happen next, and never able to get news. But when this battle is over, perhaps life will be as it was, only under York instead of Lancaster, and the girls can go to our cousins for their education.'

'Yes.'

'And your boy Thomas will be old enough to leave home soon. He should live with his kinsmen, he should learn to be a gentleman.'

'No,' I say with such sudden emphasis that she turns and looks at me.

'What's wrong?'

'I will keep my sons with me,' I say. 'My boys are not to be taken from me.'

'They will need a proper education; they will need to serve in the household of a lord. Your father will find someone, their own godfathers might . . .'

'No,' I say again. 'No, Mother, no. I cannot consider it. They are not to leave home.'

'Child?' She turns my face to the moonlight so that she can see me more clearly. 'It's not like you to take a sudden whim over nothing. And every mother in the world has to let her sons leave home and learn to be men.'

'My boys are not to be taken from me.' I can hear my voice tremble. 'I am afraid . . . I am afraid for them. I fear . . . I fear for them. I don't even know what. But I cannot let my boys go among strangers.'

She puts her warm arm around my waist. 'Well, it is natural enough,' she says gently. 'You lost your husband, you are bound to want to keep your boys safe. But they will have to go some day, you know.'

I do not yield to her gentle pressure. 'It is more than a whim,' I say. 'It feels more . . .'

'Is it a Seeing?' she asks, her voice very low. 'Do you know that something could happen to them? Have you come into the Sight, Elizabeth?'

I shake my head and the tears come. 'I don't know, I don't know. I can't tell. But the thought of them going from me, and being cared for by strangers, and me waking in the night and not knowing that they are under my roof, waking in the morning and not hearing their voices, the thought of them being in a strange room, served by strangers, not able to see me – I can't bear it. I can't even bear the thought of it.'

She gathers me into her arms. 'Hush,' she says. 'Hush. You need not think of it. I will speak to your father. They need not go until you are happy about it.' She takes my hand. 'Why, you are icy cold,' she says, surprised. She touches my face with sudden certainty. 'This is not a whim when you are both hot and cold in moonlight. This is a Seeing. My dear, you are warned of danger to your sons.'

I shake my head. 'I don't know. I can't be sure. I just know that no one should ever take my boys from me. I should never let them go.'

She nods. 'Very well. You have convinced me, at least. You have seen some danger for your boys if they are taken from you. So be it. Don't cry. You shall keep your boys close at hand and we will keep them safe.'

Then I wait. He told me clearly enough that I would never see him again, so I wait for nothing, knowing full well that I am waiting for nothing. But somehow I cannot help but wait. I dream of him: passionate, longing dreams that wake me in the darkness, twisted up in the sheet, sweaty with desire. My father asks me why I am not eating. Anthony shakes his head at me in mocking sorrow.

My mother snaps one bright-eyed glance at me and says, 'She is well. She will eat.'

My sisters whisper to ask me if I am pining for the handsome king, and I say sharply, 'There would be little point in that.'

And then I wait.

I wait for another seven nights and another seven days, like a maiden in a tower in a fairy tale, like Melusina bathing in the fountain in the forest, waiting for a chevalier to come riding the untrodden ways and love her. Each evening I draw up the loop of thread a little closer until on the eighth day there is a little chink of metal against stone and I look into the water and see a flash of gold. I bend down to pull it out. It is a ring of gold, simple and pretty. One side is straight, but the other is forged into points, like the points of a crown. I put it on the palm of my hand, where he left his kiss, and it looks like a miniature coronet. I slip it on my finger, on my right hand – I tempt no misfortune by putting it on my wedding finger – and it fits me perfectly and suits me well. I take it off with a shrug as if it were not the highest quality

Burgundian-forged gold. I tuck it into my pocket, and I walk home with it safe in my keeping.

And there – without warning – there is a horse at the door and a rider sitting tall on it, a banner over his head, the white rose of York uncurling in the breeze. My father stands in the open doorway reading a letter. I hear him say, 'Tell His Grace I shall be honoured. I will be there the day after tomorrow.'

The man bows in the saddle, throws a casual salute to me, wheels his horse and rides away.

'What is it?' I ask, coming up the steps.

'A muster,' my father says grimly. 'We are all to go to war again.'

'Not you!' I say in fear. 'Not you, Father. Not again.'

'No. The king commands me to provide ten men from Grafton and five from Stony Stratford. Fitted and kitted to march under his command against the Lancaster king. We are to change sides. That was an expensive dinner we gave him, as it turned out.'

'Who is to lead them?' I am so afraid that he will say my brothers. 'Not Anthony? Not John?'

'They are to serve under Sir William Hastings,' he says. 'He will put them in among trained troops.'

I hesitate. 'Did he say anything else?'

'This is a muster,' my father says irritably. 'Not an invitation to a May Day breakfast. Of course he didn't say anything except that they would be coming through in the morning, the day after tomorrow, and the men must be ready to fall in then.'

He turns on his heel and goes into the house, and leaves me with the gold ring, shaped like a crown, spiky in my pocket.

My mother suggests at breakfast that my sisters and I, and the two cousins who are staying with us, might like to watch the army go by, and see our men go off to war.

'Can't think why,' my father says crossly. 'I would have thought you would have seen enough of men going to war.'

'It looks well to show our support,' she says quietly. 'If he wins, it will be better for us if he thinks we sent the men willingly. If he loses, no one will remember we watched him go by, and we can deny it.'

'I am paying them, aren't I? I am arming them with what I have? The arms I have left over from the last time I went out, which, as it happens, was against him? I am rounding them up, and sending them out, and buying boots for those who have none. I would think I was showing support!'

'Then we should do it with a good grace,' my mother says.

He nods. He always gives way to my mother in these matters. She was a duchess: married to the royal Duke of Bedford when my father was nothing but her husband's squire. She is the daughter of the Count of Saint-Pol, of the royal family of Burgundy, and she is a courtier without equal.

'I would like you to come with us,' she goes on. 'And we could perhaps find a purse of gold from the treasure room, for His Grace.'

'A purse of gold! A purse of gold! To wage war on King Henry? Are we Yorkists now?'

She waits till his outrage has subsided. 'To show our loyalty,' she says. 'If he defeats King Henry and comes back to London victorious, then it will be his court, and his royal favours that are the source of all wealth and all opportunity. It will be he who distributes the land and the patronage and he who allows marriages. And we have a large family, with many girls, Sir Richard.'

For a moment we all freeze with our heads down expecting one of my father's thunderous outbursts. Then, unwillingly, he laughs. 'God bless you, my spellbinder,' he says. 'You are right, as you are always right. I will do as you say, though it goes against the grain, and you can tell the girls to wear white roses, if they can get any this early.'

She leans over to him and kisses him on the cheek. 'The dog roses are in bud in the hedgerow,' she says. 'It's not as good as full bloom but he will know what we mean, and that is all that matters.'

Of course, for the rest of the day, my sisters and cousins are in a frenzy, trying on clothes, washing their hair, exchanging ribbons and rehearsing their curtseys. Anthony's wife Elizabeth and two of our quieter companions say that they won't come, but all my sisters are beside themselves with excitement. The king and most of the lords of his court will go by. What an opportunity to make an impression on the men who will be the new masters of the country! If they win.

'What will you wear?' Margaret asks me, seeing me aloof from the excitement.

'I shall wear my grey gown, and my grey veil.'

'That's not your best, it's only what you wear on Sundays. Why wouldn't you wear your blue?'

I shrug. 'I am going since Mother wants us to go,' I say. 'I don't expect anyone to look twice at us.' I take the dress from the cupboard and shake it out. It is slim cut with a little half-train at the back. I wear it with a girdle of grey falling low over my waist. I don't say anything to Margaret, but I know it is a better fit than my blue gown.

'When the king himself came to dinner at your invitation?' she exclaims. 'Why wouldn't he look twice at you? He looked well enough the first time. He must like you – he gave your land back, he came to dinner. He walked in the garden with you. Why wouldn't he come to the house again? Why wouldn't he favour you?'

'Because between then and now, I got what I wanted and he did not,' I say crudely, tossing the dress aside. 'And it turns out he is not as generous a king as those in the ballads. The price for his kindness was high, too high for me.'

'He never wanted to have you?' she whispers, appalled.

'Exactly.'

'Oh my God, Elizabeth. What did you say? What did you do?'

'I said no. But it was not easy.'

She is deliciously scandalised. 'Did he try to force you?'

'Not much, it doesn't matter,' I mumble. 'And it's not as if I was anything to him but a girl on the roadside.'

'Perhaps you shouldn't come tomorrow,' she suggests. 'If he offended you. You can tell Mother that you're ill. I'll tell her, if you like.'

'Oh I'll come,' I say, as if I don't care either way.

In the morning I am not so brave. A sleepless night and a piece of bread and beef for breakfast does not help my looks. I am pale as marble, and though Margaret rubs red ochre into my lips I still look drawn, a ghostly beauty. Among my brightly dressed sisters and my cousins I, in my grey gown and headdress, stand out like a novice in a nunnery. But when my mother sees me she nods, pleased. 'You look like a lady,' she says. 'Not like some peasant girl tricked out in her best to go to a fair.'

As a reproof this is not successful. The girls are so delighted to be allowed to the muster at all that they don't in the least mind being reproached for looking too bright. We walk together down the road to Grafton and see before us, at the side of the highway, a straggle of a dozen men armed with staves, one or two with cudgels: father's recruits. He has given them all a badge of a white rose and reminded them that they are now to fight for the House of York. They used to be foot soldiers for Lancaster; they must remember that they are now turncoats. Of course, they are indifferent to the change of loyalty. They are fighting as he bids them for he is their landlord, the owner of their fields, their cottages, almost everything they see around them. His is the mill where they grind their corn; the ale house where they drink pays rent to him. Some of them have never been beyond the lands he owns. They can hardly imagine a world in which 'Squire' does not simply mean Sir Richard Woodville, or his son after him. When he was Lancaster so were they. Then he was given the title Rivers, but they were still his and he theirs. Now he sends them out to fight for York, and they will do their best, as always. They have been promised payment for fighting and that their widows and children will be cared for if they fall. That is all they need to know. It does not make them an inspired army, but they raise a ragged cheer for my father and pull off their hats with appreciative smiles for my sisters and me, and their wives and children bob curtseys as we come towards them.

There is a burst of trumpets, and every head turns towards the noise. Around the corner, at a steady trot, come the king's colours and trumpeters, behind them the heralds, behind them the yeomen of his household, and in the middle of all this bellow and waving pennants there he is.

For a moment I feel as if I will faint, but my Mother's hand is firm under my arm, and I steady myself. He raises his hand in the signal for halt and the cavalcade comes to a standstill. Following the first horses and riders is a long tail of men at arms, behind them, other new recruits, looking sheepish like our men, and then a train of wagons with food, supplies, weapons, a great gun carriage drawn by four massive shire horses, and a trail of ponies and women, camp followers and vagrants. It is like a small town on the move: a small deadly town, on the move to do harm.

King Edward swings down from his horse and goes to my father, who bows low. 'All we could muster, I am afraid, Your Grace. But sworn to your service,' my father says. 'And this, to help your cause.'

My mother steps forward and offers the purse of gold. King Edward takes it and weighs it in his hand and then kisses her heartily on both cheeks. 'You are generous,' he says. 'And I will not forget your support.'

His gaze goes past her to me, where I stand with my sisters and we all curtsey together. When I come up he is still looking at me and there is a moment when all the noise of the army and the horses and the men falling in freezes into silence, and it is as if there is only he and I alone, in the whole world. Without thinking what I am doing, as if he has wordlessly called me, I take a step toward him, and then another, until I have walked past my father and mother and am face to face with him, so close that he might kiss me, if he wished.

'I can't sleep,' he says so quietly that only I can hear. 'I can't sleep, I can't sleep. I can't sleep.'

'Nor I.'

'You neither?'

'No.'

'Truly?'

'Yes.'

He sighs a deep sigh as if he is relieved. 'Is this love then?'

'I suppose so.'

'I can't eat.'

'No.'

'I can't think of anything but you. I can't go on another moment like this, I can't ride out into battle like this. I am as foolish as a boy. I am mad for you, like a boy. I cannot be without you, I will not be without you. Whatever it costs me.'

I can feel my colour rising like heat in my cheeks, and for the first time in days I can feel myself smile. 'I can't think of anything but you,' I whisper. 'Nothing. I thought I was sick.'

The ring like a crown is heavy in my pocket, my headdress is pulling at my hair; but I stand without awareness, seeing nothing but him, feeling nothing but his warm breath on my cheek and scenting the smell of his horse, the leather of his saddle, and the smell of him: spices, rose water, sweat.

'I am mad for you,' he says.

I feel my smile turn up my lips as I look into his face at last. 'And I for you,' I say quietly. 'Truly.'

'Well then, marry me.'

'What?'

'Marry me. There is nothing else for it.'

I give a nervous little laugh. 'You are joking with me.'

'I mean it. I think I will die if I don't have you. Will you marry me?'

'Yes,' I breathe.

'Tomorrow morning, I will ride in early. Marry me tomorrow morning at your little chapel. I will bring my chaplain, you bring witnesses. Choose someone you can trust. It will have to be a secret for a while. Do you want to?'

'Yes.'

For the first time he smiles, a warm beam that spreads across his fair broad face. 'Good God, I could take you in my arms right now,' he says.

'Tomorrow,' I whisper.

'At nine in the morning,' he says.

He turns to my father.

'Can we offer you some refreshment?' my father asks, looking from my flushed face to the smiling king.

'No, but I will take supper with you tomorrow, if I may,' he says. 'I will be hunting near by, and I hope to have a good day.' He bows to my mother and to me, he throws a salute at my sisters and cousins, and he swings up into his saddle. 'Fall in,' he says to the men. 'It's a short march and a good cause and dinner when you stop. Be true to me and I will be a good lord to you. I have never lost a battle and you will be safe with me. I will take you out to great plunder and bring you safe home again.'

It is exactly the right thing to say to them. At once they look more cheerful and shuffle to the rear of the line, and my sisters wave their white budding roses, and the trumpeters sound, and the whole army goes forward again. He nods at me, unsmiling, and I raise my hand in farewell. 'Tomorrow,' I whisper as he goes.

I doubt him, even as I order my mother's pageboy to wake early in the morning and come to the chapel ready to sing a psalm. I doubt him even when I go to my mother and tell her the King of England himself has said that he wants to marry me in secret, and will she come and be witness, and bring her lady-in-waiting, Catherine. I doubt him when I stand in my best blue gown in the cold morning air of the little chapel. I doubt him right up to the moment when I hear his quick stride up the short aisle, until I feel his arm around my waist and his kiss on my mouth, and I hear him say to the priest, 'Marry us, Father. I am in a hurry.'

The boy sings his psalm, and the priest says the words. I give my oath and he gives his. Dimly, I see my mother's delighted face and the colours of the stained-glass window throwing a rainbow at our feet on the stone floor of the chapel.

Then the priest says, 'And the ring?'

And the king says. 'A ring! I am a fool! I forgot! I don't have a ring for you.' He turns to my mother. 'Your Ladyship, can you lend me a ring?'

'Oh, but I have one,' I say, almost surprised at myself. 'I have one here.' From my pocket I take the ring that I have drawn so slowly and so patiently out of the water, the ring shaped like the crown of England that came with watery magic to bring me my heart's desire, and the King of England himself puts it on my finger for my wedding ring. And I am his wife.

And Queen of England – or, at any rate, the York Queen of England.

His arm is tight around my waist as the boy sings the bidding, then the king turns to my mother and says, 'Your Ladyship? Where can I take my bride?'

My mother smiles and gives him a key. 'There is a hunting lodge by the river.' She turns to me. 'River Lodge. I had it made ready for you.'

He nods and sweeps me from the little chapel and lifts me onto his big hunter. He mounts behind me and I feel his arms tighten around me as he takes up the reins. We go at a walk along the riverbank and when I lean back I can feel his heart beating. We can see the little lodge through the trees and there is a curl of smoke from the chimney. He swings down from his horse and lifts me off and takes the animal to the stalls at the back of the house while I open the door. It is a simple place with a fire burning in the hearth, a jug of wedding ale and two cups on the wooden table, two stools set for eating the bread and cheese and meat, and a large wooden bed, made up with the best linen sheets. The room goes dark as he comes in the doorway, ducking his tall head under the beams.

'Your Grace . . .' I start and then I correct myself. 'My Lord. Husband.'

'Wife,' he says with quiet satisfaction. 'To bed.'

The morning sun, which was so bright on the beams and the limewashed ceiling when we went to bed, is turning the place golden in the late afternoon when he says to me, 'Thank the Lady of Heaven that your father asked me to dinner. I am weak with hunger. I am dying of hunger. Let me out of bed, you witch.'

'I offered you bread and cheese two hours ago,' I point out, 'but you would not let me go three steps to the table to fetch it for you.'

'I was busy,' he says and pulls me back to his naked shoulder. At the smell of him and the touch of his skin I feel my desire for him rise again and we move together. When we lie back, the room is rosy with the sunset and he gets out of bed. 'I must wash,' he says. 'Shall I bring you a jug of water from the yard?'

His head brushes the ceiling, his body is perfect. I look him over with satisfaction, like a horsedealer looks at a beautiful stallion. He is tall and lean, his muscles hard, his chest broad, his shoulders strong. He smiles at me and my heart turns over for him. 'You look as if you would eat me up,' he says.

'I would,' I say. 'I cannot think how to sate my desire for you. I think I will have to keep you prisoner here and eat you up in little cutlets, day after day.'

'If I kept you prisoner I would devour you in one greedy swallow,' he chuckles. 'But you would not get out till you were with child.'

'Oh!' The most delightful thought now strikes me. 'Oh, I shall give you sons, and they will be princes.'

'You will be the mother of the King of England, and the mother of the House of York, which will rule for ever, please God.'

'Amen,' I say devoutly, and I feel no shadow, no shiver, no sense of unease. 'God send you safely home to me from your battle.'

'I always win,' he says in his supreme confidence. 'Be happy, Elizabeth. You will not lose me on the battlefield.'

'And I shall be queen,' I say again. For the first time I understand, truly understand, that if he comes home from the battle and the true king, Henry, is dead, then this young man will be the undisputed King of England – and I shall be first in the land.

After dinner he takes his leave of my father and sets off to ride to Northampton. His pageboy has come to the stable and fed and watered the horses and has them ready at the door. 'I will come back tomorrow night,' he says. 'I must see my men and raise my army, all day. But I shall be with you at dusk.'

'Come to the hunting lodge,' I whisper. 'And I will have dinner there for you like a good wife.'

'Tomorrow evening,' he promises. Then he turns to my father and mother and thanks them for their hospitality, nods to their bows and leaves.

'His Grace is very attentive to you,' my father remarks. 'Don't you let your head be turned.'

'Elizabeth is the most beautiful woman in England,' my mother replies smoothly. 'And he likes a pretty face; but she knows her duty.'

Then I have to wait again. All through the evening when I play cards with my boys and then hear them say their prayers and get ready for bed. All through the night when though I am exhausted and deliciously sore I cannot sleep. All through the next day when I walk and talk as if I were in a dream waiting for night until the moment that he ducks his head under the doorway and comes into the little room and takes me into his arms and says, 'Wife, let us go to bed.'

Three nights pass in this haze of pleasure, until the last morning when he says, 'I have to go, my love, and I will see you when it is all over.' It is as if someone has thrown icy water in my face and I gasp and say: 'You are going to war?'

'I have my army mustered, and my spies tell me that Henry is commanded by his wife to meet her on the east coast with her troops. I shall go at once and bring him to battle and then march to meet her as soon as she lands.'

I clutch at his shirt as he pulls it on. 'You will not go right now?'

'Today,' he says, gently pushing me away, and continuing to dress.

'But I cannot bear it without you.'

'No. But you will. Now listen.'

This is a different man from the entranced young lover of our three-night honeymoon. I have been thoughtless of everything but our pleasure; but he has been planning. This is a king defending his kingdom. I wait to hear what he will command. 'If I win, and I will win, I will come back for you, and as soon as we can, we will announce our marriage. There will be many who will not be pleased, but it is done, and all they can do is accept it.'

I nod. I know that his great advisor, Lord Warwick, is planning his marriage with a French princess, and Lord Warwick is accustomed to commanding my young husband.

'If luck goes against me and I am dead, then you will say nothing of this marriage and these days.' He raises his hand to silence my objection. 'Nothing. You would gain nothing for being the widow of a dead imposter, whose head will be stuck on the gates of York. It would be your ruin. As far as anyone knows you are the daughter of a family loyal to the House of Lancaster. You should stay that way. You will remember me in your prayers, I hope. But it will be a secret between you and me and God. And two of us will be silent for sure, for one of us is God and the other is dead.'

'My mother knows . . .'

'Your mother knows the best way to keep you safe will be to silence her pageboy and her lady-in-waiting. She is prepared for that already, she understands, and I have given her money.'

I swallow a sob. 'Very well.'

'And I should like you to marry again. Choose a good man, one who will love you and care for the boys, and be happy. I would want you to be happy.'

I bow my head in speechless misery.

'Now, if you find you are with child, you will have to leave England,' he commands. 'Tell your mother at once. I have spoken to her and she knows what to do. The Duke of Burgundy commands all of Flanders, and he will give you a house of your own for kinship with your mother and for love of me. If you have a girl you can wait your time, get a pardon from Henry, and come back to England. If you leave it for a year, you will be deliciously notorious – men will be mad for you. You will be the beautiful widow of a dead pretender. Enjoy it all for my sake, I beg you.

'But if you have a boy, it's a different matter altogether. My son will be heir to the throne. He will be the York heir. You will have to keep him safe. You may have to put him into hiding till he is old enough to claim his rights. He can live under an assumed name, he can live with poor people. Don't be falsely proud. Hide him somewhere safe until he is old enough and strong enough to claim his inheritance. Richard and George, my brothers, will be his uncles and his guardians. You can trust them to protect any son of mine. It may be that Henry and his son die young and then your son will be the only heir to the throne of England. I don't count the Lancaster woman Margaret Beaufort. My boy should have the throne. It is my wish that he has the throne if he can win it, or if Richard and George can win it for him. Do you understand? You must hide my son in Flanders and keep him safe for me. He could be the next York king.'

'Yes,' I say simply. I see that my grief and my fear for him is no longer a private matter. If we have made a child in these long nights of lovemaking then he is not just a child of love, he is an heir to the throne, a claimant, a new player in the long deadly rivalry between the two houses of York and Lancaster.

'This is hard for you,' he says, seeing my pale face. 'My intention is that it should never happen. But remember, your refuge is Flanders if you have to keep my son safe. And your mother has money and knows where to go.'

'I will remember,' I say. 'Come back to me.'

He laughs. It is not forced, it is the laugh of a happy man, confident in his luck and his abilities. 'I will,' he says. 'Trust me. You have married a man who is going to die in his bed, preferably after making love to the most beautiful woman in England.'

He holds out his arms and I step towards him and feel the warmth of his embrace. 'Make sure you do,' I say. 'And I will make sure that the most beautiful woman in your eyes is always me.'

He kisses me, but briskly, as if his mind is already elsewhere, and he detaches himself from my clasping hands. He has gone from me long before he ducks his head to get through the doorway, and I see that his page has brought his horse round to the door and is ready to go.

I run outside to wave to him and he is already up in the saddle. His horse is dancing on the spot; he is a great chestnut beast, strong and powerful. He arches his neck and tries to rear against Edward's tight rein. The King of England towers against the sun on his great war horse and for a moment I too believe that he is invincible. 'God speed, good luck!' I call, and he salutes me and wheels his horse, and rides out, the rightful King of England, to fight the other rightful King of England for the kingdom itself.

I stand with my hand raised in farewell until I cannot see his standard with the white rose of York carried before him, until I cannot hear the hoofbeats of his horse, until he has quite gone from me; and then, to my horror, my brother Anthony, who has seen all of this, who has been watching for who knows how long, steps out from the shadow of the tree and walks towards me.

'You whore,' he says.

I stare at him as if I don't understand the meaning of the word. 'What?'

'You whore. You have shamed our house and your name and the name of your poor dead husband who died fighting that usurper. God forgive you, Elizabeth. I am going at once to tell my father, and he will put you in a nunnery, if he does not strangle you first.'

'No!' I stride forward and grab at his arm but he shakes me off.

'Don't touch me, you slut. D'you think I want your hands on me after they have been all over him?'

'Anthony, it is not what you think!'

'My eyes deceive me?' he spits savagely. 'It is an enchantment? You are Melusina? A beautiful goddess bathing in the woods and he that just departed was a knight sworn to your service? This is Camelot now? An honourable love? This is poetry and not the gutter?'

'It is honourable!' I am driven to reply.

'You don't know the meaning of the word. You are a slut and he will pass you on to Sir William Hastings when they next ride by, as he does with all his sluts.'

'He loves me!'

'As he tells each and every one.'

'He does. He is coming back to me . . .'

'As he always promises.'

Furious, I thrust my left fist towards him and he ducks away, expecting a punch in the face. Then he sees the gleam of gold on my finger and he all but laughs. 'He gave you this? A ring? I am supposed to be impressed by a love-token?'

'It is not a love-token, it is a wedding ring. A proper ring given in marriage. We are married.' I make my announcement in triumph; but I am instantly disappointed.

'Dear God, he has fooled you,' he says, anguished. He takes me into his arms and presses my head against his chest. 'My poor sister, my poor fool.'

I struggle free. 'Let me go, I am nobody's fool. What are you saying?'

He looks at me with sorrow but his mouth is twisted into a bitter smile. 'Let me guess, was this a secret wedding, in a private chapel? Did none of his friends and courtiers attend? Is Lord Warwick not to be told? Is it to be kept private? Are you to deny it, if asked?'

'Yes. But . . .'

'You are not married, Elizabeth. You have been tricked. It was a pretend service that has no weight in the eyes of God nor of man. He has fooled you with a trumpery ring and a pretend priest so that he could get you into bed.'

'No.'

'This is the man who hopes to be King of England. He has to marry a princess. He's not going to marry some beggarly widow from the camp of his enemy, who stood out on the road to plead with him to restore her dowry. If he marries an Englishwoman at all she will be one of the great ladies of the Lancaster court, probably Warwick's daughter Isabel. He's not going to marry a girl whose own father fought against him. He's more likely to marry a great princess of Europe, an Infanta from Spain or a Dauphine from France. He has to marry to set himself more safely on the throne, to make alliances. He's not going to marry a pretty face for love. Lord Warwick would never allow it. And he is not such a fool as to go against his own interests.'

'He doesn't have to do what Lord Warwick wants! He's the king.'

'He is Warwick's puppet,' my brother says cruelly. 'Lord Warwick decided to back him, just as Warwick's father backed Edward's father. Without the support of Warwick neither your lover nor his father would have been able to make anything of his claim to the throne. Warwick is the Kingmaker and he has made your lover into King of England. Be very sure he will make the queen too. He will chose who Edward is to marry, and Edward will marry her.'

I am stunned into silence. 'But he didn't. He can't. Edward married me.'

'A play, a charade, mumming, nothing more.'

'It wasn't. There were witnesses.'

'Who?'

'Mother, for one,' I say eventually.

'Our mother?'

'She was witness, along with Catherine, her lady-in-waiting.'

'Does Father know? Was he there?'

I shake my head.

'There you are then,' he says. 'Who are your many witnesses?'

'Mother, Catherine, the priest and a boy singer,' I say.

'Which priest?'

'One I don't know. The king commanded him there.'

He shrugs. 'If he was a priest at all. He is more likely some fool or mummer pretending as a favour. Even if he is ordained, the king can still deny that the marriage was valid and it is the word of three women and a boy against the King of England. Easy enough to get you three arrested on some charge and held for a year or so until he is married to whatever princess he chooses. He has played you and Mother for fools.'

'I swear to you that he loves me.'

'Maybe he does,' he concedes. 'As maybe he loves each and every one of the women he has bedded, and there are hundreds of them. But when the battle is over and he is riding home and sees another pretty girl by the roadside? He will forget you within a sennight.'

I rub my hand against my cheek and find that my cheeks are wet with tears. 'I'm going to tell Mother what you said,' I say weakly. It is the threat of our childhood; it didn't frighten him then.

'Let's both go to her. She won't be happy when she realises that she has been fooled into pushing her daughter into dishonour.'

We walk in silence through the woods and then over the footbridge. As we go by the big ash tree I glance at the trunk. The looped thread has gone; there is no proof that the magic was ever there. The waters of the river where I dragged my ring from the flood have closed over. There is no proof that the magic ever worked. There is no proof that there is such a thing as magic at all. All I have is a little gold ring shaped like a crown that may mean nothing.

Mother is in the herb garden at the side of the house and, when she sees my brother and I walking together in stubborn silence, a pace apart, saying nothing, she straightens up with the herbs in her basket and waits for us to come towards her, readying herself for trouble.

'Son,' she greets my brother. Anthony kneels for her blessing and she puts her hand on his fair head and smiles down on him. He rises to his feet and takes her hand in his.

'I think the king has lied to you and to my sister,' he says bluntly. 'The marriage ceremony was so secret that there is nobody of any authority to prove it. I think he went through the sham ceremony to have the bedding of her, and he will deny that they were married.'

'Oh, do you?' she says, unruffled.

'I do,' he says. 'And it won't be the first time he has pretended marriage to a lady in order to bed her. He has played this game before and the woman ended with a bastard and no wedding ring.'

My mother, magnificently, shrugs her shoulders. 'What he has done in the past is his own affair,' she says. 'But I saw him wedded and bedded and I wager that he will come back to claim her as his wife.'

'Never,' Anthony says simply. 'And she will be ruined. If she is with child she will be utterly disgraced.'

My mother smiles up at his cross face. 'If you were right and he was going to deny the marriage then her prospects would be poor indeed,' she agrees.

I turn my head from them. It is only a moment since my lover was telling me how to keep his son safe. Now this same child is described as my ruin.

'I am going to see my sons,' I say coldly to them both. 'I won't hear this and I won't speak of it. I am true to him and he will be true to me, and you will be sorry that you doubted us.'

'You are a fool,' my brother says, unimpressed. 'I am sorry for that, at least.' And to my mother he says, 'You have taken a great gamble with her, a brilliant gamble; but you have staked her life and happiness on the word of a known liar.'

'Perhaps,' my mother says, unmoved. 'And you are a wise man, my son, a philosopher. But some things I know better than you, even now.'

I stalk away. Neither of them calls me back.

I have to wait, the whole kingdom has to wait again to hear who to hail as king, who shall command. My brother Anthony sends a man north, scouting for news, and then we all wait for him to come back to tell us if the battle has been joined, and if King Edward's luck has held. Finally, in May, Anthony's servant comes home and says he has been in the far north, near to Hexham, and met a man who told him all about it. A bad battle, a bloody battle. I hesitate in the doorway; I want to know the outcome, not the details. I don't have to see a battle to imagine it any more; we have become a country accustomed to tales of the battlefield. Everyone has heard of the armies drawn up in their positions, or seen the charge, the falling back and the exhausted pause while they regroup. Or everyone knows someone who has been in a town where the victorious soldiers came through determined to carouse and rob and rape; everyone has stories of women running to a church for sanctuary, screaming for help. Everyone knows that these wars have torn our country apart, have destroyed our prosperity, our friendliness between neighbours, our trust of strangers, the love between brothers, the safety of our roads, the affection for our king; and yet nothing seems to stop the battles. We go on and on seeking a final victory and a triumphant king who will bring peace; but victory never comes and peace never comes and the kingship is never settled.

Anthony's messenger gets to the point. King Edward's army has won, and won decisively. The Lancaster forces were routed and King Henry, the poor wandering lost King Henry who does not know fully where he is, even when he is in his palace at Whitehall, has run away into the moors of Northumberland, a price on his head as if he were an outlaw, without attendants, without friends, without even followers, like a borderer rebel as wild as a chough.

His wife, Queen Margaret of Anjou, my mother's one-time dearest friend, is fled to Scotland with the prince their heir. She is defeated, and her husband is vanquished. But everyone knows that she will not accept her defeat, she will plot and scheme for her son, just as Edward told me, that I must plot and scheme for ours. She will never stop until she is back in England and the battle is drawn up again. She will never stop until her husband is dead, her son is dead, and she has no one left to put on the throne. This is what it means to be Queen of England in this country today. This is how it has been for her for nearly ten years, ever since her husband became unfit to rule and his country became like a frightened hare thrown into a field before a pack of hunting dogs, darting this way and that. Worse, I know that this is how it will be for me, if Edward comes home to me and names me as the new queen, and we make a son and heir. The young man I love will be king of an uncertain kingdom, and I will have to be a claimant queen.

And he does come. He sends me word that he has won the battle and broken the siege of Bamburgh Castle, and will call in as his army marches south. He will come for dinner, he writes to my father, and in a private note to me he scribbles that he will stay the night.

I show the note to my mother. 'You can tell Anthony that my husband is true to me,' I say.

'I shan't tell Anthony anything,' she says unhelpfully.

My father, at any rate, manages to be pleased at the prospect of a visit from the victor. 'We were right to give him our men,' he says to my mother. 'Bless you for that, love. He is the victorious king and you have put us on the winning side once more.'

She smiles at him. 'It could have gone either way, as always,' she says. 'And it is Elizabeth who has turned his head. It is her he is coming to see.'

'Do we have some well-hung beef?' he asks. 'And John and the boys and I will go hawking and get you some game.'

'We'll give him a good dinner,' she reassures him. But she does not tell my father that he has greater cause for celebration: that the King of England has married me. She stays silent, and I wonder if she too thinks that he is playing me false.

There is no sign of what my mother thinks, one way or another, when she greets him with a low curtsey. She shows no familiarity, as a woman might do to her son-in-law. But she treats him with no coldness, as surely she would if she thought he had made fools of us both? Rather, she greets him as a victorious king and he greets her as a great lady, a former duchess, and both of them treat me as a favoured daughter of the house.

Dinner is as successful as it is bound to be, given that my father is filled with bluster and excitement, my mother as elegant as always, my sisters in their usual state of stunned admiration, and my brothers furiously silent. The king bids his farewell to my parents and rides off down the road as if going back to Northampton, and I throw on my cape and run down the path to the hunting lodge by the river.

He is there before me, his big war horse in the stall, his page-boy in the hay loft, and he takes me into his arms without a word.

I say nothing too. I am not such a fool as to greet a man with suspicion and complaints, and besides, when he touches me all I want is his touch, when he kisses me, all I want are his kisses, and all I want to hear are the sweetest words in the world, when he says: 'Bed, Wife.'

In the morning I am combing my hair before the little silvered mirror and pinning it up. He stands behind me, watching me, sometimes taking a lock of golden hair and winding it round his finger to see it catch the light. 'You aren't helping,' I say, smiling.

'I don't want to help, I want to hinder. I adore your hair, I like to see it loose.'

'And when shall we announce our marriage, my lord?' I ask, watching his face in the reflection.

'Not yet,' he says swiftly, too swiftly: this is an answer prepared. 'My Lord Warwick is hell-bent on me marrying the Princess Bona of Savoy, to guarantee peace with France. I have to take some time to tell him it cannot be. He will need to get used to the idea.'

'Some days?' I suggest.

'Say weeks,' he prevaricates. 'He will be disappointed and he has taken God knows what bribes to bring this marriage about.'

'He is disloyal? He is bribed?'

'No. Not he. He takes the French money but not to betray me: we are as one. We have known each other since boyhood. He taught me how to joust, he gave me my first sword. His father was like a father to me. Truly, he has been like an older brother to me. I would not have fought for my right to the throne if he had not been with me. His father took my father up to the very throne and made him heir to the King of England, and in his turn Richard Neville has supported me. He is my great mentor, my great friend. He has taught me almost everything I know about fighting and ruling a kingdom. I have to take the time to tell him about us, and explain that I could not resist you. I owe him that.'

'He is so important to you?'

'The greatest man in my life.'

'But you will tell him, you will bring me to court,' I say, trying to keep my voice light and inconsequential. 'And present me to the court as your wife.'

'When the time is right.'

'May I at least tell my father, so that we can meet openly as husband and wife?'

He laughs. 'As well tell the town crier. No, my love, you must keep our secret for a little while longer.'

I take my tall headdress with the sweeping veil and tie it on, saying nothing. It gives me a headache with the weight of it.

'You do trust me, don't you, Elizabeth?' he asks sweetly.

'Yes,' I lie. 'Completely.'

Anthony stands beside me as the king rides away, his hand raised in a salute, a false smile on his face. 'Not going with him?' he asks sarcastically. 'Not going to London to buy new clothes? Not going to be presented at court? Not attending the thanksgiving mass as queen?'

'He has to tell Lord Warwick,' I say. 'He has to explain.'

'It will be Lord Warwick who will explain to him,' my brother says bluntly. 'He will tell him that no king of England can afford to marry a commoner, no king of England would marry a woman who is not a proven virgin. No king of England would marry an Englishwoman of no family and no fortune. And your precious king will explain that it was a wedding witnessed by no lord nor court official, that his new wife has not even told her family, that she wears her ring in her pocket; and they will both agree it can be ignored as if it had never happened. As he has done before, so he will do again, as long as there are foolish women in the kingdom – and that is to say for ever.'

I turn to him and at the pain on my face he stops taunting me. 'Ah, Elizabeth, don't look like that.'

'I don't care if he doesn't acknowledge me, you fool,' I flare out. 'It's not a question of wanting to be queen; it's not even a question of wanting honourable love any more. I am mad for him, I am madly in love with him. I would go to him if I had to walk barefoot. Tell me: I am one of many. I don't care! I don't care for my name or for my pride any more. As long as I can have him once more that's all I want, just to love him; all I want to be certain of is that I will see him again, that he loves me.'

Anthony folds me in his arms and pats my back. 'Of course he loves you,' he says. 'What man could not? And if he does not, then he is a fool.'

'I love him,' I say miserably. 'I would love him if he were a nobody.'

'No you wouldn't,' he says gently. 'You are your mother's child through and through; you don't have the blood of a goddess in you for nothing. You were born to be queen and maybe everything will come out well. Maybe he loves you and will stand by you.'

I tilt my head back to scan his face. 'But you don't believe it.'

'No,' he says honestly. 'To tell you the truth, I think you have seen the last of him.'

## SEPTEMBER 1464

He sends me a letter. He addresses me as Lady Elizabeth Grey and inside he writes 'my love'; he does not say 'wife', so he gives me nothing that can prove our marriage if he should deny it. He writes that he is busy but will send for me shortly. The court is at Reading, he will speak to Lord Warwick soon. The council is meeting, there is so much to do. The lost king, Henry, has still not been captured; he is out somewhere in the hills of Northumberland; but the queen has fled to her homeland of France demanding help, so an alliance with France is more important than ever before, to cut her out of the French councils, and make sure she cannot have allies. He does not remark that a French marriage would do this for him. He says he loves me, he burns up for me. Lover's words, lover's promises: nothing binding.

The same messenger brings a summons for my father to attend the court at Reading. It is a standard letter, every nobleman in the country will have had the same. My brothers Anthony, John, Richard, Edward, and Lionel are to go with him. 'Write and tell me everything about it,' my mother commands my father as we watch them mount up. They make a little army themselves, my mother's fine brood of sons.

'He will be calling us to announce his wedding to the French princess,' my father grumbles, bending over to tighten his girth under the saddle flap. 'And much good an alliance with the French will do us. Much good it has ever done us before. Still, it will have to be done if Margaret of Anjou is to be silenced. And a French bride would welcome you at her court, a kinswoman.'

My mother does not even blink at the prospect of Edward's French bride. 'Write and tell me at once,' she says. 'And God go with you, my husband, and keep you safe.'

He leans down from the saddle to kiss her hand and then turns his horse's head down the road to the south. My brothers twirl their whips, raise their hats, bellow a farewell. My sisters wave, my sister-in-law Elizabeth curtseys to Anthony, who raises his hand to her, my mother and to me. His face is grim.

But it is Anthony who writes to me two days later, and it is his manservant who rides like a madman to bring me his letter.

*Sister,*

*This is your triumph, and I am glad to my heart for you. There has been an earth-shaking quarrel between the king and Lord Warwick, for My Lord brought a marriage contract to the king for him to marry Princess Bona of Savoy, as everyone was expecting. The king, with the contract before him and the pen in his hand, raised his head and told His Lordship that he could not marry the princess for – actually – he was already married. You could have heard a feather fall; you could hear the angels gasp. I swear I heard Lord Warwick's very heart pound as he asked the king to repeat what he had said. The king was white as a girl but he faced Lord Warwick (which I would not want to do myself) and told him that all his plans and all his promises were as nothing. His Lordship took the king by the arm as if he were a boy and hustled him from the room into a privy chamber, leaving the rest of us boiling with gossip and amazement like neeps seething in a stew.*

*I took the chance to pin our father into the corner and tell him that I thought the king might announce his marriage to you, so as to prevent us looking as great fools as Lord W – but even in that moment I confess to you that I feared that the king might be admitting marriage to another lady. There has been another lady mentioned of noble birth, better than ours, actually, and she has his son. Forgive me, Sister, but you don't know how bad his reputation has been. So Father and I were like hares in March, jumping at nothing, while the privy-chamber door stayed shut and the king was locked away with the man who made him and who – God knows – might just as quickly unmake him again.*

*Of course Lionel wanted to know what we were whispering about, and John too. Thank God, Edward and Richard had gone out, so there were only two extra to tell; but they couldn't believe it any more than Father, and I had much to do to keep the three of them quiet. You can imagine what it was like.*

*An hour must have passed but no one could bear to leave the council chamber until they had the end of this story. Sister, they were pissing in the fireplaces rather than leave the great hall – and then the door opened and the king came out looking shaken and Lord Warwick came out looking grim and the king put on his happiest smile and said, 'Well, my lords, I thank you for your patience. I am happy and proud to tell you that I am married to Lady Elizabeth Grey,' and he nodded towards my father and I swear he shot me a look which begged me to keep Father quiet, so I got hold of the old man's shoulder and leaned hard to keep him anchored to the ground. Edward got the other side of him as ballast, and Lionel crossed himself like he was an archbishop already. Father and I bowed proudly and simpered about ourselves, as if we had known all along and only failed to mention that we were now brother and father-in-law to the King of England from sheer delicacy.*

*John and Richard stumbled in at this most inconvenient moment and we had to mutter to them that the world was turned upside down and they did better than you can imagine. They managed to close their mouths and stood beside Father and me, and people took our dumbstruck faces for quiet pride. We were a quartet of idiots trying to look suave. You cannot imagine the bluster and the shouting and the complaints and the trouble which followed. Nobody in my hearing dared to suggest that the king had stooped too low, but I know that behind me and on either side there were men who think so, and will go on thinking so. Still, the king kept his fair head high and brazened it out and Father and I went and stood on either side of him, and all my brothers stood behind us and no one can deny that we are a handsome family, or at the very least tall, and the thing is done, nobody can now deny it. You can tell Mother that her great gamble has paid a thousandfold: you will be Queen of England and we will be England's ruling family, even if no one in England wants us.*

*Father kept his mouth shut till we were clear of the court but I swear his eyes were rolling in his head like Idiot Jim at Stony Stratford, till we got to our lodgings and I could tell him what had been done and how it had been done – at least as far as I knew – and now he is aggrieved that nobody told him, since he would have managed it so well and been so discreet – but given that he is father-in-law to the King of England I think he will forgive you and Mother for keeping your women's toils to yourselves. Your brothers went out and got drunk on credit, as anyone would do. Lionel swears he will be Pope.*

*Your new husband is clearly stunned by the row that has broken on his head, and he will find it hard to reconcile with his former master Lord Warwick, who is dining apart tonight and could make a dangerous enemy. We are to dine with the king and his interests are ours. The world has changed for us Rivers and we are become so great that I confidently expect us to flow up hills. We are now passionate Yorkists and you can expect Father to plant white roses in his hedgerows and wear a bloom in his hat. You can tell Mother that whatever magic she deployed to bring this about has the stunned admiration of her husband and sons. If the magic was nothing more than your beauty, we admire that too.*

*You are now summoned to be presented at court, here at Reading. The king's order will be sent tomorrow. Sister, be warned by me and please come dressed modestly and with only a small escort. It will not avert envy but we should try not to make matters worse than they already are. We have made enemies of every family in the kingdom. Families that we do not even know will be cursing our luck and wishing us to fall. Ambitious fathers with pretty daughters will never forgive you. We will have to be on our guard for the rest of our lives. You have put us into great opportunity but also great risk, my sister. I am brother-in-law to the King of England, but I must say tonight my greatest hope is to die in my bed, at peace with the world, as an old man.*

*Your brother,*
*Anthony*

*But I think, in the meantime, before my peaceful death, I shall ask him to make me a duke.*

My mother plans our journey to Reading and the summoning of our family as if she were a queen militant. Every relation that would benefit from our rise or might contribute to our position is commanded from every corner of England, and even our Burgundy family – her kinsmen – are invited to come to London for my coronation. She says that they will give me the royal and noble status that we need, and besides, in the state the world is in, it is always wise to have powerful relatives for support or refuge.

She starts to draw up a list of eligible lords and ladies for my brothers and sisters to marry; she starts to consider noble children who will be made wards and can be raised in a royal nursery to our profit. She understands, and she starts to teach me, how the patronage and power of the English court works. She knows it well enough. She was married into the royal family with her first husband, the Duke of Bedford. Then she was second lady in the kingdom under the Lancaster queen; now she will be second lady under the York queen: me. No one knows better than she how to plough the furrow that is royal England.

She sends a string of instructions to Anthony to order tailors and sempstresses so that I shall have new dresses waiting for me, but she takes his advice that we should enter into our greatness quietly, and without any sign of glorying in this leap from being of the defeated House of Lancaster to being new partners of the victorious House of York. My sisters, cousins and sister-in-law are to ride with us to Reading but there is to be no great train with standards and trumpets. Father writes to her that there are many who begrudge us our prosperity, but the ones that he fears above all are the king's greatest friend Sir William Hastings, the king's great ally Lord Warwick, and the king's close family: his mother, sisters and his brothers, as they have the most to lose from new favourites at court.

I remember Hastings looking at me as if I were roadside merchandise, a pedlar's pack, the very first time that I met the king, and I promise myself that he will never look at me in that way again. Hastings, I think I can manage. He loves the king like no other, and he will accept any choice that Edward makes, and defend it too. But Lord Warwick frightens me. He is a man who will stop at nothing to get his own way. As a boy he saw his father rebel against his lawful king and set up a rival house in the name of York. When his father and Edward's father were killed together, he at once continued his father's work and saw Edward crowned king, a boy of only nineteen. Warwick is thirteen years his senior: an adult man compared with a boy. Clearly he has planned all along to put a boy on the throne and to rule from the shadows. Edward's choice of me will be the first declaration of independence from his mentor, and Warwick will be quick to prevent any others. They call him the Kingmaker and when we were Lancastrians we said that the Yorks were nothing but puppets and he and his family were the puppet masters. Now I am married to Warwick's puppet and I know that he will try to set me dancing to his tune as well. Still, there is no time to do anything but bid farewell to my boys, make them promise to obey their tutors and be good, mount the new horse that the king has sent me for the journey, and with my mother at my side and my sisters following behind me take the road to Reading and to the future that waits for me.

I say to my mother, 'I am afraid.'

She brings her horse beside mine and she puts back the hood of her cape so that I can see the smiling confidence in her face. 'Perhaps,' she says. 'But I was at the court of Queen Margaret d'Anjou; I swear you cannot be a worse queen than her.'

Despite myself, I giggle. This comes from a woman who was Margaret of Anjou's most trusted lady-in-waiting and the first lady of her court. 'You have changed your tune.'

'Aye, for now I am in a different choir. But it is true nonetheless. You could not be a worse queen for this country than she was, God help her, wherever she is now.'

'Mother – she was married to a husband who was out of his wits for half of the time.'

'And whether he was saintly, sane or raving mad she always went her own way. She took a lover,' she says cheerfully, ignoring my scandalised gasp. 'Of course she did. Where d'you think she got her son Edward? Not from the king, who was struck deaf and dumb for nearly the whole year that the child was conceived and born. I expect you to do better than her. You cannot doubt that you can do better than her. And Edward cannot help but do better than a sainted half-wit, God bless the poor man. And as for the rest, you should give your husband a son and heir, protect the poor and innocent, and further the hopes of your family. That is all you need to do, and you can do that. Any ninny with an honest heart, a scheming family and an open purse can do that.'

'There will be many people who hate me,' I say. 'Many who hate us.'

She nods. 'Then make sure that you get the favours that you want and the places that you need before they take the ear of the king,' she says simply. 'There are only so many great positions for your brothers, there are only a few noblemen for your sisters to marry. Make sure that you get everything you want in the first year, and then you have taken the high ground, and are in battle array. We are ready for whatever comes against us and even if your influence declines with the king then we are still safe.'

'My Lord Warwick . . .' I say nervously.

She nods. 'He is our enemy,' she says. It is the declaration of a blood feud. 'You will watch him, and you will be wary of him. We will all be on our guard against him. Him and the king's brothers: George, the Duke of Clarence, who is always so charming, and the boy Richard, the Duke of Gloucester. They too will be your enemies.'

'Why the king's brothers?'

'Your sons will disinherit them. Your influence will turn the king from them. They have been three fatherless boys together, they have fought side by side for their family. He called them the three sons of York; he saw a sign for the three of them in the heavens. But now he will want to be with you, not with them. And the grants of lands and wealth that he might have given to them will come to you and yours. George was the heir after Edward, Richard the heir after him. As soon as you have a boy they drop one place.'

'I am going to be Queen of England,' I protest. 'You make it sound like a battle to the death.'

'It is a battle to the death,' she says simply. 'That is what it means to be Queen of England. You are not Melusina, rising from a fountain to easy happiness. You will not be a beautiful woman at court with nothing to do but make magic. The road you have chosen will mean that you have to spend your life scheming and fighting. Our task, as your family, is to make sure you win.'

*In the darkness of the forest he saw her, and whispered her name, Melusina, and at that summoning she rose out of the water and he saw that she was a woman of cool and complete beauty to the waist, and below that she was scaled, like a fish. She promised him that she would come to him and be his wife, she promised him that she would make him as happy as a mortal woman can, she promised him that she would curb her wild side, her tidal nature, that she would be an ordinary wife to him, a wife that he could be proud of; if he in return would let her have a time when she could be herself again, when she could return to her element of water, when she could wash away the drudgery of a woman's lot and be, for just a little while, a water goddess once more. She knew that being a mortal woman is hard on the heart, hard on the feet. She knew that she would need to be alone in the water, under the water, the ripples reflected on her scaly tail now and then. He promised her that he would give her everything, everything she wanted, as men in love always do. And she trusted him despite herself, as women in love always do.*

My father and all my brothers ride out of Reading to greet us, so I might enter the town with my kinsmen at my side. There are crowds along the road and hundreds watching my father pull off his hat as he rides towards me, and then dismounts and kneels to me in the dust, honouring me as queen.

'Get up, Father!' I say alarmed.

He rises slowly and bows again. 'You must become accustomed, Your Grace,' he says to me, his head bent to his knees.

I wait till he comes up smiling at me. 'Father, I don't like to see you bow to me.'

'You are Queen of England, now, Your Grace. Every man but one must bow to you.'

'But you will still call me Elizabeth, Father?'

'Only when we are alone.'

'And you will give me your blessing?'

His wide smile assures me that everything is the same as ever.

'Daughter, we have to play at being kings and queens. You are the newest and most unlikely queen to a new and unlikely house. I never dreamed that you would capture a king. I certainly never thought that this lad would capture a throne. We are making a new world here, we are forming a new royal family. We have to be more royal than royalty itself or nobody will believe us. I can't say I quite believe it myself.'

My brothers all jump down from their horses, doff their caps, and kneel to me on the public highway. I look down at Anthony who called me a whore and my husband a liar. 'You can stay down there,' I say. 'Who is right now?'

'You are,' he says cheerfully, rising up, kissing my hand, and remounting his horse. 'I give you joy of your triumph.'

My brothers come around me and kiss my hand. I smile down at them; it is as if we are all about to burst out laughing at our own presumption. 'Who'd have thought it?' John says wonderingly. 'Who would ever have dreamed it?'

'Where is the king?' I ask as we start our small procession through the gates of the town. The streets are lined on either side with townspeople, guildsmen, apprentices, and there is a cheer for my beauty and laughter at our procession. I see Anthony flush when he hears a couple of bawdy jokes and I put my hand on his gloved fist, clenched on the pommel of his saddle. 'Hush,' I say. 'People are bound to make mock. This was a secret wedding, we cannot deny it, and we will have to live down the scandal. And you don't help me at all if you look offended.'

At once he assumes the most ghastly simper. 'This is my court smile,' he says out of the corner of his upturned mouth. 'I use it when I talk to Warwick or the royal dukes. How d'you like it?'

'Very elegant,' I say, trying not to laugh. 'Dear God, Anthony, d'you think we will get through this all right?'

'We will get through it triumphantly,' he says. 'But we must stick together.'

We turn up the high street and now there are hastily made banners and pictures of saints held from the overhanging windows to welcome me to the city. We ride to the abbey; and there, in the centre of his court and advisors, I see him, Edward, dressed in cloth of gold with a scarlet cape and a scarlet hat on his head. He is unmistakable, the tallest man in the crowd, the most handsome, the undoubted King of England. He sees me, and our eyes meet, and it is once again as if no one else is there. I am so relieved to see him that I give him a little wave, like a girl, and instead of waiting for me to halt my horse and dismount and approach him up the carpet, he breaks away from them all and comes quickly to my side and lifts me off my horse and into his arms.

There is a roar of delighted applause from the onlookers and a shocked silence from the court at this passionate breach of protocol.

'Wife,' he says in my ear. 'Dear God, I am so glad to have you in my arms.'

'Edward,' I say. 'I have been so afraid!'

'We have won,' he says simply. 'We will be together for ever. I shall make you Queen of England.'

'And I shall make you happy,' I say, quoting the marriage vows. 'I shall be bonny and blithe at bed and board.'

'I don't care a damn about dinnertime,' he says vulgarly, and I hide my face against his shoulder and laugh.

I still have to meet his mother; and Edward takes me to her private chambers before dinner. She was not present during my welcome from the court, and I am right to read this as her first snub, the first of many. He leaves me at her door. 'She wants to see you alone.'

'How do you think she will be?' I ask nervously.

He grins. 'What can she do?'

'That is the very thing I would like to know before I go in to face her,' I say drily and walk past him as they throw open the doors to her presence chamber. My mother and three of my sisters come with me as a makeshift court, my newly declared ladies-in-waiting, and we step forward with all the eagerness of a coven of witches dragged to trial.

The dowager Duchess Cecily is seated on a great chair covered by a cloth of estate, and she does not trouble herself to rise to greet me. She is wearing a gown encrusted with jewels at the hem and the breast, and a large square headdress that she wears proudly, like a crown. Very well, I am her son's wife but not yet an ordained queen. She is not obliged to curtsey to me, and she will think of me as a Lancastrian, one of her son's enemies. The turn of her head and the coldness of her smile convey very clearly that to her I am a commoner, as if she herself had not been born an ordinary English woman. Behind her chair are her daughters Anne, Elizabeth and Margaret, dressed quietly and modestly so as not to outshine their mother. Margaret is a pretty girl: fair and tall like her brothers. She smiles shyly at me, her new sister-in-law, but nobody steps forward to kiss me, and the room is as warm as a lake in December.

I curtsey low, but not very low, to Duchess Cecily, out of respect to my husband's mother and behind me I see my mother sweep her grandest gesture and then stand still, her head up, a queen herself, in everything but a crown.

'I will not pretend that I am happy with this secret marriage,' the dowager duchess says rudely.

'Private,' my mother interrupts smartly.

The duchess checks, amazed, and raises her perfectly arched eyebrows. 'I beg your pardon, Lady Rivers. Did you speak?'

'Neither my daughter nor your son would so far forget themselves as to marry in secret,' my mother says, her Burgundy accent suddenly revived. It is the very accent of elegance and high style for the whole of Europe. She could not remind everyone more clearly that she is the daughter of the Count of Saint-Pol, Burgundian royalty by birth. She was on first-name terms with the queen who she alone persists in calling Margaret d'Anjou, with much emphasis on the 'd' of the title. She was the Duchess of Bedford by her first marriage to a duke of the royal blood, and the head of the

Lancaster court when the woman seated so proudly before us was born nothing more than Lady Cecily Neville of Raby Castle. 'Of course it was not a secret wedding. I was there and so were other witnesses. It was a private wedding.'

'Your daughter is a widow and years older than my son,' Her Grace says, joining battle.

'He is hardly an inexperienced boy. His reputation is notorious. And there are only five years between them.'

There is a gasp from the duchess's ladies and a flutter of alarm from her daughters. Margaret looks at me with sympathy as if to say there is no escaping the humiliation to come. My sisters and I are like standing stones, as if we were dancing witches under a sudden enchantment.

'And the good thing,' my mother says, warming to her theme, 'is that we can at least be sure that they are both fertile. Your son has several bastards, I understand, and my daughter has two handsome legitimate boys.'

'My son comes from a fertile family. I had eight boys,' the dowager duchess says.

My mother inclines her head and the scarf on her headdress billows like a sail filled with the swollen breeze of her pride. 'Oh, yes,' she remarks. 'So you did. But of that eight, only three boys left, of course. So sad. As it happens, I have five sons. Five. And seven girls. Elizabeth comes from fertile royal stock. I think we can hope that God will bless the new royal family with issue.'

'Nonetheless she was not my choice, nor the choice of the Lord Warwick,' Her Grace repeats, her voice trembling with anger. 'It would mean nothing if Edward were not king. I might overlook it if he were a third or fourth son to throw himself away . . .'

'Perhaps you might. But it does not concern us. King Edward is the king. The king is the king. God knows, he has fought enough battles to prove his claim.'

'I could prevent him being king,' she rushes in, temper getting the better of her, her cheeks scarlet. 'I could disown him, I could deny him, I could put George on the throne in his place. How would you like that – as the outcome of your so-called private wedding, Lady Rivers?'

The duchess's ladies blanch and sway back in horror. Margaret, who adores her brother, whispers, 'Mother!' but dares say no more. Edward has never been their mother's favourite. Edmund, her beloved Edmund, died with his father at Wakefield and the Lancastrian victors stuck their heads on the gates of York. George, his brother, younger again and his mother's darling, is the pet of the family. Richard, the youngest of all, is the dark-haired runt of the litter. It is incredible that she should talk of putting one son before another, out of order.

'How?' my mother says sharply, calling her bluff. 'How would you overthrow your own son?'

'If he was not my husband's child . . .'

'Mother!' Margaret wails.

'And how could that be?' demands my mother, as sweet as poison. 'Would you call your own son a bastard? Would you name yourself a whore? Just for spite, just to throw us down, would you destroy your own reputation and put cuckold's horns on your own dead husband? When they put his head on the gates of York they put a paper crown on him to make mock. That would be nothing to putting cuckold's horns on him now. Would you dishonour your own name? Would you shame your husband worse than his enemies did?'

There is a little scream from the women, and poor Margaret staggers as if to faint. My sisters and I are half fish, not girls; we just goggle at our mother and the king's mother head to head, like a pair of slugging battleaxemen in the jousting ring, saying the unthinkable.

'There are many who would believe me,' the king's mother threatens.

'More shame to you then,' my mother says roundly. 'The rumours about his fathering reached England. Indeed. I was among the few who swore that a lady of your house would never stoop so low. But I heard, we all heard, gossip of an archer named – what was it –' She pretends to forget and taps her forehead. 'Ah, I have it: Blaybourne. An archer named Blaybourne, who was supposed to be your amour. But I said, and even Queen Margaret d'Anjou said, that a great lady like you would not so demean herself as to lie with a common archer and slip his bastard into a nobleman's cradle.'

The name Blaybourne drops into the room with a thud like a cannonball. You can almost hear it roll to a standstill. My mother is afraid of nothing.

'And anyway, if you can make the lords throw down King Edward, who is going to support your new King George? Could you trust his brother Richard not to have his own try at the throne in his turn? Would your kinsman Lord Warwick, your great friend, not want the throne on his own account? And why should they not feud amongst themselves and make another generation of enemies, dividing the country, setting brother against brother again, destroying the very peace that your son has won for himself and for his house? Would you destroy everything for nothing but spite? We all know the House of York is mad with ambition; will we be able to watch you eat yourselves up like a frightened cat eats her own kittens?'

It is too much for her. The king's mother puts out a hand to my mother as if to beg her to stop. 'No, no. Enough. Enough.'

'I speak as a friend,' my mother says quickly, as sinuous as a river eel. 'And your thoughtless words against the king will go no further. My girls and I would not repeat such a scandal, such a treasonous scandal. We will forget that you ever said such a thing. I am only sorry that you even thought of it. I am amazed that you should say it.'

'Enough,' the king's mother repeats. 'I just wanted you to know that this ill-conceived marriage is not my choice. Though I see I must accept it. You show me that I must accept it. However much it galls me, however much it denigrates my son and my house, I must accept it.' She sighs. 'I will think of it as my burden to bear.'

'It was the king's choice, and we must all obey him,' my mother says, driving home her advantage. 'King Edward has chosen his wife and she will be Queen of England and the greatest lady – bar none – in the land. And no one can doubt that my daughter will make the most beautiful Queen that England has ever seen.'

The king's mother, whose own beauty was famous in her day, when they called her the Rose of Raby, looks at me for the first time without pleasure. 'I suppose so,' she says grudgingly.

I curtsey again. 'Shall I call you Mother?' I ask cheerfully.

As soon as the ordeal of my welcome from Edward's mother is over, I have to prepare for my presentation to the court. Anthony's orders from the London dressmakers have been delivered in time and I have a new gown to wear in the palest of grey, trimmed with pearls. It is cut low in the front with a high girdle of pearls and long silky sleeves. I wear it with a conical high headdress which is draped with a scarf of grey. It is both gloriously rich and beguilingly modest, and when my mother comes to my room to see that I am dressed she takes my hands and kisses me on both cheeks. 'Beautiful,' she says. 'Nobody could doubt that he married you for love at first sight. Troubadour love, God bless you both.'

'Are they waiting for me?' I ask nervously.

She nods her head to the chamber outside my bedroom door. 'They are all out there: Lord Warwick and the Duke of Clarence and half a dozen others.'

I take a deep breath, and I put my hand to steady my headdress, and I nod to my maids-in-waiting to throw open the double doors, and I raise my head like a queen, and walk out of the room.

Lord Warwick, dressed in black, is standing at the fireside, a big man, in his late thirties, shoulders broad like a bully, stern face in profile as he is watching the flames. When he hears the door opening he turns and sees me, scowls and then pastes a smile on his face. 'Your Grace,' he says and bows low.

I curtsey to him but I see his smile does not warm his dark eyes. He was counting on Edward remaining under his control. He had promised the King of France that he could deliver Edward in marriage. Now everything has gone wrong for him and people are asking if he is still the power behind this new throne, or if Edward will make his own decisions.

The Duke of Clarence, the king's beloved brother George, is beside him looking like a true York prince, golden-haired, ready of smile, graceful even in repose, a handsome dainty copy of my husband. He is fair and well made, his bow is as elegant as an Italian dancer's and his smile is charming. 'Your Grace,' he says. 'My new sister. I give you joy of your surprise marriage and wish you well in your new estate.'

I give my hand and he draws me to him and kisses me warmly on both cheeks. 'I do truly wish you much joy,' he says cheerfully. 'My brother is a fortunate man indeed. And I am happy to call you my sister.'

I turn to the Earl of Warwick. 'I know that my husband loves and trusts you as his brother and his friend,' I say. 'It is an honour to meet you.'

'The honour is all mine,' he says curtly. 'Are you ready?'

I glance behind me: my sisters and mother are lined up to follow me in procession. 'We are ready,' I say, and with the Duke of Clarence on one side of me and the Earl of Warwick on the other, we march slowly to the abbey chapel through a crowd which parts as we come towards them.

My first impression is that everyone I have ever seen at court is here, dressed in their finest to honour me, and there are a few hundred new faces too, who have come in with the Yorks. The lords are in the front with their capes trimmed with ermine, the gentry behind them with chains of office and jewels on display. The aldermen and councillors of London have trooped down to be presented, the city fathers among them. The civic leaders of Reading are there, struggling to see and be seen around the big bonnets and the plumes, behind them the guildsmen of Reading and gentry from all England. This is an event of national importance; anyone who could buy a doublet and borrow a horse has come to see the scandalous new queen. I have to face them all alone, flanked by my enemies, as a thousand gazes take me in: from my slippered feet to my high headdress and airy veil, take in the pearls on my gown, the carefully modest cut, the perfection of the lace piece which hides and yet enhances the whiteness of the skin of my shoulders. Slowly, like a breeze going through tree tops, they doff their hats and bow, and I realise that they are acknowledging me as queen, queen in the place of Margaret of Anjou, Queen of England, the greatest woman in the realm, and nothing in my life will ever be the same again. I smile from side to side, acknowledging the blessings and the murmurs of praise, but I find that I am tightening my grip on Warwick's hand, and he smiles down at me, as if he is pleased to sense my fear, and he says, 'It is natural for you to be overwhelmed, Your Grace.' It is, indeed, natural for a commoner but would never have occurred to a princess, and I smile back at him and cannot defend myself, and cannot speak.

That night in bed, after we have made love, I say to Edward, 'I don't like the Earl of Warwick.'

'He made me what I am today,' he says simply. 'You must love him for my sake.'

'And your brother George? And William Hastings?'

He rolls onto his side and grins at me. 'These are my companions and my brothers-in-arms,' he says. 'You are marrying into an army at war. We cannot choose our allies, we cannot choose our friends. We are just glad of them. Love them for me, beloved.'

I nod as if obedient. But I think I know my enemies.

## MAY 1465

The king decides that I shall have the most glorious coronation that England has ever seen. This is not solely as a compliment to me. 'We make you queen, undoubted queen, and every lord in the kingdom will bow his knee to you. My mother—' He breaks off and grimaces. 'My mother will have to show you homage as part of the celebrations. Nobody will be able to deny that you are queen and my wife. It will silence those who say our marriage is not valid.'

'Who says?' I demand. 'Who dares say?'

He grins at me. He is a boy still. 'D'you think I would tell you and have you turn them into frogs? Never mind who speaks against us. They don't matter as long as all they do is whisper in corners. But a great coronation for you also declares my position as king. Everyone can see that I am king and that poor thing Henry is a beggar somewhere in Cumbria and his wife a pensioner of her father in Anjou.'

'Hugely grand?' I say, not wholly welcoming the thought.

'You will stagger under the weight of your jewels,' he promises me.

In the event, it is even richer than he predicted, richer than I could have imagined. My entrance to London is by London Bridge, but the dirty old highway is transformed with wagon on wagon load of sparkling sand into a road more like a jousting arena. I am greeted by players dressed as angels, their costumes made from peacock feathers, their dazzling wings like a thousand eyes of blue and turquoise and indigo. Actors make a tableau of the Virgin Mary and the saints, I am exhorted to be virtuous and fertile. The people see me indicated as the choice of God for Queen of England. Choirs sing as I enter the city, rose petals are showered down on me. I am myself, my own tableau: the Englishwoman from the House of Lancaster come to be the Queen of York. I am an object of peace and unity.

I spend the night before my coronation at the grand royal apartments in the Tower, newly decorated for my stay. I don't like the Tower: it gives me a shudder as I am carried shoulder high in a litter under the portcullis, and Anthony at my side glances up at me.

'What's the matter?'

'I hate the Tower, it smells damp.'

'You have grown choosy,' Anthony says. 'You are spoiled already, now that the king has given you great places of your own, the manor of Greenwich, and Sheen as well.'

'It's not that,' I say, trying to name my unease. 'It is as if there are ghosts here. Are my boys staying here tonight?'

'Yes, the whole family is here in the royal rooms.'

I make a little grimace of unease. 'I don't like my boys being here,' I say. 'This is an unlucky place.'

Anthony crosses himself and jumps from his horse to lift me down. 'Smile,' he commands me under his breath.

The Lieutenant of the Tower is waiting to welcome me and give me the keys: this is no time for foreseeing, or for ghosts of boys lost long ago.

'Most gracious Queen, greetings,' he says, and I take Anthony's hand and smile, and hear the crowd murmur that I am a beauty beyond their imaginings.

'Nothing exceptional,' Anthony says for my ears only, so that I have to turn my head and stop myself giggling. 'Nothing compared to our mother, for instance.'

Next day is my coronation at Westminster Abbey. For the court herald, bellowing names of dukes and duchesses and earls, it is a roster of the greatest and most noble families in England and Christendom. For my mother, carrying my train with the king's sisters Elizabeth and Margaret, it is her triumph; for Anthony, a man so much of the world and yet so detached from it, I think it is a ship of fools and he would wish himself far away; and for Edward it is a vivid statement of his wealth and power to a country hungry for a royal family of wealth and power. For me it is a blur of ceremonial in which I feel nothing but anxiety: desperate only to walk at the right speed, to remember to slip off my shoes and go barefoot at the brocade carpet, to accept the two sceptres in each hand, to bare my breast for the holy oil, to hold my head steady for the weight of the crown.

It takes three archbishops to crown me, including Thomas Bourchier, and an abbot, a couple of hundred clergy and a full thousand choristers to sing my praises and call down God's blessing on me. My kinswomen escort me; it turns out I have hundreds of them. The king's family come first, then my own sisters, my sister-in-law Elizabeth Scales, my cousins, my Burgundy cousins, my kinswomen that only my mother can trace, and every other beautiful lady that can scrape an introduction. Everyone wants to be a lady at my coronation, everyone wants a place at my court.

By tradition, Edward is not even with me. He watches from behind a screen, my young sons with him: I may not even see him, I cannot catch courage from his smile. I have to do this all entirely alone, with thousands of strangers watching my every movement. Nothing is to detract from my rise from gentrywoman to Queen of England, from mortal to a being divine: next to God. When they crown me and anoint me with the holy oil I become a new being, one above mortals, only one step below angels, beloved and the elect of heaven. I wait for the thrill down my spine of knowing that God has chosen me to be Queen of England; but I feel nothing but relief that the ceremony is over and apprehension at the massive banquet to follow.

Three thousand noblemen and their ladies sit down to dine with me and each course has nearly twenty dishes. I put off my crown to eat, and put it back on again between every course. It is like a prolonged dance where I have to remember the steps and it goes on for hours. To shield me from prying eyes, the Countess of Shrewsbury and the Countess of Kent kneel to hold a veil before me when I eat. I taste every dish out of courtesy but I eat almost nothing. The crown presses down like a curse on my head and my temples throb. I know myself to have ascended to the greatest place in the land and I long only for my husband and my bed.

There is a moment at one point in the evening, probably around the tenth course, when I actually think that this has been a terrible mistake and I would have been happier back at Grafton, with no ambitious marriage and no ascent to the rank of royals. But it is too late for regrets and, even though the finest of dishes taste of nothing in my weariness, I must still smile and smile, and put my heavy crown back on and send out the best dishes to the favourites of the king.

The first go out to his brothers, George the golden young man, Duke of Clarence, and the youngest York boy, twelve-year-old Richard, Duke of Gloucester, who smiles shyly at me and dips his head when I send him some braised peacock. He is as unlike his brothers as is possible, small and shy and dark-haired, slight of build and quiet while they are tall and bronze-headed and filled with their own importance. I like Richard on sight, and I think he will be a good companion and playmate to my boys, who are only a little younger than him.

At the end of the dinner, when I am escorted back to my chambers by dozens of noblemen and hundreds of clergy, I hold my head high as if I am not weary, as if I am not overwhelmed. I know that I have become something more than a mortal woman today: I have become half a goddess. I have become a divinity something like my ancestress Melusina, who was born a goddess and became a woman. She had to forge a hard bargain with the world of men to move from one world to another. She had to surrender her freedom in the water to earn her feet, so that she could walk beside her husband on the earth. I can't help but wonder what I will have to lose in order to be queen.

They put me to bed in Margaret of Anjou's bed, in the echoing royal bedchamber, and I wait, the cover of cloth of gold up to my ears, until Edward can get away from the feasting and join me. He is escorted into my bedroom by half a dozen companions and menservants and they formally undress him and leave him only when he is in his nightgown. He sees my wide-eyed gaze and laughs as he closes the door behind them.

'We are royal now,' he says. 'These ceremonies have to be endured, Elizabeth.'

I reach out my arms for him. 'As long as you are still you, even underneath the crown.'

He throws off his gown and comes naked to me, his shoulders broad, his skin smooth, the muscles moving in thigh and belly and flank. 'I am yours,' he says simply, and when he slides into the cold bed beside me I quite forget that we are queen and king and think only of his touch and my desire.

The following day there is a great tournament and the noblemen enter the lists in beautiful costumes, with poetry bellowed by their squires. My boys are in the royal box with me, their eyes wide and their mouths open at the ceremony, the flags, the glamour and the crowds, the enormity of the first great joust they have ever seen. My sisters and Elizabeth – Anthony's wife – are seated beside me. We are starting to form a court of beautiful women; already people are speaking of an elegance which has never before been seen in England.

The Burgundian cousins are out in force, their armour the most stylish, their poetry the best for metre. But Anthony, my brother, is superb: the court goes mad over him. He sits a horse with such grace and he carries my favour and breaks the lances of a dozen men. No one can match his poetry either. He writes in the romantic style of the southern lands; he tells of joy with a tinge of sadness, a man smiling at tragedy. He composes poems about love which can never be fulfilled, of hopes that summon a man across a desert of sand, a woman across a sea of water. No wonder every lady at court falls in love with him. Anthony smiles, picks up the flowers that they throw into the arena, and bows, hand on his heart, without asking any lady for her favour.

'I knew him when he was just my uncle,' Thomas remarks.

'He is the favourite of the day,' I say to my father, who comes to the royal box to kiss my hand.

'What is he thinking of?' he demands of me, puzzled. 'In my day we killed an opponent, not made a poem about them.'

Anthony's wife Elizabeth laughs. 'This is the Burgundian way.'

'These are chivalrous times,' I tell my father, smiling at his broad-faced puzzlement.

But the winner of the day is Lord Thomas Stanley, a handsome man who lifts his visor and comes for his prize pleased to have won. The motto of his family is shown proudly on his standard: '*Sans changer*'.

'What does it mean?' Richard mutters to his brother.

'Without changing,' Thomas says. 'And you would know if you studied rather than wasting your time.'

'And do you never change?' I ask Lord Stanley. He looks at me: the daughter of a family that has changed completely, turned from one king to another, a woman who has changed from being a widow into being a queen, and he bows. 'I never change,' he says. 'I support God and the king and my rights, in that order.'

I smile. Pointless to ask him how he knows what God wants, how he knows which king is rightful, how he can be sure that his rights are just. These are questions for peace, and our country has been at war too long for complicated questions. 'You are a great man in the jousting arena,' I remark.

He smiles. 'I was lucky not to be listed against your brother Anthony. But I am proud to joust before you, Your Grace.'

I bend from the queen's box to give him the prize of the tournament, a ruby ring, and he shows me that it is too small for his big hand.

'You must marry a beautiful lady,' I tease him. 'A virtuous woman, whose price is beyond rubies.'

'The finest lady in the kingdom is married and crowned.' He bows to me. 'How shall we – who are neglected – bear our unhappiness?'

I laugh at this, it is the very language of my kinsmen, the Burgundians who have made flirtation a form of high art. 'You must endeavour,' I say. 'So formidable a knight should found a great house.'

'I will found my house, and you will see me win again,' he says, and at his words, for some reason, I feel a little shiver. This is a man who is not just strong in the jousting arena, I think. This is a man who would be strong on the battlefield. This is a man without scruple who will pursue his own interest. Formidable indeed. Let us hope he is true to his motto and never changes from his loyalty to our House of York.

*When the goddess Melusina fell in love with the knight he promised her that she would be free to be herself if she would only be his wife. They settled it that she would be his wife and walk on feet but once a month, she might go to her own chamber, fill a great bath with water, and, for one night only, be her fishy self. And so they lived in great happiness for many years. For he loved her and he understood that a woman cannot always live as a man. He understood that she could not always think as he thought, walk as he walked, breathe the air that he took in. She would always be a different being from him, listening to a different music, hearing a different sound, familiar with a different element.*

*He understood that she needed her time alone. He understood that she had to close her eyes and sink beneath the glimmer of the water and swish her tail and breathe through her gills and forget the joys and the trials of being a wife – just for a while, just once a month. They had children together, and they grew in health and beauty; he grew more prosperous and their castle was famous for its wealth and grace. It was famous also for the great beauty and sweetness of its lady, and visitors came from far away to see the castle, its lord, and his beautiful mysterious wife.*

As soon as I am crowned queen I set about establishing my family, and my mother and I become the greatest matchmakers in the kingdom.

'Will this not cause more enmity?' I ask Edward. 'My mother has a list of lords for my sisters to marry.'

'You have to do it,' he assures me. 'They complain that you are a poor widow from a family of unknowns. You have to improve your family by marrying them to the nobility.'

'We are so many, I have so many sisters, I swear we will take up all the eligible young men. We will leave you with a dearth of lords.'

He shrugs. 'This country has been divided into either York or Lancaster for too long. Make me another great family that will support me when York wavers, or when Lancaster threatens. You and I need to link ourselves to the nobility, Elizabeth. Give your mother free rein, we need cousins and in-laws in every county in the land. I shall ennoble your brothers, and your Grey sons. We need to create a great family around you, both for your position and for your defence.'

I take him at his word and I go to my mother and find her seated at the great table in my rooms, with pedigrees and contracts and maps all around her, like a commander raising troops.

'I see you are the goddess of love,' I observe.

She glances up at me, frowning in concentration. 'This is not love, this is business,' she says. 'You have your family to provide for, Elizabeth, and you had better marry them to wealthy husbands or wives. You have a lineage to create. Your task as queen is to watch and order the nobility of your country, no man must grow too great, no lady can fall too low. I know this: my own marriage to your father was forbidden, and we had to beg pardon from the king, and pay a fine.'

'I would have thought that would have put you on the side of freedom and true love?'

She laughs shortly. 'When it was my freedom and my love affair: yes. When it is the proper ordering of your court: no.'

'You must be sorry that Anthony is already married now that we could command a great match for him?'

My mother frowns. 'I am sorry that she is barren and in poor health,' she says bluntly. 'You can keep her at court as a lady-in-waiting and she is of the best family; but I don't think she will give us sons and heirs.'

'You will have dozens of sons and heirs,' I predict, looking at her long lists of names and the boldly drawn arrows between the names of my sisters and the names of English noblemen.

'I should do,' she says with satisfaction. 'And not one of them less than a lord.'

So we have a month of weddings. Every sister of mine is married to a lord, except for Katherine, where I go one better and betroth her to a duke. He is not yet ten years old, a sulky child, Henry Stafford, the little Duke of Buckingham. Warwick had him in mind for his daughter Isabel. But as the boy is a royal ward since the death of his father, he is at my disposal. I am paid a fee to guard him, and I can do with him what I want. He is an arrogant rude boy to me; he thinks he is of such a great family, he is so filled with pride in himself that I take a pleasure in forcing this young pretender to the throne into marriage with Katherine. He regards her, and all of us, as unbearably beneath him. He thinks he is demeaned by marriage to us, and I hear he tells his friends, boasting like a boy, that he will have his revenge, and we will fear him one day, he will make me sorry that I insulted him, one day. This makes me laugh; and Katherine is glad to be a duchess even with a sulky child for a husband.

My twenty-year-old brother John, who is luckily still single, will be married to Lord Warwick's aunt, Lady Catherine Neville. She is dowager Duchess of Norfolk, having wedded and bedded and buried a duke. This is a slap in the face to Warwick and that alone gives me mischievous joy, and, since his aunt is all but one hundred years old, marriage to her is a jest of the most cruel sort. Warwick will learn who makes the alliances in England now. Besides, she must soon die, and then my brother will be free again and wealthy beyond belief.

For my son, my darling Thomas Grey, I buy little Anne Holland. Her mother, the Duchess of Exeter, my husband's own sister, charges me four thousand marks for the privilege and I note the price of her pride and pay it, so that Thomas can inherit the Holland fortune. My son will be as wealthy as any prince in Christendom. I rob the Earl of Warwick of this prize too – he wanted Anne Holland for his nephew and it was all but signed and sealed; but I outbid him by a thousand marks – a fortune, a king's fortune, which I can command and Warwick cannot. Edward makes Thomas Marquis of Dorset to match his prospects. I shall have a match for my son Richard Grey as soon as I can see a girl who will bring him a fortune, in the meantime he will be knighted.

My father becomes an earl, Anthony does not gain the dukedom that he joked about, but he does get the lordship of the Isle of Wight, and my other brothers get their places in royal service or in the church. Lionel will be a bishop as he wanted. I use my great position as queen to put my family into power, as any woman would do, and indeed as any woman risen to greatness from nothing would be advised to do. We will have our enemies – we have to make connections and allies. We have to be everywhere.

By the end of the long process of marriage and ennoblement no man can live in England without encountering one of my family: you cannot make a trade, plough a field, or try a case without meeting one of the great Rivers family or their dependants. We are everywhere; we are where the king has chosen to place us. And should the day come that everyone turns against him, he will find that we, the Rivers run deep and strong, a moat around his castle. When he loses all other allies we will still be his friends, and now we are in power.

We are loyal to him and he cleaves to us. I swear to him my faith and my love and he knows there is no woman in the world who loves him more than I do. My brothers and my father, my cousins and my sisters, and all our new husbands and wives promise him their absolute loyalty, whatever comes, whoever comes against us. We make a new family neither Lancaster nor York, we are the Woodville family enobled as Rivers and we stand behind the king like a wall of water, and half the kingdom can hate us but now I have made us so powerful that I do not care.

Edward settles to the business of governing a country that is accustomed to having no king at all. He appoints justices and sheriffs to replace men killed in battle; he commands them to impose law and order in their counties. Men who have seized the chance to make war on their neighbours have to return to their own bounds. The soldiers discharged from one side or another have to go back to their homes. The warring bands who have taken their chance to ride out and terrorise must be hunted down, the roads have to be made safe again. Edward starts the hard work of making England a country at peace with itself once more. A country at peace instead of a country at war.

Then, finally, there is an end to the constant warfare when we capture the former King Henry, half lost and half-witted in the hills of Northumberland, and Edward orders him to be brought to the Tower of London, for his own safety and for ours. He is not always in his right mind, God keep him. He moves into the rooms in the Tower and seems to know where he is; he seems to be glad to be home after his wandering. He lives quietly, communing with God, a priest at his side night and day. We don't even know if he remembers his wife or the son she told him was his; certainly, he never speaks of them nor asks for them in faraway Anjou. We don't know for sure if he always remembers that once he was king. He is lost to the world, poor Henry, and he has forgotten everything that we have taken from him.

# SUMMER 1468

Edward trusts Warwick with an embassy to France and Warwick seizes the opportunity to get away from England and away from court. He cannot bear the rising of our tide and the slow decline of his own hopes. He plans to make a treaty with the King of France and promises him that the government of England is still in his gift; and that he is going to choose the husband for the York heiress Margaret. But he is lying, and everyone knows that his days of power are over. Edward listens to my mother, to me, and to his other advisors, who say that the dukedom of Burgundy has been a faithful friend where France is a constant enemy, and that an alliance with Burgundy could be made for the good of trade, for the sake of our cousinship, and could be cemented with the marriage of Edward's sister Margaret to the new duke himself: Charles, who has just inherited the rich lands of Burgundy.

Charles is a key friend to England. The Duke of Burgundy owns all the lands of Flanders, as well as his own dukedom of Burgundy, and so commands all the lowlands of the north, all the lands between Germany and France, and the rich lands in the south. They are great buyers of English cloth, merchants and allies to us. Their ports face ours across the English sea; their usual enemy is France and they look to us for alliance. These are traditional friends of England and now – through me – kinsmen to the English king.

All this is planned without reference to the girl herself, of course; and Margaret comes to me when I am walking in the garden at Westminster Palace, all in a fluster, as someone has told her that her betrothal to Dom Pedro of Portugal is to be put aside and she is now to be sold to the highest bidder, either to Louis of France for one of the French princes, or to Charles of Burgundy.

'It'll be all right,' I say to her, tucking her hand in mine so she can walk beside me. She is only twenty-two and she was not raised to be the sister of a king. She is not accustomed to the way that her husband-to-be can change with the needs of the moment, and her mother, torn between her divided loyalties to her rivalrous sons, has quite failed to care for her daughters.

When Margaret was a little girl, she thought she would be married to an English lord and live in an English castle, raising children. She even dreamed of being a nun – she shares her mother's enthusiasm for the Church. She did not realise, when her father claimed the throne and her brother won it, that a price must always be paid for power, and it will be paid by her as well as the rest of us. She doesn't realise yet that though men go to war it is women who suffer – perhaps more than anyone.

'I won't marry a Frenchman, I hate the French,' she says hotly. 'My father fought them, he would not have wanted me to marry a Frenchman. My brother should not think of it. I don't know why my mother considers it. She was with the English army in France; she knows what the French are like. I am of the House of York, I don't want to be a Frenchwoman!'

'You won't be,' I say steadily. 'That is the plan of the Earl of Warwick and he no longer has the ear of the king. Yes, he takes French bribes and he favours France; but my advice to the king is that he should make an alliance with the Duke of Burgundy and that will be a better alliance for you. Just think – you will be my kinswoman! You will marry the Duke of Burgundy and live in the beautiful palace at Lille. Your husband-to-be is an honoured friend of the House of York, and my kinsman through my mother. He is a good friend, and from his palace you will be able to come on visits home. And when my daughters are old enough I shall send them to you, to teach them the elegant court life at Burgundy. There is nowhere more fashionable and more beautiful than the court of Burgundy. And as Duchess of Burgundy you shall be godmother to my sons. How will that be?'

She is partly comforted. 'But I am of the House of York,' she says again. 'I want to stay in England. At least until we have finally defeated the Lancastrians, and I want to see the christening of your son, the first York prince. Then I shall want to see him made Prince of Wales . . .'

'You shall come to his christening, whenever he comes to us,' I promise her. 'And he will know his aunt is his good guardian. But you can further the needs of the House of York in Burgundy. You will keep Burgundy a friend to York and to England, and if ever Edward is in trouble he will know that he can call on the Burgundy wealth and arms. And if ever again he is in danger from a false friend he can come to you for help. You will like to be our ally over the sea. You will be our haven.'

She drops her little head on my shoulder. 'Your Grace, my sister,' she says. 'It is hard for me to go away. I have lost a father and I am not sure that my brother is not still in danger. I am not sure that he and George are true friends, I am not certain that George does not envy Edward, and I am afraid of what my Lord Warwick might do. I want to stay here. I want to be with Edward and with you. I love my brother George; I don't want to leave him at this time. I don't want to leave my mother. I don't want to leave home.'

'I know,' I say gently. 'But you can be a powerful and good sister to Edward and to George as the Duchess of Burgundy. We will know that there is always one country that we can depend on to stand our friend. We will know that there is a beautiful duchess who is a Yorkist through and through. You can go to Burgundy and have sons, York sons.'

'D'you think I can found a house of York overseas?'

'You will found a new line,' I assure her. 'And we will be glad to know that you are there, and we will visit you.'

She puts a brave face on it, and Warwick puts a two-faced face on it and escorts her to the port of Margate, and we wave her away, our little duchess, and I know that of all of Edward's brothers and sisters, George the unfaithful and Richard the boy, we have just sent away the most loving, the most loyal, the most reliable Yorkist of them all.

To Warwick this is another defeat at my hands and at the hands of my family. He promised that Margaret would have a French husband but he has to take her to the Duke of Burgundy. He planned to make an alliance with France and he said that he had control of the decision-making in England. Instead, we are to marry into the royal House of Burgundy: my mother's family, and everyone can see that England is commanded by the Rivers family and that the king listens only to us. Warwick escorts Margaret on her wedding journey with a face as if he is sucking lemons and I laugh behind my hand to see him overpowered and outnumbered by us, and think myself safe from his ambition and his malice.

# SUMMER 1469

I am wrong, I am so wrong. We are not so powerful, we are not powerful enough. And I should have taken more care. I did not think, and I, of all people, who was afraid of Warwick before I had even met him, should have thought of his envy and his enmity. I did not foresee – and I of all queens with growing sons of my own should have foreseen – that Warwick and Edward's bitter mother might come together and think to place another York boy on the throne in place of the first boy they had chosen, that the Kingmaker would make a new king.

I should have been more aware of Warwick, as my family pushed him out of his offices and won the lands that he might have wanted for himself. I should have seen also that George, the young Duke of Clarence, was bound to interest him. George is a son of York like Edward, but malleable, easily tempted, and above all unmarried. Warwick looked at Edward and me and the growing strength and wealth of the Rivers that I have put around Edward, and began to think that perhaps he might make another king, another king again, a king who would be more obedient to him.

Three beautiful daughters, we have, one newborn, and we are hoping – with rising anxiety – for a son, when Edward gets news of a rebel in Yorkshire calling himself Robin. Robin of Redesdale, a fanciful name meaning nothing, a petty rebel hiding himself behind a legendary name, raising troops, slandering my family, and demanding justice and freedom and the usual nonsense by which good men are tempted from minding their fields to go to their deaths. Edward pays little attention at first, and I, foolishly, think nothing of it at all. Edward is on pilgrimage with my family, my Grey sons Richard and Thomas and his young brother Richard, showing himself to the people and giving thanks to God, and I am travelling to meet him with the girls and, though we write every day, we think so little of the uprising that he does not even mention it in his letters.

Even when my father remarks to me that someone is paying these men, they are not armed with pitchforks, they have good boots and they are marching in good order, I pay him no attention. Even when he says, a few days later, that these are men who belong to someone: peasants or tenants or men sworn to a lord, I hardly listen to his hard-won wisdom. Even when he points out to me that no man takes up his scythe and thinks he will go and fight in a war; someone, his lord, has to give the order. Even then, I pay him no attention. When my brother John says that this is Warwick's country and most likely the rebels are raised by Warwick's men, I still think nothing of it. I have a new baby and my world revolves around her carved gold-painted crib. We are on progress in south-east England where we are beloved, the summer is fine and I think, when I think at all, that the rebels will most likely go home in time to bring in the harvest, and the unrest will go quiet of its own accord.

I am not concerned until my brother John comes to me, his face grave, and swears that there are hundreds, perhaps thousands of men in arms, and it has to be the Earl of Warwick about his old business of making mischief, as no one else could muster so many. He is king-making again. Last time he made Edward to replace King Henry, this time he wants to make George, Duke of Clarence, brother to the king, the son of no importance, to replace my husband Edward. And so to replace me and mine as well.

Edward meets me at Fotheringhay, as we had arranged, quietly furious. We had planned to enjoy the beautiful house and grounds in the midsummer weather and then travel on to the prosperous town of Norwich together, for a great ceremonial entry to this most wealthy city. Our plan was to knit ourselves into the pilgrimages and feasts of the country towns, to dispense justice and patronage, to be seen as the king and queen at the heart of their people – nothing like the mad king in the Tower and his madder queen in France.

'But now I have to go north and deal with this,' Edward complains to me. 'There are new rebellions coming up like springs in a flood. I thought it was one discontented squire but the whole of the north seems to be taking up arms again. It is Warwick, it must be Warwick, though he has said not a word to me. But I asked him to come to me; and he has not come. I thought that was odd – but I knew he was angry with me – and now this very day I hear that he and George have taken ship. They have gone to Calais together. God damn them, Elizabeth, I have been a trusting fool. Warwick has fled from England, George with him, they have gone to the strongest English garrison, they are inseparable, and all the men who say they are out for Robin of Redesdale are really paid servants of George or Warwick.'

I am aghast. Suddenly the kingdom which had seemed quiet in our hands is falling apart.

'It must be Warwick's plan to use all the tricks against me that he and I used against Henry.' Edward is thinking aloud. 'He is backing George now, as he once backed me. If he goes on with this, if he uses the fortress of Calais as his jumping point to invade England, it will be a brothers' war as it was once a cousins' war. This is damnable, Elizabeth. And this is the man I thought of as my brother. This is the man who all but put me on the throne. This is my kinsman and my first ally. This was my greatest friend!'

He turns from me so I cannot see the anger and the distress in his face, and I can hardly breathe at the thought of this great man, this tremendous commander of men, coming against us.

'You are sure? George is with him? And they have gone to Calais together? He wants the throne for George?'

'I am sure of nothing,' he shouts in exasperation. 'This is my first and foremost friend and with him is my own brother. We have been shoulder to shoulder on the battlefield, we have been brothers in arms as well as kinsmen. At the battle of Mortimer's Cross, there were three suns in the sky, I saw them myself, three suns: everyone said that was a sign from God for me and for George and for Richard, the three sons of York. How can one son leave the others? And who else betrays me with him? If I cannot trust my own brother who will stand by me? My mother must know of this: George is her darling. He will have told her he is plotting against me and she has kept his secret. How can he betray me? How can she?'

'Your mother?' I repeat. 'Your mother, backing George against you? Why would she do such a thing?'

He shrugs. 'The old story. Whether I am my father's son. Whether I am legitimate, born and bred a York. George is saying that I am a bastard, and that makes him the true heir. God knows why she would support this. She must hate me for marrying you and taking your part more than I even dreamed.'

'How dare she!'

'I can trust no one but you and yours,' Edward exclaims. Everyone else I trust is cut out from under my feet and now I hear that this Robin in Yorkshire has a list of demands that he wants me to meet, and that Warwick has announced to the people that he thinks they are reasonable. Reasonable! He promises that he and George will land with an army to remonstrate with me. Remonstrate! I know what he means by that! Is this not the very thing we did to Henry? Do I not know how a king is destroyed? Did Warwick's father not take my very own father to remonstrate with King Henry, planning to cut him from his wife and from his allies? Did he not teach my father how to cut off a king from his wife, from his allies? And now he thinks to destroy me with the same trick. Does he think that I am a fool?'

'And Richard?' I ask anxiously, thinking of his other brother, the shy boy who has become a quiet and thoughtful young man. 'Where are Richard's loyalties? Does he side with his mother?'

It is his first smile. 'My Richard stays true to me, thank God,' he says briefly. 'Richard is always true to me. I know you think him an awkward sulky boy, I know your sisters laugh at him, but he is honest and faithful to me. Whereas George can be bribed to left or to right. He is a greedy child, not a man. God only knows what Warwick has promised him.'

'I can tell you that,' I reply fiercely. 'It's easy. Your throne. And my daughters' inheritance.'

'I shall keep them all.' He takes my hands and kisses them. 'I swear I shall keep them all. You go to the city of Norwich as we planned. Do your duty, play the queen, look as if you are untroubled. Show them a smiling and confident face. And I will go and scotch this snakes' plot before it gets out of the ground.'

'Do they admit that they hope to overthrow you? Or do they insist they just want to remonstrate with you?'

He grimaces. 'It is more that they will overthrow you, sweetheart. They want your family and your advisors exiled from my court. Their great complaint is that I am ill advised and that your family are destroying me.'

I gasp. 'They are slandering me?'

'It is a cover, a mumming,' he says. 'Don't regard it. It is the usual song of this not being a rebellion against the king but against his evil advisors. I sang this song myself as did my father, as did Warwick against Henry. Then, we said that it was all the fault of the queen and the Duke of Somerset. Now, they say it is your fault and your family around you. It is easy to blame the wife. It is always easier to accuse the queen of being a bad influence than to declare yourself against the king. They want to destroy you and your family, of course. Then, once I am alone before them, without friends and family, they will destroy me. They will force me to declare our marriage a sham, our girls all bastards. They will make me name George as my heir, perhaps to cede my throne to him. I have to drive them to open opposition where I can defeat them. Trust me, I will keep you safe.'

I put my forehead to his. 'I wish I had given you a son,' I say very low. 'Then they would know that there could be only one heir. I wish I had given you a prince.'

'Time enough for that,' he says steadily. 'And I love our girls. A son will come, I don't doubt it, beloved. And I will keep the throne safe for him. Trust me.'

I let him go. We both have work to do. He rides out from Fotheringhay behind a harshly rippling standard and surrounded by a guard ready for battle to go to Nottingham to the great castle there, and wait for the enemy to show himself. I go on to Norwich with my daughters, to act as if England is all mine, as if it is all still a fair garden for the rose of York, and I fear nothing. I take my Grey sons with me. Edward offered to have them ride with him, for a first taste of battle, but I am fearful for them and I take them with me and the girls. So I have two very sulky young men, aged fifteen and thirteen, as I make my progress to Norwich and nothing will please them, as they are missing their first battle.

I have a state entry and choirs singing and flowers thrown down before me, and plays extolling my virtue and welcoming my girls. Edward bides his time in Nottingham, summoning his soldiers again, waiting for his enemy to land.

While we wait, playing our different parts, wondering when our enemies will come, and where they will land, we hear more news. In the city of Calais, with special permission from the Pope – which must have been sought and gained in secret by our own archbishops – George has married Warwick's daughter, Isabel Neville. He is now Warwick's son-in-law and, if Warwick can put George on Edward's throne, Warwick will make his own daughter queen, and she will take my crown.

I spit like a cat at the thought of our turncoat archbishops writing to the Pope in secret to aid our enemies, of George before the altar with Warwick's girl, and of Warwick's long slow-burning ambition. I think of the pale-faced girl, one of the only two Neville girls, for Warwick has no son of his own and cannot seem to get any more children, and I swear that she will never wear the crown of England while I live. I think of George, turning his coat like the spoiled boy he is, and falling in with Warwick's plans like the stupid child he is, and I swear vengeance on them both. I am so certain that it will come to a battle, and a bitter battle between my husband and his former tutor in war Warwick, that I am taken by surprise, just as Edward is taken by surprise, when Warwick lands without warning, and meets and smashes the gathering royal army at Edgecote Moor near Banbury, before Edward is even out of Nottingham Castle.

It is a disaster. Sir William Herbert, the Earl of Pembroke, lies dead on the field, a thousand Welshmen around him, his ward the Lancaster boy Henry Tudor left without a guardian. Edward is on the road to London, riding as fast as he can to arm the city for siege, about to warn them that Warwick is in England, when armed figures block the road before him.

Archbishop Neville, Warwick's kinsman appointed by us, steps up and takes Edward his own king prisoner, telling him, as he is surrounded, that Warwick and George are already in the kingdom, and the royal army has already been defeated. It is over, Edward is beaten, even before battle is declared, even before he had his war horse harnessed. The wars, which I thought had ended in peace, our peace, are over with our defeat, without Edward even drawing his sword, and the House of York will be founded on the puppet plaything George and not on my unborn son.

I am at Norwich, pretending to confidence, pretending to queenly grace, when they bring me a mud-stained messenger from my husband. I open the letter:

*Dearest wife,*

*Prepare yourself for bad news.*

*Your father and your brother were taken at a battle near Edgecote fighting for our cause and Warwick has them. I too am a prisoner, held at Warwick's castle of Middleham. They took me on the road on my way to you. I am unhurt, as are they.*

*Warwick has named your mother as a sorceress and he says that our marriage was an act of witchcraft by you and her. So be warned: both of you are in grave danger. She must leave the country at once: they will have her strangled as a witch if they can. You too should prepare for exile.*

*Get yourself and our daughters to London as fast as you can, arm the Tower for a siege and raise the city. As soon as the city is set for siege you must take the girls and go to safety to Flanders. The charge of witchcraft is very grave, beloved. They will execute you if they think they can make it stick. Keep yourself safe above anything else.*

*If you think it best, send the girls away at once, secretly and place them with humble people in hiding. Don't be proud, Elizabeth, choose a refuge where no one will look. We have to live through this if we want to fight to claim our own again.*

*I am more grieved at bringing you and them into danger than anything else in the world. I have written to Warwick to demand to know the ransom that he wants for the safe return of your father and your brother John. I don't doubt he will send them back to you and you can pay whatever he demands from the Treasury.*
*Your husband,*
*The one and only King of England,*

*Edward*

A knock at the door of my presence chamber and the flinging open of the door makes me leap to my feet, expecting, I don't know, the Earl of Warwick himself, with a bundle of greenwood stakes for burning me and my mother; but it is the Mayor of Norwich, who greeted me with such rich ceremony only days before.

'Your Grace, I have urgent news,' he says. 'Bad news. I am sorry.'

I take a little breath to steady myself. 'Tell me.'

'It is your father, and your brother.'

I know what he is going to say. Not from foreknowledge, but from the way his round face is creased with worry at the thought of the pain he is bringing me. I know it from the way that the men behind him gather together, awkward as people who bring the worst tidings. I know it from the way that my own ladies-in-waiting sigh like a breeze of mourning and gather behind my chair.

'No,' I say. 'No. They are prisoners. They are held by Englishmen of honour. They must be ransomed.'

'Shall I leave you?' he asks. He looks at me as if I am sick. He does not know what to say to a queen who came into his town in glory and will leave it in mortal danger. 'Shall I go, and come back later, Your Grace?'

'Tell me,' I say. 'Tell me now, the worst there is, and I will bear it somehow.'

He glances at my women for help and then his dark eyes come back to me. 'I am sorry, Your Grace. Sorrier than I can rightly say. Your father Earl Rivers and your brother Sir John Woodville were taken in battle – a new battle between new enemies – the king's army against the king's own brother George, the Duke of Clarence. The duke seems to be in alliance now with the Earl of Warwick against your husband – perhaps you knew? In alliance against your gracious husband and you. Your father and brother were taken fighting for Your Grace, and they have been executed. They were beheaded.' He snatches one quick look at me. 'They would not have suffered,' he volunteers. 'I am sure it was quick.'

'The charge?' I can hardly speak. My mouth is numb as if someone had punched me in the face. 'They were fighting for an ordained king against rebels. What could anyone say against them? What could be the charge?'

He shakes his head. 'They were executed on the word of Lord Warwick,' he says quietly. 'There was no trial, there was no charge. It seems my Lord Warwick's own word is now law. He had them beheaded without trial or sentence, without justice.

Shall I give the orders for you to be escorted to London? Or shall I arrange for a ship? Will you go overseas?'

'I am to go to London,' I say. 'It is my capital city, it is my kingdom. I am not a foreign queen to run to France. I am an Englishwoman. I live and die here.' I correct myself. 'I will live and fight here.'

'May I offer you my deepest condolences? To you and to the king?'

'Do you have news of the king?'

'We were hoping that your gracious self could reassure us?'

'I have heard nothing,' I lie. They will not learn from me that the king is a prisoner in Middleham Castle, that we are defeated. 'I will leave this afternoon, within two hours, tell them. I will ride to claim my city of London and then we will reclaim England. My husband has never lost a battle. He will defeat his enemies and bring all traitors to trial and justice.'

He bows, they all bow, and go out backwards. I sit on my chair like a queen, the gold cloth of estate over my head, until the door has closed on them and then I say to my ladies, 'Leave me. Prepare for our journey.'

They flutter and they hesitate. They long to pause and pet me, but they see the grimness in my face and they trail away. I am alone in the sunlit room and I see that the chair that I am sitting on is chipped, the carving under my hand is faulty. The cloth of estate over my head is dusty. I see that I have lost my father and my brother, the kindest most loving father that a daughter ever had, and a good brother. I have lost them for a chipped chair and a dusty cloth. My passion for Edward and my ambition for the throne put us, all of us, into the very forefront of the battle and cost me this first blood: my darling brother and the father I love.

I think of my father putting me on my first pony and telling me to lift up my chin and keep my hands down, to keep tight hold of the reins, to tell the pony who is master. I think of him cupping my mother's cheek in his hand and telling her that she is the cleverest woman in England and he will be guided by none but her; and then going his own way. I think of him falling in love with her when he was her first husband's squire and she his lady, who should never even have looked at him. I think of him marrying her the moment she was widowed, in defiance of all the rules, and them being called the handsomest couple in England, married for love, which nobody but the two of them would have dared to do. I think of him at Reading, as Anthony described him, pretending to know everything and with his eyes rolling in his head. I could even laugh for love of him, thinking of him telling me that he can only call me Elizabeth in private, now I am queen, and that we must become accustomed. I think of how he puffed out his chest when I told him that I was marrying his son to a duchess, and that he himself would be an earl.

And then I think of how my mother will take her loss, and that it will be me who has to tell her that he had a traitor's death for fighting in my cause, after fighting all his life for the other side. I think of all of this, and I feel weary and sick to my soul, wearier and sicker than I have ever felt in all my life, even worse than when Father came home from the battle of Towton and said that our cause was lost, even worse than when my husband never came home at all from St Albans and they told me he died bravely in a charge against the Yorks.

I feel worse than I have ever done before, because now I know that it is easier to take a country into war than to bring it to live at peace, and a country at war is a bitter place to live, a risky place to have daughters, and a dangerous place to hope for a son.

I am welcomed in London as a heroine, and the city is all for Edward; but it will make no difference if that butcher Warwick kills him in prison. I make my home for now in the well-fortified Tower of London with my girls and my Grey sons – they are obedient, scared as puppies now that they see that not every battle is won, and not every beloved son comes safe home. They are shaken by the loss of their uncle John and they ask every day for the safety of the king. We are all grieving: my girls have lost a good grandfather and a beloved uncle, and know that their father is in dreadful danger. I write to my kinsman the Duke of Burgundy and ask him to prepare a safe hiding place in Flanders for me, my Grey sons and my royal girls. I tell him that we must find a little town, one of no importance, and a poor family who can pretend to take in English cousins. I must find somewhere for my daughters to hide that they will never be found.

The duke swears he will do more than this. He will support the City if they turn out for me and for York. He promises men and an army. He asks me what news I have of the king. Is he safe?

I cannot write to reassure him. The news of my husband is inexplicable. He is a king in captivity, just like the poor King Henry. How can such a thing be? How can such a thing continue? Warwick is still holding him at Middleham Castle, and persuading the lords to deny that Edward was ever king. There are those who say that Edward will be offered the choice: either to abdicate his throne for his brother, or climb the scaffold. Warwick will have either the crown or his head. There are those who say it is only days now before we hear that Edward is thrown down and fled to Burgundy; or dead. I have to listen to such gossip in the place of news, and I wonder if I am to be widowed in the same month that I have lost my father and my brother. And how shall I bear that?

My mother comes to me in the second week of my vigil. She comes from our old home at Grafton, dry-eyed and somehow bowed, as if she has taken a wound to her belly and is bent over the pain. The moment that I see her I know that I won't have to tell her that she is a widow. She knows she has lost the great love of her life, and her hand rests on the knot of her girdle all the time, as if to hold in a mortal wound. She knows that her husband is dead, but no one has told her how he died, or why. I have to take her into my private room, close the door on the children, and find the words to describe the death of her husband and son. And it was a shameful death, for good men, at the hand of a traitor.

'I am so sorry,' I say. I kneel at her feet and clasp her hands. 'I am so sorry, Mother. I will have Warwick's head for this. I will see George dead.'

She shakes her head. I look up at her and see lines on her face that I swear were never there before. She has lost the glow of a contented woman and her joy has fallen away from her face and left weary lines.

'No,' she says. She pats my plaited hair and says, 'Hush, hush. Your father would not have wanted you to grieve. He knew the risks well enough. It was not his first battle, God knows. Here.' She reaches inside her gown and gives me a handwritten note. 'His last letter to me. He sends me his blessing and his love to you. He wrote it as they told him he would be released. I think he knew the truth.'

My father's handwriting is clear and bold as his speech. I cannot believe I will not hear the one and see the other again and again.

'And John . . .' She breaks off. 'John is a loss to me and to his generation,' she says quietly. 'Your brother John had his whole life before him.'

She pauses. 'When you raise a child and he becomes a man you start to think that he is safe, that you are safe from heartbreak. When a child gets through all the illnesses of childhood, when a plague year comes and takes your neighbours' children and yet your boy lives, you start to think he will be safe for ever. Every year you think another year away from danger, another year towards becoming a man. I raised John, I raised all my children, breathless with hope. And we married him to that old woman for her title and her fortune and we laughed knowing that he would outlive her. It was a great joke to us, knowing that he was such a young husband, to such an old woman. We laughed to make mock of her age knowing her to be so much closer to the grave than he. And now she will see him buried and keep her fortune. How can such a thing be?'

She breathes a long sigh, as if she is too tired for anything more. 'And yet I should know. Of all the people in the world I should have known. I have the Sight, I should have seen it all, but some things are too dark to foresee. These are hard times and England is a country of sorrows. No mother can be sure that she will not bury her sons. When a country is at war, cousin against cousin, brother against brother, no boy is safe.'

I sit back on my heels. 'The king's mother, Duchess Cecily, shall know this pain. She will have this pain that you are feeling. She will know the loss of her son George,' I spit. 'I swear it. She will see him die the death of a liar and a turncoat. You have lost a son and so shall she, my word on it.'

'So will you, by that rule,' my mother warns me. 'More and more deaths, and more feuds, and more fatherless children, and more widowed brides. Do you want to mourn for your missing son in future days, as I am doing now?'

'We can reconcile after George,' I say stubbornly. 'They must be punished for this. George and Warwick are dead men from this day. I swear it, Mother. They are dead men from this day.' I rise up and go to the table. 'I will tear a corner from his letter,' I say. 'I will write their deaths in my own blood on my father's letter.'

'You are wrong,' she says quietly, but she lets me cut a corner from the letter and give it back to her.

There is a knock at the door and I wipe the tears from my face before I let my mother call 'Enter', but the door is flung open without ceremony and Edward, my darling Edward, strolls into the room as if he had been out for a day's hunting and thought he would surprise me by coming home early.

'My God! It is you! Edward! It is you? It is really you?'

'It is me,' he confirms. 'I greet you too, My Lady Mother Jacquetta.'

I fling myself at him and as his arms come around me I smell his familiar scent and feel the strength of his chest, and I sob at the very touch of him. 'I thought you were in prison,' I say. 'I thought he was going to kill you.'

'Lost his nerve,' he says shortly, trying to stroke my back and take down my hair at the same time. 'Sir Humphrey Neville raised Yorkshire for Henry, and when Warwick went against him nobody supported him, he needed me. He started to see that nobody would have George for king, and I would not sign away my throne. He hadn't bargained for that. He didn't dare behead me. To say truth, I don't think he could find a headsman to do it. I am crowned king: he can't just lop off my head as if it were firewood. I am ordained, my body is sacred. Not even Warwick dares to kill a king in cold blood.

'He came to me with the paper of my abdication and I told him that I couldn't see my way to signing. I was happy to stay in his house. The cook is excellent and the cellar better. I told him I was happy to move my whole court to Middleham Castle if he wanted me as a guest for ever. I said I could see no reason why my rule should not run from his castle, at his expense. But that I would never deny who I am.'

He laughs, his loud confident laugh. 'Sweetheart, you should have seen him. He thought if he had me in his power, that he had the crown at his bidding. But he found me unhelpful. It was as good as a mumming to see him puzzle as to what to do. Once I heard you were safely in the Tower I wasn't afraid of anything. He thought I would break when he took hold of me, and I didn't even bend. He thought I was still the little boy who adored him. He didn't realise that I am a grown man. I was a most agreeable guest. I ate well and when friends came to see me I demanded that they be entertained royally. First I asked to walk in the gardens, then in the forest. Then I said I should like to ride out, and what would be the harm in letting me go hunting? He started to let me ride out. My council came and demanded to see me and he did not know how to refuse them. I met them and passed the odd law or two so that everyone knew nothing had changed, I was still reigning as king. It was hard not to laugh in his face. He thought to imprison me and found instead he was merely bearing the cost of a full court. Sweetheart, I asked for a choir while I dined, and he could not see how to refuse me. I hired dancers and players. He started to see that merely holding the king is not enough: you have to destroy him. You have to kill him. But I gave him nothing; he knew I would die before I gave him anything.

'Then one fine morning – four days ago – his grooms made the mistake of giving me my own horse, my war horse Fury, and I knew he could outrun anything in their stables. So I thought I would ride a little further, and a little faster than usual, that's all. I thought I might be able to ride to you – and I have done.'

'It is over?' I ask incredulously. 'You got away?'

He grins in his pride like a boy. 'I would like to see the horse that could catch me on Fury,' he said. 'They had left him in the stable for two weeks feeding him oats. I was at Ripon before I could draw breath. I couldn't have pulled him up if I had wanted to!'

I laugh, sharing his delight. 'Dear God, Edward, I have been so afraid! I thought I would never see you again. Beloved, I thought I would never ever see you again.'

He kisses my head and strokes my back. 'Did I not say when we first married that I will always come back to you? Did I not say I would die in my bed with you as my wife? Have you not promised to give me a son? D'you think any prison could keep me from you, ever?'

I press my face to his chest as if I would bury myself into his body. 'My love. My love. So will you go back with your guards and arrest him?'

'No, he's too powerful. He still commands most of the north. I hope we can make peace again. He knows this rebellion has failed. He knows it is over. He is cunning enough to know that he has lost. He and George and I will have to patch together some reconciliation. They will beg my pardon and I will forgive them.

But he has learned that he cannot keep me and hold me. I am king now, he can't reverse that. He is sworn to obey me as I have sworn to rule. I am his king. It is done. And the country has no appetite for another war between more rival kings. I don't want a war. I have sworn to bring the country justice and peace.'

He pulls the final pins from my hair and rubs his face against my neck. 'I missed you,' he said. 'And the girls. I had a bad moment or two when they first took me into the castle and I was in a cell with no windows. And I am sorry about your father and brother.'

He raises his head and looks at my mother. 'I am more sorry for your loss than I can say, Jacquetta,' he says frankly. 'These are the fortunes of war, and we all know the risks; but they took two good men when they took your husband and son.'

My mother nods. 'And what will be your terms for reconciliation with the man who killed my husband and my son? I take it you will forgive him that also?'

Edward makes a grimace at the hardness in her voice. 'You will not like it,' he warns us both. 'I shall make Warwick's nephew Duke of Bedford. He is Warwick's heir; I have to give Warwick a stake in our family, the royal family, I have to tie him in to us.'

'You give him my old title?' my mother asks incredulously. 'The Bedford title? My first husband's name? To a traitor?'

'I don't care if his nephew has a dukedom,' I say hastily. 'It is Warwick who killed my father, not the boy. I don't care about his nephew.'

Edward nods. 'There is more,' he says uncomfortably. 'I shall give our daughter Elizabeth in marriage to young Bedford. She will make the alliance firm.'

I turn on him. 'Elizabeth? My Elizabeth?'

'Our Elizabeth,' he corrects me. 'Yes.'

'You will promise her in marriage, a child of not yet four years old, to the family of the man who murdered her grandfather?'

'I will. This has been a cousins' war. It has to be a cousins' reconciliation. And you, beloved, will not stop me. I have to bring

Warwick to peace with me. I have to give him a great share of the wealth of England. This way I even give him a chance at his line inheriting the throne.'

'He is a traitor and a murderer, and you think you will marry my little daughter to his nephew?'

'I do,' he says firmly.

'I swear that it will never happen,' I say fiercely. 'And more: I tell you this. I foresee it will never happen.'

He smiles. 'I bow to your superior foreknowledge,' he says and sweeps a magnificent bow at my mother and me. 'And only time will prove your foreseeing true or false. But in the meantime, while I am King of England with the power to give my daughter in marriage to whom I wish, I shall always do my very best to stop your enemies ducking you two as a pair of witches, or strangling you at the crossroads. And I tell you, as I am king, the only way to make you and every woman and her son in this kingdom as safe as she should be, is to find a way to stop this warfare.'

## AUTUMN 1469

Warwick returns to court as a beloved friend and loyal mentor. We are to be as a family that suffers occasional quarrels, but loves one another withal. Edward does this rather well. I greet Warwick with a smile as warm as a frozen fountain dripping with ice. I am expected to behave as if this man is not the murderer of my father and brother, and the gaoler of my husband. I do as I am commanded: not a word of my anger escapes me, but Warwick knows without any telling that he has made a dangerous enemy for the rest of his life.

He knows I can say nothing, and his small bow when he first greets me is triumphant. 'Your Grace,' he says suavely.

As ever with him, I feel at a disadvantage, like a girl. He is a great man of the world and he was planning the fortunes of this kingdom when I was minding my manners to my Lady Grey, my husband's mother, and obeying my first husband. He looks at me as if I should still be feeding the hens at Grafton.

I want to be icy, but I fear I appear only sulky. 'Welcome back to court,' I say unwillingly.

'You are always gracious,' he replies with a smile. 'Born to be queen.'

My son Thomas Grey makes a small exclamation of anger, raging like the boy he is, and takes himself out of the room.

Warwick beams at me. 'Ah, the young,' he says. 'A promising boy.'

'I am only glad he was not with his grandfather and beloved uncle at Edgecote Moor,' I say, hating him.

'Oh, so am I!'

He may make me feel like a fool, and like a woman who can do nothing; but what I can do, I will. In my jewellery box is a dark locket of black tarnished silver and inside it, locked in the darkness, I have his name: Richard Neville, and that of George, Duke of Clarence, written in my blood on the piece of paper from the corner of my father's last letter. These are my enemies. I have cursed them. I will see them dead at my feet.

# WINTER 1469–70

At the very darkest hour of the longest night in the heart of the winter solstice my mother and I go down to the River Thames, black as glass. The path from the Palace of Westminster garden runs alongside the water, and the river is high tonight, but very dark in the darkness. We can hardly see it; but we can hear it, washing against the jetty and slapping against the walls, and we can feel it, a black wide presence, breathing like a great sinuous animal, heaving gently, like the sea. This is our element: I inhale the smell of the cold water like someone scenting their own land after a long exile.

'I have to have a son,' I say to my mother.

And she smiles and says, 'I know.'

In her pocket she has three charms on three threads and, careful as a fisherman baiting a line, she throws each of them into the river and gives me the thread to hold. I hear a little splash as each one falls into the water, and I am reminded of the golden ring that I drew from the river five years ago at home.

'You choose,' she says to me. 'You choose which one you draw out.' She spreads out the three threads in my left hand and I hold them tightly.

The moon comes out from behind the cloud. It is a waning moon, fat and silvery, it draws a line of light along the dark water and I choose one thread and hold it in my right hand. 'This one.'

'Are you sure?'

'Yes.'

At once she takes a pair of silver scissors from her pocket and cuts the other two threads so whatever was tied on is swept away into the dark waters.

'What were they?'

'They are the things that will never happen; they are the future that we will never know. They are the children who will not be born and the chances that we won't take and the luck that we won't have,' she says. 'They are gone. They are lost to you. See instead what you have chosen.'

I lean over the palace wall to draw on the thread and it comes from the water, dripping. At the end is a silver spoon, a beautiful little silver spoon for a baby, and when I catch it in my hand I see, shining in the moonlight, that it is engraved with a coronet and the name 'Edward'.

We keep Christmas in London as a feast of reconciliation, as if a feast will make a friend of Warwick. I am reminded of all the times that poor King Henry tried to bring his enemies together and make them swear friendship, and I know that others at the court see Warwick and George as honoured guests and laugh behind their hands.

Edward orders that it should be done grandly and nearly two thousand noblemen of England sit down to dinner with us on Twelfth Night, Warwick chief amongst them all. Edward and I wear our crowns and the newest fashions in the richest cloths. I wear only silver white and cloth of gold in this winter season and they say that I am the White Rose of York, indeed.

Edward and I give gifts to a thousand of the diners, and favours to them all. Warwick is a most popular guest and he and I greet each other with absolute courtesy. When commanded by my husband, I even dance with my brother-in-law George: hand to hand and smiling into his handsome, boyish face. Again, it strikes me how like my husband Edward he is: a smaller daintier version of Edward's blond handsomeness. Again I am struck by how people like him on sight. He has all of the York easy charm and none of Edward's honour. But I don't forget and I don't forgive.

I greet his new bride Isabel, Warwick's daughter, with kindness. I welcome her to my court and wish her very well. She is a poor, thin, pale girl, looking rather aghast at the part she has to play in her father's scheme of things. Now she is married into the most treacherous and dangerous family in England, at the court of the king that her husband betrayed. She is in need of a little kindness and I am sisterly and loving to her. A stranger at court, visiting us in this most hospitable season, would think that I love her as a kinswoman. He would think I had not lost a father, a brother. He would think that I have no memory at all.

I don't forget. And in my jewellery case is a dark locket, and in the dark locket there is the corner of the page of my father's last letter, and on that scrap of paper, written in my own blood, are the names Richard Neville, Earl of Warwick and George, Duke of Clarence. I don't forget, and one day they will know that.

Warwick remains enigmatic, the greatest man in the kingdom after the king. He accepts the honours and favours that are shown him with icy dignity, as a man to whom everything is due. His accomplice, George, is like a hound puppy, jumping and fawning. Isabel, George's wife, sits with my ladies, between my sisters and my sister-in-law Elizabeth, and I cannot help but smile when I see her turn her head away from her husband's dancing, or the way she flinches as he shouts out toasts in honour of the king. George, so fair-headed and round-faced, has always been a beloved boy of the Yorks, and at this Christmas feast he acts towards his older brother not only as if he has been forgiven, but also as if he will always be forgiven anything. He is the spoilt child of the family – he really believes he can do no wrong.

The youngest York brother, Richard, Duke of Gloucester, now seventeen and a handsome slight boy, may be the baby of the family but he has never been the favourite. Of all the York boys he is the only one to resemble his father and he is dark and small-boned, a little changeling beside the big-boned handsome York line. He is a pious young man, thoughtful; most at home in his great house in the north of England where he lives a life of duty and austere service to his people. He finds our glittering court an embarrassment, as if we were aggrandising ourselves as pagans at a Christian feast. He looks on me, I swear it, as if I were a dragon sprawled greedily over treasure, not a mermaid in silver water. I guess that he looks at me with both desire and fear. He is a child, afraid of a woman that he could never understand. Beside him, my Grey sons, only a little younger, are worldly and cheerful. They keep inviting him out to hunt with them, to go drinking in the ale houses, to roister round the streets in masks, and he, nervously, declines.

News of our Christmas feast goes all around Christendom. The new court in England is said to be the most beautiful, elegant, mannered and gracious court in Europe. Edward is determined that the English court of York shall become as famous as Burgundy for fashion and beauty and culture. He loves good music and we have a choir singing or musicians playing at every meal; my ladies and I learn the court dances, and compose our own. My brother Anthony is a great guide and advisor in all of this. He has travelled in Italy and speaks of the new learning and the new arts, of the beauty of the ancient cities of Greece and of Rome and how their arts and their studies can be made new. He speaks to Edward of bringing in painters and poets and musicians from Italy, of using the wealth of the crown to found schools and universities. He speaks of the new learning, of new science, of arithmetic and astronomy and everything new and wonderful. He speaks of arithmetic which starts with the number zero, and tries to explain how this transforms everything. He speaks of a science that can calculate distances that cannot be measured: he says it should be possible to know the distance to the moon. Elizabeth, his wife, watches him quietly, and says that he is a magus, a wise man. We are a court of beauty, grace and learning, and Edward and I command the best of everything.

I am amazed at the cost of running a court, of the price of all this beauty, even the charges for food, of the continual demands from every courtier for a hearing, for a place, for a slice of land or a favour, for a post where he can levy taxes or for help in claiming an inheritance.

'This is what it is to be a king,' Edward says to me as he signs the last of the day's petitions. 'As King of England I own everything. Every duke and earl and baron holds his lands at my favour; every knight and squire below him has a stream from the river. Every petty farmer and tenant and copyholder and peasant below him depends on my favour. I have to give out wealth and power in order to keep the rivers flowing. And if it goes wrong, at the least sign of it going wrong, there will be someone saying that they wished Henry was back on the throne, that it was better in the old days. Or that they think his son Edward, or George might do a more generous job. Or, surely to God, there is another claimant to the throne somewhere – Margaret Beaufort's son Henry, let's have the Lancaster boy for a change – who might speed the flow. To keep my power I have to give it away in carefully spaced and chosen pitchers. I have to please everyone. But none too much.'

'They are money-grubbing peasants,' I say irritably. 'And their loyalty goes with their interest. They think of nothing but their own desires. They are worse than serfs.'

He smiles at me. 'They are indeed. Every one of them. And each of them wants their little estate and their little house just as I want my throne and as much as you wanted the manor of Sheen, and places for all your kinsmen. We are all anxious for wealth and land and I own it all, and have to give it out carefully.'

## SPRING 1470

As the weather turns warmer and it starts to grow brighter in the mornings and the birds start to sing in the gardens of Westminster Palace, Edward's informers bring him reports from Lincolnshire of another uprising in favour of Henry, the king, as though he were not forgotten by everyone else in the world, living quietly in the Tower of London, more an anchorite than a prisoner.

'I shall have to go,' Edward says to me, letter in his hand. 'If this leader, whoever he is, is a forerunner for Margaret of Anjou, then I have to defeat him before she lands her army in his support. It looks like she plans to use him to test the support of her cause, to have him take the risk of raising troops, and when she sees he has raised an English army for her, she will land her French one and then I will have to face them both.'

'Will you be safe?' I ask. 'Against this person who has not even the courage to have a name of his own?'

'As always,' he says steadily. 'But I won't let the army go out without me again. I have to be there. I have to lead.'

'And where is your loyal friend Warwick?' I ask acidly. 'And your trusted brother George? Are they recruiting for you? Are they hurrying to be at your side?'

He smiles at my tone. 'Ah, you are mistaken, little Queen of Mistrust. I have a letter here from Warwick offering to raise men to march with me, and George says he will come too.'

'Then you make sure that you watch them in battle,' I say, completely unconvinced. 'They will not be the first men to bring soldiers to the battlefield and change sides at the last moment. When the enemy is before you, cast an eye behind you to see what your true and loyal friends are doing at the rear.'

'They have promised their loyalty,' he soothes me. 'Truly, my dearest. Trust me. I can win battles.'

'I know you can, I know you do,' I say. 'But it is so hard to see you march out. When will it end? When will they stop raising an army for a cause which is over?'

'Soon,' he says. 'They will see we are united and we are strong. Warwick will bring in the north to our side and George will prove to be a true brother. Richard is with me as always. I will come home as soon as this man is defeated. I will come home early and I will dance with you on May Day morning and you will smile.'

'Edward, you know, just this once, this one time, I think I cannot bear to see you go. Cannot Richard command the army? With Hastings? Can you not stay with me? This time, just this time.'

He takes my hands and presses them against his lips. He is not affected by my anxiety but amused by it. He is smiling. 'Oh why? Why this time? Why does this time matter so much? Do you have something to tell me?'

I cannot resist him. I am smiling in return. 'I do have something to tell you. But I have been saving it.'

'I know. I know. Did you think I didn't know? So tell me, what is this secret that I am supposed not to have any idea about?'

'It should bring you home safely to me,' I say. 'It should bring you home quickly to me, and not send you out in your pomp.'

He waits, smiling. He has been waiting for me to tell him as I have been revelling in the secret. 'Tell me,' he says. 'This has been a long time coming.'

'I am with child again,' I say. 'And this time I know it is a boy.'

He scoops me to him and holds me gently. 'I knew it,' he says.

'I knew that you were with child. I knew it in my bones. And how can you know it is a boy, my little witch, my enchantress?'

I smile up at him, secure in women's mysteries. 'Ah, you don't need to know how I know,' I say. 'But you can know that I am certain. You can be sure of it. Know this. We will have a boy.'

'My son, Prince Edward,' he says.

I laugh, thinking of the silver spoon that I drew out of the silvery river on midwinter's eve. 'How do you know that his name will be Edward?'

'Of course it will. I have been determined on it for years.'

'Your son, Prince Edward,' I repeat. 'So make sure you are home safely, in time for his birth.'

'Do you know when?'

'In the autumn.'

'I will come home safely to bring you peaches and salt cod. What was it you wanted so much when you were big with Cecily?'

'Samphire,' I laugh. 'Fancy you remembering! I could not have enough of it. Make sure you come home to bring me samphire and anything else I crave. This is a boy, this is a prince; he must have whatever he desires. He will be born with a silver spoon.'

'I shall come home to you. And you are not to worry. I don't want him born with a frown.'

'Then you beware of Warwick and your brother. I don't trust them.'

'Promise to rest and be happy and make him strong in your belly?'

'Promise to come back safe and make him strong in his inheritance,' I counter.

'It is a promise.'

He was wrong. Dear God, Edward was so wrong. Not, thank God, about winning the battle; for that was the battle that they called Lose-coat Field, when the bare-footed fools fighting for a lack-wit king were in such a rush to run away that they dropped their weapons and even their coats to escape from the charge led by my husband who was fighting his way through them, to keep his promise to me, to come home in time to bring me peaches and samphire.

No, he was wrong about the loyalty of Warwick and George his brother, who – it turned out – had planned and paid for the uprising and had decided this time to be certain of Edward's defeat. They were going to kill my Edward and put George on the throne. His own brother and Warwick, who had been his best friend, had decided together that the only way to defeat Edward was to stab him from behind on the battlefield, and they would have done it too; but for the fact that he rode so fast in the charge that no man could catch him.

Before the battle had even begun Lord Richard Welles, the petty leader, had gone down on his knees to Edward, confessed the plan and showed Warwick's orders and George's money. They paid him to lead an uprising in the name of King Henry, but in truth it was only a feint to draw Edward into battle and to kill him there. Warwick had learned his lesson truly. He had learned that you cannot hold a man like my Edward. He has to be dead to be defeated. George, his own brother, had overcome his fraternal affection. He was ready to slit his brother's throat on the battlefield and to wade through his blood to get to the crown. The two of them had bribed and ordered poor Lord Welles to raise a battle to bring Edward into danger, and then found once again that Edward was too much for them. When Edward saw the evidence against them he summoned them as kinsmen, the friend who had been an older brother to him and the youth who was his brother indeed; and when they did not come he knew what to think of them at last, and he summoned them as traitors to answer to him: but they were long gone.

'I shall see them dead,' I say to my mother as we sit before an open window in my privy chamber at Westminster Palace, spinning wool and gold thread to make yarn for a costly cloak for the baby. It will be purest lambswool and priceless gold, a cloak fit for a little prince, the greatest prince in Christendom. 'I shall see the two of them dead. I swear it, whatever you say.'

She nods at the spindle in her hand and the wool I am carding. 'Don't put ill-wishing into his little cape,' she says.

I stop the wheel and put the wool to one side. 'There,' I say. 'The work can wait; but the ill-wishing cannot.'

'Did you know: Edward promised a safe conduct to Lord Richard Welles if he would confess his treason and reveal the plot; but when he did so, he broke his word and killed him?'

I shake my head.

My mother's face is grave. 'Now the Beaufort family are in mourning for their kinsman Welles, and Edward has given a new cause to his enemies. He has broken his word, too. No one will trust him again, no one will dare to surrender to him. He has shown himself a man who cannot be trusted. As bad as Warwick.'

I shrug. 'These are the fortunes of war. Margaret Beaufort knows them as well as I. And she will have been unhappy anyway, since she is the heir to the House of Lancaster and we summoned her husband Henry Stafford to march out for us.' I give a hard laugh. 'Poor man, caught between her and our summons.'

My mother can't hide her smile. 'No doubt she was on her knees all the while,' she says cattily. 'For a woman who boasts that she has the ear of God she has little benefit to show for it.'

'Anyway, Welles doesn't matter,' I say. 'Alive or dead. What matters is that Warwick and George will be heading for the court of France, speaking ill of us, and hoping to raise an army. We have a new enemy, and this one is in our own house, our own heir. What a family the Yorks are!'

'Where are they now?' my mother asks me.

'At sea, heading for Calais, according to Anthony. Isabel is big with child, on board ship with them, and no one to care for her but her mother, the Countess of Warwick. They will be hoping to enter Calais and raise an army. Warwick is beloved there. And if they put themselves in Calais we will have no safety at all with them waiting just over the sea, threatening our ships, half a day's sail away from London. They must not enter Calais; we have to prevent it. Edward has sent the fleet to sea but our ships will never catch them in time.'

I rise to my feet and lean out of the open window into the sunshine. It is a warm day. The River Thames below me sparkles like a fountain, it is calm. I look to the south-west. There is a line of dark clouds on the horizon as if there might be dirty weather at sea. I put my lips together and I blow a little whistle.

Behind me, I hear my mother's spindle laid aside, and then I hear the soft sound of her whistle also. I keep my eye on the line of clouds and I let my breath hiss like the wind of a storm. She comes to stand behind me, her arm around my broad waist. Together we whistle gently into the spring air, blowing up a storm.

Slowly but powerfully the dark clouds pile up, one on top of another, until there is a great thunderhead of threatening dark cloud, south, far away, over the sea. The air freshens. I shiver in the sudden chill and we turn from the cooler, darkening day and close the window on the first scud of rain.

'Looks like a storm out at sea,' I remark.

A week later my mother comes to me with a letter in her hand. 'I have news from my cousin in Burgundy. She writes that George and Warwick were blown off the coast of France and then nearly wrecked in terrible seas off Calais. They begged the fort to let them enter for the sake of Isabel, but the castle would not admit them and they had the chain up across the entrance to the port. A wind got up from nowhere and the seas nearly drove them on to the walls. The fort would not let them in, they could not land the boat in high seas. Poor Isabel went into labour in the middle of the storm. They were tossed about for hours, and her baby died.'

I cross myself. 'God bless the poor little one,' I say. 'Nobody would have wished that on them.'

'Nobody did,' my mother says robustly. 'But if Isabel had not taken ship with traitors then she would have been safe in England with midwives and friends to care for her.'

'Poor girl,' I say, a hand on my own big belly. 'Poor girl. She has had little joy from her grand marriage. D'you remember her at court at Christmas?'

'There is worse news,' my mother goes on. 'Warwick and George have gone to his great friend King Louis of France and now the two of them have met with Margaret d'Anjou at Angers, and another plot is spinning, just as we have been spinning here.'

'Warwick still goes on against us?'

My mother makes a grimace. 'He must be a determined man indeed to see his own grandchild still-born while his family is on the run, and go from a near shipwreck straight to forswear his oaths of loyalty. But nothing stops him. You would think a storm out of a blue sky would make him wonder, but nothing makes him wonder. Now he is courting Margaret d'Anjou, that he once fought against. He had to spend half an hour on his knees to beg the forgiveness of her, his greatest enemy. She would not see him without his act of contrition. God bless her, she always did take herself very high.'

'What d'you think he plans?'

'It is the French King who is planning the dance now. Warwick thinks he is Kingmaker but now he is a puppet. They call Louis of France the spider, and I must say he spins a finer thread even than us. He wants to bring down your husband and diminish our country. He is using Warwick and Margaret d'Anjou to do it. Margaret's son, the so-called Prince of Wales, Prince Edward of Lancaster, is to marry Warwick's younger daughter Anne to bind their lying parents together in a pact they cannot dishonour.

Then I imagine they will all come to England to free Henry from the Tower.'

'That little thing Anne Neville?' I demand, immediately diverted. 'They would give her to that monster Edward, to make sure her father does not play false?'

'They will,' my mother agrees. 'She is only fourteen and they are marrying her to a boy who was allowed to choose how to execute his enemies when he was eleven years old. He was raised to be a devil. Anne Neville must be wondering if she is rising to be Queen or falling among the damned.'

'But it changes everything for George,' I say, thinking aloud. 'It was one thing to fight his brother the King when he hoped to kill him and succeed him – but now? Why would he fight Edward when he gains nothing for himself? Why would he fight his brother to put the Lancaster king and then the Lancaster prince on the throne?'

'I suppose he didn't think such a thing would happen when he set sail with a wife near her time, and a father-in-law determined to win the crown. But now he has lost his son and heir and his father-in-law has a second daughter who could be queen. George's prospects are changed very much. He should have the sense to see that. But d'you think he has?'

'Someone should advise him.' Our eyes meet. I never have to spell things out for my mother: we understand each other so well.

'Shall you visit the king's mother before dinner?' Mother asks me.

I take my foot from the pedal of the spinning wheel and stop it with my hand. 'Let's go and see her now,' I suggest.

She is sitting with her women sewing an altar cloth. One of them is reading from the Bible as they work. She is famously devout; her suspicion that we are not as saintly as she, worse, perhaps pagans, worst of all, perhaps witches, is just one of the many fears she holds against me. The years have not improved her view of me. She did not want me to marry her son, and even now, though I have proved my fertility and myself a good wife for him, she hates me still. Indeed, she has been so discourteous that Edward has given her Fotheringhay to keep her from court. As for me, I am not impressed by her sanctity: if she is such a good woman, then she should have taught George better. If she had the ear of God, she would not have lost her son Edmund and her husband. I curtsey to her as we enter and she rises to curtsey low to me. She nods her women to pick up their work and go to one side. She knows I am not visiting her to enquire after her health. There is still no great love lost between us and never will be.

'Your Grace,' she says levelly. 'I am honoured.'

'My Lady Mother,' I say, smiling. 'The pleasure is mine.'

We all sit simultaneously in order to avoid the issue of priority, and she waits for me to speak.

'I am so concerned for you,' I say sweetly. 'I am sure you are worried about George, so far from home, proclaimed as a traitor, and all but entrapped with the traitor Warwick, estranged from his brother and from his family. His first baby lost, his own life in such danger.'

She blinks. She had not anticipated my concern for her favourite George. 'Of course I wish he were reconciled to us,' she says cautiously. 'It is always sad when brothers quarrel.'

'And now I hear that George is abandoning his own family,' I say plaintively. 'A turncoat – not just against his brother but against you and against his own house.'

She looks at my mother for an explanation.

'He has joined Margaret d'Anjou,' my mother says bluntly. 'Your son, a Yorkist, is going to fight for the Lancastrian King. Shameful.'

'He will be defeated for certain: Edward always wins,' I say. 'And then he must be executed as a traitor. How can Edward spare him, even for brotherly love, if George takes up the Lancaster colours? Think of him dying with a red rose at his collar! The shame for you! What would his father have said?'

She is truly aghast. 'He would never follow Margaret of Anjou,' she says. 'His father's greatest enemy?'

'Margaret of Anjou put George's father's head on a spike on the walls of York, and now he serves her,' I say thoughtfully. 'How can any of us ever forgive him?'

'It cannot be so,' she says. 'He might be tempted to join Warwick. It is hard for him to always come second to Edward, and . . .' She breaks off but we all know that George is jealous of everyone: his brother Richard, Hastings, me and all of my kin. We know she has filled his head with wild thoughts that Edward is a bastard and so he is the true heir. 'And besides, what—'

'What good does it do him?' I supplement smoothly. 'I see what you think of him. Indeed, he always thinks of nothing but his gain and never of loyalty or his word or his honour. He is all George and no York.'

She flushes at that but she cannot deny that George has been the most selfish spoiled boy that ever turned coat.

'He thought when he went with Warwick that Warwick would make him king,' I say bluntly. 'Then they found that nobody would have George for king if they could have Edward. Only two people in the country think George is a better man than my husband.'

She waits.

'George himself and you,' I say precisely. 'Then he fled with Warwick because he did not dare face Edward after betraying him again. And now he finds that Warwick's plan has changed. Warwick will not put George on the throne. He will marry Anne his daughter to Edward of Lancaster, he will put the young Edward of Lancaster on the throne and become father-in-law to the King of England that way. George and Isabel are no longer his choice for King and Queen of England. Now it is Edward of Lancaster and Anne. The best that George can hope for is to be brother-in-law to the usurping Lancaster King of England instead of brother to the rightful York king.'

George's mother nods.

'Little profit for him,' I observe. 'For a great deal of work, and dreadful danger.'

I let her think on this for a moment. 'Now, if he were to turn his coat again and come back to his brother penitent and truly loyal, Edward would have him back,' I say. 'Edward would forgive him.'

'He would?'

I nod. 'I can promise it.' I don't add that I will never forgive him and that he and Warwick are dead men to me, and have been ever since they executed my father and brother after the battle of Edgecote Moor, and they will be dead men hereafter, whatever they do. Their names are in the black locket in my jewellery case and their names will never see the light again until they themselves are in the eternal darkness.

'It would be such a good thing if George, a young man without good advisors, could hear from someone, in private, in secret, that he could come back safely to his brother,' my mother observes at random, looking out of the window at the scudding clouds. 'Sometimes a young man needs good advice. Sometimes he needs to be told that he has taken a wrong turning but that he can come back to the high road. A young man such as George should not be fighting for Lancaster, dying with a red rose on his collar. A young man like George should be with his family, with his brothers who love him.' She pauses to let his mother think this through. It is really beautifully done.

'If only someone could tell him that he was welcome at home then you would have your son back, the brothers would be reunited, York would fight for York once more, and George would lose nothing. He would be brother to the King of England and he would be Duke of Clarence as he has always been. We could undertake that Edward would restore him. There lies his future. This other way he is – what would one call him?' She pauses to wonder what one would call Cecily's favourite son, then she finds the words: 'An utter numpty.'

The king's mother rises to her feet; my mother gets up too. I stay seated, smiling up at her, letting her stand before me. 'I always so enjoy talking with you both,' she says, her voice trembling with anger.

Now I rise, my hand on my spreading belly, and I wait for her to curtsey to me. 'Oh, me too. Good day, My Lady Mother,' I say pleasantly.

And so it is done, as easily as an enchantment. Without another word said, without Edward even knowing, a lady from the king's mother's court decides to visit her great friend, George's wife, poor Isabel Neville. The lady, heavily veiled, takes a boat, goes to Angers, finds Isabel, wastes no time on her crying in her room, finds George, tells him of his mother's tender love and her concerns for him. George tells her in return of his increasing discomfort with the allies to whom he is not only sworn but also married. God, he thinks, does not bless their union since their baby died in the storm, and nothing has gone right for him since he married Isabel. Surely, nothing as unpleasant as this should ever happen to George? Now he finds himself in the company of his family's enemies and – far worse for him – in second place again. Turncoat George says that he will come to England with the invading army of Lancaster but as soon as he sets foot in his beloved brother's kingdom he will tell us where they have landed, and what is their strength. He will seem to stand by them as brother-in-law to the Lancaster Prince of Wales until the battle is joined and then he will attack them from behind, and fight his way through to his brothers once more. He will be a son of York, one of the three sons of York again. We can rely on him. He will destroy his present friends, and his wife's own family. He is loyal to York. In his innermost heart, he has always been loyal to York.

My husband brings this encouraging news to me, unaware that this is the doing of women, spinning their toils around men.

I am resting on my day bed, one hand on my belly, feeling the baby move.

'Isn't this wonderful?' he asks me, truly delighted. 'George will come back to us!'

'I know that you love George,' I say. 'But even you have to admit he is an absolute crawling thing, loyal to no one.'

My generous-hearted husband smiles. 'Oh, he is George,' he says kindly. 'You can't be too hard on him. He has always been everyone's favourite, he has always been one to please himself.'

I find a smile in return. 'I am not too hard on him,' I say. 'I am glad he has come back to you.' And inwardly, I say to myself: But he is a dead man.

# SUMMER 1470

I am running behind my husband, my hand on my large belly, down the long winding corridors of the Palace of Whitehall. Servants run behind us carrying goods. 'You can't go. You swore to me you would be with me for the birth of our baby. It will be a boy, your son. You must be with me.'

He turns, his face grave. 'Sweetheart, our son will have no kingdom if I don't go. Warwick's brother-in-law, Henry Fitzhugh, has raised Northumberland. There's no doubt in my mind that Warwick will strike in the north, and then Margaret will land her army in the south. She will come straight to London to free her husband from the Tower. I have to go, and I have to go fast. I have to deal with the one and then turn and march south to catch the other before she comes here for you. I don't dare even stop for the pleasure of arguing with you.'

'What about me? What about me and the girls?'

He is muttering orders to the clerk, who runs behind him with a writing desk as he strides towards the stables. He pauses to shout orders at his equerries. Soldiers are rushing to the armoury to draw their weapons and breastplates, sergeants are bawling at them to fall in. The great wagons are being loaded again with tents, weapons, food, gear. The great army of York is on the march again.

'You have to go to the Tower,' he swings round to order me. 'I have to know you are safe. All of you, your mother as well, go to the royal rooms in the Tower. Prepare for the baby there. You know I will come to you as soon as I can.'

'When the enemy is in Northumberland? Why should I go to the Tower when you are riding out to fight an enemy hundreds of miles away?'

'Because only the devil knows for sure where Warwick and Margaret will land,' he says briefly. 'I'm guessing they'll split into two battles and land one to support the uprising in the north and the other in Kent. But I don't know. I've not heard from George. I don't know what they plan. Suppose they sail up the Thames while I am fighting in Northumberland? Be my love, be brave, be a queen: go to the Tower with the girls and keep yourselves safe. Then I can fight and win and come home to you.'

'My boys?' I whisper.

'Your boys will come with me. I shall keep them as safe as I can but it is time they played their part in our battles, Elizabeth.'

The baby turns inside me as if he is protesting too, and I am silenced by the heave of the movement. 'Edward, when will we ever be safe?'

'When I have won,' he says steadily. 'Let me go and win now, beloved.'

I let him go. I think no power in the world would have stopped him, and I tell the girls that we are staying in London at the Tower, one of their favourite palaces, and that their father and their half-brothers have gone to fight the bad men who still hanker after the old King Henry, though he is a prisoner at the Tower himself, silent in his rooms on the floor just below us. I tell them that their father will come home safe to us. When they cry for him in the night, for they have bad dreams about the wicked queen and the mad king, and their bad uncle Warwick, I promise them that their father will defeat the bad people and come home. I promise he will bring the boys safely back. He has given his word. He has never failed. He will come home.

But this time, he does not.

This time, he does not.

He and his brothers in arms, my brother Anthony, his brother Richard, his beloved friend Sir William Hastings and his loyal supporters, are shaken awake at Doncaster in the early hours of the morning by a couple of the king's minstrels who, coming drunkenly home from whoring, happen to glance over the castle walls and see torches on the road. The enemy advance guard, marching at night, a sure sign of Warwick in command, is only an hour away, perhaps only moments away, coming to snatch the king before he can meet with his army. The whole of the north is up against the king and ready to fight for Warwick, and the royal party will be taken in a moment. Warwick's influence runs deep and wide in this part of the world, and Warwick's brother and Warwick's brother-in-law have turned out against Edward and are fighting for their kinsman and for King Henry, and will be at the castle gate within an hour. There is no doubt in anyone's mind that this time Warwick will not take prisoners.

Edward dispatches my boys to me and then he, Richard, Anthony and Hastings fling themselves on their horses and ride away in the night, desperate not to be taken by Warwick or his kinsmen, certain that this time there will be a summary execution for them. Warwick tried once to capture and keep Edward, as we have captured and kept Henry, and learned that there is no victory as final as death. He will never again imprison Edward and wait for everyone to concede defeat. This time he wants him dead.

Edward rides out into the darkness with his friends and kinsmen and has no time to send to me, to tell me where to meet him, he cannot even write to me to tell me where he is going. I doubt that he knows himself. All he is doing is getting away from certain death. Thoughts of how to return will come later. Now, tonight, the king is running for his life.

## AUTUMN 1470

The news comes to London in unreliable rumours, and it is all, always bad. Warwick lands in England, as Edward predicted, but what he did not predict is the rush of nobles to the traitor's side, in support of the king they have left to rot in the Tower for the last five years. The Earl of Shrewsbury joins him. Jasper Tudor – who can raise most of Wales – joins him. Lord Thomas Stanley – who took the ruby ring at my coronation joust and told me that his motto was 'Without Changing' – joins him. A whole host of lesser gentry follow these influential commanders, and Edward is swiftly outnumbered in his own kingdom. All the Lancaster families are finding and polishing their old weapons, hoping to march out to victory once again. It is as he warned me: he could not spread out the wealth quickly enough, fairly enough, to enough people. We could not spread the influence of my family far enough, deep enough. And now they think they will do better under Warwick and the mad old king than under Edward and my family.

Edward would have been killed on the spot if they had caught him; but they have missed him – that much is clear. But nobody knows where he is, and someone comes to the Tower once a day to assure me that they have seen him, and that he was dying of his wounds, or that they have seen him and he is fleeing to France, or that they have seen him on a bier and he is dead.

My boys arrive at the Tower travel-stained and weary, furious that they did not get away with the king. I try not to hang on to them, or kiss them more often than morning and night, but I can hardly believe that they have come safely back to me. Just as I cannot believe that my husband and my brother have not.

I send to Grafton for my mother to come to us in the Tower. I need her advice and company, and if we are indeed lost and I have to go abroad I will want her with me. But the messenger comes back and his face is grave.

'Your Lady Mother is not at her home,' he says.

'Where is she?'

He looks shifty, as if he wishes someone else could tell me bad news. 'Tell me at once,' I say, my voice sharp with fear. 'Where is she?'

'She is under arrest,' he says. 'Orders of the Earl of Warwick. He has ordered her arrest and his men came to Grafton and took her away.'

'Warwick has my mother?' I can hear my heart thudding in my ears. 'My mother is a prisoner?'

'Yes.'

I hear a rattling noise and I see that my hands are shaking so badly that my rings are clicking against the arms of the chair. I take a breath to steady myself, and grip tight to stop myself shaking. My son Thomas comes closer to stand on one side of my chair. Richard steps up to the other.

'On what charge?'

I think: it cannot be treason: nobody could argue that my mother has done more than advise me. Nobody could charge her with treason when she has been a good mother-in-law to the crowned king and a loving companion to his queen. Not even Warwick could stoop so low as to charge a woman with treason and behead her for loving her daughter. But this is a man who killed my father and my brother without reason. His desire must only be to break my heart and rob Edward of the support of my family. This is a man who will kill me if he ever gets hold of me.

'I am so sorry, Your Grace . . .'

'What charge?' I demand. My throat is dry and I give a little cough.

'Witchcraft,' he says.

There is no need of a trial to put a witch to death, though no trial has ever failed: it is easy to find people to witness on oath that their cows died or that their horse threw them because a witch had overlooked them. But in any case, there is no need of either witnesses or a trial. A single priest is all that is needed to attest a witch's guilt, or a lord like Warwick can simply declare her guilty, and no one will defend her. Then she can be strangled and buried at the village crossroads. They usually get the blacksmith to strangle the woman since he, by virtue of his trade, has big strong hands. My mother is a tall woman, a famous beauty with a long slim neck. Any man could choke the life out of her in minutes. It does not need to be a brawny blacksmith. Any one of Warwick's guard could easily do it; would do it, in a moment, on a word, gladly on Warwick's word.

'Where is she?' I demand. 'Where has he taken her?'

'Nobody at Grafton knew where they were going,' the man says. 'I asked everyone. A troop of horse came, and they made your mother ride pillion behind their commanding officer, and they took her north. They told no one where they were going. They just said that she was under arrest for witchcraft.'

'I must write to Warwick,' I say quickly. 'Go and eat and get a fresh horse. I shall need you to travel as fast as you can. Are you ready to leave at once?'

'At once,' he says, bows and goes out.

I write to Warwick demanding her release. I write to every archbishop we once commanded, and anyone who I think would speak for us. I write to my mother's old friends and family attached to the House of Lancaster. I even write to Margaret Beaufort, who as the heir of the House of Lancaster may have some influence. Then I go to my chapel, the Queen's Chapel, and I get down on my knees all night to pray that God will not allow this wicked man to take this good woman, who is blessed with nothing more than a sacred foresight, a few pagan tricks and a total lack of deference. At dawn, I write her name on a dove's feather and send it floating downstream to warn Melusina that her daughter is in danger.

Then I have to wait for news. For a whole week I have to wait, hearing nothing and fearing the very worst. Daily, people come to tell me that my husband is dead. Now I fear they will say the same of my mother, and I will be utterly alone in the world. I pray to God, I whisper to the river: Someone has to save my mother. Then, at last, I hear that she is freed, and two days later she comes to me in the Tower.

I run into her arms and I cry as if I were her daughter of ten years old. She holds me and she rocks me as if I were still her little girl, and when I look up into her beloved face I see there are tears on her own cheeks.

'I'm safe,' she says. 'He didn't hurt me. He didn't put me to question. He held me only for a few days.'

'Why did he let you go?' I ask. 'I wrote to him, I wrote to everybody, I prayed and I wished; but I didn't think he would show you any mercy.'

'Margaret d'Anjou,' she answers with a wry smile. 'Of all the women in the world! She commanded him to release me as soon as she heard that he had arrested me. We were good friends once, and we are kinswomen still. She remembered my service at her court and she ordered Warwick to release me, or face her extreme displeasure.'

I give an incredulous laugh. 'She commanded him to release you, and he obeyed?'

'She is his daughter's mother-in-law now, as well as his queen,' my mother points out. 'And he is her sworn ally and counting on her army to support him as he recaptures the country. And I was her companion when she came to England as a bride, and her friend through all the years of her queenship. I was of the House of Lancaster then, as we all were, until you married Edward.'

'It was good of her to save you,' I concede.

'This is a cousins' war indeed,' my mother says. 'We all have those we love on the other side. We all have to face killing our own family. Sometimes we can be merciful. God knows, she is not a merciful woman; but she thought she would be merciful to me.'

I am sleeping uneasily in the rich royal apartments of the Tower of London, the flicker of moonlight reflected from the river onto the drapes over my bed. I am lying on my back, the weight of the baby heavy on my belly, an ache in my side, drifting between sleep and wakefulness when I see, as bright as moonlight on the arras above me, my husband's face, gaunt and aged, bent low over the galloping mane of his horse, riding like a madman through the night, less than a dozen men around him.

I give a little cry and turn on the pillow. The rich embroidery presses against my cheek and I sleep again; but again I wake to the image of Edward riding hard through darkness on a strange road.

I half wake, crying out against the picture in my mind, and as I drift between sleeping and wakefulness, I see a small fishing port, Edward, Anthony, William and Richard hammering on a door, arguing with a man, hiring his boat, forever looking over their shoulders to the west, for their enemies. I hear them promise the ship's master anything, anything! if he will launch his little ship and take them to Flanders. I see Edward strip off his great coat of furs and offer it as payment. 'Take it,' he says. 'It's worth more than your boat twice over. Take it and I will think it a service.'

'No,' I say in my sleep. Edward is leaving me, leaving England, leaving me and breaking his word that he would be with me for the birth of our son.

The seas are high outside the harbour, the dark waves topped with white foam. The little ship rises and falls, rolling between the waves, water breaking over the bows. It seems impossible that it should climb to the top of the waves, and then it crashes down in the troughs. Edward stands at the stern, clutching to the side for support, thrown about by the movement of the boat, looking back at the country he called his own, watching for the flare of the torches of the men coming after him. He has lost England. We have lost England. He claimed the throne and he was crowned king. He crowned me as queen and I believed that we were established. He never lost a battle; but Warwick has been too much, too fast, too duplicitous for him. Edward is heading for exile, just as Warwick did. He is heading out into a vicious storm, just as Warwick did. But Warwick went straight to the King of France and found an ally and an army. I cannot see how Edward will ever return.

Warwick is back in power, and now it is my husband and my brother Anthony and my brother-in-law Richard who are the fugitives, and God knows what wind will ever blow them back to England again. And the girls and I, and the baby in my belly, are the new hostages, the new prisoners. I may be in the royal apartments of the Tower for now, but soon I shall be in the rooms below, with the bars over the window, and King Henry will sleep in this bed again, and I shall be the one that people say should, for Christian charity, be released, so that I do not die in prison, without sight of the free sky.

'Edward!' I see him look up, almost as if he can hear me call for him in my sleep, in my dream. 'Edward!' I cannot believe that he could leave me, that we could have lost our fight for the throne. My father laid down his life that I might be queen; my brother died beside him. Are we now to be nothing but pretenders, dismissed after a few years of good luck? A king and a queen who over-reached themselves and for whom the luck ran out? Are my girls to be the daughters of an attainted traitor? Are they to marry small squires on country estates and hope to live down their father's shame? Is my mother to greet Margaret of

Anjou on her knees, and hope to worm her way back into favour again? Am I to have the choice of living in exile or living in prison? And what of my son, the baby not yet born? Is Warwick likely to let him live – he who lost his own grandson and only heir, as we closed the gates of Calais to him, his daughter losing her baby in rough seas with a witch's wind blowing them on shore?

I scream out loud: 'Edward! Don't leave me!' and the terror in my voice starts me into full wakefulness, and next door my mother lights a candle from the fire, and opens the door. 'Is he coming? The baby? Is he early?'

'No. I had a dream. Mother, I had a most terrible dream.'

'There, there, never mind,' she says, quick to comfort. She lights candles at my bedside, she stirs up the fire with a kick from her slippered foot. 'There, Elizabeth. You're safe now.'

'We're not safe,' I say certainly. 'That's the very thing.'

'Why, what did you dream?'

'It was Edward, on a ship, in a storm. It was night, the seas were huge. I don't even know if his ship will get through. It's an ill wind that blows no good, Mother, and he was facing an ill wind. It was our wind. It was the gale we called up to blow George and Warwick away. We called it up but it has not blown away. Edward is in a storm of our making. Edward was dressed like a servant, a poor man: he had nothing, nothing but the clothes he stood up in. He had given away his coat. Anthony was there; he didn't even have his cape. William Hastings was with them, and Edward's brother Richard. They were all that had survived, they were all that could run. They were . . .' I close my eyes trying to remember. 'They were leaving us, Mother. Oh Mother, he's left England, he's left us. He's lost. We're lost. Edward has gone, Anthony too. I am sure of it.'

She takes my cold hands and rubs them in her own. 'Perhaps it was just a bad dream,' she says. 'Perhaps nothing but a dream. Women with child, near their time, have strange fancies, vivid dreams . . .'

I shake my head, I throw back the covers. 'No. I am certain. It was a Seeing. He is defeated. He has run away.'

'D'you think he has gone to Flanders?' she asks. 'To take refuge with his sister, the Duchess Margaret, and Charles of Burgundy?'

I nod. 'Of course. Of course he has. And he will send for me, I don't doubt him. He loves me, and he loves the girls, and he swore he would never leave me. But he has gone, Mother. Margaret of Anjou must have landed, and she will be marching here, to London, to free Henry. We have to go. I have to get the girls away. We can't be here when her army comes in. They will imprison us for ever if they find us here.'

My mother throws a shawl around my shoulders. 'Are you sure? Can you travel? Shall I send a message to the docks and shall we take a ship?'

I hesitate. I am so afraid of the voyage when my baby is near to his time. I think of Isabel, crying out in pain on a rocking ship and nobody to help her with the birth, the baby dying and not even a priest to christen him. I can't face what she had to face, with the wind screaming in the rigging. I am afraid that the wind I whistled up, is still blowing down the sea roads, its ill-nature unsatisfied by the death of one baby, looking around the horizon for unsteady sails. If that wind sees me and my girls on the heaving sea then we will be drowned.

'No, I can't bear it. I don't dare. I am too afraid of the wind. We'll go into sanctuary. We'll go to Westminster Abbey. They won't dare hurt us there. We'll be safe there. The Londoners love us still and Queen Margaret wouldn't break sanctuary. If King Henry is in his wits he would never let her break sanctuary. He believes in the power of God working in the world. He will respect sanctuary and make Warwick leave us alone. We'll take the girls and my Grey sons and go into sanctuary. At least until my son is born.'

## NOVEMBER 1470

When I had heard of desperate men claiming sanctuary by hanging on to the ring on the church door and yelling defiance at the thief-takers, or dashing up the aisle and putting their hand on the high altar as if they were playing a childhood game of tag, I always thought that they must live thereafter on the wine of the Mass and the bread of the Host, and sleep in the pews pillowed on hassocks. It turns out that it is not as bad as this. We live in the crypt of the church built in St Margaret's churchyard, within the precincts of the abbey. It is a little like living in a cellar, but we can see the river from the low windows on one side of the room and we can glimpse the highway through the grille in the door, on the other side. We live like a poor family, dependent on the goodwill of Edward's supporters and the citizens of London, who love the family of York and continue to do so, even though the world has changed again, the family of York is in hiding, and King Henry is acclaimed king once more.

Warwick, the ascendant Lord Warwick, the murderer of my father and brother and the kidnapper of my husband, enters London in triumph, George his unhappy son-in-law at his side. George may be a spy in their ranks, secretly on our side, or he may have turned his coat and turned it again and now hopes for crumbs from the Lancaster royal table. At any rate, he gets no message to me, nor does anything to guarantee my safety. He bobs along in the wake of the Kingmaker, as if he had no brother, no sister-in-law, perhaps still hoping for a chance at being king himself.

Warwick, triumphant, takes his old enemy King Henry from the Tower and proclaims him fit to rule and fully restored. He is now the liberator of his king and the saviour of the House of Lancaster, and the country is filled with joy. King Henry is confused by this turn of events, but they explain to him, slowly and kindly once a day, that he is king again, and that his cousin Edward of York has gone away. They may even tell him that we, Edward's family, are hiding in Westminster Abbey for he orders – or they order in his name – that the sanctuary of the holy places shall be observed, and we are safe in our self-imposed prison.

Every day, the butchers send us meat, the bakers send us bread, even the milkmaids from the green fields of the city bring us pails of milk for the girls, and the fruit-sellers from Kent bring the best of the crop to the abbey and leave it at the door for us. They tell the churchwardens that it is for the 'poor queen' at her time of trouble, and then they remember that there is a new queen, Margaret of Anjou, only waiting for a fair wind to set sail and return to her throne, and they trip over their words and finally say, 'You know who I mean. But make sure she has it, for fruit from Kent is very good for a woman near her time. It will make the baby come easier. And tell her that we wished her well and we will come again.'

It is hard for my girls to have so little news of their father, hard for them to be kept inside in the few small rooms, since they were born to the best of things. They have lived all their lives in the greatest palaces of England; now they are confined. They can stand on a bench to look out of the windows at the river, where the royal barge used to take them up and down between one palace and another, or they can take turns to get on a chair and look out of the grating at the streets of London, where they used to ride and hear people bless their names and their pretty faces. Elizabeth, my oldest girl, is only four years old, but it is as if she understands that a time of great sorrow and difficulty has come on us. She never asks me where her tame birds are, she never asks for the servants who used to pet her and play with her, she never asks for her golden top or her little dog, or her precious toys. She acts as if she had been born and bred in this little space, and she plays with her baby sisters as if she were a paid nursemaid, ordered to be cheerful. The only question she poses is: where is her father? – and I have to learn to become accustomed to her looking up at me, a little puzzled frown on her round face, asking, 'Is my father the king here yet, Lady Mother?'

It is hardest of all on my boys, who are like confined lion cubs in the small space and prowl around, bickering. In the end, my mother sets them exercises, sword play with broom handles, poems to learn, jumping and catching games that they have to do every day, and they keep a score and hope that it will make them stronger in the battle they long for, which will restore Edward to the throne.

As the days grow shorter and the nights grow darker I know that my time is coming and my baby is due. My great terror is that I will die here, in childbirth, and my mother will be left here alone, in our enemy's city, guarding my children.

'Do you know what will happen?' I ask her bluntly. 'Have you foreseen it? And what will happen to my girls?'

I see some knowledge in her eyes but the face she turns to me is untroubled. 'You aren't going to die, if that's what you're asking,' she says bluntly. 'You are a healthy young woman and the king's council is sending Lady Scrope to care for you, and a pair of midwives. There is no reason to think that you will die, any more than there was with any of the others. I expect you to survive this, and to have more children.'

'The baby?' I ask, trying to read her face.

'You know he is healthy,' she says, smiling. 'Anyone who has felt that child kick knows he is strong. There is no reason for you to fear.'

'But there is something,' I say certainly. 'You foresee something about Edward, my baby prince Edward.'

She looks at me for a moment and then she decides to speak honestly. 'I can't see him becoming king,' she says. 'I have read the cards and I have looked at the reflection of the moon on the water. I have tried asking the crystal, and looking into the smoke. Indeed, I have tried everything I know which is inside the laws of God and is allowed in this holy space. But to tell you the truth, Elizabeth: I cannot see him being king.'

I laugh out loud. 'Is that it? Is that all? Dear God, Mother, I cannot see his own father being king again, and he is crowned and ordained! I cannot see myself being queen again, and I have had the holy oil on my breast and the sceptres in my hand. I don't hope for a Prince of Wales here, just a healthy boy. Just let him be born strong and grow to be a man and I will be content. I don't need him to be King of England. I just want to know that he and I will live through this.'

'Oh, you'll live through this,' she says. An airy wave of her hand dismisses the cramped rooms, the girls' truckle beds in one corner, the servants' straw mattresses on the floor in another, the poverty of the space, the chill of the cellar, the damp in the stone of the walls, the smoking fire, the dauntless courage of my children, who are forgetting that they ever lived anywhere better. 'This is nothing. I expect to see us rise from this.'

'How?' I ask her disbelievingly.

She leans over and she puts her mouth to my ear. 'Because your husband is not growing vines and making wine in Flanders,' she says. 'He is not carding wool and learning to weave. He is equipping an expedition, making allies, raising money, planning to invade England. The London merchants are not the only ones in the country who prefer York to Lancaster. And Edward has never lost a battle. D'you remember?'

Uncertainly, I nod. Even though he is defeated and in exile, it is true that he has never lost a battle.

'So when he comes against Henry's forces, even when they are captained by Warwick and driven on by Margaret of Anjou, don't you think he will win?'

It is not a proper confinement, as a queen should be confined, with a ceremonial retirement from court six weeks before the date of the birth, and a closing of the shutters and a blessing of the room.

'Nonsense,' my mother says buoyantly. 'You retired from daylight itself, didn't you? Confinement? I should think no queen has ever been so confined. Who has ever been confined to sanctuary before?'

It is not a proper royal birth with three midwives and two wet nurses, and rockers and noble godmothers and mistresses of the nursery standing by, and ambassadors waiting with rich gifts. Lady Scrope is sent by the Lancaster court to make sure that I have everything I need, and I think this a gracious gesture from the Earl of Warwick to me. But I have to bring my baby into the world with no waiting husband and court at the door, and almost none to help me, and his godfathers are the Abbot of Westminster and the Prior, and his godmother is Lady Scrope: the only people who are with me, neither great lords of the land nor foreign kings, the usual godfathers for a royal baby, but good and kind people who have been trapped at Westminster with us.

I call him Edward, as his father wants, and as the silver spoon from the river predicted. Margaret of Anjou, with her invasion fleet held in port by storms, sends me a message to tell me to call him John. She does not want another Prince Edward in England to rival her son. I ignore her words as from a nobody. Why would I listen to the preferences of Margaret of Anjou? My husband named him Edward, and the silver spoon came from the river with his name on it. Edward he is: Edward, Prince of Wales he shall be, even if my mother is right and he is never Edward the king.

Amongst ourselves we call him Baby, and no one calls him the Prince of Wales, and I think as I drift into sleep after the birth, all warm with him in my arms, half drunk from the birthing cup that they have given me, that perhaps this baby will not be king. There have been no cannons fired for him and no bonfires lit on hilltops. The fountains and conduits of London have not run with wine, the citizens are not drunk with joy, there are no announcements of his arrival racing to the great courts of Europe. It is like having an ordinary baby, not a prince. Perhaps he will be an ordinary boy and I will become an ordinary woman again. Perhaps we will not be great people, chosen by God, but just happy.

## WINTER 1470–71

We spend Christmas in sanctuary. The London butchers send us a fat goose and my boys and little Elizabeth and I play cards and I make sure that I lose a silver sixpence to her, and send her to bed thrilled to be a serious gamester. We spend Twelfth Night in sanctuary, and Mother and I compose a play for the children with costumes and masks and enchantments. We tell them our family story of Melusina, the beautiful woman, half girl, half fish, who is found in the fountain in the forest and marries a mortal for love. I wrap myself in a sheet, which we tie at the feet to make a great tail and I let down my hair and when I rise up from the floor the girls are transported by the fish-woman Melusina and the boys applaud. My mother enters with a paper horse's head taped on the stick of a broom; wearing the doorman's jerkin, and a paper crown. The girls don't recognise her at all and watch the play as if we were paid mummers at the greatest court in the world. We tell them the story of the courtship of the beautiful woman who is half fish and how her lover persuades her to leave her watery fountain in the wood and take her chance in the great world. We tell only half the story: that she lives with him and gives him beautiful children and they are happy together.

There is more to the story than this, of course. But I find that I don't want to think about marriages for love that end in separation. I don't want to think about being a woman who cannot live in the new world that is being made by men. I don't want to think of Melusina rising from her fountain and confining herself to a castle while I am held in sanctuary, and all of us, daughters of Melusina, are trapped in a place where we cannot wholly be ourselves.

*Melusina's mortal husband loved her, but she puzzled him. He did not understand her nature and he was not content to live with a woman who was a mystery to him. He allowed a guest to persuade him to spy on her. He hid behind the hangings in her bath house and saw her swim beneath the water of her bath, saw – horrified – the gleam of ripple on scales, learnt her secret: that although she loved him, truly loved him, she was still half woman and half fish. He could not bear what she was, and she could not help but be who she was. So he left her, because in his heart he feared that she was a woman with a divided nature – and he did not realise that all women are creatures of divided nature. He could not stand to think of her secrecy, that she had a life hidden from him. He could not, in fact, tolerate the truth that Melusina was a woman who knew the unknown depths, who swam in them.*

*Poor Melusina, who tried so hard to be a good wife, had to leave the man who loved her and go back to the water, finding the earth too hard. Like many women, she was unable to fit exactly with her husband's view. Her feet hurt: she could not walk in the path of her husband's choosing. She tried to dance to please him, but she could not deny the pain. She is the ancestress of the royal house of Burgundy, and we, her descendants, still try to walk in the paths of men, and sometimes we too find the way unbearably hard.*

I hear that the new court has a merry Christmas feast. Henry the king is back in his senses and the House of Lancaster is triumphant. From the windows of the sanctuary we can see the barges going up and down the river as the noblemen go from their riverside palaces to Whitehall. I see the Stanley barge go by. Lord Stanley, who kissed my hand at my coronation tournament, and told me his motto was '*Sans changer*', was one of the first to greet Warwick when he landed in England. It turns out he is a Lancaster man after all; maybe he will be unchanging for them.

I see the Beaufort barge with the flag of the red dragon of Wales flying at the stern. Jasper Tudor, the great power of Wales, is taking his nephew young Henry Tudor to court to visit the king, his kinsman. Half outlaw, half prince. Jasper will be back in the castles of Wales again and Lady Margaret Beaufort will weep tears of joy all over her fourteen-year-old son, Henry Tudor, I don't doubt. She was parted from him when we put him with good York guardians, the Herberts, and she had to endure the prospect of him marrying the Yorkist Herbert girl. But now William Herbert lies dead in our service, and Margaret Beaufort has her son back in her keeping. She will be pushing him forward at court, pushing him forward for favours and places. She will want his titles restored, she will want his inheritance guaranteed. George, Duke of Clarence, stole both the title and the lands, and she will have named them in her prayers ever since. She is a most ambitious woman, and determined mother. I don't doubt she will have the earldom of Richmond off George within the year and, if she can, her son will be named as the Lancaster heir after the prince.

I see Lord Warwick's barge, the most beautiful on the river, his rowers going in time to the beat of the drummer in the stern, moving swiftly against the tide as if nothing can stop his onward progress, not even the flow of the river. I even make him out, standing in the prow of the boat as if he would rule the very water of the river, his hat pulled off and held in his hand so that he can feel the cold air in his dark hair. I purse my lips to whistle up a wind but I let him go. It makes no difference.

Warwick's older daughter Isabel may be hand in hand with my

brother-in-law George in the seats at the back of the barge as they go past my subterranean prison. Perhaps she remembers the Christmas that she came to court as an unwilling bride and I was kind to her, or perhaps she prefers to forget the court where I was the Queen of the White Rose. George will know I am here, the wife of his brother, the woman who stayed loyal when he did not; living in poverty, living in half-darkness. He will know I am here; he may even feel me watching him, my narrowed eyes overlooking him – this man who was once George of the House of York, and is now a favoured kinsman at the court of Lancaster.

My mother puts her hand on my arm. 'Don't ill-wish them,' she warns me. 'It comes back on you. It is better to wait. Edward is coming. I don't doubt it. I don't doubt him for a moment. This time will be like a bad dream. It is as Anthony says: shadows on the wall. What matters is that Edward musters an army big enough to defeat Warwick.'

'How can he?' I say, looking out at the city that now declares itself all for Lancaster. 'How can he even begin?'

'He has been in touch with your brothers, and with all our kinsmen. He is raising his forces, and he has never lost a battle.'

'He has never fought Warwick. And Warwick taught him everything he knows about war.'

'He is king,' she says. 'Even if they now say that it meant nothing. He was crowned, he is divinely ordained, he has had the holy oil on his breast – they cannot deny that he is king. Even if another crowned and ordained king sits on the throne. But Edward is lucky, and Henry is not. Perhaps it comes down only to that: if you are a lucky man. And the Yorks are a lucky house.' She smiles. 'And of course he has us. We can wish him well, no harm in a little spell for good luck. And if that does not improve his chances then nothing will.'

## SPRING 1471

My mother brews up tisanes and leans from the window and pours them into the river, whispering words that no one can hear, throws powder on the fires to make them burn green and smoke. She never stirs the children's porridge without whispering a prayer, turns her pillow over twice before she gets into bed, claps her shoes together before putting them on to rid them of bad luck.

'Does any of it mean anything?' my son Richard asks me, one eye on his grandmother, who is twisting a plait of ribbon and whispering over it.

I shrug. 'Sometimes,' I say.

'Is it witchcraft?' he asks nervously.

'Sometimes.'

Then in March my mother tells me. 'Edward is coming to you, I am sure of it.'

'You have foreseen it?' I ask.

She giggles. 'No, the butcher told me.'

'What did the butcher tell you? London is filled with gossip.'

'Yes, but he had a message from a man in Smithfield who serves the ships that go to Flanders. He saw a little fleet sailing northwards in the worst weather, and one of them was flying the Sun in Splendour: the badge of York.'

'Edward is invading?'

'Perhaps at this very moment.'

In April, in the early hours of the night, I hear the sound of cheering from the streets outside and I jump from my bed and go to the window to listen. The abbey serving girl pounds on the door and comes running into the room and babbles, 'Your Grace! Your Grace! It is him. It is the king. Not King Henry, the other king. Your king. The York king. King Edward!'

I draw my nightgown around me and put my hand to the plait of my hair. 'Here now? Are they cheering for him?'

'Cheering for him now!' she exclaims. 'Lighting torches to guide him on his way. Singing and throwing down gold coins before him. Him, and a band of soldiers. And he must be coming here!'

'Mother! Elizabeth! Richard! Thomas! Girls!' I call out. 'Get up! Get dressed! Your father is coming. Your father is coming to us!' I seize the serving girl by the arm. 'Get me hot water to wash in and the best gown I have. Leave the firewood, it doesn't matter. Who's going to sit by that paltry fire ever again?' I push her from the room to fetch the water and I pull my hair out of the night-time plait as Elizabeth comes running into my room her big eyes wide. 'Is it the Bad Queen coming? Lady Mother, is the Bad Queen here?'

'No, sweetheart! We are saved. It is your own good father coming to visit us. Can't you hear them cheering?'

I stand her up on a stool to the grille in the door then I splash water on my face and twist my hair up under my headdress. The girl brings me my gown and ties it up, fumbling with the ribbons, and then we hear the thunder of his knock at the door and Elizabeth screams and jumps down to open it, and then falls back as he comes in, taller and graver than she remembers him, and in a moment I have run to him, barefoot as I am, and I am in his arms again.

'My son,' he demands after he has held me and kissed me and

rubbed his rough chin against my cheek. 'Where is my son? Is he strong? Is he well?'

'He is strong and well. He is five months old this month,' my mother says as she brings him in, swaddled tightly, and sweeps Edward a great curtsey. 'And you are welcome home, son Edward, Your Grace.'

Gently he puts me aside and goes swiftly to her. I had forgotten that he could move so lightly on his feet, like a dancer. He takes his son from my mother's arms and though he whispers, 'Thank you,' he does not even see her: he is quite distracted. He takes the baby over to the light of the window, and Baby Edward opens his dark-blue eyes and yawns, his rosebud mouth opening wide, and he looks into the face of his father as if to return the intense grey-eyed scrutiny.

'My son,' he says quietly. 'Elizabeth, forgive me, that you had to give birth to him here. I would not have had that for the world.'

I nod in silence.

'And he is baptised and named Edward as I wanted?'

'He is.'

'And he thrives?'

'We are just starting to feed him solid food,' my mother says proudly. 'And he is taking to it. He sleeps well and he is a bright, clever boy. Elizabeth has nursed him herself, and no one could have been a better wet nurse to him. We have made you a little prince here.'

Edward looks at her. 'Thank you for his care,' he says. 'And for staying with my Elizabeth.' He looks down. His daughters, Elizabeth, Mary and Cecily, are gathered around him, gazing up at him as if he were some strange beast, a unicorn perhaps, who has suddenly cantered into their nursery.

Gently he kneels so that he does not tower above them, still holding the baby in the crook of his arm. 'And you are my girls, my princesses,' he says quietly to them. 'Do you remember me? I have been away a long time, more than half a year; but I am your father. I have been away from you for far too long; but there was never a day when I did not think of you and your beautiful mother and swear that I would come home to you and set you in your rightful places again. Do you remember me?'

Cecily's lower lip trembles, but Elizabeth speaks: 'I remember you.' She puts her hand on his shoulder and looks into his face without fear. 'I am Elizabeth, I am the oldest. I remember you; the others are too small. Do you remember me, your Elizabeth? Princess Elizabeth? One day I shall be Queen of England like my mother.'

We laugh at that, and he gets to his feet again, hands the baby to my mother and takes me into his arms. Richard and Thomas step forward and kneel for his blessing.

'My boys,' he says warmly. 'You must have hated it, cooped up in here.'

Richard nods. 'I wish I had been with you, Sire.'

'Next time you shall,' Edward promises him.

'How long have you been in England?' I ask, my words muffled as he starts to pull my hair down. 'Have you an army?'

'I came with your brother and with my true friends,' he says. 'Richard my brother, your brother Anthony, Hastings, of course, the ones who went into exile with me. And now others are coming to my side. George my brother has left Warwick and will fight for me. He and Richard and I embraced each other as brothers once more, before the very walls of Coventry, under the nose of Warwick. George has brought Lord Shrewsbury over to us. And Sir William Stanley has come over to my side. There will be others.' I think of the power of Warwick and the Lancastrian affinity, and the French army that Margaret will bring, and I know that it is not enough.

'I can stay tonight,' he says. 'I had to see you. But tomorrow I have to go to war.'

I can hardly believe him. 'You will never leave me tomorrow?'

'Sweetheart, I took a risk just coming here. Warwick is holed up in Coventry and will neither surrender nor give battle for he knows that Margaret of Anjou is coming with her army and together they will make a mighty force. George came out and is with us and he has brought Shrewsbury and his tenants; but it's not enough. I have to take Henry as a hostage, and ride out to face her. They will be hoping that I will be cornered here, but I will take the battle to them and, if I am lucky, then I will meet Warwick and defeat him before I have to meet Margaret and defeat her.'

My mouth grows dry and I swallow in fear at the thought of him facing one great general, and then the great army of Margaret. 'The French army will come with Margaret?'

'The miracle is that she has not yet landed. We were both ready to sail at the same time. We were about to race each other to England. We have both been pinned down by the weather since February. She had her fleet ready to sail from Honfleur nearly a month ago and she has been out and driven back by a storm over and over again. There was a gap in the wind in my favour for no more than a day. It was like magic, my love, and we got away, blown all the way to Yorkshire. But at least it gives me the chance to take them one at a time and not face a united army led by the two of them at once.'

I glance at my mother at the mention of the storm but her face is smilingly innocent. 'You will not go tomorrow?'

'Sweetheart, you have me tonight. Shall we spend the time talking?'

We turn and go into my chamber and he closes the door with a kick of his foot. He takes me into his arms as he always does. 'Bed, Wife,' he says.

He takes me as he has always done, passionately, as a dry man slaking his thirst. But for once, tonight, he is a different man. The smell of his hair and his skin is the same, and that is enough to make me beg for his touch, but after he has had me, he holds me tightly in his arms, as if for once the pleasure is not enough. It is as if he wants something more from me.

'Edward?' I murmur. 'Are you all right?'

He does not answer but buries his head against my shoulder and my neck as if he would block out the world with the warmth of my flesh.

'Sweetheart, I was afraid,' he says. I can hardly hear him he speaks so low. 'Sweetheart, I was most afraid.'

'Of what?' I ask, a foolish question of a man who has had to flee for his life and put together an army in exile and is facing the most powerful army in Christendom.

He turns and lies on his back, his hand still gripping me close to his side so I press against him from breastbone to toes.

'When they said Warwick was coming for me, and George with him, I knew this time he would not take me and hold me. I knew this time it would be my death. I have never thought anyone would kill me before, but I knew Warwick would, and I knew George would let him.'

'But you got away.'

'I ran,' he said. 'It was not a careful retreat, my love, it was not a manoeuvre. It was a rout. I ran in fear of my life, and all the time I knew myself for a coward. I ran and left you.'

'It is not cowardice to get away from an enemy,' I say. 'Anyway, you have come back to face him.'

'I ran and I left you and the girls to face him,' he says. 'I find I don't think well of myself for that. I didn't run to London for you. I didn't get here and make a desperate stand. I ran to the nearest port and I took the first boat.'

'Anyone would have done so. I never blamed you.' I lean up on my elbow and look down into his face. 'You had to get away to get an army together and come back to save us. Everyone knew that. And my brother went with you, and your brother Richard. They judged it the right thing to do as well.'

'I don't know what they felt while they were running like deer, but I know what I felt. I was as scared as a child with a bully coming after him.'

I fall silent. I don't know how to comfort him, or what to say.

He sighs. 'I have been fighting for my kingdom or for my life ever since I was a boy. And in all that time I never thought I might lose. I never thought I would be captured. I never thought I would die. It's odd, isn't it? You will think me foolish. But in all that long time, even when my father was killed and my brother too, I never thought it could happen to me. I never thought it would be my head chopped off and stuck on a spike on the city walls. I thought myself unbeatable, invulnerable.'

I wait.

'And now I know I am not,' he says. 'I have told no one this. I will tell no one but you. But I am not the man you married, Elizabeth. You married a boy who knew no fear. I thought that meant I was brave. But I was not brave – I was just lucky. Until now. Now I am a man and I have felt fear and fled from it.'

I am about to say something to comfort him, a sweet lie; but then I think I will tell him the truth. 'It's a fool who is afraid of nothing,' I say. 'And a brave man is one who knows fear and rides out and faces it. You ran then, but you are back now. Are you going to run away from battle tomorrow?'

'God, no!'

I smile. 'Then you are the man I married. For the man I married was a brave young man, and you are a brave man still. The man I married had not known fear, nor had he a son, nor did he know love. But all these things have come to us and we are changed by them, but not spoiled by them.'

He looks at me gravely. 'You mean this?'

'I do,' I say. 'And I too have been very afraid; but I am not afraid with you here again.'

He draws me even closer. 'I think I will sleep now,' he says, comforted like a little boy, and I hold him tenderly, as if he were my little boy.

I wake in the morning wondering at my joy, at the silky feel of my skin, at the warmth in my belly, at my sense of renewal and life, and then he stirs beside me and I know that I am safe, that he is safe, that we are together once more, and that this is why I have woken with sunshine on my bare skin. Then, in the next moment, I remember that he must go. And though he is now stirring, he is not smiling this morning. That shakes me again. Edward is always so confident, but this morning his face is grim.

'Don't say one word to delay me,' he says, getting out of the bed and throwing on his clothes. 'I cannot bear to go. I cannot stand to leave you again. If you hold me back, I swear I will falter. Smile, and wish me good luck, sweetheart. I need your blessing, I need your courage.'

I swallow my fear. 'You have my blessing,' I say, strained. 'Always you have my blessing. And all the good luck in the world.' I try to sound bright, but my voice quavers. 'Are you going right away?'

'I am going to fetch Henry that they have been calling king,' he says. 'I will take him with me as a hostage. I saw him yesterday at his rooms in the Tower, before I came to you. He knew me. He said that he knew he would be safe with me, his cousin. He was like a child, poor thing. He did not seem to know that he had been king again.'

'There is only one King of England,' I say staunchly. 'And there has only been one King of England since you were crowned.'

'I shall see you in a few days,' he says. 'And I'll go now without saying goodbye to your mother or the girls. It's better like this. Let me go quickly.'

'Won't you even have breakfast?' I don't mean to wail, but I can hardly bear to let him go.

'I'll eat with the men.'

'Of course,' I say brightly. 'And my boys?'

'I'll take them with me. They can serve as messengers. I'll keep them as safe as I can.'

I feel my heart plunge in terror for them too. 'Good,' I say. 'Besides, you will be back within the week, won't you?'

'God willing,' he says.

This is the man who used to swear to me that he was born to die in his bed with me beside him. Never before has he said 'God willing'. Always before it has been his will – not God's.

He pauses in the doorway. 'If I die, then get yourself and the children away to Flanders,' he says. 'There is a poor house at Tournai where a man owes me a favour. He is a bastard cousin or something to your mother's family. He would take you in as his kinswoman. He has a story ready to account for you. I went to see him and we agreed how it should be done in time of need. I have paid him money already, and written his name down for you. It is on the table in your room. Read it and then burn it. You can stay with him and when the hunt is over you can get a house of your own. But hide there for a year or two. When my son is grown he can claim his own, perhaps.'

'Don't speak of it,' I say fiercely. 'You have never lost a battle, you never lose. You will be home within the week, I know it.'

'It's true,' he says. 'I have never lost a battle.' He manages a grim smile. 'But I have never come against Warwick himself before. And I can't muster enough men in time. But I am in the hands of God and with His will, we will win.'

And with that, he is gone.

It is Easter Saturday, it is dusk, and the church bells of London slowly start to peal, one after another. The city is quiet, still sombre from the prayers of Good Friday, apprehensive: a capital city which had two kings and now has no king at all, as

Edward has marched out and taken Henry in his train. If they are both killed what will become of England? What will become of London? What will become of me, and my sleeping children?

Mother and I have spent the day sewing, playing with the children, and tidying our four rooms. We said our prayers for Easter Saturday and we boiled and painted eggs, ready to give as gifts for Easter Day. We heard mass and received Holy Communion. If anyone reports on us to Warwick they will have to say that we were calm; they will say we seemed confident. But now, as the afternoon goes grey, we stand together by the little window over the river that passes so close below us. Mother swings open the casement to listen to the quiet ripples, as if the river might whisper news of Edward's army, and whether the son of York can rise again like a Lenten lily, this spring, as he rose once before.

Warwick has left his stronghold at Coventry for a heavy-footed march to London, certain that he can beat Edward. The Lancastrian lords have flocked to his standard, half of England is with him, and the other half is waiting for Margaret of Anjou to land on the south coast. The witch's wind that trapped her in harbour has died down: we are unprotected.

Edward collects men from the city and then the suburbs of London and then he heads north to meet Warwick. His brothers Richard and George go with him and ride down the line of the foot soldiers, reminding them that York has never lost a battle with their King at the head. Richard is beloved of all the men. They trust him, though he is still only eighteen. George is followed by Lord Shrewsbury and his army of men and there are others who will follow George into battle and don't care which side they are on as they follow their landlord. Altogether, they are an army of about nine thousand men, no more. William Hastings rides at Edward's right hand, faithful as a dog. My brother Anthony brings up the rear, watching the road behind, sceptical as always.

It is getting dark and they are starting to think of making a camp for the evening, when Richard and Thomas Grey, sent out by Edward to go before the army on the great north road to scout the land ahead, come riding back. 'He's here!' says Thomas. 'Your Grace! Warwick is here, in force, and they're drawn up outside Barnet, in battle formation, on a ridge of high ground that runs west–east across the road. We won't be able to get past. He must know we are coming: he is ready for us. He's blocked our way.'

'Hush, lad,' Hastings says heavily. 'No need to tell the whole army. How many?'

'I couldn't see. I don't know. It's getting too dark. More than us.'

Edward and Hastings exchange one hard look. 'Many more?' Hastings asks.

Richard comes up behind his brother. 'Looks like twice our number, sir. Perhaps three times.'

Hastings leans out of the saddle towards him. 'And keep that to yourself too,' he says. He nods the boys away, and turns to Edward. 'Shall we fall back, wait for morning? Perhaps fall back to London? Hold the Tower? Set a siege? Hope for reinforcements from Burgundy?'

Edward shakes his head. 'We'll go on.'

'If the boys are right, and Warwick is on high ground, with double our numbers and waiting for us . . .' Hastings does not need to finish the prediction. Edward's only hope against a greater army was surprise. Edward's battle style is the rapid march and the surprise attack; but Warwick knows this. It was Warwick who taught Edward his generalship. He is thoroughly prepared for him. The master is meeting his pupil and he knows all the tricks.

'We'll go on,' Edward says.

'We won't see where we're going in half an hour,' Hastings says.

'Exactly,' Edward replies. 'And neither will they. Have the men march up in silence, give the order: I want absolute silence. Have them line up, battle-ready, facing the enemy. I want them in position for dawn. We'll attack with first light. Tell them no fires, no lights: silence. Tell them that word is from me. I shall come round and whisper to them. I want not a word.'

George and Richard, Hastings and Anthony nod at this and start to ride up and down the line, ordering the men to march in utter silence and, when the word is given, to set camp at the foot of the ridge, facing the Warwick army. Even as they set off in silence up the road, the day gets darker and the horizon of the ridge and the silhouettes of the standards disappear into the night sky. The moon is not yet risen, the world dissolves into black.

'That's all right,' Edward says, half to himself, half to Anthony. 'We can hardly see them, and they are up against the sky. They won't see us at all, looking downhill into the valley, all they will see is darkness. If we're lucky, and it is misty in the morning, they won't know we are here at all. We will be in the valley, hidden by cloud. They will be where we can see them, like pigeons on a barn roof.'

'You think they will just wait till morning?' Anthony asks him. 'To be picked off like pigeons on a barn roof?'

Edward shakes his head. 'I wouldn't. Warwick won't.'

As if to agree, there is a mighty roar, terribly close, and the flames of Warwick's cannon spit into the darkness, illuminating, in a tongue of yellow fire, the dark waiting army massed above them.

'Dear God, there are twenty thousand of them at least,' Edward swears. 'Tell the men to keep silent, pass the word. No return fire, tell them, I want them as mice. I want them as sleeping mice.'

There is a low laugh as some joker gives a whispered mouse-squeak. Anthony and Edward hear the hushed command go down the line.

The cannons roar again and Richard rides up, his horse black in the darkness, all but invisible. 'Is that you, brother? I can see nothing. The shot is going clear over our heads, praise God. He has no idea where we are. He has the range wrong; he thinks we are half a mile further back.'

'Tell the men to keep silent and he won't know till morning,' Edward says. 'Richard, tell them they must lie low: no lights, no fires, absolute silence.' His brother nods and turns into the darkness again. Edward summons Anthony with a crook of his finger. 'Take Richard and Thomas Grey, and get a good mile away, light two or three small fires, spaced out, like we were setting up camp where the shot is falling. Then get clear of them. Give them something to aim at. The fires can die down at once: don't go back to them and get yourself hit. Just keep them thinking we are distant.'

Anthony nods and goes.

Edward slides from his horse Fury, and the pageboy steps forward and takes the rein. 'See he is fed, and take the saddle off him, and drop the bit from his mouth but leave the bridle on,' Edward orders. 'Keep the saddle at your side. I don't know how long a night we will have. And then you can rest, boy, but not for long. I shall need him ready a good hour before dawn, maybe more.'

'Yes, Sire,' the lad says. 'They're passing out feed and water for the horses.'

'Tell them to do it in silence,' the king repeats. 'Tell them I said so.'

The lad nods, and takes the horse a little way from where the lords are standing.

'Post a watch,' Edward says to Hastings. The cannons roar out again making them jump at the noise. They can hear the whistle of the balls overhead and then the thud as they fall too far south, well behind the line of the hidden army. Edward chuckles. 'We won't sleep much, but they won't sleep at all,' he says. 'Wake me after midnight, about two.'

He swings his cloak from his shoulders and spreads it on the ground. He pulls his hat from his head and puts it over his face. In moments, despite the regular bellow of the cannon and the thud of the shot, he is asleep. Hastings takes his own cloak and drapes it, as tenderly as a mother, over the sleeping king. He turns to George, Richard and Anthony, 'Two-hour watches each?' he asks. 'I'll take this one, then I'll wake you, Richard, and you and George can check the men, and send out scouts, then you, Anthony.' The three men nod.

Anthony wraps his cloak around him and lies down near to the king. 'George and Richard together?' he asks softly of Hastings.

'I would trust George as far as I would throw a cat,' Hastings says quietly. 'But I would trust young Richard with my life. He will keep his brother on our side until battle is joined. And won, God willing.'

'Bad odds,' says Anthony thoughtfully.

'I've never known worse,' Hastings says cheerfully. 'But we have right on our side, and Edward is a lucky commander, and the three sons of York are together again. We might survive, please God.'

'Amen to that.' Anthony crosses himself, and goes to sleep.

'Besides,' Hastings says quietly to himself, 'there's nothing else we can do.'

I do not sleep in the sanctuary at Westminster, and my mother keeps a vigil with me. A few hours before dawn, when it is at its very darkest and the moon is going down, my mother swings open the casement window and we stand side by side as the great dark river goes by. Gently I breathe out into the night and in the cold air my breath makes a cloud, like a mist. My mother beside me sighs and her breath gathers with mine and swirls away. I breathe out again and again, and now the mist is gathering on the river, grey against the dark water, a shadow on blackness. My mother sighs and the mist is rolling out down the river, obscuring the other bank, holding the darkness of the night. The starlight is hidden by it, as the mist thickens into fog and starts to spread coldly along the river, through the streets of London, and away, north and west, rolling up the river valleys, holding the darkness into the low ground, so that even though the sky slowly lightens, the land is still shrouded, and Warwick's men, on the high ridge outside Barnet, waking in the cold hour before dawn, looking down the slope for their enemy, can see nothing below them but a strange inland sea of cloud that lies in heavy bands along the valley, can see nothing of the army that is enveloped and silent in the obscuring darkness beneath them.

'Take Fury,' Edward says to the page quietly. 'I fight on foot. Get me my battleaxe and sword.' The other lords, Anthony, George, Richard and William Hastings, are already armed for the slugging terror of the day, their horses taken out of range, saddled and bridled, prepared – though no one says it – for flight if everything should go wrong, or for a charge if things go well.

'Are we ready now?' Edward asks Hastings.

'As ready as ever,' William says.

Edward glances up at the ridge, and suddenly says, 'Christ save us. We're wrong.'

'What?'

The mist is broken for just a small gap and it shows the king that he is not drawn up opposite Warwick's men, troop facing troop, but too far to the left. The whole of Warwick's right wing has nothing against them. It is as if Edward's army is too short by a third. Edward's army overlaps slightly to the left. His men there will have no enemy: they will plunge forward against no resistance and break the order of the line, but on his right he is far too short.

'It's too late to regroup,' he decides. 'Christ help us that we are starting wrong. Sound the trumpets, our time is now.'

The standards lift up, the pennants limp in the damp air, rising out of the mist like a sudden leafless forest. The trumpets bellow, thick and muffled in the darkness. It is still not dawn and the mist makes everything strange and confusing. 'Charge,' says Edward, though his army can hardly see his enemy, and there is a moment of silence when he senses the men are as he is, weighted down with the thick air, chilled to their bones with the mist, sick with fear. 'Charge!' Edward bellows and ploughs his way uphill, as with a roar his men follow him to Warwick's army, who, starting up out of sleep, eyes straining, can hear them coming, and see glimpses now and then, but can be certain of nothing until, as if they have burst through a wall, the army of York with the king, toweringly tall, at their head, whirling a battleaxe, comes at them like a horror of giants out of the darkness.

In the centre of the field the king presses forward and the Lancastrians fall back before him, but on the wing, that fatal empty right side, the Lancastrians can push down, bear down, outnumbering the fighting York army, hundreds of them against the few men on the right. In the darkness and in the mist the outnumbered York men start to fall, as the left wing of Warwick's army pushes down the hill, and stabbing, clubbing, kicking and beheading, forces their way closer and closer to the heart of the Yorkists. A man turns and runs, but gets no further than a couple of paces before his head is burst open by a great swing from a mace, but that first movement of flight creates another. Another York soldier, seeing more and more men pouring down the hill towards them and with no comrade at his side, turns and takes a couple of steps into the safety and shelter of the mist and the darkness. Another follows him, then another. One goes down with a sword thrust through his back, and his comrade looks behind, his white face suddenly pale in the darkness, and then he throws down his weapon and starts to run. All along the line men hesitate, glance behind them at the tempting safety of the darkness, look ahead and hear the great roar of their enemy, who can sense victory, who can hardly see their hands before their faces but who can smell blood and smell fear. The unopposed Lancastrian left wing races down the hill and the York right flank dare not stand. They drop their weapons and go like deer, running as a herd, scattering in terror.

The Earl of Oxford's men, fighting for Lancaster, are on their trail at once, baying like hunting dogs, following the smell since they are still blind in the mist, with the earl cheering them on until the battlefield is behind them and the noise of the battle muffled in the fog, and the fleeing Yorkists lost, and the earl realises that his men are running on their own account, heading for Barnet and the ale shops, already settling to a jog, wiping their swords and boasting of victory. He has to gallop around them to overtake them, block the road with his horse. He has to whip them, he has to have his captains swear at them and chivvy them. He has to lean down from his saddle and run one of his own men through the heart, and curse the others before he can bring them to a standstill.

'The battle isn't done, you whoresons!' he yells at them. 'York is still alive, so is his brother Richard, so is his brother the turncoat George! We all swore the battle would end with their deaths. Come on! Come on! You have tasted blood, you have seen them run. Come and finish them, come and finish the rest. Think of the plunder on them! They are half beaten, they are lost. Let's make the rest run, let's make them skip. Come on, lads, come on, let's go, let's see them run like hares!'

Driven into order and persuaded into ranks, the men turn and the earl dashes them at a half-run back from Barnet towards the battle, his flag before him with its emblem of the Streaming Sun proudly raised. He is blinded by the mist, and desperate to rejoin Warwick, who has promised wealth to every man at his side today. But what de Vere of Oxford does not know, as he leads his troop of nine hundred men, is that the battle lines have swung round. The breaking of the York right wing and their pressing forward of their left has pushed the battlefield off the ridge and the line of battle now runs up and down the London road.

Edward is at the heart of it still; but he can feel he is losing ground, dropping back off the road as Warwick's men push them harder and harder. He starts to feel the sense of defeat, and this is new to him: it tastes like fear. He can see nothing in the mist and the darkness but the attackers who come, one after the other, out of the mist before him, and he responds with the instincts of a blind man to the rush of the men who come, and then come again, and again, with a sword or an axe or sometimes a scythe.

He thinks of his wife and his baby son, waiting for him and depending on his victory. He has no time to think what will happen to them if he fails. He can feel his own soldiers around him, giving way, as if they are being thrust back by the sheer weight of Warwick's extra men. He can feel himself wearying at the unstoppable approach of his enemies, the constant demand that he should swing, thrust, spear, kill: or be killed. In the rhythm of his endurance he has a glimpse, almost a vision it is so bright, of his brother Richard: swinging, spearing, going on and on, and yet feeling his sword arm grow tired and fail. He has a picture in his mind of Richard alone on a battlefield, without him, turning to face a charge without a friend at his side, and it makes him angry and he bellows, 'York! God and York!'

De Vere of Oxford, bringing his troops in at a run, gives the order to charge, seeing the battle line before him, expecting to take his men into the rear of the York lines, knowing he will wreak havoc, coming out of the mist at them, as good as fresh Lancaster reinforcements, as terrifying as an ambush. In the darkness they rush, swords and weapons drawn and already bloody, into the rear – not of the York soldiers – but of his own army, the Lancaster line, who have turned in the battle and are off the hill.

'Traitor! Treason!' screams a man, stabbed from behind who looks round and sees de Vere. A Lancastrian officer looks over his shoulder and sees the most dreaded sight on the battlefield: fresh soldiers, coming up from the rear. In the mist he cannot see the flag clearly but he sees, he is sure he sees, the Sun in Splendour, the York standard, fluttering proudly over fresh troops who are running up the road from Barnet, their swords out before them, battleaxes swinging, their mouths gaping as they bellow in their powerful charge. The banner of the Streaming Sun of Oxford, he mistakes for the emblem of York. He and his men have soldiers of York before them, pressing them hard, fighting like men with nothing to lose, but more and more of them coming out of the mist, from behind, like an army of spectres, is more than any man can stand.

'Turn! Turn!' Somebody bellows in a panic, and another voice shouts, 'Regroup! Regroup! Fall back!' And the orders are right, but the voices are filled with panic and the men turn from the York enemy before them to find another army behind them. They cannot recognise their allies. They think themselves surrounded and outnumbered and certain of death, and the heart goes out of them in a rush.

'De Vere!' shouts the Earl of Oxford, seeing his men attacking his own side. 'De Vere! For Lancaster! Hold! Hold! In the name of God, hold!' But it is too late. Those who now recognise the Oxford standard with the Streaming Sun, and see de Vere laying about him in the middle of the confusion, and shouting to bring his men to order, think that he has turned his coat in mid-battle – as men do – and those who are close enough, his old friends, turn on him like furious dogs to kill him as a thing worse than the enemy: a traitor on the battlefield. But in the mist and the chaos most of the Lancaster forces know only that an untold enemy is before them, pressing forward with soldiers of clouds, and now a fresh battalion has come from behind, and the darkness and fog on the road could hide more on every side. Who knows how many soldiers will rise out of the river? Who knows what horror, that Edward, married to a witch, might conjure from rivers and springs and streams? They can hear the sounds of battle and the screams of the wounded but they cannot see their lords, they cannot recognise their commanders. The battlefield is shifting; they cannot even be sure of their comrades in the eerie half-light. Hundreds throw down their weapons and start to run. Everyone knows that this is a war in which no prisoners will be taken. It is death to be on the losing side.

Edward, stabbing and slicing, in the very heart of the battle, William Hastings on his shield arm, his sword out, his knife in his other hand, bellows, 'Victory to York! Victory to York!' and his soldiers believe that mighty shout, and so does the Lancaster army, attacked from the front in darkness, attacked from the rear in mist, and now leaderless, as Warwick shouts for his page to save him, flings himself on his waiting horse, and gallops away.

It is a signal for the battle to break into a thousand adventures. 'My horse!' Edward yells for his page. 'Get me Fury!' And William cups his hands and throws the king upwards into the saddle, seizes his own bridle and scrambles on to his own charger, races after his lord and master and dearest friend, and the York lords go at a headlong gallop after Warwick, cursing him for getting away.

My mother straightens up with a sigh, and together the two of us close the window. We are both pale from watching all night. 'It is over,' she says with certainty. 'Your enemy is dead. Your first and most dangerous enemy. Warwick will make no more kings. He will have to meet the King of Heaven and explain what he thinks he has been doing to this poor kingdom here below.'

'My boys are safe, I think?'

'I am sure of it.'

My hands are curled into claws like a cat. 'And George, Duke of Clarence?' I ask. 'What do you think for him? Tell me he is dead on the battlefield!'

My mother smiles. 'He is on the winning side as usual,' she says. 'Your Edward has won this battle and loyal George is at his side. You may find that you have to forgive George for the death of your father and brother. I may have to leave my vengeance to God. George may survive. He is the king's own brother, after all.

Would you kill a royal prince? Could you bring yourself to kill a prince of the House of York?'

I open my jewellery box and take out the black enamelled locket. I press the little catch and open it. There are the two names, George, Duke of Clarence, Richard Neville, Earl of Warwick, written on the scrap of paper torn from my father's last letter. The letter that he wrote in hope to my mother, speaking of his ransom, never dreaming that those two, that he had known all his life, would kill him for no better reason than spite. I tear it in half and the piece that says Richard Neville, Earl of Warwick I scrunch in my hand. I do not even trouble to throw it into the fire. I let it fall on the floor and I tread it into the rushes. It can be dust. The name of George I put back in my locket and into my jewellery case. 'George will not survive,' I say flatly. 'If I myself have to hold a pillow over his face when he is sleeping in bed under my roof, a guest in my own house, under my protection, my husband's beloved kin. George will not survive. A son of the House of York is not inviolate. I will see him dead. He can be sweetly sleeping in his bed in the Tower of London itself and I will still see him dead.'

Two days I have with Edward when he comes home from the battle, two days when we move back to the royal apartments at the Tower hastily cleaned and poor Henry's things tossed to one side. Henry, the poor mad king, is returned to his old chambers with the bars on the windows, and kneels in prayer. Edward eats as if he has starved for weeks, wallows like Melusina in a deep long bath, takes me without grace, without tenderness, takes me as a soldier takes his doxy, and sleeps. He wakes only to announce to the London citizens that stories of Warwick's survival are untrue: he saw the man's body himself. He was killed while he was escaping from the battle, fleeing like a coward, and Edward orders that this body be shown in St Paul's Cathedral so that there can be no doubt that the man is dead. 'But I'll have no dishonouring of him,' he says.

'They put our father's head on a spike on York gate,' George reminds him. 'With a paper crown on his head. We should put Warwick's head on a spike on London Bridge, and quarter his dead body and send it round the kingdom.'

'That's a pretty plan you propose for your father-in-law,' I observe. 'Will it not disturb your wife a little, as you dismember her father? Besides, I thought you had sworn to love and follow him?'

'Warwick can be buried with honour by his family at Bisham Abbey,' Edward rules. 'We are not savages. We don't make war on dead bodies.'

Two days and two nights we have together, but Edward watches for a messenger, and keeps his troop armed and ready, and then the messenger comes. Margaret of Anjou has landed at Weymouth, too late to support her ally but ready to fight her cause alone. At once we get reports of the rise of England. Lords and squires who would not turn out their men for Warwick feel it is their duty to support the queen when she comes armed for battle, and her husband Henry is held by us, her enemy. People start to say that this is the last battle, the one that will count: one last battle, which will mean everything. Warwick is dead, there are no intermediaries. It is the queen of Lancaster against King Edward, the royal House of Lancaster against the royal House of York, and every man in every village in the kingdom has to make a choice; and many choose her.

Edward commands his lords in every county to come to him fully armed with their proper number of men, demands that every town send him troops and money to pay them, exempts no one. 'I have to go again,' he says at dawn. 'Keep my son safe, whatever happens.'

'Keep yourself safe,' I reply. 'Whatever happens.'

He nods, he takes my hand and puts my palm to his mouth, folds my fingers over the kiss. 'You know that I love you,' he says.

'You know I love you as much today as I did when you stood under the oak tree?'

I nod. I cannot speak. He sounds like a man saying farewell.

'Good,' he says briskly. 'Remember if it goes wrong you are to take the children to Flanders? Remember the name of the little boatman at Tournai where you are to go and hide?'

'I remember,' I whisper. 'But it won't go wrong.'

'God willing,' he says, and with those last words he turns on his heel and goes out to face another battle.

The two armies race, the one against the other, Margaret's army heading for Wales to gather reinforcements, Edward in pursuit, trying to cut her off. Margaret's force, commanded by the Earl of Somerset, with her son, the vicious young prince, commanding his own troop, charges through the countryside going west to Wales, where Jasper Tudor will raise the Welsh for them and where the Cornishmen will meet them. Once they get into the mountains of Wales they will be unbeatable. Jasper Tudor and his nephew Henry Tudor can give them safe haven and ready armies. Nobody will be able to get them out of the fortresses of Wales, and they can amass forces at their leisure and march on England in strength.

With Margaret travels little Anne Neville, Warwick's youngest daughter, the Prince's bride, reeling at the news of the death of her father, the betrayal of her brother-in-law George, Duke of Clarence, and abandoned by her mother, who has taken to a nunnery in her grief at the loss of her husband. They must be a desperate trio, everything staked on victory, and so much lost already.

Edward, chasing out from London, gathering troops as he goes, is desperate to catch them before they cross the great River Severn and disappear into the mountains of Wales. Almost certainly, it cannot be done. It is too far to go and too fast to march, and his troops, weary from the battle at Barnet, will never get there in time.

But Margaret's first crossing point at Gloucester is barred to her. Edward's command is that they should not be allowed across the river to Wales, and the fort of Gloucester holds for Edward and bars the ford. The river, one of the deepest and most powerful in England, is up, and flowing fast. I smile at the thought of the waters of England turning against the French queen.

Instead, Margaret's army has to drive itself north and go on upriver to find another place where the army can get across; and now Edward's army is only twenty miles behind them, trotting like hunting dogs, whipped on by Edward and his brother Richard. That night, the Lancastrians pitch their camp in an old ruined castle just outside Tewkesbury, sheltered from the weather by the tumbling walls, certain of crossing the river by the ford in the morning. They wait, with some confidence, for the exhausted army of York, marching straight from one battle to this next, and now run ragged by a forced march of thirty-six miles in the one day, across the breadth of the country. Edward may catch his enemy, but he may have drained the spirit of his own soldiers in the dash to the battle. He will get there; but with broken-winded soldiers, fit for nothing.

# 3 MAY 1471

Queen Margaret and her hapless daughter-in-law, Anne Neville, commandeer a nearby house called Payne's Place, and wait for the battle which they believe will make them queen and Princess of Wales. Anne Neville spends the night on her knees, praying for the soul of her father, whose body is exposed, for every citizen to see, on the steps before the altar at St Paul's in London. She prays for the grief of her mother, who landing in England, learned before her feet had dried that her husband was defeated, killed fleeing from a battle, and that she was a widow. The widowed duchess, Anne of Warwick, refused to go a step further with the Lancaster army and shut herself up in Beaulieu Abbey, abandoning both her daughters to their opposed husbands: one married to the Lancaster prince and the other to the York duke. Little Anne prays for the fate of her sister Isabel, tied for life to the turncoat George, and now a York countess once more, whose husband will fight on the other side of the battle tomorrow. She prays as she always does that God will send the light of His reason to her young husband Prince Edward of Lancaster, who grows more perverse and vicious every day, and she prays for herself, that she may survive this battle and somehow come home again. She no longer knows quite what her home might be.

Edward's army is commanded by the men he loves: the

brothers he would gladly die beside, if it is God's will that they should die that day. His fears ride with him; he knows what defeat is like now, and he will never forget it again. But he knows also that there is no avoiding this battle: he has to chase it with the fastest forced march that England has ever seen. He might well be afraid; but if he wants to be king he will have to fight, and fight better than he has ever done before. His brother Richard, Duke of Gloucester orders the troop at the front of them all, leads with his fierce bright loyal courage. Edward takes the battle in the centre, and William Hastings, who would lay down his life to block an ambush from reaching the king, defends at the rear. For Anthony Woodville, Edward has a special need.

'Anthony, I want you and George to take a small company of spearmen, and hide in the trees to our left,' Edward says quietly. 'You'll do two tasks there. One, you'll watch that Somerset sends no troops out from the castle ruins to surprise us on our left, and you will watch the battle and make a charge when you think we need it.'

'You trust me this much?' Anthony asks, thinking of days when the two young men were enemies and not brothers.

'I do,' Edward says. 'But, Anthony – you know you are a wise man, a philosopher, and death and life are alike to you?'

Anthony grimaces. 'I have only a little learning, but I am very attached to my life, Sire. I have not yet risen to detachment.'

'Me too,' Edward says fervently. 'And I am much attached to my cock, brother. Make sure your sister can put another prince in the cradle,' he says baldly. 'Save my balls for her, Anthony!'

Anthony laughs and throws a mock salute. 'Will you signal in time of need?'

'You will see my need clearly enough. My signal will be when I look like I am losing,' he says flatly. 'Don't leave it till then is all I ask.'

'I'll do my best, Sire,' Anthony agrees equably, and turns to march his company of two hundred spearmen into hiding.

Edward waits only till he can see they are in position, and

invisible to the Lancaster force behind the castle walls on the hill, and then he gives an order to his cannon. 'Fire!' At the same time Richard's troop of archers let loose a rain of arrows. The shot of the cannon hits the crumbling masonry of the old castle and blocks of stone tumble down with the cannonballs on the heads of the men sheltering below. There is a scream as one man gets an arrow agonisingly in his face, and then a dozen more yells as the accurate arrows hail down on them. The castle proves to be more ruin than fortress. There is no shelter behind the walls and the collapsing arches and falling stone are more of a danger than a refuge. The men scatter out, some of them charging downhill before they are given the command to advance, some of them turning towards Tewkesbury in retreat. Somerset bellows for the army to group and charge down the hill to the king's troop below them; but already his men are on the run.

Yelling in rage, and helped by the fall of the ground, running faster and faster, the Lancaster troops hurl themselves down and aim at the heart of the York forces, where the tall king, his crown on his helmet, is ready for them. Edward is lit by a bright merciless joy that he has come to know from a boyhood of battles. As soon as the Lancaster men plough towards him through the first rank, he greets them with his broadsword in one hand and an axe in the other. His long hours of training at the joust, on foot in the arena, come into play, and his movements are as swift and as natural as those of a baited lion: a thrust, a snarl, a turn, a stab. The men keep coming at him and he never hesitates. He stabs to unguarded throats, up and under the helmet. He slices cleverly at a man's sword arm from the unprotected armpit upwards. He kicks a man in the groin and, as the victim doubles up, he brings down the axe on his head, shattering his skull.

As soon as the shock of the impact throws the York troops back, the flank commanded by Richard comes in at the side and starts to hack and stab, a merciless butchery with the young duke at the very heart of the battle, small, vicious, a killer in the field, an apprentice of terror. The determined push of Richard's men breaks the onward charge of the Lancastrians and they check. As always in the hand-to-hand fighting there is a lull as even the strongest men catch their breath; but in this pause the Yorks push forward, headed by the king with Richard at his side, and start to press the Lancastrians back up the hill to their refuge.

There is a yell, a cold terrifying yell of determined men from the wood to the left of the battle, where no one knew that soldiers were hiding. And two hundred, though it looks like two thousand, spearmen, deadly armed but lightly footed, come running rapidly towards the Lancastrians, the greatest knight in England, Anthony Woodville, far ahead in the lead. Their spears are stretched out before them, hungry for a strike, and the Lancastrian soldiers look up from their slugging battle and see them let fly, like a man might see a storm of lightning bolts: death coming too fast to avoid.

They run, they can bear to do nothing else. The spears come at them like two hundred blades on a single lethal weapon. They can hear the howl of them through the air before the screams as they reach their targets. The soldiers thrash themselves to run back up the hill and Richard's men follow them and cut them down without a moment's mercy, Anthony's men closing on them fast, pulling out swords and knives. The Lancaster soldiers run towards the river and wade across, or swim across or, weighed down by their armour, drown in a frenzy of struggling in the reeds. They run towards the park, and Hastings' men close up and hack at them as if they were hares at the end of a harvest when the reapers form a circle around the last stand of wheat and scythe down the frightened beasts. They turn to run towards the town and Edward's own troop with Edward at their head chases them like exhausted deer, and catches them for butchery. The boy they call Prince Edward, Edward of Lancaster, Prince of Wales, is among them, just outside the city walls, and they cut them all down in the charge, with flashing swords and bloodied blades among screams for mercy, without pity.

'Spare me! Spare me! I am Edward of Lancaster, I am born to be king, my mother—' The rest of it is lost in a gurgle of royal blood, as a foot soldier, a common man, puts his knife into the young prince's throat and so ends the hopes of Margaret of Anjou and the life of her son and the Lancaster line, for the profit of a handsome belt and engraved sword.

It is no sport for the king; it is a deathly ugly business, and Edward rests on his sword, and cleans his dagger, and watches his men slit throats, cut guts, smash skulls, and break legs until the Lancaster army is crying on the ground, or has run far away, and the battle, this battle at least, is won.

But there is always an aftermath and it is always messy. Edward's joy in the battle does not extend to killing prisoners or torturing captives. He does not even relish a judicial beheading, unlike most of the other warlords of his time. But Lancaster lords have claimed sanctuary in the Abbey of Tewkesbury and cannot be allowed to stay there or given safe conduct home. 'Get them out,' Edward says curtly to Richard his brother, the two united in a desire to finish it. He turns to the Grey boys, his step-sons. 'You go and find the living Lancaster lords from the battlefield and take their weapons off them and put them under arrest.'

'They claim sanctuary,' Hastings points out. 'They are in the abbey, hanging on to the high altar. Your own wife survives only because sanctuary was honoured. Your only son was born safe in sanctuary.'

'A woman. A baby,' Edward says curtly. 'Sanctuary is for the helpless. Duke Edmund of Somerset is not helpless. He is a death-dealing traitor and Richard here will pull him out of the abbey and on to the scaffold in Tewkesbury marketplace. Won't you, Richard?'

'Yes,' Richard says shortly. 'I have a greater respect for victory than for any sanctuary,' and he puts his hand on his sword hilt and goes to break down the door of the abbey, though the Abbot clings to his sword arm and begs him to fear the will of God and show mercy. The army of York does not listen. It is beyond forgiveness. Richard's men drag out screaming supplicants, and Richard and Edward watch their men knife prisoners who are begging to be ransomed in the churchyard, where they cling to gravestones, begging the dead to save them, till the abbey steps are slippery with blood and the sacred ground smells like a butcher's shop, as if nothing were sacred. For nothing is sacred in England any more.

## 14 MAY 1471

We are waiting for news in the Tower when the sound of cheering tells me that my husband is coming home. I run down the stone stairs, my heels clacking, the girls behind me, but when the gate opens and the horses rattle in it is not my husband but my brother Anthony at the head of the troop, smiling at me.

'Sister, give you joy, your husband is well and has won a great battle. Mother, give me your blessing, I have need of it.'

He jumps from his horse and bows to me, and then turns to our mother and doffs his cap and kneels to her as she puts her hand on his head. There is a moment of quietness as she touches him. This is a real blessing, not the empty gesture that most families make. Her heart goes out to him, her most talented child, and he bows his fair head to her. Then he gets up and turns to me.

'I'll tell you all about it later but be sure he won a great victory. Margaret of Anjou is in our keeping, our prisoner. Her son is dead: she has no heir. The hopes of Lancaster are down in blood and mud. Edward would be with you but he has marched north where there are more uprisings for Neville and Lancaster. Your sons are with him and are well and in good heart. Me, he sent here to guard you and London. The men of Kent are up against us, and Thomas Neville is supporting them. Half of them are good men, ill led, but the other half are nothing but thieves looking for plunder. The smallest and most dangerous part are those who think they can free King Henry and capture you, and they are sworn to do so. Neville is on his way to London with a small fleet of ships. I'm to see the mayor and the city fathers and organise the defence.'

'We are to be attacked here?'

He nods. 'They are defeated, their heir is dead, but still they take the war onwards. They will be choosing another heir for Lancaster: Henry Tudor. They will be swearing for revenge. Edward has sent me to your defence. At the worst I am to organise your retreat.'

'Are we in real danger?'

He nods. 'I am sorry, sister. They have ships and the support of France, and Edward has taken the whole army north.' He bows to me and he turns, and marches into the Tower bellowing to the constable that the mayor shall be admitted at once and that he wants a report on the Tower's preparedness for siege.

The men come in and confirm that Thomas Neville has ships in the sea off Kent, and he has sworn he will support a march by the men of Kent by sailing up the Thames and taking London. We have just won a dramatic battle, and killed a boy, the heir to the claim, and should be safe; but we are still endangered. 'Why would he do it? I demand. 'It is over. Edward of Lancaster is dead, his cousin Warwick is dead, Margaret of Anjou is captive, Henry is our prisoner held here in this very Tower? Why would a Neville have ships off Gravesend and hope to take London?'

'Because it is not over,' my mother observes. We are walking on the leads of the Tower, Baby in my arms to take the air, the girls walking with us. Mother and I, looking down can see Anthony supervising the rolling out of cannon to face downriver, and ordering sacks of river sand to stack behind the doors and windows of the White Tower. Looking downriver we can see the men working in the docks piling sandbags and putting water buckets at the ready, fearful of fire in the warehouses when Neville brings his ships upriver.

'If Neville takes the Tower, and Edward were to be defeated in the north, then it all starts again,' my mother points out. 'Neville can release King Henry. Margaret can reunite with her husband, perhaps they can make another son. The only way to end their line for sure, the only way to end these wars for ever, is death. The death of Henry. We have scotched the heir, now we have to kill the father.'

'But Henry has other heirs,' I say. 'Even though he has lost his son. Margaret Beaufort, for one. The House of Beaufort goes on with her son, Henry Tudor.'

My mother shrugs. 'A woman,' she says. 'Nobody is going to ride out to put a queen on this throne. Who could hold England but a soldier?'

'She has a son, the Tudor boy.'

My mother shrugs. 'Nobody is going to ride out for a stripling. Henry Tudor doesn't matter. Henry Tudor could never be King of England. Nobody would fight for a Tudor against a Plantagenet king. The Tudors are only half royal and that from the French royal family. He is no threat to you.' She glances down the white wall to the barred window, where the forgotten King Henry has been returned to his prayers again. 'No, once he is dead, the Lancaster line is over and we are all safe.'

'But who could bring themselves to kill him? He is a helpless man, a half-wit. Who could have such a hard heart as to kill him when he is our prisoner?' I lower my voice – his rooms are just below us. 'He spends his days on his knees before a prie-dieu and gazing without speaking out of the window. To kill him would be like massacring a fool. And there are those who say he is a holy fool. There are those who say he is a saint. Who would dare murder a saint?'

'I hope your husband will do it,' my mother says bluntly. 'For the only way to make the English throne safe is to hold a pillow on his face and help him to lasting sleep.'

A shadow goes across the sun and I hold my baby Edward to me, as if to prevent him hearing such bitter counsel. I shudder as if it is my own death that my mother is foreseeing.

'What's the matter?' she asks me. 'Are you chilled? Shall we go in?'

'It's the Tower,' I say irritably. 'I have always hated the Tower. And you: saying such vile things, as to murder a prisoner in the Tower, who has no defence! You shouldn't even speak of such things, especially not before Baby. I wish this was over and we could go back to Whitehall Palace.'

From far below my brother Anthony looks up and waves to me to signal that the cannon are in place and we are ready.

'Soon we will be able to go,' my mother says comfortingly. 'And Edward will come home, and you will be safe again with Baby.'

But that night the alarm sounds and we all jump from our beds and I snatch up Baby and the girls come running to me, and Anthony throws open my bedchamber door and says, 'Be brave, they are coming upriver and there will be firing. Keep away from the windows.'

I slam and bar the shutters on the windows, draw the curtains around the big bed, and jump inside with the girls and Baby and listen. We can hear the crump of the cannons firing and the whistle of cannonballs in the air, and then we hear the thud as they hit the walls of the Tower, and Elizabeth, my oldest daughter, looks at me white-faced, her little lower lip trembling, and whispers, 'Is it the Bad Queen?'

'Your father has beaten the Bad Queen and she is our prisoner as the old king is too,' I say, thinking of Henry in the rooms below us and wondering if anyone will have thought to close his shutters or keep him away from the windows. It would serve Neville right and save us all a great deal of trouble if he were to kill his own king with a cannon shot tonight.

There is a roar from our cannons on their mountings before the Tower and the windows light up briefly with the blaze of the firing. Elizabeth shrinks back against me. 'That is our cannon, shooting the bad men's ships,' I say cheerfully. 'It is a cousin of Warwick, Thomas Neville, who is too stupid to know that the war is over and that we have won.'

'What does he want?' Elizabeth asks.

'He wants to start it all again,' I say bitterly. 'But your uncle Anthony is ready for him, and he has the London-trained bands ready on the walls of London, and all the apprentice boys – they like a fight – are ready to defend the City. And then your father will come home.'

She looks at me with her huge grey eyes. She always thinks more than she says, my little Elizabeth. She has been at war since she was a baby, she knows even now that she is a piece on the chessboard of England. She knows that she is to be traded, she knows that she has a value, she knows that she has been in danger all her life. 'And will it end then?' she asks me.

'Yes,' I promise her doubtful little face. 'It will end then.'

Three days we are under siege, three days of shelling and then the assaults from the men of Kent and the Neville ships with Anthony and our kinsman, Henry Bourchier, the Earl of Essex, organising the defence. Each day more of my family and kin stream into the Tower, my sisters and their husbands, Anthony's wife, my former ladies-in-waiting, all thinking it the safest place in a city under siege, until Anthony decrees we have enough officers and enough men for a counter-attack.

'How far away is Edward?' I ask nervously.

'Last I heard, he was four days away,' he says. 'Too far. We don't dare wait for him to come. And I think we can beat them with the forces I have.'

'What if you lose?' I ask nervously.

He laughs. 'Then, sister queen, you must be queen militant and command the defence of the Tower yourself. You can hold out for days. What we have to do is drive them back now, before they start to come any closer. If they tighten the siege on the Tower or increase the cannon fire, or if, God forbid, they get in somehow, you could die before Edward gets home.'

I nod. 'Go on then,' I say grimly. 'Attack them.'

He bows. 'Spoken like a true Yorkist,' he says. 'All the York family are a bloodthirsty lot, born and raised on the battlefield. Let us hope that when we finally have peace they don't kill each other out of sheer habit.'

'Let's get peace first before we worry about the York brothers spoiling it,' I say.

At dawn Anthony is ready. The London-trained bands are well armed and well drilled. This is a city that has been at war for sixteen years, and every apprentice has a weapon and knows how to use it. The men of Kent, under the command of the Neville forces, are encamped all around the Tower and the City walls but they are sleeping when the postern gate to the Tower opens and Anthony and his men quietly file out. I hold the gate for them, Henry Bourchier is the last to go. 'Your Grace, my cousin, bolt it behind us and get you into safety,' he says to me.

'No, I'll wait here,' I say. 'If it goes wrong for you, I shall be here to let my brother in and you all with him.'

He smiles at that. 'Well, I hope we will come back with a victory,' he says.

'God speed,' I reply.

I should close and bolt the gate behind them but I do not. I stand in the gateway to watch. I think of myself as a heroine in a story, the beautiful queen who sends out her knights to battle and then watches over them like an angel.

At first, it looks like that. My brother, bareheaded, in his beautifully engraved breastplate, goes quietly towards the camp, his broadsword in his hand, followed by his men, our loyal friends and those of our affinity. In the moonlight they look like cavaliers on a quest, the river gleaming behind them, the night sky dark above them. The rebels are camped in the field by the river; more of them are quartered in the narrow dirty streets around. They are poor men; there are a few with tents and shelters but most are sleeping on the ground beside campfires. The streets outside the city walls are full of alehouses and whorehouses and half the men are drunk. Anthony's force forms into three, and then at the whispered word everything changes. They put their helmets on their heads, they drop their visors over their kindly eyes, they draw their swords, they release the heavy ball of their maces, they turn from mortals into men of metal.

I somehow sense the change that comes over them as I stand at the gate watching, and even though I have sent them out to battle and it is me they are defending, I have a feeling that something bad and bloody is about to happen. 'No,' I whisper, as if I would stop them as they start to run forward, their swords drawn, their axes swinging.

Sleeping men stumble up with a cry of fright and get a blade in the heart or an axe through the head. There is no warning: they come out of dreams of victory, or dreams of home, into a cold blade and an agonising death. The dozing sentries jump awake and scream the alarm, silenced by a dagger through the throat. They flail about. One man falls into the flames of the fire and screams in agony, but nobody stops to help him. Our men kick the campfire embers and some of the tents and the blankets catch fire and the horses rear up and neigh in fear as their fodder blazes up before them. At once the whole camp is awake and running in panic as Anthony's men go through them like silent killers, stabbing men on the ground as they roll over and try to wake, pushing men down as they rise up, slitting an unarmed man's belly, clubbing a man as he reaches for his sword. The army from Kent rolls out of sleep and starts to run. Those that are not brought down grab what they can and dash away. They rouse the men in the streets beside the Tower and some come running towards the field and Anthony's men turn on them with a roar and charge at them, their swords already red with blood, and the rebels, country boys most of them, turn and run.

Anthony's men give chase but he calls them back: he won't leave the Tower undefended. A group he sends down to the quayside to capture the Neville ships; the rest head back to the Tower, their voices loud and excited in the coldness of the morning. They shout at each other of a man stabbed in his sleep, of a woman rolling over to be beheaded, of a horse breaking its own neck, rearing from the fire.

I open the sally-port gate for them. I don't want to greet them, I don't want to see any more, I don't want to hear any more. I go up to my rooms, gather my mother, my girls and Baby, and bolt our bedroom door in silence, as if I fear my own army. I have heard men tell of many battles in this cousins' war and they always spoke of heroism, of the courage of men, and of the power of their comradeship, of the fierce anger of battle and of the brotherhood of survival. I have heard ballads about great battles, and poems about the beauty of a charge and the grace of the leader. But I did not know that war was nothing more than butchery, as savage and unskilled as sticking a pig in the throat and leaving it to bleed to make the meat tender. I did not know that the style and nobility of the jousting arena had nothing to do with this thrust and stab. Just like killing a screaming piglet for bacon after chasing it round the sty. And I did not know that war thrilled men so: they come home like laughing schoolboys filled with excitement after a prank; but they have blood on their hands and a smear of something on their cloaks and the smell of smoke in their hair and a terrible ugly excitement in their faces.

I understand now why they break into convents, force women against their will, defy sanctuary to finish the killing chase. They arouse in themselves a wild vicious hunger more like animals than men. I did not know that war was like this. I feel I have been a fool not to know, since I was raised in a kingdom at war and am the daughter of a man captured in battle, the widow of a knight, the wife of a merciless soldier. But I know now.

## 21 MAY 1471

Edward rides in at the head of his men, looking like a king coming home in glory, no trace of battle in his bearing, on his horse or on his gleaming harness. Richard is one side of him, George the other, my sons, thrilled, behind them. The York boys are come to their own again, the three of them as one, and London goes mad with joy to see them. Three dukes, six earls and sixteen barons ride in with them, all of them heartfelt Yorkists and sworn to be faithful. Who would have thought that we had so many friends? Not me, when I was in a sanctuary that was more like a prison, bearing the child that is heir to this glory in darkness and fear and all but alone.

Behind their train comes Margaret of Anjou, white-faced and grim, seated on a litter drawn by mules. They don't exactly bind her hands and feet and put a silver chain around her throat but I think everyone understands well enough that this woman is defeated and will not rise from her defeat. I take Elizabeth with me when I greet Edward at the gate of the Tower because I want my little daughter to see this woman who has been a terror to her for all her five years, to see her defeated and to know that we are all safe from the one she calls the Bad Queen.

Edward greets me formally before the cheering crowd but whispers in my ear, 'I can't wait to get you alone.'

But he has to wait. He has knighted half the city of London in thanks for their fidelity and there is a banquet to celebrate their rise to greatness. In truth, we all have much to be thankful for. Edward has fought for his crown again, and won again, and I am still the wife of a king who has never been beaten in battle. I put my mouth to his ear and whisper back, 'I can't wait either, husband.'

We go to bed late, in his chambers, and half the guests are drunk and the others beside themselves with happiness to find themselves at a York court again, and Edward pulls me down beside him and takes me as if we were newly married in the little hunting lodge by the river, and I hold him again, as the man who saved me from poverty and the man who saved England from constant warfare, and I am glad that he calls me 'Wife, my darling wife'.

He says against my hair. 'You held me when I was afraid, my love. I thank you for that. It's the first time I have had to go out knowing that I might lose. It made me sick with fear.'

'I saw a battle. Not even a battle, a massacre,' I say, my forehead against his chest. 'It's a terrible thing, Edward. I didn't know.'

He lies back, his face grim. 'It is a terrible thing,' he says. 'And there is no one who loves peace more than a soldier. I will bring this country to peace and to loyalty to us. I swear it. Whatever I have to do to bring it about. We have to stop these endless battles. We have to bring this war to an end.'

'It's vile,' I say. 'There is no honour in it at all.'

'It has to end,' he says. 'I have to end it.'

We are both silent, and I expect him to sleep but instead he lies thoughtful, his arms folded behind his head, staring at the golden tester over the bed, and when I say, 'What is it, Edward? Is something troubling you?'

He says slowly, 'No, but there is something I have to do before I can sleep at peace tonight.'

'Shall I come with you?'

'No, love, this is men's work.'

'What is it?'

'Nothing. Nothing for you to worry about. Nothing. Go to sleep. I will come back to you later.'

I am alarmed now. I sit up in bed. 'What is it, Edward? You look – I don't know – what is the matter? Are you ill?'

He gets out of bed with sudden decision and pulls on his clothes. 'Peace, beloved. I have to go and do something, and when it is done I shall be able to rest. I shall be back within the hour. Go to sleep and I will wake you and have you again.'

I laugh at that, and lie back but, when he is dressed and gone quietly from the room, I slip from the bed and I pull on my night-gown. On my bare feet, making no noise, I tiptoe through the privy chamber and out into the presence chamber. The guards are silent at the door and I nod at them without a word, and they lift their halberds and let me pass. I pause at the head of the stairs and look down. The stair rails curl round and round inside the well of the building and I can see Edward's hand going down and down to the floor below us, where the old king has his rooms. I see Richard's dark head far below me, at the old king's doorway, as if he is waiting to enter; and I hear George's voice floating up the stairwell. 'We thought you had changed your mind!'

'No. It has to be done.'

I know then what they are about, the three golden brothers of York who won their first battle under three suns in the sky, who are so blessed by God that they never lose. But I do not call out to stop them. I do not run downstairs and catch Edward's arm and swear that he shall not do this thing. I know that he is in two minds; but I do not throw my opinion on the side of compassion, of living with an enemy, of trusting to God for our safety. I do not think: If they do this, what might someone do to us? I see the key in Edward's hand, I hear the turning of the lock, I hear the door open to the king's rooms, and I let the three of them go in, without a word from me.

Henry, madman or saint, is a consecrated king: his body is sacred. He is in the heart of his own kingdom, his own city, his own tower: he must be safe here. He is guarded by good men. He is a prisoner of honour to the House of York. He should be as secure as if he were in his own court: he trusts to us for his safe keeping.

He is one frail man to three young warriors. How can they not be merciful? He is their cousin, their kinsman, and they all three once swore to love and be faithful to him. He is sleeping like a child when the three come into the room. What will happen to us all if they can bring themselves to murder a man as innocent and helpless as a sleeping boy?

I know this is why I have always hated the Tower. I know this is why the tall dark palace on the edge of the Thames has always filled me with foreboding. This death has been on my conscience before we even did it. How heavily it will sit with me from now on only God and my conscience knows. And what price will I have to pay for my part in it, for my silent listening, without a word of protest?

I don't go back to Edward's bed. I don't want to be in his bed when he comes back to me with the smell of death on his hands. I don't want to be here, in the Tower at all. I don't want my son to sleep here, in the Tower of London, supposedly the safest place in England, where armed men can walk into the room of an innocent and hold a pillow over his face. I go to my own rooms and I stir up the fire and I sit beside the warmth all night long, and I know without doubt that the House of York has taken a step on a road that will lead us to hell.

## SUMMER 1471

I am seated with my mother on a raised bed of camomile, the warm scent of the herb all around us, in the garden of the royal manor of Wimbledon, one of my dower houses, given to me as Queen, and still one of my favourite country houses. I am picking out colours for her embroidery. The children are down at the river, feeding ducks with their nursemaid. I can hear their high voices in the distance, calling the ducks by the names they have given them, and scolding them when they don't respond. Now and then I can hear the distinctive squeak of joy from my son. Every time I hear his voice my heart lifts that I have a boy, and a prince, and that he is a happy baby; and my mother, thinking the same, gives a little nod of satisfaction.

The country is so settled and peaceful one would think there had never been a rival king and armies marching at double time to face each other. The country has welcomed the return of my husband; we have all rushed towards peace. More than anything else, we all want to get on with our lives under a fair rule, and forget the loss and pain of the last sixteen years. Oh, there are a few who hold out: Margaret Beaufort's son, now the most unlikely heir to the Lancaster line, is holed up in Pembroke Castle in Wales with his uncle, Jasper Tudor, but they cannot last for long. The world has changed and they will have to sue for peace. Margaret Beaufort's own husband, Henry Stafford, is a Yorkist now and fought on our side at Barnet. Perhaps only she, stubborn as a martyr, and her silly son are the last Lancastrians left in the world.

I have a dozen shades of green laid out on my white-gowned knee, and my mother is threading her needle, holding it up to the sky to see better, bringing it closer to her eyes and then further away again. I think it is the first time in my life I have ever seen a trace of weakness in her. 'Can't you see to thread your needle?' I ask her, half amused.

And she turns and smiles at me and says, quite easily, 'My eyes are not the only things that are failing me, and my thread is not the only thing that is blurred. I shan't see sixty, my child. You should prepare yourself.'

It is as if the day has suddenly gone cold and dark. 'Shan't see sixty!' I exclaim. 'Why ever not? Are you ill? You said nothing! Shall you see the physician? We must go back to London?'

She shakes her head and sighs. 'No, there is nothing for a physician to see, and thank God, nothing that some fool with a knife would think he could cut out. It is my heart, Elizabeth. I can hear it. It is beating wrongly – I can hear it skip a beat, and then go slowly. It will not beat strongly again, I don't think. I don't expect to see many more summers.'

I am so aghast I don't even feel sorrow. 'But what shall I do?' I demand, my hand on my belly, where another new life is beginning. 'Mother, what shall I do? You can't think of it! How shall I manage?'

'You can't say I haven't taught you everything,' she says with a smile. 'Everything I know and everything I believe I have taught you. And some of it may even be true. And I am sure that you are safe on your throne at last. Edward has England in his hand, he has a son to come after him, and you have another baby on the way.' She puts her head on one side as if she is listening to some distant whisper. 'I can't tell. I don't think this is your second boy; but I know you will have another boy,

Elizabeth, I am sure of that. And what a boy he will be! I am sure of that too.'

'You must be with me for the birth of another prince. You would want to see a Prince of York christened as he should be,' I say plaintively, as if promising her a treat if she will only stay. 'You would be his godmother. I would put him in your keeping. You could choose his name.'

'Richard,' she says at once. 'Call him Richard.'

'So get well and stay with me and see Richard born,' I urge her.

She smiles and I see now the telltale signs that I had not seen before. The weariness even when she holds herself upright in her chair, the creamy colour of her face, and the brown shadows under her eyes. How could I not have seen these before? I who love her so well that I kiss her cheek every day and kneel for her blessing – how could I not have noticed that she has grown so thin?

I throw the silks aside and kneel at her feet, clasp her hands, suddenly feel that they are bony, suddenly notice they are freckled with age. I look up into her tired face. 'Mother, you have been with me through everything. You will never leave me now?'

'Not if I could choose to stay,' she says. 'But I have felt this pain for years, and I know it is coming to an end.'

'Since when?' I ask fiercely. 'How long have you felt this pain?'

'Since the death of your father,' she says steadily. 'The day they told me that he was dead, that they had beheaded him for treason, I felt something move deep inside me, like my heart breaking; and I wanted to be with him, even in death.'

'But not to leave me!' I cry selfishly. And then cleverly I add, 'And surely, you cannot bear to leave Anthony?'

She laughs at that. 'You both are grown,' she says. 'You both can live without me. You must both learn to live without me. Anthony will go on a pilgrimage to Jerusalem as he longs to do. You will see your son grow to be a man. You will see our little Elizabeth marry a king and have a crown of her own.'

'I'm not ready!' I cry out like a desolate child. 'I can't manage without you!'

She smiles gently, touches my cheek with her thin hand. 'Nobody is ever ready,' she says tenderly. 'But you will manage without me, and through you, and your children, I will have founded a line of kings in England. Queens as well, I think.'

## SPRING 1472

I am in the last months of my pregnancy and the court is at the beautiful Nonesuch Palace at Sheen, a palace for springtime, when we are all convulsed by the enormous, delicious scandal of the marriage of Edward's brother Richard. All the more wonderful since who would ever have thought Richard would be scandalous? George, yes, with his incessant seeking of his own interest. George would always give the gossip grinders sackfuls of grist since he cares for no one but George himself. No honour, no loyalty, no affection prevents George from suiting himself.

Edward, too, will go his own way and care nothing what people say of him. But Richard! Richard is the good boy of the family, the one who works hardest at being strong, who studies so that he can be clever, who prays devoutly so that he can be favoured by God, who tries so hard for his mother's love and always knows he is eclipsed. For Richard to cause a scandal is like my best hound dog suddenly declaring that she won't hunt any more. It is quite out of nature.

God knows, I try to love Richard, since he has been a true friend to my husband, and a good brother. I should love him: he stood by my husband without thinking twice of it when they had to flee England on a tiny fishing boat; he endured exile with him, and came home with him to risk his life half a dozen times. And always, Edward said, that if Richard had the left wing he could be sure that the left wing would hold. If Richard's troop was bringing up the rear he knew there would be no surprise attack from the road behind. Edward trusts Richard as a brother and a vassal, and loves him dearly – why can I not? What is it about the young man that makes me want to narrow my eyes when I look at him, as if there is some flaw that escapes me? But now this young puppy, not yet twenty years old, has become a hero, a hero from a ballad.

'Who would have thought that dull little Richard would have such passion in him?' I demand of Anthony, who is seated at my feet in a bower looking down to the river. My ladies are around me with half a dozen young men from Edward's court singing and playing with a ball and generally idling and flirting. I am plaiting primroses for a crown for the victor of a race they are going to run later.

'He is deep,' Anthony pronounces, making my sixteen-year-old son Richard Grey choke with laughter.

'Hush,' I say to him. 'Respect for your uncle, please. And pass me some leaves.'

'Deep and passionate,' Anthony continues. 'And all of us thought he was nothing but dull. Amazing.'

'Actually, he is passionate,' my son volunteers. 'You underrate him because he is not grand and loud like the other York brothers.'

My son Thomas Grey nods beside him. 'That's right.'

Anthony raises an eyebrow at the implied criticism of the King. 'You two go and get them ready for their race,' I say, sending them away.

The court has been transfixed by poor little Anne Neville, the young widow of the boy Prince Edward of Lancaster. Brought to London as part of our victory parade after the battle of Tewkesbury, the girl and her fortune were immediately spotted by George, Duke of Clarence, as his way to the entire Warwick fortune. With the Neville girls' mother, the poor Countess of Warwick, taking herself off to a nunnery in complete despair,

George planned to gain everything. He owned half of the Warwick fortune already through his marriage to Isabel Neville, and then he made a great show of taking her young sister into safe keeping. He took little Anne Neville, condoled with her on the death of her father and the absence of her mother, congratulated her on her escape from her nightmare marriage to the little monster, Prince Edward of Lancaster, and thought to keep her under his protection, housed with his wife, her sister, and hold her fortune in his sticky hands.

'It was chivalrous,' Anthony says to irritate me.

'It was an opportunity, and I wish I had seen it first,' I reply.

Anne, a pawn in her father's game for power, widow of a monster, daughter of a traitor, was still only fifteen when she came to live with her sister and her husband George, Duke of Clarence. She had no idea, no better than my kitten, as to how she would survive in this kingdom of her enemies. She must have thought that George was her saviour.

But not for long.

Nobody knows quite what happened after that; but something went wrong with George's agreeable plan to own both Neville girls, and keep their enormous fortune to himself. Some say that Richard, visiting George's grand house, met Anne again – his childhood acquaintance – and they fell in love, and that he rescued her like a knight in a fable from a visit which was nothing less than imprisonment. They say George had her disguised as a kitchen maid, to keep her away from his brother. They say he had her locked in her room. But true love prevailed and the young duke and the young widowed princess fell into each other's arms. At all events, this version of the story is all desperately romantic and wonderful. Fools of all ages enjoy it very much.

'I like it told that way,' my brother Anthony says. 'I am thinking of composing a rondel.'

But there is another version. Other people, who admire Richard, Duke of Gloucester as much as I, say that he saw in the newly widowed lonely girl a woman who could deliver to him the popularity in the north of England that her maiden name commands, who could bring him massive lands that adjoin what he has already got from Edward, and give him a fortune in her dowry, if only he could steal it from her mother. A young girl who was so alone and so unprotected that she could not refuse him. A girl so accustomed to being ordered that she could be bullied into betraying her own mother. This version suggests that Anne, imprisoned by one York brother, was kidnapped by another and forced to marry him.

'Less pretty,' I observe to Anthony.

'You could have stopped it,' he says to me with one of his sudden moments of seriousness. 'If you had taken her into your keeping, if you had made Edward order Richard and George not to pull her apart like dogs over a bone.'

'I should have done,' I say. 'For now Richard has one Neville girl, the Warwick fortune, and the support of the north, and George has the other. That's a dangerous combination.'

Anthony raises an eyebrow. 'You should have done it because it was the right thing to do,' he says to me with all of an older brother's pomposity. 'But I see you are still only thinking of power and profit.'

## APRIL 1472

My mother's skill at foretelling the future is borne out. Less than a year after she warned me her heart would not last much longer, she complains of fatigue and keeps to her rooms. The baby I was carrying in the garden the day of the primrose races came early, and for the first time I go into my confinement without my mother's company. I send her messages from my darkened room and she replies cheerfully from hers. But when I come out with a frail new-born girl, I find my mother in her chamber, too weary to rise. I take the baby girl, light as a little bird, and lay her in my mother's arms every afternoon. For a week or two, the two of them watch the sun sink below the level of the window, and then like the gold of the sunset they slip away from me together.

At dusk, on the last day of April, I hear a calling noise, like a white-winged barn owl, and I go to my window and push open the shutters and look out. There is a waning moon rising off the horizon, white against a white sky; it too is wasting away, and in its cold light I can hear a calling, like a choir, and I know it is not the music of owls, nor singers nor nightingales, but Melusina. Our ancestor goddess is calling around the roof of the house, for her daughter Jacquetta of the House of Burgundy is dying.

I stand and listen to the eerie whistling for a while and then I swing the shutters closed and go to my mother's room. I don't hurry. I know there is no need to hurry to her any more. The new baby is in her arms as she lies in her bed, the little head pressed to my mother's cheek. They are both pale as marble, they are both lying with their eyes shut, they both seem to be peacefully asleep as the shadows of the evening darken the room. The moonlight on the water outside the chamber window throws the reflection of ripples onto the whitewashed ceiling of the room, so they look as if they are underwater, floating with Melusina in the fountain. But I know that they are both gone from me, and our water mother is singing them on their journey down the sweet river to the deep springs of home.

## SUMMER 1472

The pain of my mother's death is not closed for me by her funeral; it is not healed with the months that go slowly by. Every morning, I wake and miss her, as much as the first morning. Every day I have to remember that I cannot ask her opinion, or quarrel with her advice, or laugh at her sarcasm, or look for the guidance of her magic. And every day I find I blame George, Duke of Clarence even more for the murder of my father and my brother. I believe it was at the news of their deaths at his hand, under the orders of Warwick, that my mother's loving heart broke, and if they had not been traitorously killed by him then she too would be alive today.

It is summer, a time for thoughtless pleasure, but I take my sorrow with me, through the picnics and days as we travel through the countryside, on the long rides and nights under a harvest moon. Edward makes my son Thomas the Earl of Huntingdon and it does not cheer me. I don't speak of my sadness to anyone but Anthony, who has lost his mother too. And we hardly ever speak of her. It is as if we cannot bring ourselves to speak of her as dead, and we cannot lie to ourselves that she is still alive. But I blame George, Duke of Clarence, for her heartbreak and her death.

'I hate George of Clarence more than ever,' I say to Anthony as we ride down the road to Kent together, a banquet ahead of us and a week spent travelling in the green lanes between the apple orchards. My heart should be light as the court is happy. But my sense of loss comes with me like a hawk on my wrist.

'Because you're jealous,' my brother Anthony says provocatively, one hand holding the reins of his horse, the other leading my young son, Prince Edward, on his little pony. 'You are jealous of anyone Edward loves. You are jealous of me, you are jealous of William Hastings, you are jealous of anyone who entertains the king, and takes him out whoring, and brings him home drunk and amuses him.'

I shrug my shoulders, indifferent to Anthony's teasing. I have long known that the king's pleasure in deep drinking with his friends and visiting other women is part of his nature. I have come to tolerate it, especially as it never takes him far from my bed, and when we are there together it is as if we were married in secret that very morning. He has been a soldier on campaign, far from home, with a hundred doxies at his command; he has been an exile in cities where women have hurried to comfort him, and now he is the King of England and every woman in London would be glad to have him – I truly believe that half of them have had him. He is the king. I never thought I was marrying an ordinary man, with moderate appetites. I never expected a marriage where he would sit quietly at my feet. He is the king: he is bound to go his own way.

'No, you are wrong. Edward's whoring doesn't trouble me. He is the king, he can take his pleasures where he wants. And I am the queen, and he will always come home to me. Everyone knows that.'

Anthony nods, conceding the point. 'But I don't see why you concentrate your hatred on George. The king's entire family are as bad as each other. His mother has loathed you and all of us since we first emerged at Reading, and Richard is more awkward and surly every day. Peace doesn't suit him, for sure.'

'Nothing about us suits him,' I say. 'He is as unlike his two brothers as chalk to cheese: small and dark, and so anxious about his health and his position and his soul; always hoping for a fortune and saying a prayer.'

'Edward lives as if there is no tomorrow, Richard as if he wants no tomorrow, and George as though someone should give it to him for free.'

I laugh. 'Well, I would like Richard better if he was as bad as the rest of you,' I remark. 'And since he has been married, he is even more righteous. He has always looked down on us Rivers; now he looks down on George too. It is that pompous saintliness that I cannot stomach. He looks at me sometimes as if I were some kind of . . .'

'Some kind of what?'

'Some kind of fat fishwife.'

'Well,' my brother says. 'To be honest, you're getting no younger, and in certain lights, y'know . . .'

I tap him on the knee with my riding crop and he laughs and winks at Baby Edward on his little pony.

'I don't like how he has taken all the north into his keeping. Edward has made him overly great. He has made him a prince in his own principality. It is a danger to us, and to our heirs. It is to divide the kingdom.'

'He had to reward him with something. Richard has laid down his life on Edward's gambles over and over again. Richard won the kingdom for Edward: he should have his share.'

'But it makes Richard all but a king in his own domain,' I protest. 'It gives him the kingdom of the north.'

'Nobody doubts his loyalty but you.'

'He is loyal to Edward, and to his house, but he doesn't like me or mine. He envies me everything I have, and he doesn't admire my court. And what does that mean when he thinks of our children? Will he be loyal to my boy, because he is Edward's boy too?'

Anthony shrugs. 'We are raised up, you know. You have brought us up very high. There are a lot of people who think we ride higher than our deserts, and on nothing more than your roadside charms.'

'I don't like how Richard married Anne Neville.'

Anthony laughs shortly. 'Oh sister, nobody liked to see Richard, the wealthiest young man in England, marry the richest young woman in England, but I never thought to see you take the side of George, Duke of Clarence!'

I laugh unwillingly. George's outrage at having his heiress sister-in-law snatched from his own house by his own brother has entertained us all for half the year.

'Anyway, it is your husband who has obliged Richard,' Anthony remarks. 'If Richard wanted to marry Anne for love he could have done so, and been rewarded by her love. But it took the king to declare her mother's fortune should be divided between the two girls. It took your honourable husband to declare the mother legally dead – though I believe the old lady stoutly protests her continuing life, and demands the right to plead for her own lands – and it was your husband who took all the fortune from the poor old lady to give to her two daughters, and thus, and so conveniently, to his brothers.'

'I told him not to,' I say irritably. 'But he paid no attention to me on this. He always favours his brothers, and Richard far above George.'

'He is right to prefer Richard but he should not break his own laws in his own kingdom,' Anthony says with sudden seriousness. 'That's no way to rule. It is unlawful to rob a widow and he has done just that. And she is the widow of his enemy and in sanctuary in a nunnery. He should be gracious to her, he should be merciful. If he were a truly chivalrous knight he would encourage her to come out of the nunnery and take up her lands, protect her daughters and curb the greed of his brothers.'

'The law is what powerful men say it shall be,' I say irritably. 'And sanctuary is not unbreakable. If you were not a dreamer, far away in Camelot, you would know that by now. You were at Tewkesbury, weren't you? Did you see the sanctity of holy ground then when they dragged the lords from the abbey and stabbed them in the churchyard? Did you defend sanctuary then? For I heard everyone unsheathed their swords and cut down the men who were coming with their sword hilts held out?'

Anthony shakes his head. 'I am a dreamer,' he concedes. 'I don't deny it; but I have seen enough to know the world. Perhaps my dream is of a better one. This York reign is sometimes too much for me, you know, Elizabeth. I cannot bear what Edward does when I see him favour one man and disregard another, and for no reason but that it makes himself stronger or his reign more secure. And you have made the throne your fief: you distribute favours and wealth to your favourites, not to the deserving. And the two of you make enemies. People say that we care for nothing but our own success. When I see what we do, now that we are in power, I sometimes regret fighting under the white rose. I sometimes think that Lancaster would have done just as well, or at any rate no worse.'

'Then you forget Margaret of Anjou and her mad husband,' I say coldly. 'My mother herself said to me on the day we rode out for Reading that I could not do worse than Margaret of Anjou and I have not done so.'

He concedes the point. 'All right. You and your husband are no worse than a madman and a harpy. Very good.'

I am surprised at his gravity. 'It is as the world is, my brother,' I remind him. 'And you too have had your favours from the king and me. And now you are Earl Rivers and brother-in-law to the king, and uncle to the king to be.'

'I thought we were doing more than lining our own pockets,' he says. 'I thought we were doing more than putting a king and a queen on the throne who were only better than the worst that could be. You know, sometimes I would rather be in a white tabard with a red cross, fighting for God in the desert.'

I think of my mother's prediction that Anthony's spirituality will one day triumph over his Rivers worldliness and he will leave me. 'Ah don't say that,' I say. 'I need you. And as Baby grows and has his own prince's council he will need you. I can think of no man better fitted to guide him and teach him than you. There's no knight in England better read. There's no poet in England who can fight as well. Don't say you will go, Anthony. You know you have to stay. I can't be queen without you. I can't be me without you.'

He bows to me with his twisted smile and takes my hand and kisses it. 'I won't leave you while you have need of me,' he promises. 'I will never willingly leave you while you need me. And, for sure, good times are coming soon.'

I smile; but he makes the optimistic words sound like a lament.

## SEPTEMBER 1472

Edward beckons me to one side after dinner one evening at Windsor Castle and I go to him smiling. 'What do you want, husband? Do you want to dance with me?'

'I do,' he says. 'And then I am going to get hugely drunk.'

'For any reason?'

'None at all. Just for pleasure. But before all that, I have to ask you something. Can you take another lady into your rooms as a lady-in-waiting?'

'Do you have someone in mind?' I am instantly alert to the danger that Edward has a new flirt that he wants to palm off on me, and that he thinks I will make her my lady-in-waiting to make his seduction the more convenient. This must show in my face, for he gives a whoop of laughter and says, 'Don't look so furious. I wouldn't foist my whores upon you. I can house them myself. No, this is a lady of unimpeachable family. None other than Margaret Beaufort, the last of the Lancastrians.'

'You want her to serve me?' I ask incredulously. 'You want her to be one of my ladies?'

He nods. 'I have reason. You remember she is newly married to Lord Thomas Stanley?'

I nod.

'He is declared our friend, he is sworn to our support, and his army sat on the sidelines and saved us at the battle of Blore Heath though he was promised to Margaret of Anjou. With his fortune and influence in the country I do need to keep him on our side. He had our permission to marry her well enough, and now he has done it, and seeks to bring her to court. I thought we could give her a position. I must have him on my council.'

'Isn't she wearisomely religious?' I ask unhelpfully.

'She is a lady. She will adapt her behaviour to yours,' he says equably. 'And I need her husband close to me, Elizabeth. He is an ally who will be of importance both now and in the future.'

'If you ask it so sweetly, what can I do but say yes?' I smile at him. 'But don't blame me if she is dull.'

'I will not see her, nor any woman, if you are before me,' he whispers. 'So don't trouble yourself as to how she behaves. And in a little while, when she asks for her son Henry Tudor to come home again, he may – as long as she is loyal to us, and he can be persuaded to forget his dreams of being the Lancaster heir. They will both come to court and serve us and everyone will forget there was ever such a thing as a House of Lancaster. We'll marry him to some nice girl of the House of York that you can pick out for him and the House of Lancaster will be no more.'

'I will invite her,' I promise him.

'Then tell the musicians to play something merry and I will dance with you.'

I turn and nod to the musicians and they confer for a moment and then play the newest tune, straight from the Burgundian court where Edward's sister Margaret is continuing the York tradition of making merry and the Burgundian tradition of high fashion. They even call the dance 'Duchess Margaret's jig', and Edward sweeps me onto the floor and whirls me in the quick steps until everyone is laughing and clapping in a circle around us, and then taking their turn.

The music ends and I spin away to a quieter corner and Anthony my brother offers me a glass of small ale. I drink it thirstily. 'So, do I still look like a fat fishwife?' I demand.

'Oho, that stung did it?' he grins. He puts his arms around me and hugs me gently. 'No, you look like the beauty you are, and you know it. You have that gift, which our mother had, of growing older and becoming more lovely. Your features have changed from being merely those of a pretty girl to being those of a beautiful woman with a face like a carving. When you are laughing and dancing with Edward you could pass for twenty, but when you are still and thoughtful you are as lovely as the statues they are carving in Italy. No wonder women loathe you.'

'As long as men do not,' I smile.

# JANUARY 1473

In the cold days of January Edward comes to my rooms where I am seated before the fire, a footstool before me so I can put my feet up. As he sees me sitting, uncharacteristically idle, he checks in the doorway and nods to the men behind him and to my women and says, 'Leave us.' They go out with a little bustle, the newly arrived Lady Margaret Stanley among them, fluttering as women always do around Edward – even the holy Margaret Stanley.

He nods at their backs as they close the door behind them. 'Lady Margaret? She is merry and good company for you?'

'She is well enough,' I say, smiling up at him. 'She knows, and I know, that she rode in the Tudor barge past my window when I was in sanctuary and she enjoyed her moment of triumph then. And she knows, and I know, that I have the upper hand now. We don't forget that. We aren't men to clap each other on the back and say "No hard feelings" after a battle. But we know also that the world has changed and we have to change too, and she never says a word to suggest that she wishes her son were acknowledged heir to the Lancaster throne, rather than Baby is to the York.'

'I came to speak to you about Baby,' Edward says. 'But I see that you should be speaking to me.'

I widen my eyes and smile up at him. 'Oh? About what?'

He gives a little laugh and pulls a cushion off a settle and drops it to the floor so he can sit beside me. The freshly strewn herbs on the floor beneath his cushion release the scent of water mint. 'Do you think I am blind? Or just stupid?'

'Neither, my lord,' I say flirtatiously. 'Should I?'

'In all the time I have known you, you have always seated yourself as your mother taught you. Straight upright in a chair, feet together, hands in your lap or resting on the arms of the chair. Isn't that how she taught you to sit? Like a queen? As if she knew all along you would have a throne?'

I smile. 'She probably did know, actually.'

'And so now I find you lazing about in the afternoon, feet on a footstool.' He leans back and lifts the hem of my gown so that he can see my stockinged feet. 'Shoes off! I am scandalised. You are clearly becoming a slattern and my royal court is run by a hedgerow slut, just as my mother warned me.'

'And so?' I ask, unmoved.

'And so, I know you are with child. For the only time you ever sit with your feet up is when you are with child. And that is why I ask you if you think I am blind or just stupid?'

'I think you are as fertile as a bull in a water meadow, if you want to know what I think!' I exclaim. 'Every other year I have a baby to you.'

'And all the others,' he says unrepentantly. 'Don't forget them. So when is this precious one due?'

'In the summer,' I say. 'And more than that . . .'

'Yes?'

I pull his fair head towards me, and whisper in his ear. 'I think he will be a boy.'

His head jerks up, his face filled with joy. 'You do? You have signs?'

'Women's fancies,' I say; thinking of my mother with her head on one side as if she were listening for the sound of little feet in riding boots clattering across heaven. 'But I think so. I hope so.'

'A boy born to the Yorks at a time of peace,' he says longingly.

'Ah, my dear, you are a good wife. You are my beauty. You are my only love.'

'So what about all the others?'

He dismisses the mistresses and their babies with one wave of his hand. 'Forget them. I have. The only woman in the world for me is you. Now as always.'

He kisses me gently, holding back his usual ready arousal. We will not be lovers again until after the baby is born and I have been churched. 'My darling,' he whispers to me.

We sit for a little while in silence, watching the fire. 'But what did you come to see me for?' I ask.

'Ah, yes. This should make no difference, I think. I want to send Baby to start his little kingdom in Wales. To Ludlow Castle.'

I nod. This is how it has to be. This is what it means to have a prince and not a girl. My oldest darling daughter Elizabeth can stay with me until she is married, but my son has to go and serve his apprenticeship as a king. He has to go to Wales, for he is Prince of Wales, and he has to rule it with his own council.

'But he is not yet three,' I say plaintively.

'Old enough,' my husband says. 'And you shall travel to Ludlow with him, if you think you are strong enough, and order it just as you wish, and make sure that he has the companions and tutors that you want. And I will appoint you to his council and you can choose the other members, and you will guide him and order his studies and his life until he is fourteen.'

I pull Edward's face towards me again and I kiss his mouth. 'Thank you,' I say. He is leaving my son in my keeping when most kings would say that the boy has to live only with men, taken away from the counsels of women. But Edward makes me the guardian of my son, honours my love for him, respects my judgement. I can bear the separation from Baby if I am to appoint his council, for it means that I shall visit him often and his life shall still be in my keeping.

'And he can come home for feast days and holy days,' Edward says. 'I shall miss him too, you know. But he has to be in his principality. He has to make a start at ruling. Wales has to know their prince, and learn to love him. He has to know his land as from childhood, and thus we keep their loyalty.'

'I know,' I say. 'I know.'

'And Wales has always been loyal to the Tudors,' Edward adds, almost as an aside. 'And I want them to forget him.'

I consider carefully who shall have the raising of my boy in Wales, and who shall head his council and rule Wales for him until he is of age, and then I come to the decision I would have made if I had picked the first name that came to mind, without thinking. Of course. Who else would I trust with the most precious possession in the world?

I go to my brother Anthony's rooms, which are set back from the main stair, overlooking the private gardens. His door is guarded by his manservant, who swings it open and announces me in a respectful whisper. I cross through his presence chamber and knock on the door of his private room, and enter.

He is seated at a table before the fire, a glass of wine in his hand, a dozen well-sharpened quills before him, sheets of expensive paper covered with crossed-through lines. He is writing, as he does most afternoons when the early darkness of winter drives everyone indoors. He writes every day now, and he no longer posts his poems in the joust: they are too important to him.

He smiles and sets a chair for me close to the fire. He puts a footstool under my feet without comment. He will have guessed that I am with child. Anthony has the eyes of a poet as well as the words. He doesn't miss much.

'I am honoured,' he says with a smile. 'Do you have a command for me, Your Grace, or is this a private visit?'

'It is a request,' I say. 'Because Edward is going to send Baby to Wales to set up his court, and I want you to go with him as his chief advisor.'

'Won't Edward send Hastings?' he asks.

'No, I am to appoint Baby's council. Anthony, there is much profit to be won from Wales. It needs a strong hand, and I would want it to be under our family's command. It can't be Hastings, or Richard. I don't like Hastings, and I never will, and Richard has the Neville lands in the north – we can't let him have the west too.'

Anthony shrugs. 'We have enough wealth and influence, don't we?'

'You can never have too much.' I state the obvious. 'And anyway, the most important thing is that I want you to have the guardianship of Baby.'

'You'd better stop calling him Baby if he is to be Prince of Wales with his own court,' my brother reminds me. 'He will be moving to a man's estate, his own command, his own court, his own country. Soon you will be seeking a princess for him to marry.'

I smile into the warm flames. 'I know, I know. We are considering it already. I can't believe it. I call him Baby because I like to remember how he was when he was in his gowns, but he has his short clothes and he has his own pony now, and is growing every day. I change his riding boots every quarter.'

'He's a fine little boy,' Anthony says. 'And though he takes after his father I sometimes think I see his grandfather in him. You can see he is a Woodville, one of ours.'

'I won't have anyone but you be his guardian,' I say. 'He must be raised as a Rivers at a Rivers court. Hastings is a brute, and I wouldn't trust the care of my cat to either of Edward's brothers: George thinks of nothing but himself and Richard is too young. I want my Prince Edward to learn from you, Anthony. You wouldn't want anyone else to influence him, would you?'

He shakes his head. 'I wouldn't have him raised by any of them. I didn't realise the king was setting him up in Wales so soon.'

'This spring,' I say. 'I don't know how I shall bear to let him go.'

Anthony pauses. 'I won't be able to take my wife with me,' he says. 'If you thought she might be the Lady of Ludlow. She is not strong enough, and this year she is worse than ever, weaker.'

'I know. If she wants to live at court I will see she is well cared for. But you would not stay behind for her?'

He shakes his head. 'God bless her, no.'

'So you will go?'

'I will, and you can visit us,' Anthony says grandly. 'At our new court. Where will we be? Ludlow?'

I nod. 'You can learn Welsh and become a bard,' I say.

'Well, I can promise to bring up the boy as you and our family would wish,' he says. 'I can keep him to his learning and to his sports. I can teach him what he will need to be a good king of York. And it is something, to raise a king. It is a legacy to leave: that of making the boy who will be king.'

'Enough to sacrifice your pilgrimage for another year?' I ask.

'You know I can never refuse you. And your word is the king's command and nobody can refuse that. But in truth, I would not refuse to serve the young Prince Edward: it will be something to be guardian of such a boy. I should be proud to have the making of the next King of England. And I will be glad to be at the court of the Prince of Wales.'

'Do I always have to call him that now? Is he not to be Baby any more?'

'You do.'

## SPRING 1473

The young Edward, Prince of Wales and his uncle Earl Rivers, my Grey son Richard, now Sir Richard by order of his stepfather the king, and I make a grand progress to Wales so the little prince can see his country and be seen by as many people as possible. His father says that this is how we make our rule secure: we show ourselves to the people, and by demonstrating our wealth, our fertility and our elegance we make them feel secure in their monarchy.

We go by slow stages. Edward is strong but he is not yet three years old and riding all day is too tiring for him. I order that he shall have a rest every afternoon, and go to bed in my chamber, early at night. I am glad of the leisurely pace on my own account, riding pillion so that I can sit sideways as the new curve of my belly is starting to show. We reach the pretty town of Ludlow without incident and I decide to stay in Wales with my first-born son for the first half-year, until I am certain that the household is organised for his comfort and safety, and that he is settled and happy in his new home.

He is all delight; there is no regret for him. He misses the company of his sisters but he loves being the little Prince at his own court, and he enjoys the company of his half-brother, Richard, and his uncle. He starts to learn the land around the castle, the deep valleys and beautiful mountains. He has the servants who have been with him since babyhood. He has new friends in the children of his court, who are brought to learn and play with him, and he has the watchful care of my brother. It is I who cannot sleep for the week before I am due to leave him. Anthony is at ease, Richard is happy, and Baby is joyous in his new home.

Of course, it is almost unbearable for me to leave him, for we have not been an ordinary royal family. We have not had a life of formality and distance. This boy was born in sanctuary under threat of death. He slept in my bed for the first few months of his life – unheard of for a royal prince. He had no wet nurse, I suckled him myself, and it was my fingers that his little hands gripped as he first learned to walk. Neither he, nor any of the others, were sent away to be raised by nurses or in a royal nursery at another palace. Edward has kept his children close, and this, his oldest son, is the first to leave us to take up his royal duties. I love him with a passion: he is my golden boy, the boy who came at last to secure my position as queen and to give his father, then nothing more than a York pretender, a stronger claim to the throne. He is my prince, he is the crown of our marriage, he is our future.

Edward comes to join me for my last month at Ludlow in June, bringing the news that Anthony's wife, Lady Elizabeth, has died. She had been in ill health for years with a wasting sickness. Anthony orders masses said for her soul, and I, secretly and ashamed of myself, start to wonder who might be the next wife for my brother.

'Time enough for that,' Edward says. 'But Anthony will have to play his part for the safety of the kingdom. He might have to marry a French princess. I need allies.'

'But not go from home,' I say. 'And not leave Edward?'

'No. I see he has made Ludlow his own. And Edward will need him here when we leave. And we must leave soon. I have given orders that we will go within the month.'

I gasp, though in truth I have known that this day must come.

'We will come again to see him,' he promises me. 'And he will come to us. No need to look so tragic, my love. He is starting his work as a prince of the House of York: this is his future. You must be glad for him.'

'I am glad,' I say, without any conviction at all.

When it is time for me to go I have to pinch my cheeks to bring colour into them, and bite my mouth to stop myself crying. Anthony knows what it costs me to leave the three of them, but Baby is happy, confident that he will come to court in London soon on a visit, enjoying his new freedom and the importance of being the prince in his own country. He lets me kiss him, and hold him without wriggling. He even whispers in my ear, 'I love you Mama,' then he kneels for my blessing; but he comes up smiling.

Anthony lifts me into the pillion saddle behind my master of horse and I hold on tightly to his belt. I am awkward now, in the seventh month of my pregnancy. A sudden wave of the darkest anxiety comes over me, and I look from my brother to my two sons, real fear clutching at me. 'Take care,' I say to Baby.

'Look after him,' I say to Anthony. 'Write to me. Don't let him take jumps on his pony. I know that he wants to, but he's too small. And don't let him get chilled. Don't let him read in poor light, and keep him away from anyone with illness. If there is plague in the town then take him right away.' I cannot think what I should warn them against, I am just flooded with anxiety as I look from one smiling face to another. 'Really,' I say weakly. 'Really, Anthony: guard him.'

He steps up to the horse and takes hold of the toe of my boot and shakes it gently. 'Your Grace,' he says simply. 'Really. I am here to guard him. I will guard him. I will keep him safe.'

'And you,' I whisper. 'You keep safe too. Anthony, I feel so afraid, but I don't know what to fear. I don't know what to say. I want to warn you but I don't know what danger there is.' I look over to where my son Richard Grey is leaning against the castle gateway, a young man grown tall and handsome. 'And my Grey son,' I say. 'My Richard. I cannot tell you why but I am fearful for you all.'

He steps back and shrugs his shoulders. 'Sister mine,' he says tenderly. 'There is always danger. Your sons and I will be men, and we will face it like men. Don't you go frightening yourself with imaginary threats. And have a safe journey and a safe confinement. We are all hoping for another prince as good as this one!'

Edward gives the order to move out and leads the way, his standard going before him, his household guard around him. The royal procession starts to unroll like a scarlet ribbon through the castle gates, the bright red of the livery studded with the rippling standards. The trumpets sound, the birds fly up from the castle roofs and whirl in the sky announcing that the king and queen are leaving their precious son. I cannot stop the onward march, and I should not stop it. But I look back over my shoulder at my little son, at my grown son, and at my brother, until the fall of the road from the inner keep down to the outer wall has hidden them, and I see them no more. And when I can see them no more I am filled with such darkness that for a moment I think night has fallen and there will never be a dawn again.

## JULY 1473

We halt at the town of Shrewsbury on the way back to London in the last days of July for me to go into confinement in the guest rooms of the great abbey. I am glad to be out of the glare and the heat of summer and into the coolness of the shuttered room. I have ordered them to set a fountain in the corner of my stone-walled chambers, and the drip, drip of the water soothes me as I lie on the day bed and wait for my time.

This is a town built around the sacred well of St Winifred, and as I listen to the dripping fountain of her water and hear the ringing of the hours for prayer I think of the spirits that move in waters of this wet land, both the pagan and the holy, Melusina and Winifred, and how the springs and streams and rivers speak to all men, but perhaps especially to women, who know in their own bodies the movement of the waters of the earth. Every holy site in England is a well or a spring; the baptismal fonts are filled with holy water that goes back, blessed, to the earth. It is a country for Melusina, and her element is everywhere, sometimes flowing in the rivers, sometimes hidden underground but always present.

In the middle of August the pains start, and I turn my head to the fountain and listen to the trickle as if I were seeking the voice of my mother in the water. The baby comes easily, as I thought he would, and he is a boy, as my mother knew he would be.

Edward comes into the chamber, though men are supposed to be banned until I have been churched. 'I had to come and see you,' he says. 'A son. Another son. God bless you and keep you both. God bless you, my love, and thank you for your pains to give me another boy.'

'I thought you did not mind if it was a boy or a girl,' I tease him.

'I love my girls,' he says at once. 'But the House of York needed another boy. He can be a companion to his brother Edward.'

'Can we call him Richard?' I ask.

'I thought Henry?'

'Henry for the next one,' I say. 'Let's call this boy Richard. My mother herself named him to me.'

Edward bends over the cradle where the tiny boy is sleeping, and then he understands my words. 'Your mother? She knew you would have a boy?'

'Yes, she knew,' I say, smiling. 'Or at any rate, she pretended to know. You remember my mother. It was always one part magic and one part nonsense.'

'And is this our last boy? Did she say? Or do you think there will be another?'

'Why not another?' I say lazily. 'If you still want me in your bed, that is. If you have not had enough of me? If you are not tired of me? If you don't prefer your other women?'

He turns from the cradle and comes to me. His hands slide under my shoulder blades and lift me up to his mouth. 'Oh, I still want you,' he says.

# SPRING 1476

I am proved right, it was by no means my last confinement. My husband continued as fertile as the bull in the water meadow that I accused him of being. In the second year after the birth of Richard, I was pregnant again and in November I had another baby, a girl that we called Anne. Edward rewards me for my labours by making my son Thomas Grey, Marquis of Dorset and I marry him to a pleasant girl – an heiress to a mighty fortune. Edward had hoped for a boy and we had promised to name him George, as a compliment to the other York duke, and so that there are, once again, three boys of York named Edward, Richard and George; but the duke shows no sign of gratitude. He was a spoiled greedy boy and he has grown into a disappointed, bad-tempered man. He is in his mid-twenties now, and his rosebud mouth has drooped into a sneer of disdain. He gloried at being one of the sons of York when he was a hopeful boy; since then he was first in line for the throne of England as Warwick's chosen heir, and then displaced when Warwick favoured Lancaster. When Edward won back the throne George became first in line to inherit, but then was pushed down to second at the birth of my baby, Prince Edward. Since the birth of Prince Richard, George drops down to third in line to the throne of England. Indeed, every time I have a son, the Duke George drops down one more step away from the throne and deeper and deeper into jealousy. And since Edward is famously uxorious, and I am famously fertile, George's inheritance of the throne has become a most unlikely event and he is the Duke of Disappointment.

Richard, the other York brother, does not seem to mind this, but he turns against us after the Yorks come back from France without fighting a war but winning a peace. My husband the king, and every man and woman of sense throughout the entire country are all rejoicing that Edward has made a peace with France that should last for years, in which they will pay us a fortune not to claim our lands in France. Everyone is delighted to escape a costly and painful foreign war except Duke Richard, the boy who was raised on a battlefield and now cites the rights of Englishmen over our lands in France, clings to the memory of his father, who spent much of his life fighting the French, and all but calls his brother the king a lazy coward in not leading yet another expensive and dangerous expedition.

Edward laughs his good-tempered laugh, and lets the insult go, but Richard storms off to his lands in the north, taking his obedient wife Anne Neville with him, and sets himself up as a northern princeling, refusing to come south to us, believing himself to be the only true York of England, the only true heir to his father in his enmity with France.

Nothing troubles Edward, and he is smiling when he comes to find me in the stables, where I am looking over a new mare, a gift from the King of France, to mark the new friendliness between our countries. She is a beautiful horse, but nervous at the new surroundings, and will not even come near me, though I have a tempting apple in my hand.

'Your brother came to me today to ask permission to go on pilgrimage, and leave Edward in the care of his half-brother Sir Richard for a little while.'

I come out of the stable and close the door carefully behind me to keep the horse safely inside. 'Why? Where does he want to go?'

'He wants to go to Rome,' Edward says. 'He tells me he wants time away from the world.' He gives me an odd crooked smile.

'Seems that Ludlow has given him a taste for solitude. He wants to be a saint. He tells me he wants to find the poet in himself. He says he wants silence and the deserted road. He wants to find silence and wisdom.'

'Oh nonsense,' I say, with a sister's scorn. 'He has always had this idea of going away. He has been planning to go to Jerusalem ever since he was a boy. He loves to travel and he thinks that the Greeks and the Moslems know everything. He may want to go but his life and his work are here. Just tell him no, and make him stay.'

Edward hesitates. 'He has a great desire to do this, Elizabeth. And he is one of the greatest knights of Christendom. I don't think anyone can defeat him at the joust when he is on his day. And his poetry is as fine as that written by anyone. His reading and his knowledge is so wide, and his command of languages is greater than anyone else in England. He is not an ordinary man. Perhaps it is his destiny to go far and learn more. He has served us well, none better, and if God has called him to travel perhaps we should let him go.'

The mare comes and puts her head over the half-door to sniff at my shoulder. I stand still, so as not to frighten her. Her warm oaty breath blows on my neck. 'You're very tender of his talents,' I say suspiciously. 'Why are you so admiring of him all of a sudden?'

He shrugs his shoulders and at that small gesture, wife-like, I am on to him. I step forward and take both his hands in mine so he cannot escape my scrutiny. 'So who is she?'

'What? What are you talking about?'

'The new one. The new whore. The one who likes Anthony's poetry,' I say bitingly. 'You never read it yourself. You never had such a high opinion of his learning and his destiny before. So someone has been reading to you. My guess is that *she* has been reading it to you. And if my guess is right, she knows it because he has been reading it to her. And probably Hastings knows her as well, and all of you think she is utterly lovely. But you will be bedding her; and the others sniffing round like dogs. You have a new and agreeable whore, and that I understand. But if you think you are going to share her stupid opinions with me then she will have to go.'

He looks away from me, at his boots, at the sky, at the new mare.

'What's her name? I ask. 'You can tell me that, at least.'

He pulls me towards him and folds me in his arms. 'Don't be angry, beloved,' he whispers in my ear. 'You know there is only you. Only ever you.'

'Me and a score of others,' I say irritably, but I don't pull away from him. 'They go through your bedroom like a May Day procession.'

'No,' he says. 'Truly. There is only you. I have only one wife. I have a score of whores, perhaps hundreds. But only one wife. That is something, is it not?'

'Your whores are young enough to be my daughters,' I say crossly. 'And you go out into the City to chase them. And the City merchants complain to me that their wives and their daughters are not safe from you.'

'No,' my husband says with the vanity of a handsome man. 'They are not. I hope that no woman can resist me. But I never took anyone by force, Elizabeth. The only woman who ever resisted me was you. D'you remember drawing that dagger on me?'

I smile despite myself. 'Of course I do. And you swearing that you would give me the scabbard; but it would be the last thing you ever gave me.'

'There is no one like you.' He kisses my brow and then my closed eyelids and then my lips. 'There is no one but you. No one but my wife holds my heart in her beautiful hands.'

'So what is her name?' I ask as he kisses me into peace. 'What's the name of the new whore?'

'Elizabeth Shore,' he says, his lips on my neck. 'But that doesn't matter.'

Anthony comes to my rooms as soon as he arrives at court, having made the journey from Wales, and I greet him at once with an absolute refusal to let him go away.

'No, truly, my dear,' he says. 'You have to let me go. I am not going to Jerusalem, not this year, but I want to travel to Rome and confess my sins. I want to be away from the court for a while and think of things that matter and not things that are of the everyday. I want to ride from monastery to monastery and rise at dawn to pray and, where there is no religious house for me to spend the night, I want to sleep under the stars and seek God in the silence.'

'Won't you miss me?' I ask, child-like. 'Won't you miss Baby? And the girls?'

'Yes, and that's why I don't even consider a crusade. I can't bear to be away for months. But Edward is settled in Ludlow with his playmates and his tutors, and young Richard Grey is a fine companion and model for him. It is safe to leave him for a little while. I have a longing to travel the deserted roads, and I have to follow it.'

'You are a son of Melusina,' I say, trying to smile. 'You sound like her when she had to be free to go into the water.'

'It's like that,' he agrees. 'Think of me as swimming away and then the tide will bring me back.'

'Your mind is made up?'

He nods. 'I have to have silence to hear the voice of God,' he says. 'And silence to write my poetry. And silence to be myself.'

'But you will come back?'

'Within a few months,' he promises.

I stretch out my hands to him and he kisses them both. 'You must come back,' I say.

'I will,' he says. 'I have given my word that only death will take me from you and yours.'

# JULY 1476

He is as good as his word and returns from his trip to Rome in time to meet us at Fotheringhay in July. Richard has planned and organised a solemn reburial of his father and his brother Edmund, who were killed in battle, made mock of and hardly buried at all. The House of York rallies together for the funeral and the memorial service and I am glad Anthony comes home in time to bring Prince Edward to honour his grandfather.

Anthony is as brown as a Moor and full of stories. We steal away together to walk in the gardens of Fotheringhay. He was robbed on the road; he thought he would never get away with his life. He stayed one night beside a spring in a forest and could not sleep for the certainty that Melusina would rise out of the waters. 'And what would I say to her?' he demands plaintively. 'How confusing for us all if I fell in love with my great-grandmother.'

He met the Holy Father, he fasted for a week and saw a vision, and now he is determined one day to set out again, but this time go further afield. He wants to lead a pilgrimage to Jerusalem.

'When Edward is a man and comes to his own estate, when he is sixteen, I will go,' he says.

I smile. 'All right,' I agree easily. 'That's years and years away. Ten years from now.'

'It seems a long time now,' Anthony warns me. 'But the years will go quickly.'

'Is this the wisdom of the travelling pilgrim?' I laugh at him.

'It is,' he agrees. 'Before you know it, he will be a young man standing taller than you, and we will have to consider what sort of a king we have made. He will be Edward V and he will inherit a throne peacefully, please God, and continue the royal House of York without challenge.'

For no reason at all, I shiver.

'What is it?'

'Nothing, I don't know. A shiver of cold: nothing. I know he will make a wonderful king. He's a real York and a real son of the house of Rivers. There could be no better start for a boy.'

## DECEMBER 1476

Christmas comes, and my darling son Prince Edward comes home to Westminster for the feast. Everyone marvels at how he has grown. He is seven next year, and a straight-standing, handsome, fair-headed boy with a quickness of understanding and an education that is all from Anthony, and the promise of good looks and charm that is all his father's.

Anthony brings both my sons to me, Richard Grey and Prince Edward, for my blessing and then releases them to find their brothers and sisters.

'I miss you all three. So much,' I say.

'And I you,' he says, smiling at me. 'But you look well, Elizabeth.'

I make a face. 'For a woman who is sick every morning.'

He is delighted. 'You are expecting a baby again?'

'Again, and given the sickness, they all think it will be a boy.'

'Edward must be delighted.'

'I assume so. He shows his delight by flirting with every woman within a hundred miles.'

Anthony laughs. 'That's Edward.'

My brother is happy. I can tell at once, from the easy set of his shoulders and the relaxed lines around his eyes. 'And what about you? Do you still like Ludlow?'

'Young Edward and Richard and I have things just as we want

them,' he says. 'We are a court devoted to scholarship, chivalry, jousting and hunting. It is a perfect life for all three of us.'

'He studies?'

'As I report to you. He is a clever boy and a thoughtful one.'

'And you don't let him take risks hunting?'

He grins at me. 'Of course I do! Did you want me to raise a coward for Edward's throne? He has to test his courage in the hunting field and in the jousting arena. He has to know fear and look it in the face and ride towards it. He has to be a brave king, not a fearful one. I would serve you both very ill if I steered him away from any risk and taught him to fear danger.'

'I know, I know,' I say. 'It is just that he is so precious . . .'

'We are all precious,' Anthony declares. 'And we all have to live a life with risk. I am teaching him to ride any horse in the stable and to face a fight without a tremble. That will keep him safer than trying to keep him on safe horses and away from the jousting arena. Now, to far more important things. What have you got me for Christmas? And are you going to name your baby for me, if you have a boy?'

The court prepares for the Christmas feast with its usual extravagance and Edward orders new clothes for all the children and ourselves as part of the pageant which the world expects from England's handsome royal family. I spend some time every day with the little Prince Edward. I love to sit beside him when he sleeps, and listen to his prayers as he goes to bed, and summon him to my rooms for breakfast every day. He is a serious little boy, thoughtful, and he offers to read to me in Latin, Greek or French until I have to confess that his learning far surpasses my own.

He is patient with his little brother Richard, who idolises him, following him everywhere at a determined trot, and he is tender to baby Anne, hanging over her cradle and marvelling at her little hands. Every day we compose a play or a masque, every day we go hunting, every day we have a great ceremonial dinner and dancing and an entertainment. People say that the Yorks have an enchanted court, an enchanted life, and I cannot deny it.

There is only one thing which casts a shadow on the days before Christmas: George the Duke of Dissatisfaction.

'I do think your brother grows more peculiar every day,' I complain to Edward when he comes to my rooms in Whitehall Palace to escort me to dinner.

'Which one?' he asks lazily. 'For you know I can do nothing right in the eyes of either. You would think they would be glad to have a York on the throne and peace in Christendom, and one of the finest Christmas feasts we have ever arranged; but no: Richard is leaving court to go back north as soon as the feast is over, to demonstrate his outrage that we are not slogging away in a battle with the French, and George is simply bad-tempered.'

'It is George's bad temper which is troubling me.'

'Why, what has he done now?' he asks.

'He has told his server that he will not eat anything sent to him from our table,' I say. 'He has told him he will only eat privately, in his own room, after the rest of us have had dinner. When we send him a dish down the room to him as a gesture of courtesy for him to taste, he will refuse it. I hear he plans to send it back to us as an open insult. He will sit at the dinner table in company with an empty plate before him. He will not drink either. Edward, you will have to speak to him.'

'If he is refusing drink it is more than an insult, it is a miracle!' Edward smiles. 'George cannot refuse a glass of wine, not if it came from the devil himself.'

'It is no laughing matter if he uses our dinner table to insult us.'

'Yes, I know. I have spoken to him.' He turns to the retinue of lords and ladies who are forming a line behind us. 'Give us a moment,' he says and draws me off to a window bay where he can talk without being overheard. 'Actually, it's worse than you know, Elizabeth. I think he is spreading rumours against us.'

'Saying what?' I ask. George's resentment of his older brother was not satisfied by his failed rebellion and forgiveness. I had hoped he would settle to being one of the two greatest dukes in England. I had thought he would be happy with his wife, the whey-faced Isabel, and her enormous fortune, even though he lost control of his sister-in-law Anne when she married Richard. But like any mean, ambitious man, he counts his losses more than his gains. He begrudged Richard his wife, little Anne Neville. He begrudged Richard the fortune that she brought him. He cannot forgive Edward for giving Richard permission to marry her, and he watches every grant that Edward makes to my family and kinsmen, every acre of land Edward gives to Richard. You would think England was a tiny field that he feared losing a row of peas, such is his anxious suspicion. 'What can he say against us? You have been ceaselessly generous to him.'

'He is saying again that my mother betrayed my father and that I am a bastard,' he says, his mouth to my ear.

'For shame! That old story!' I exclaim.

'And he is claiming that he made an agreement with Warwick and Margaret of Anjou which said that at Henry's death he should be king. So that he is rightful king now, as Henry's appointed heir.'

'But he killed Henry himself!' I exclaim.

'Hush, hush. Nothing of that.'

I shake my head and the veil from my headdress dances in my agitation. 'No. You must not be mealy-mouthed about that now, not between the two of us in private. You said at the time that his heart gave out, and that was good enough for everyone. But George cannot pretend that he is the man's chosen and named heir when he was his murderer.'

'He says worse,' my husband warns.

'Of me?' I guess.

He nods. 'He says that you—' He breaks off and looks round

to see that no one is in earshot. 'He says that you are a w . . .' His voice is so low he cannot speak the word.

I shrug my shoulders. 'A witch?'

He nods.

'He is not the first to say so. I suppose he will not be the last. While you are King of England he cannot hurt me.'

'I don't like it being said about you. Not just for your reputation but for your safety. It is a dangerous name to attach to a woman, whoever her husband might be. And besides, everyone always goes on to say that our marriage was an enchantment. And that leads them to say that there was no true marriage at all.'

I give a little hiss like an angry cat. I care less about my own reputation: my mother taught me that a powerful woman will always attract slander; but those who say that I am not truly married would make bastards of my sons. This is to disinherit them. 'You will have to silence him.'

'I have spoken to him, I have warned him. But I imagine that, despite it all, he is making a cause against me. He has followers, more every day, and I think he may be in touch with Louis of France.'

'We have a peace treaty with King Louis.'

'Doesn't stop him meddling. I think nothing will ever stop him meddling. And George is fool enough to take his money and cause me trouble.'

I look around. The court is waiting for us. 'We have to go into dinner,' I say. 'What are you going to do?'

'I shall speak to him again. But in the meantime, don't send him any dishes from our table. I don't want him making a show of refusing them.'

I shake my head. 'Dishes go to favourites,' I say. 'He is no favourite of mine.'

The King laughs and kisses my hand. 'Don't turn him into a toad either, my little witch,' he says in a whisper.

'I don't need to. He's that in his heart already.'

Edward does not tell me what he says to this, his most difficult brother, and not for the first time I wish my mother was still with me: I need her advice. After a few weeks of sulking and refusing to dine with us, stalking around the palace as if he were afraid to sit down, drawing away from me as if my very gaze might turn him to stone, George announces that Isabel, in the last months of her pregnancy, is ill: sickened by the air, he announces pointedly, and he is taking her from court.

'Perhaps it's for the best,' my brother Anthony says to me hopefully one morning as we walk back to my rooms after mass. My ladies are behind me, except for Lady Margaret Stanley who is still on her knees in chapel, bless her. She prays like a woman who has sinned against the Holy Ghost itself, but I know for a fact that she is innocent of everything. She does not even bed her husband; I think she is quite without desire. My guess is that nothing stirs that celibate Lancastrian heart but ambition.

'He has everyone asking what Edward has done to anger him, and he is insulting to both of you. He's got people talking about whether Prince Edward resembles his father, and how anyone can know if he is your true-born son, since he was born in sanctuary without proper witnesses. I asked Edward for permission to challenge him to a joust. He cannot be allowed to speak of you as he does. I want to defend your name.'

'What did Edward say?'

'He said better to ignore him than give any support to his lies by challenging them. But I don't like it. And he abuses you and our family, our mother too.'

'It's nothing to what he does to his own,' I remark. 'He calls our mother a witch, but his own he names as a whore. He is not a man who is afraid to slander. I am surprised his mother does not order his silence.'

'I think she has done so, and Edward has reprimanded him in private, but nothing will stop him. He is beside himself with spite.'

'At least if he is away from court he will not be forever whispering in corners and refusing to dance.'

'As long as he does not plot against us. Once he is far away in his house surrounded by his retainers, Edward will know nothing of who he is summoning, till he has men in the field again, and Edward has a rebellion on his hands.'

'Oh, Edward will know,' I say shrewdly. 'He will have men watching George. Even I have a paid servant in his house. Edward will have dozens. I will know what he is doing before he does it.'

'Who is your man?' Anthony asks.

I smile. 'It does not have to be a man to watch and understand and report. I have a woman in his household and she tells me everything.'

My spy, Ankarette, sends me weekly reports, and she tells me that George is indeed receiving letters from France, our enemy. Then just before Christmas Day she writes of the failing health of his wife, Isabel. The little duchess gives birth to another child, her fourth, but does not recover her strength, and only weeks after her confinement she gives up the struggle to live, turns her face away from the world and dies.

I pray for her soul with genuine feeling. She was a terribly unlucky girl. Her father Warwick adored her and thought he would make her a duchess, and then thought he could make her husband a king. But instead of a handsome York king, her husband was a sulky younger son who turned his coat not once but twice. After she lost her first baby in the wild seas in the witches' wind off Calais she had two more children, Margaret and Edward. Now they will have to manage without her. Margaret is a bright clever girl, but Edward is slow in understanding, perhaps even simple. God help both of them with George as their only parent. I send a letter expressing my sorrow and the court wears mourning for her – the daughter of a great earl, and the wife of a royal duke.

## JANUARY 1477

We mourn for her, but George has barely buried her, barely blown out the candles, before he comes strutting back to court, full of plans for a new wife, and this time he is aiming high. Charles of Burgundy, the husband of our Margaret of York, has died in battle and left his daughter Mary a duchess and heiress of one of the wealthiest duchies in Christendom.

Margaret, always a Yorkist, and fatally blind to the faults of her family, suggests that her brother George, so fortunately free, should marry her stepdaughter – thereby consulting the needs of her York brother more than her Burgundy ward; or so I think. George, of course, is at once on fire with ambition. He announces to Edward that he will take either the Duchess of Burgundy or the Princess of Scotland.

'Impossible,' Edward says. 'He is faithless enough when he has a duke's income paid by me. If he were as rich as a prince with an independent fortune, none of us would be safe. Think of the trouble he would cause for us in Scotland! Dear God, think of him bullying our sister Margaret in Burgundy! She's only just widowed, her stepdaughter newly orphaned. I would as willingly send a wolf to the two of them as George.'

## SPRING 1477

George broods over his brother's refusal and then we hear outrageous news, news so extraordinary that we start by thinking it must be an exaggerated rumour: it cannot be true. George suddenly declares that Isabel died not of childbed fever; but of poisoning, and bundles the poisoner into jail.

'Never!' I exclaim to Edward. 'Has he run mad? Who would have hurt Isabel? Who has he arrested? Why?'

'It is worse than arrest,' he says. He looks quite stunned by the letter in his hand. 'He must be crazed. He has rushed this woman servant before a jury and ordered them to find her guilty of murder, and he has had her beheaded. She is dead already. Dead on George's word, as if there were no law of the land. As if he were a greater power than the law, greater than the King. He is ruling my kingdom as if I had allowed tyranny.'

'Who is she? Who was she?' I demand. 'The poor serving girl?'

'"AnkaretteTwynho",' he says, reading the name from the letter of complaint. 'The jury says he threatened them with violence and made them bring in a verdict of guilty, though there was no evidence against her but his oath. They say they did not dare refuse him, and that he forced them to send an innocent woman to her death. He accused her of poison and witchcraft, and of serving a great witch.' He raises his eyes from the letter and sees my white face. 'A great witch? Do you know anything of this, Elizabeth?'

'She was my spy in his household,' I confess quickly. 'But that is all. I had no need to poison poor little Isabel. What would I gain from it? And witchcraft is nonsense. Why would I cast a spell on her? I didn't like her, nor her sister, but I wouldn't ill-wish them.'

He nods. 'I know. Of course you didn't have Isabel poisoned. But did George know that the woman he accused was in your pay?'

'Perhaps. Perhaps. Why else would he accuse her? What else could she have done to offend him? Does he mean to warn me? To threaten us?'

Edward throws down the letter on the table. 'God knows! What does he hope to gain by murdering a servant woman but to cause more trouble and gossip? I shall have to act on this, Elizabeth. I can't let it go.'

'What will you do?'

'He has a little group of his own advisors: dangerous, dissatisfied men. One of them is certainly a practising fortune-teller, if not worse. I shall arrest them. I shall bring them to trial. I shall do to his men what he has done to your servant. It can serve as a warning for him. He cannot challenge us or our servants without risk to himself. I only hope he has the sense to see it.'

I nod. 'They cannot hurt us?' I ask. 'These men?'

'Only if you believe, as George seems to think, that they can cast a spell against us.'

I smile in the hope of hiding my fear. Of course I believe that they can cast a spell against us. Of course I fear that they have already done so.

I am right to be troubled. Edward arrests the notorious sorcerer Thomas Burdett, and two others, and they are put to question and a farrago of stories of black arts and threats and enchantments starts to spill out.

My brother Anthony finds me leaning my heavy belly on the river wall and staring into the water at Whitehall Palace on a sunny May afternoon. Behind me, in the gardens, the children are playing a game of bat and ball. By the outraged cries of cheating, I guess that my son Edward is losing and taking advantage of his status as Prince of Wales to change the score. 'What are you doing here?' Anthony asks.

'I am wishing this river was a moat that could keep me and mine safe from enemies without.'

'Does Melusina come when you call her from the waters of the Thames?' he asks with a sceptical smile.

'If she did, I would have her hang George, Duke of Clarence alongside his wizard. And I would have her do that to them both at once, without more words.'

'You don't believe that the man could hurt you from ill-wishing?' he demands. 'He is no wizard. There is no such thing. It is a fairy tale to frighten children, Elizabeth.' He glances back at my children, who are appealing to Elizabeth for a ruling on a dropped catch.

'George believes him. He paid him good money to foretell the King's death and then some more to bring it about by overlooking. George hired this wizard to destroy us. Already his spells are in the air, in the earth, even in the water.'

'Oh nonsense. He is no more a wizard than you are a witch.'

'I don't claim to be a witch,' I say quietly. 'But I have Melusina's inheritance. I am her heir. You know what I mean: I have her gift, just as Mother did. Just as my daughter Elizabeth has. The world sings to me and I hear the song. Things come to me; my wishes come true. Dreams speak to me. I see signs and portents. And sometimes I know what will happen in the future. I have the Sight.'

'These could all be revelations from God,' he says firmly. 'This is the power of prayer. All the rest is wishful thinking. And women's nonsense.'

I smile. 'I think they are from God. I never doubt it. But God speaks to me through the river.'

'You are a heretic and a pagan,' he says with brotherly scorn. 'Melusina is a fairy story; but God and His Son are your avowed faith. For heaven's sake, you have founded religious houses and chantries and schools in His name. Your love of rivers and streams is a superstition, learned from our mother, like that of ancient pagans. You can't puddle them up into a religion of your own, and then frighten yourself with devils of your own devising.'

'Of course, brother,' I say with my eyes cast down. 'You are a nobleman of learning: I am sure you know best.'

'Stop!' he throws up a hand, laughing. 'Stop. You need not think I am going to try to debate with you. You have your own theology, I know. Part fairy tale and part Bible and all nonsense. Please, for all of our sakes, make it a secret religion. Keep it to yourself. And don't frighten yourself with imaginary enemies.'

'But I do dream true.'

'If you say so.'

'Anthony, my whole life is a proof of magic, that I can foresee.'

'Name one thing.'

'Did I not marry the King of England?'

'Did I not see you stand out in the road like the strumpet you are?'

I exclaim against his crow of laughter. 'It was not like that! It was not like that! And besides, my ring came to me from the river!'

He takes my hands and kisses them both. 'It is all nonsense,' he says gently. 'There is no Melusina but an old, half-forgotten story that Mother used to tell us at bedtime. There is no enchantment but Mother encouraging you with play. You have no powers. There is nothing but what we can do as sinners under the will of God. And Thomas Burdett has no powers but ill-will and a huckster's promise.'

I smile at him and I don't argue. But in my heart I know that there is more.

'How did the story of Melusina end?' my little boy Edward asks me that night when I am listening to his bedtime prayers. He is sharing a room with his three-year-old brother Richard and both boys look at me hopefully, wanting a story to delay their bedtime.

'Why would you ask?' I sit on a chair beside their fire and draw a footstool towards me so I can put up my feet to rest. I can feel the new baby stir in my body. I am six months into my time, and what feels like a lifetime yet to go.

'I heard My Lord Uncle Anthony speak to you of her today,' Edward says. 'What happened after she came out of the water and married the knight?'

'It ends sadly,' I say. I gesture to them that they must get into bed, and they obey me but two pairs of unblinking, bright eyes watch me over their covers. 'The stories differ. Some people say that a curious traveller came to their house and spied on her and saw her becoming a fish in her bath. Some say her husband broke his word that she was free to swim alone, and spied on her and saw her become fish again.'

'But why would he mind? Edward asks sensibly. 'Since she was half fish when he met her?'

'Ah, he thought he could change her to be the woman he wanted,' I say. 'Sometimes a man likes a woman, but then hopes he can change her. Perhaps he was like that.'

'Is there any fighting in this story?' Richard asks sleepily as his head droops to the pillow.

'No, none,' I say. I kiss Edward's forehead and then I go to the other bed and kiss Richard. They both still smell like babies, of soap and warm skin. Their hair is soft and smells of fresh air.

'So what happens when he knows she is half fish?' Edward whispers as I go to the door.

'She takes the children and leaves him,' I say. 'And they never meet again.'

I blow out a branch of candles but leave the other burning. The firelight in the little grate makes the room warm and cosy.

'That's really sad,' Edward says mournfully. 'Poor man, that he could not see his children or his wife again.'

'It is sad,' I say. 'But it is just a story. Perhaps there is another ending that people forgot to tell. Perhaps she forgave him and went back to him. Perhaps he turned into a fish for love and swam after her.'

'Yes.' A happy boy, he is easily comforted. 'Goodnight, Mama.'

'Good night and God bless you both.'

*When he saw her, the water lapping on her scales, head down in the bath he had built especially for her, thinking that she would like to wash – not to revert to fish – he had that instant revulsion that some men feel when they understand, perhaps for the first time, that a woman is truly 'other'. She is not a boy though she is weak like a boy, nor a fool though he has seen her tremble with feeling like a fool. She is not a villain in her capacity to hold a grudge, nor a saint in her flashes of generosity. She is not any of these male qualities. She is a woman. A thing quite different to a man. What he saw was a half-fish, but what frightened him to his soul was the being which was a woman.*

George's malice to his brother becomes horribly apparent in the days of the trial of Burdett and his conspirators. When they hunt for evidence the plot unravels to reveal a tangle of dark promises and threats, recipes for poisoned capes, a sachet of ground glass, and outright curses. In Burdett's papers they find not only a chart of days drawn up to foretell Edward's death, but a set of spells designed to kill him. When Edward shows them to me I cannot stop myself shivering. I tremble as if I had an ague. Whether they can cause death or not, I know that these ancient drawings on dark paper have a malevolent power. 'They make me cold,' I say. 'They feel so cold and damp. They feel evil.'

'Certainly they are evil evidence,' Edward says grimly. 'I would not have dreamed that George could have gone so far against me. I would have given the world for him to live at peace with us, or at the very least to keep this quiet. But he hired such incompetent men that now everyone knows that my own brother was conspiring against me. Burdett will be found guilty and he will hang for his crime. But it is bound to come out that George directly commissioned him. George is guilty of treason too. But I cannot put my own brother on trial!'

'Why not?' I ask sharply. I am seated on a low cushioned stool by the fire in my bedroom, wearing only my fur-lined night cape. We are on our way to our separate beds, but Edward cannot keep his trouble to himself any longer. Burdett's slimy spells may not have hurt his health, but they have darkened his spirit. 'Why can you not put George on trial and send him to a traitor's death? He deserves it.'

'Because I love him,' he says simply. 'As much as you do your brother Anthony. I cannot send him to the scaffold. He is my little brother. He has been at my side in battle. He is my kinsman. He is my mother's favourite. He is our George.'

'He has been on the other side in battle too,' I remind him. 'He has been a traitor to you and your family more than once already. He would have seen you dead if he and Warwick had caught you and you had not escaped. He named me as a witch, he had my mother arrested, he stood by and watched as they killed my father and my brother John. He lets neither justice nor family feeling block his way. Why should you?'

Edward, seated in the chair on the other side of the fire, leans forward. His face in the flickering light looks old. For the first time I see the weight of years and kingship on him. 'I know. I know. I should be harder on him, but I cannot. He is my mother's pet, he is our little golden boy. I cannot believe he is so—'

'Vicious,' I give him the word. 'Your little pet has become vicious. He is a grown dog now, not a sweet puppy. And he has a bad nature that has been spoiled from birth. You will have to deal with him, Edward, mark my words. When you treat him with kindness he repays you with plots.'

'Perhaps,' he says and sighs. 'Perhaps he will learn.'

'He will not learn,' I promise. 'You will only be safe from him when he is dead. You will have to do it, Edward. You can only choose the when and the where.'

He gets up and stretches and goes to the bed. 'Let me see you into your bed, before I go to my own rooms. I shall be glad when the baby is born and we can sleep together again.'

'In a minute,' I reply. I lean forward and look into the embers. I am the heiress to a water goddess, I never see well in flames, but in the gleam of the ashes I can make out George's petulant face and something behind him, a tall building, dark as a fingerpost – the Tower. It is always a dark building for me, a place of death. I shrug my shoulders. Perhaps it means nothing.

I rise up and go to bed and huddle under the covers and Edward takes my hands to kiss me goodnight.

'Why, you're chilled,' he says in surprise. 'I thought the fire was warm enough.'

'I hate that place,' I say at random.

'What place?'

'The Tower of London. I hate it.'

George's familiar, the traitor Burdett, protests his innocence on the scaffold at Tyburn before a cat-calling crowd and is hanged anyway; but George, learning nothing from the death of his man, rides in a fury from London and marches into the king's council meeting at Windsor Castle and repeats the speech, shouting it in Edward's face.

'Never!' I say to Anthony. I am quite scandalised.

'He did! He did!' Anthony is choking with laughter trying to describe the scene to me in my rooms at the castle, my ladies seated in my presence chamber, Anthony and I tucked away in my private rooms for him to tell me the scandalous news. 'There is Edward, standing at least seven feet tall from sheer rage. There is the Privy Council looking quite aghast. You should have seen their faces, Thomas Stanley's mouth open like a fish! Our brother Lionel clutching his cross on his chest in horror. There is George, squaring up to the king and bellowing his script like a mummer. Of course it makes no sense to half of them, who don't realise George is doing the scaffold speech from memory, like a strolling player. So when he says "I am an old man, a wise man . . ." they are all utterly confused.'

I give a little shriek of laughter. 'Anthony! They were not!'

'I swear to you, we none of us knew what was happening except Edward and George. Then George called him a tyrant!'

My laughter abruptly dies. 'In his own council?'

'A tyrant and a murderer.'

'He called him that?'

'Yes. To his face. What was he talking about? The death of Warwick?'

'No,' I say shortly. 'Something worse.'

'Edward of Lancaster? The young Prince?'

I shake my head. 'That was in battle.'

'Not the old king?'

'We never speak of it,' I say. 'Ever.'

'Well, George is going to speak of it now. He looks like a man ready to say anything. You know he is claiming that Edward is not even a son of the House of York? That he is a bastard to Blaybourne the archer? So that George is the true heir?'

I nod. 'Edward will have to silence him. This cannot go on.'

'Edward will have to silence him at once,' he warns me. 'Or George will bring you, and the whole House of York, down. It is as I said. Your house's emblem should not be the white rose but the old sign of eternity.'

'Eternity?' I repeat, hopeful that he is going to say something reassuring at this most dark time in our days.

'Yes, the snake which eats itself. The sons of York will destroy each other, one brother destroying another, uncles devouring nephews, fathers beheading sons. They are a house which has to have blood and they will shed their own if they have no other enemy.'

I put my hands over my belly as if to shield the child from hearing such dark predictions. 'Don't, Anthony. Don't say such things.'

'They are true,' he says grimly. 'The House of York will fall whatever you or I do, for they will eat up themselves.'

I go into my darkened bedchamber for the six weeks of my confinement, leaving the matter still unsettled. Edward cannot think what can be done. A disloyal royal brother is no new thing in England, no new thing for this family, but it is a torment for Edward. 'Leave it till I come out,' I say to him on the very threshold of my chamber. 'Perhaps he will see sense and beg for a pardon. When I come out we can decide.'

'And you be of good courage.' He glances at the shadowy room behind me, warm with a small fire, blank-walled, for they take down all images which might affect the shape of the baby waiting to be born. He leans forward. 'I shall come and visit you,' he whispers.

I smile. Edward always breaks the prohibition that the confinement chamber should be the preserve of women. 'Bring me wine and sweetmeats,' I say, naming the forbidden foods.

'Only if you will kiss me sweetly.'

'Edward, for shame!'

'As soon as you come out then.'

He steps back and formally wishes me well before the court. He bows to me, I curtsey to him, and then I step back and they close the door on the smiling courtiers and I am on my own with the nurses in the small suite of rooms, with nothing to do but wait for the new baby to come.

I have a long hard birth and at the end of it the treasure which is a boy. He is a darling little York boy, with scanty fair hair and eyes as blue as a robin's egg. He is small and light, and when they put him in my arms I have an instant pang of fear because he seems so tiny.

'He will grow,' says the midwife comfortingly. 'Small babies grow fast.'

I smile and touch his miniature hand and see him turn his head and purse his mouth.

I feed him myself for the first ten days, and then we have a big-bodied wet nurse who comes in and gently takes him from me. When I see her seated in the low chair and the steady way she takes him to her breast I am sure that she will care for him. He is christened George, as we promised his faithless uncle, and I am churched and I come out of my darkened confinement apartment into the bright sunshine of the middle of August to find that in my absence the new whore, Elizabeth Shore, is all but queen of my court. The king has given up drunken bouts and womanising in the bath houses of London. He has bought her a house near to the Palace of Whitehall. He dines with her as well as beds her. He enjoys her company and the court knows it.

'She leaves tonight,' I say briskly to Edward when, resplendent in a gown of scarlet embroidered with gold, he comes to my rooms.

'Who?' he asks mildly, taking a glass of wine at my fireside, no husband more innocent. He waves his hand and the servants whisk from the room, knowing well enough that there is trouble brewing.

'The Shore woman,' I say simply. 'Did you not think that

someone would greet me with the gossip as soon as I came out of confinement? The wonder is that they held their tongues for so long. I barely stepped out of the chapel door before they were stumbling over each other in their haste to tell me. Margaret Beaufort was particularly sympathetic.'

He chuckles. 'Forgive me. I did not know that my doings were of such great interest.'

I say nothing to this untruth. I just wait.

'Ah beloved, it was a long time,' he says. 'I know you were in your confinement and then in your time of travail and my heart went out to you, but nonetheless a man needs a warm bed.'

'I am out of confinement now,' I say smartly. 'And you will have an icy bed, it will be a pillow of frost, it will be a counterpane of snow for you; if she is not gone by tomorrow morning.'

He puts out his hand to me and I go to stand beside him. At once, the familiar touch, and the scent of his skin when I bend down to kiss his neck overwhelm me.

'Say you are not angry with me, sweetheart,' he whispers to me, his voice a lulling coo.

'You know I am.'

'Then say you will forgive me.'

'You know I always do.'

'Then say we can go to bed and be happy to be together again. You have done so well to give us another boy. You are such a joy when you are plump and newly returned to me. I desire you so much. Say we can be happy.'

'No. You say something.'

His hand slides up my arm and circles my elbow under the sleeve of my nightgown. As always his touch is as intimate as lovemaking. 'Anything. What would you have me say?'

'Say that she is gone tomorrow.'

'She is,' he says with a sigh. 'But you know, if you would but meet her you would like her. She is a joyful young woman, and well read and merry. She is a good companion. And one of the sweetest-natured girls that I have ever met.'

'She is gone tomorrow,' I repeat, ignoring the charms of Elizabeth Shore, as if I cared one way or another whether she was well read. As if Edward cared. As if he had the capacity to tell the truth about a woman. He chases after women like a randy dog after a bitch on heat. I swear he knows nothing about their reading or their temperament.

'First thing, my darling. First thing.'

# SUMMER 1477

In June Edward has George arrested for treason, and brings him before the council. Only I know what it cost my husband to accuse his brother of plotting his death. His grief and his shame he kept hidden from everyone else. At the meeting of the Privy Council there is no evidence brought; there need be no evidence. The king himself declares that treason has been committed, and no one can argue with the king on such a charge. And indeed, there is not a man there who has not had the sleeve of his jacket held by George in some dark passageway as George whispered his insane suspicions. There is not a man who has not heard the promise of advancement if he will make a party against Edward. There is not a man who has not seen George refuse any food prepared in any kitchen ordered by me, or throw salt over his shoulder before he sits down to dine at our tables, or clench his fist in the sign against witchcraft when I go by. There is not a man who does not know that George has done everything but write his own accusation of treason and sign his own confession. But none of them, even now, know what Edward wants to do about it. They find him guilty of treason but they do not set a punishment. None of them knows how far this king will go against the brother he still loves.

## WINTER 1477

We celebrate Christmas at Westminster but it is an odd Christmas with George, Duke of Clarence missing from his place in the hall, and his mother with a face like thunder. George is in the Tower, charged with treason, well served and well fed, drinking well – I don't doubt – but his namesake is in our nursery, and his true place is with us. I have all my children around me, which gives me all the joy that I could wish: Edward home from Ludlow, Richard riding with him, Thomas returned from a visit to the court of Burgundy, the other children well and strong, the new baby George in the nursery.

In January we celebrate the greatest marriage that England has ever seen when my little Richard is betrothed to the heiress Anne Mowbray. The four-year-old prince and the little girl are lifted onto the table at their wedding feast in their beautiful miniature clothes and they hold hands like a pair of little dolls. They will live apart until they are old enough to marry, but it is a great thing to have secured such a fortune for my boy; he will be the richest prince England has ever seen.

But after Twelfth Night, Edward comes to me and says that his Privy Council are pressing him to make a final decision on the fate of his brother George.

'What do you think?' I ask. I have a sense of foreboding. I

think of my three York boys: another Edward, Richard and George. What if they were to turn against each other as these have done?

'I think I have to go ahead,' he says sadly. 'The punishment for treason is death. I have no choice.'

# SPRING 1478

'You cannot dream of executing him.' His mother sweeps past me into Edward's privy chamber in her haste to speak to her son.

I rise and sweep her the smallest curtsey. 'My Lady Mother,' I say.

'Mother, I don't know what I should do.' Edward goes on one knee for her blessing and she rests her hand on his head absent-mindedly, by rote. There is no tenderness in her for Edward: she is thinking of no one but George. She dips a tiny curtsey to me and turns back to Edward.

'He is your brother. Remember it.'

Edward shrugs, his face miserable.

'Actually, he himself says he is not,' I point out. 'George claims that he is only Edward's half-brother since he says that Edward is a bastard to an English archer on you. He traduces you as well as us. He is generous in his slanders. He does not balk at libelling any of us. He calls me a witch, but he calls you a whore.'

'I don't believe he says any such thing,' she declares roundly.

'Mother, he does,' Edward replies. 'And he insults me and Elizabeth.'

She looks as if this is not such a bad thing.

'He undermines the House of York with his libels,' I say. 'And he employed a wizard to ill-wish the king.'

'He is your brother; you will have to forgive him,' she declares to Edward.

'He is a traitor; he will have to die,' I say simply. 'What else? Is it forgivable to plot the death of the king? Then why shouldn't the defeated House of Lancaster do it then? Why shouldn't the spies from France? Why shouldn't any scum from the highway come with a knife against your finest son?'

'George has been disappointed,' she says urgently to Edward, ignoring me. 'If you had let him marry the Burgundy girl, as he wanted, or let him have the Scots princess, none of this would have happened.'

'I couldn't trust him,' Edward says simply. 'Mother, there is no doubt in my mind that if he had his own kingdom he would invade mine. If he had a fortune he would only use it to raise an army to take my throne.'

'He was born to greatness,' she says.

'He was born a third son,' Edward says, finally roused to tell her the truth. 'He can only rule England if I die, and my son and heir dies too, then my second son Richard, and then my new son George. Is that what you would have preferred, Mother? Do you wish me dead, and my three precious sons too? Do you favour George so much? Do you ill-wish me as his hired wizard did? Will you order ground glass in my meat and foxglove powder in my wine?'

'No,' she says. 'No, of course not. You are your father's son and heir, and you won your throne. Your son must come after you. But George is my son. I feel for him.'

Edward grits his teeth on a hasty reply, and turns to the fireplace and stands in silence, his shoulders hunched. We all wait in silence until the king finally speaks. 'All I can do for you and for him is to let him choose the means of his death. He has to die; but if he wants a French swordsman I will send for one. It doesn't have to be the headsman for him. It can be poison if he wants it; he can take it in private. It can be a dagger on his dinner table and he can do it himself. And it will be in private: there will be no crowd, not even witnesses. It can be in his room in the Tower if he wishes. He can put himself to bed and open his wrists. There can be nobody there but the priest, if he wishes.'

She gasps. She did not expect this. I am very still, watching them both. I did not think Edward would go so far.

He looks at her stricken face. 'Mother, I am sorry for your loss.'

She is white. 'You will forgive him.'

'You can see yourself that I cannot.'

'I command it. I am your mother. You will obey me.'

'I am the king. He cannot oppose me. He must die.'

She rounds on me. 'This is your doing!'

I spread out my hands. 'George has killed himself, Lady Mother. You cannot blame me, nor Edward. He leaves the king no choice. He is a traitor to our rule and a danger to us and our children. You know what must happen to claimants to the throne. This is the way of the House of York.'

She is silent. She walks to the window and leans her head against the thick glass. I look at her back and at the rigid set of her shoulders and wonder what it must be like to know that your son will die. I once promised her the pain of a mother who knows that she has lost her son. I see it now.

'I cannot bear it,' she says, her voice strained with grief. 'This is my son, my dearest son. How can you take him from me? I would rather have died myself than see this day. This is my George, my most precious son. I cannot believe you would send him to his death!'

'I am sorry,' Edward says grimly. 'But I can see no way out of this but his death.'

'He can choose the means?' she confirms. 'You will not expose him to the headsman?'

'He can choose the means but he has to die,' Edward says. 'He has made it a matter of him or me. Of course he will have to die.'

She turns without another word and goes from the room. For a moment, for a moment only, I am sorry for her.

George, the fool, chooses a fool's death.

'He wants to be drowned in a barrel of wine.' Anthony, my brother, comes from the Privy Council meeting to find me rocking in the chair in the nursery, my baby George in my arms, and wishing that it was all over and my little prince's namesake was dead and gone.

'You are trying to be funny?'

'No, I think he is trying to be funny.'

'What does he mean?'

'I suppose what he says. He wants to be drowned in a barrel of wine.'

'He really said that? He really means it?'

'I have come from the Privy Council just now. He wants to drown in wine, if he has to die.'

'A sot's death,' I say, hating the thought of it.

'I suppose that is his joke against his brother.'

I raise my baby to my shoulder and stroke his back as if I would shield him from the cruelty of the world.

'I can think of worse ways to die,' Anthony observes.

'I can think of better. I would rather be hanged than held down in wine.'

He shrugs his shoulders. 'Perhaps he thinks he can make mock of Edward, and of the death sentence. Perhaps he thinks he will force Edward to forgive him rather than execute this drunkard's end. Perhaps he thinks the Church will protest and cause a delay and he will get away.'

'Not this time,' I say. 'His sot's luck has run out, he might as well have a drunkard's end. Where will they do it?'

'In his chamber, at the Tower of London.'

I shudder. 'God forgive him,' I say quietly. 'That is an awful way to die.'

The headsman does it, leaving his axe to one side but wearing his black mask over his face. He is a big man with strong big hands and he takes his apprentice with him. The two of them roll a barrel of malmsey wine into George's room and George the fool makes a joke of it and laughs with his mouth open wide as if already gasping for air, as his face bleaches white with fear.

They lever open the lid and find a box for George to stand on so he can lean over the top of the barrel and see his frightened face reflected back at him in the slopping surface of the wine. The smell of it fills the room. He mutters 'Amen' to the prayers of the priest as if he does not know what he is hearing.

He puts his head down to the ruby surface of the wine as if he were putting his head on the block, and he sucks great gulps of it as if he would drink the danger away, then he thrusts out his hands in the signal of assent, and the two men take his head and, holding him by the hair and the collar, plunge him down below the surface, half lifting him from the floor so his legs kick as if he is swimming, and the wine is slopped on the floor as he writhes, trying to escape. The wine cascades around their feet as the air bubbles out of him in great retching whoops. The priest steps back from the red puddle and goes on reading the last rites, his voice steady and reverent, while the two executioners hold the flailing head of the most stupid son of York deep into the barrel until his feet hang slack and there are no more bubbles of air, and the room smells like an old taproom.

That night at midnight I get up from my bed in the Palace of Westminster and go to my dressing room. On the top of a long cupboard for my furs is a little box with my private things. I open it. Inside is an old locket of silver so tarnished with age that is black as ebony. I open the catch, and there is the old scrap of paper, torn from the bottom of my father's letter. On it, written in blood, my blood, is the name George, Duke of Clarence. I screw the paper up in my fingers and I throw it on the embers of the fire and watch it twist in the heat of the ashes and then suddenly spring into flame.

'So go,' I say as George's name goes up in smoke and my curse on him is completed. 'But let you be the last York who dies in the Tower of London. Let it end here, as I promised my mother it would. Let it finish here.'

I wish I had remembered, as she taught me, that it is easier to unleash evil than call it back again. Any fool can blow up a wind, but who can know where it will blow or when it will stop?

## SUMMER 1478

I have my boy Edward, my son Sir Richard Grey and my brother Anthony come to my private apartments for me to say goodbye to them. I cannot bear to let them go from me in public. I don't want to be seen to weep as they leave. I bend to hold Edward close, as if I would never be parted from him, and he looks at me with his warm brown eyes, and holds my face in his little hands and says, 'Don't cry, Mama. There is nothing to cry about. I shall come again next Christmas. And you can visit me at Ludlow you know.'

'I know,' I say.

'And if you bring George, then I will teach him how to ride,' he promises me. 'And you can put young Richard into my keeping, you know.'

'I know.' I try to speak clearly but the tears are in my voice.

Richard hugs me around the waist. He is as tall as me now, a young man.'I will care for him,' he says. 'You must visit us. Bring all my brothers and sisters. Come for the summer.'

'I will, I will,' I say and turn to my brother Anthony.

'Trust us to take care of ourselves,' he says, before I can even start the list of things that make me fearful. 'And I will bring him safe home to you next year. And I will not leave him, not even for Jerusalem. I will not leave him till he commands me to go. All right?'

I nod, blinking away my tears. There is something that troubles me at the thought of Edward letting Anthony go from him. It is as if a shadow has fallen on us. 'I don't know why, I just always fear for him so much, whenever I have to say goodbye to the three of you. I can hardly bear to let him go.'

'I will guard him with my life,' Anthony promises. 'He is as dear to me as life itself. No harm will come to him while he is in my keeping. You have my word.'

He bows and turns to the door. Edward, beside him, does a mirror copy of the graceful gesture. Richard my son puts his fist to his chest in the salute that means 'I love you'.

'Be happy,' Anthony says. 'I have your boy safe.'

Then they are gone from me.

## SPRING 1479

My boy George, always a slight baby, starts to fail before he reaches his second birthday. The physicians know nothing, the ladies of the nursery can suggest only gruel and milk, to be fed hourly. We try it, but he grows no stronger.

Elizabeth, his thirteen-year-old sister, plays with him every day, takes his little hands and helps him to walk on his thin legs, makes up a story for every mouthful of food that he eats. But even she sees that he is not thriving. He does not grow and his little arms and legs are like sticks.

'Can we get a physician from Spain?' I ask Edward. 'Anthony always says that the Moors have the wisest men.'

His face is weary with worry and sorrow for this, a precious son. 'You can get anyone you like from anywhere,' he says. 'But Elizabeth, my love, find your courage. He is a frail little boy, and he was a tiny baby. You have done well to keep him with us this far.'

'Don't say that,' I say quickly, shaking my head. 'He will get better. The spring will come and then the summer. He will get better in the summer for sure.'

I spend hours in the nursery with my little boy on my lap, dripping gruel into his little mouth, holding his chest to my ear so I can hear the faint patter of his heart.

They tell me that we are blessed to have two strong sons: the succession to the throne of York is surely secure. I say nothing in reply to these fools. I am not nursing him for the sake of York, I am nursing him for love. I do not want him to thrive to be a prince. I want him to thrive to be a strong boy.

This is my baby boy. I cannot bear to lose him as I lost his sister. I cannot bear that he should die in my arms as she died in my mother's arms and they went away together. I haunt the nursery during the day and even at night I come to watch him sleep, and I am sure he is growing no stronger.

He is asleep on my lap one day in March, and I am rocking him in the chair and humming, without knowing I am doing so, a little song: a Burgundian lullaby half-remembered from my childhood.

The song ends, and there is silence. I still the rocking of the chair and everything is quiet. I put my ear to his little chest to hear the beating of his heart; and I cannot hear the beating of his heart. I put my cheek to his nose, his mouth to feel the warmth of his breath. There is no flutter of breath. He is still warm and soft in my arms, warm and soft as a little bird. But my George has gone. I have lost my son.

I hear the sound of the lullaby again, softly, as softly as the wind, and I know that Melusina is rocking him now, and my boy George has gone. I have lost my son.

They tell me that I still have my boy Edward, that I am lucky in that my handsome boy of eight years old is so strong and grows so well. They tell me to be glad of Richard his five-year-old brother. I smile, for I am glad of both of my boys. But that makes no difference to my loss of George, my little George with his blue eyes and his tuft of blond hair.

Five months later, I am in confinement awaiting the birth of another child. I don't expect a boy, I don't imagine that one child can replace another. But little Katherine comes at just the right time to comfort us, and there is a York princess in the cradle again and the York nursery is busy as usual. A year later and I have another baby, my little girl Bridget.

'I think this will be our last,' I say regretfully to Edward when I come out of confinement.

I had been afraid that he would note that I was growing older. But instead he smiles at me as if we were still young lovers, and kisses my hand. 'No man could have asked for more,' he says sweetly to me. 'And no queen has ever laboured harder. You have given me a great family, my love. And I am glad this will be our last.'

'You don't want another boy?'

He shakes his head. 'I want to take you for pleasure, and hold you in my arms for desire. I want you to know that it is your kiss that I want, not another heir to the throne. You can know that I love you, quite for yourself, when I come to your bed, and not as the York's brood mare.'

I tilt back my head and look at him under my eyelashes. 'You think to bed me for love and not for children? Isn't that sin?'

His arm comes around my waist and his palm cups my breast. 'I shall make sure that it feels richly sinful,' he promises me.

# APRIL 1483

The weather is cold and unseasonal and the rivers run high. We are at Westminster for the feast of Easter and I look from my window at the fullness and the fast flow of the river and think of my son Edward, beyond the great waters of the Severn River, far away from me. It is as if England is a country of intersecting waterways, lakes and streams and rivers. Melusina must be everywhere this is a country made in her element.

My husband Edward, a man of the land, has a whim to go fishing and takes himself out for the day and comes home soaking wet and merry. He insists that we eat the salmon that he caught in the river for our dinner, and it is borne into the dining room at shoulder-height with a fanfare: a royal catch.

That night he is feverish and I scold him for getting wet and cold, as if he were still a boy and could take such risks with his health. The next day he is worse and he gets up for a little while but then goes back to bed: he is too tired. The next day the physician says that he should be bled and Edward swears that they may not touch him. I tell the doctors that it shall be as the king insists; but I go to his room when he is sleeping and I look at his flushed face to reassure myself that this is nothing more than a passing illness. This is not the plague or a serious fever. He is a strong man in good health. He can take a chill and throw it off within a week.

He gets no better. And now he starts to complain of gripping pains in the belly and a terrible flush of heat. Within a week the court is in fear and I am in a state of silent terror. The doctors are useless: they don't even know what is wrong with him, they don't know what has caused his fever, they don't know what will cure it. He can keep nothing down. He vomits everything he eats, and he is fighting the pain in his belly as if it were a new war. I keep a vigil in his room, my daughter Elizabeth beside me, nursing him with two wise women that I trust. Hastings, the friend of his boyhood and his partner in every enterprise including the stupid, stupid fishing trip, keeps his vigil in the outer room. The Shore whore has taken to living on her knees at the altar in Westminster Abbey, they tell me, in an agony of fear for the man she loves.

'Let me see him,' William Hastings implores me.

I turn a cold face to him. 'No. He is sick. He needs no companion for whoring or drinking or gambling. So he has no need of you. His health has been ruined by you, and all them like you. I will nurse him to health now and, if I have my way, when he is well he will not see you again.'

'Let me see him,' he says. He does not even defend himself against my anger. 'All I want is to see him. I can't bear not to see him.'

'Wait like a dog out here,' I say cruelly. 'Or go back to the Shore whore and tell her that she can service you now, for the king has finished with you both.'

'I'll wait,' he says. 'He will ask for me. He will want to see me. He knows I am here waiting to see him. He knows I am out here.'

I walk past him to the king's bedchamber and I close the door so he cannot even glimpse the man he loves, fighting for breath in the big four-poster bed.

Edward looks up when I come in. 'Elizabeth.'

I go to him and hold his hand. 'Yes, love.'

'You remember I came home to you and told you I had been afraid?'

'I remember.'

'I am afraid again.'

'You will get well,' I whisper urgently. 'You will get well, my husband.'

He nods and his eyes close for a moment. 'Is Hastings outside?'

'No,' I say.

He smiles. 'I want to see him.'

'Not now,' I say. I stroke his head. It is burning hot. I take up a towel and soak it with lavender water and gently bathe his face. 'You are not strong enough to see anyone now.'

'Elizabeth, fetch him, and fetch everyone of my Privy Council who is in the palace. Send for Richard my brother.'

For a moment I think I have caught his sickness, as my belly turns over with such a pain; then I realise this is fear. 'You don't need to see them, Edward. All you need to do is rest and grow strong.'

'Fetch them,' he says.

I turn and say a sharp word to the nurse and she runs to the door and tells the guard. At once, the message goes out all through the court that the king has summoned his advisors, and everyone knows that he must be dying. I go to the window and stand with my back to the view of the river. I don't want to see the water, I don't want to see the glimmer of a mermaid's tail, I don't want to hear Melusina singing to warn of a death. The lords file into the room, Stanley, Norfolk, Hastings, Cardinal Thomas Bourchier, my brothers, my cousins, my brothers-in-law, half a dozen others: all the great men of the kingdom, men who have been with my husband from the days of his earliest challenge, or men like Stanley who are always perfectly aligned to the winning side. I look at them stony-faced, and they bow to me: grim-faced.

The women have propped Edward up so he can see the council. Hastings' eyes are filled with tears, his face twisted with pain. Edward reaches out a hand to him and they grip each other as if Hastings would hold him to life.

'I fear I have not long,' Edward says. His voice is a rasping whisper.

'No,' whispers Hastings. 'Don't say it. No.'

Edward turns his head and speaks to them all. 'I leave a young son. I had hoped to see him grow to a man. I had hoped to leave you with a man for king. Instead I have to trust you to care for my boy.'

I have my fist to my mouth to stop myself from crying out. 'No,' I say.

'Hastings,' Edward says.

'Lord.'

'And all of you, and Elizabeth my queen.'

I step to his bedside and he takes my hand in his, joins it with Hastings', as if he were making us wed. 'You have to work together. All of you have to forget your enmities, your rivalries, your hatreds. You all have scores to settle, you all have wrongs you can't forget. But you have to forget. You have to be as one to keep my son safe and see him to the throne. I ask you this, I demand this of you, from my deathbed. Will you do it?'

I think of all the years that I have hated Hastings, Edward's dearest friend and companion, the partner for all his drinking and whoring bouts, the friend at his side in battle. I remember how Sir William Hastings, from the very first moment, despised and looked down on me from his high horse when I stood at the roadside, how he opposed the rise of my family and always and again urged the king to listen to other advisors and employ other friends. I see him look at me and, even though tears are pouring down his face, his eyes are hard. He thinks I stood at the roadside and cast a spell on a young boy for his ruin. He will never understand what happened that day between a young man and a young woman. There was a magic: and the name of it was love.

'I will work with Hastings for my son's safety,' I say. 'I will work with all of you and forget all wrongs, to put my son safely on the throne.'

'I too,' says Hastings, and then they all say, one after another. 'And I.'

'And I'

'And I.'

'My brother Richard is to be his guardian,' Edward says. I flinch and would pull my hand away; but Hastings has it in a tight grip. 'As you wish, Sire,' he says, looking hard at me. He knows that I resent Richard, and the power of the north that he can command.

'Anthony, my brother,' I say in a whisper, prompting the king.

'No,' Edward says stubbornly. 'Richard, Duke of Gloucester is to be his guardian and Protector of the Realm till Prince Edward takes his throne.'

'No,' I whisper. If I could only get the king alone I could tell him that, with Anthony as Protector, we Rivers could hold the country safe. I don't want my power threatened by Richard. I want my son surrounded by my family. I don't want any one of the York affinity in the new government that I will make around my son. I want this to be a Rivers boy on England's throne.

'Do you so swear?' Edward says.

'I do,' they all say.

Hastings looks at me. 'Do you swear?' he asks. 'Do you swear that, just as we promise to put your son on the throne, you promise to accept Richard, Duke of Gloucester as Protector?'

Of course I do not. Richard is no friend of mine, and he commands half of England already. Why would I trust him to put my son on the throne, when he is a York prince himself? Why would he not take the chance to seize the throne for himself? And he has a son, a boy by little Anne Neville, a boy who could be Prince of Wales in place of my own prince. Why would Richard, who has fought half a dozen battles for Edward, not fight one more for himself?

Edward's face is grey with fatigue. 'Swear it, Elizabeth,' he whispers. 'For my sake. For Edward's sake.'

'Do you think it will make Edward safe?'

He nods. 'It is the only way. He will be safe if you and the lords agree, if Richard agrees.'

I am trapped. 'I swear it,' I say.

Edward releases his hard grip on our hands and falls back on his pillows. Hastings howls like a dog and puts his face down in the cover and Edward's hand finds its way blindly to touch his old friend's head as in a blessing. The others file out, Hastings and I are left on either side of the bed, and the king dying between us.

I have no time for grief, no time to measure my loss. Inside my heart is breaking for the man I love, the only man that I ever loved in all my life, the only man that I will ever love. Edward, the boy who rode up to me when I waited for him. My beloved. I have no time to think about this when my son's future and my family's prospects depend on me being hard of will and dry-eyed.

That night I write to my brother Anthony.

*The king is dead. Bring the new King Edward to London at all possible speed. Bring as many men as you can command as a royal guard – we will need them. Edward foolishly named Richard, Duke of Gloucester as protector. Richard hates you and me equally for the king's love and our own power. We must crown Edward at once and defend against the duke who will never give up the protectorate without a fight. Recruit men as you march, and collect the weapons that are stored in hiding on the way. Prepare yourself for battle, to defend our heir. I will delay announcing the death as long as I can, so Richard, who is still in the north, does not know what is happening yet. So hurry. Elizabeth*

What I don't know is that Hastings is writing to Richard, blotting the page with his tears, but legible enough, to say that the Rivers family are arming around their prince and that, if Richard wants to take up his role as protector, if he wants to guard the young Prince Edward against the boy's own rapacious family, he had better come at once, with as many men from his heartlands of the north as he can muster, before the prince is kidnapped by his own kin. He writes:

> *The king left all under your protection – goods, heir, realm. Secure the person of our sovereign Lord Edward V and get you to London before the Rivers flood us out.*

What I don't know, and what I don't allow myself to think, is that, having learned to fear the constant wars for the throne of England, I am just starting one on my own account, and that at stake this time is the inheritance and even the life of my beloved son.

He kidnaps him.

Richard moves faster and is better armed and more determined than any of us could have imagined. He moves as fast and as decisively as Edward would have done – and he is as ruthless. He waylays my son on his journey to London, dismisses the men from Wales who were loyal to him and to me, arrests my brother Anthony, my son Richard Grey and our cousin Thomas Vaughan, and takes Edward into his so-called safe keeping. My boy is not quite thirteen, in God's name. My boy is still a boy of only twelve. His voice is still fluting, his chin is smooth as a girl's, he has the softest fair down on his upper lip that you can only see when his face is in profile, against the light. And when Richard sends his loyal servants away, his uncle whom he idolises, the half-brother he loves, he defends them with a little quaver in his voice. He says that he is certain that his father would only have placed good men about him, and that he wants to keep them in his service.

He is only a boy. He has to stand up to a battle-hardened man who is determined to do wrong. When Richard says that my own brother Anthony, who has been my boy's friend and guardian and protector for all his life, and my youngest Grey son Richard, must leave his side, my little boy tries to defend them. He says that he is certain that his uncle Anthony is a good man and a fine guardian. He says his half-brother Richard has been a kinsman and a comrade to him, that he knows that his uncle Anthony has never done anything but that suits the great knight, the chivalrous knight that he is. But Duke Richard tells him that all will be resolved and in the meantime he and the Duke of Buckingham, my former ward, who I married against his will to my sister Katherine, and who now turns up in this surprising company, will be the prince's companions to London.

He is only a little boy. He has always been gently guarded. He does not know how to stand up to his uncle Richard, dressed in black and with a face like thunder, two thousand men in his train and ready to fight. So he lets his uncle Anthony go, he lets his brother Richard go. How could he save them? He cries bitterly. They tell me that. He cries like a child when no one will obey him; but he lets them go.

## MAY 1483

Elizabeth, my seventeen-year-old daughter, comes running through the shouting and the chaos of Westminster Palace. 'Mother! Lady Mother! What's happening?'

'We're going into sanctuary,' I snap. 'Hurry. Get everything you want and all the clothes for the children. And make sure they bring the carpets out of the royal rooms and the tapestries. Get all that taken into Westminster Abbey – we are going into sanctuary again. And your jewellery box, and your furs. And then go through the royal apartments and make sure they are stripping them of everything of value.'

'Why?' she asks, her pale mouth trembling. 'What has happened now? What about Baby?'

'Your brother the king has been taken by his uncle the lord protector,' I say. My words are like knives and I see them strike her. She admires her uncle Richard, she always has done. She was hoping he would care for all of us – protect us in truth. 'Your father's will has put my enemy in charge of my son. We will see what kind of a lord protector he makes. But we had better see it from safety. We go into sanctuary today, right this minute.'

'Mother.' She dances on the spot with fear. 'Should we not wait, should we not consult the Privy Council? Should we not wait here for Baby? What if Duke Richard is just bringing Baby safely to us? What if he is doing as he should, as lord protector? Protecting Baby?'

'He is King Edward to you, not Baby any more,' I say fiercely. 'And even to me. And let me tell you, child, that only fools wait when their enemies are coming, to see if they may prove to be friends. We will be as safe as I can make us. In sanctuary. And we will take your brother Prince Richard and keep him safe too. And, when the lord protector comes to London with his private army, he can persuade me that it is safe to come out.'

I speak bravely to my brave girl, now a young woman with her own life blighted by this sudden fall from being a princess of England to a girl in hiding; but in truth we are at a very low ebb when we barricade the door of St Margaret's crypt at Westminster and we are alone – my brother Lionel, Bishop of Salisbury, my grown son Thomas Grey, my little son Richard, and my girls: Elizabeth, Cecily, Anne, Katherine and Bridget. When we were last here I was big with my first boy, with every reason to hope that he would lay claim to the throne of England one day. My mother was alive, and was my companion and my greatest friend. And nobody could be afraid for long when my mother was scheming for them, and making her spells and laughing at her own ambition. My husband was alive in exile, planning his return. I never doubted that he would come. I never doubted that he would be victorious. I always knew that he never lost a battle. I knew he would come, I knew he would win, I knew he would rescue us. I knew they were bad days but I hoped for better.

Now we are here again, but this time it is hard to hope. In this season of early summer, which has always before been my favourite, filled with picnics and jousts and parties. The shade of the crypt is oppressive. It is like being buried alive. In truth, there is not much cause for hope. My boy is in enemy hands, my mother is long gone, and my husband is dead. No handsome tall man is going to hammer on the door and block the light as he comes in, calling my name. My son who was a baby then is a young boy of twelve now, and in the hands of our enemy. My girl Elizabeth, who played then so sweetly with her sisters when we were last confined, is now seventeen. She turns her pale face to me and asks what we are going to do. Last time we waited secure in the knowledge that, if we could just survive, we would be rescued. This time there are no certainties.

For nearly a week I listen at the tiny window set into the front door. From dawn till dusk I am peering through the grille, straining my ears to hear what people are doing, for the sound of the streets. When I turn from the door I go to the river and look out on the boats passing by, watching for the royal barge, listening for Melusina.

Every day I send out messengers for news of my brother and my son, and to speak to the lords who should be rising to defend us, whose liveries should be arming for us. And on the fifth day I hear it: a rising swell of noise, the cheering of the apprentice lads, and another sound beneath it, a deeper sound, a booing. I can hear the rattle of harness and the sound of many horses' hooves. It is the army of Richard, Duke of Gloucester, my husband's brother, the man he trusted with our safety, entering my husband's capital city to a mixed reception. When I look out of the window at the river there is a chain of his boats around Westminster Palace: a floating barricade, holding us captive. Nobody can come in or out.

I hear the clatter of a cavalry charge and some shouting. I start to wonder: if I had armed the city against him, declared war in the first moment, could I have stood against him now? But then I think: And what about my boy Edward in his uncle's train? What about my brother Anthony and my son Richard Grey, held hostage for my good behaviour? And yet again: Perhaps I have nothing to fear. I simply don't know. My boy is either a young king, processing in high honour to his coronation, or a kidnapped child. I don't even know which for sure.

I go to bed with that question haunting me like the beating of a drum. I lie down in my clothes and I do not sleep at all. I know that somewhere, not far from me tonight, my son is lying sleepless too. I am restless, like a woman tormented, to be with him, to see him, to tell him that he is safe with me again. I cannot believe, daughter of Melusina as I am, that I cannot squeeze through the bars of the windows and simply swim to him. He is my boy: perhaps he is afraid, maybe he is in danger. How can I not be with him?

But I have to lie still and wait for the sky to turn from deepest black to grey in the small panes of the window before I allow myself to rise up and walk down the crypt to the door and open the spy-hole to look out and see the quiet streets. Then, I realise that no one has armed to protect my boy Edward, no one is going to rescue him, no one is going to liberate me. They may have booed as the lord protector marched in at the head of his army with my son in his train, they may have raised a little riot and fought a little running scrap; but they are not arming this morning and storming his castle. Last night, I was the only one in all of London wakeful, worrying about the little king for all the long hours.

The city is waiting to see what the lord protector will do. Everything hinges on this. Is Richard, Duke of Gloucester, the beloved loyal brother of the late king, going to fulfil his brother's dying command and put his son on the throne? Is he, loyal as ever, going to play his part as lord protector and guard his nephew till the day of his coronation? Or is Richard, Duke of Gloucester, false as any Yorkist, going to take the power his brother gave him, disinherit his nephew, and put the crown on his own head, and name his own son Prince of Wales? Nobody knows what Duke Richard might do, and many – as always – want only to be on the winning side. Everyone will have to wait and see. Only I would strike him down now, if I could. Just to be on the side of safety.

I go to the low windows and I stare down at the river which

flows by so close that I could almost lean out and touch it. There is a boat with armed men at the water gate to the abbey. They are guarding me and keeping my allies from me. Any friends who try to come to me will be turned away.

'He will take the crown,' I say quietly to the river, to Melusina, to my mother. They listen to me in the flow of the waters. 'If I had to put my fortune on it I would do so. He will take the crown. All the York men are sick with ambition and Richard, Duke of Gloucester is no different. Edward risked his life, year after year, fighting for his throne. George put his head in a vat of wine rather than promise never to claim it. Now Richard rides into London at the head of thousands of armed men. He is not doing that for the benefit of his nephew. He will claim the crown for himself. He is a prince of York. He cannot help but do it. He will find a hundred reasons to do so, and years from now people will still be arguing over what he does today. But my bet is he will take the crown because he cannot stop himself, any more than George could stop being a fool or Edward stop being a hero. Richard will take the crown and he will put me and mine aside.

I pause for a moment of honesty. 'And it is my nature to fight for my own,' I say. 'I shall be ready for him. I shall be ready for the worst that he might do. I shall prepare myself to lose my son Richard Grey and my dearest brother Anthony, as I have already lost my father and my brother John. These are hard times, sometimes too hard for me. But this morning, I am ready. I will fight for my son and for his inheritance.'

Just as I am certain of my determination, there is a visitor at the sanctuary gate, an anxious tappetty tap, and then another. I walk towards the big barred door very slowly, stamping down my fear with each footstep. I open the spy-hole and there is the whore Elizabeth Shore, a hood drawn up to hide her bright-gold hair and her eyes red from weeping. Through the grille she can see my white face like a prisoner glaring out at her. 'What do you want?' I ask coldly.

She starts at my voice. Perhaps she thought I still keep an

equerry of the household and a dozen grooms of the chamber to open my door. 'Your Grace!'

'The same. What do you want, Shore?'

She disappears altogether as she curtseys so deeply that she sinks below the sight of the grille in the door, and I have a moment when I see the comical aspect of this as she rises up again like a pale moon on the horizon, into my vision. 'I am come with gifts, Your Grace,' she says clearly. Then she drops her voice. 'And news. Please admit me, for the king's own sake.'

My temper flares as she dares to mention him, then I consider that she seems to think herself still in his service and that I am still his wife, and I draw back the bolts of the door and slam them quickly shut as she darts inside like a frightened cat.

'What?' I ask flatly. 'What do you mean by coming here? Unbidden?' She comes no further into my sanctuary than the cold step of the door. She puts down a basket that she has carried like a kitchen maid. I quickly note the cured ham and the roasted chicken.

'I come from Sir William Hastings, with his greeting and the assurance of his loyalty,' she says in a rush.

'Oh, have you changed keepers? Are you his whore now?'

She looks me directly in the face and I have to stop myself gasping at her proud beauty. She is grey-eyed and fair-haired. She looks like I did, twenty years ago. She looks like my daughter Elizabeth of York: a cool English beauty, a rose of England. I could hate her for this, but I find I do not. I think that twenty years ago if Edward had been married I would have been no better than her, and become his whore rather than never know him at all.

My son Thomas Grey, comes out from the shadows of the crypt behind me and bows to her as if she were a lady. She slides a quick small smile to him as if they are good friends who need no words.

'Yes, I am Sir William's whore now,' she concurs quietly. 'The late king sent my husband abroad and he annulled our marriage.

My family will not have me home. I am without protection now that the king is dead. Sir William Hastings offered me a home and I am glad to find some safety with him.'

I nod. 'And so?'

'He asks me to be his envoy to you. He cannot come to you himself – he fears the Duke Richard's spies. But he tells you to be hopeful and that he thinks all will be well.'

'And why should I trust you?'

Thomas steps forward. 'Listen to her, Lady Mother,' he says gently. 'She loved your husband truly and she is a most honourable lady. She won't come with false counsel.'

'You go in,' I say harshly to him. 'I will deal with this woman.' I turn to her. 'Your new protector has been my enemy since he first set eyes on me,' I say roughly. 'I don't see why we would be friends now. He brought Duke Richard down on us, and supports him still.'

'He thought he was defending the young king,' she says. 'He was thinking of nothing but the young king's safety. He wants you to know this, and to know that he thinks all will be well.'

'Oh does he?' I am impressed, despite the messenger. Hastings is loyal to my husband in death as in life. If he thinks things will be all right, if he is convinced of the safety of my son, then everything might come right. 'Why is he so confident?'

She steps a little closer, so that she can whisper. 'The young king has been housed at the Bishop's Palace,' she says. 'Just near by. But the Privy Council agree that he should be housed in the royal apartments in the Tower and everything be made ready for his coronation. He is to take his place at once as the new King of England.'

'Duke Richard will crown him?'

She nods. 'The royal apartments are being made ready for him; they are fitting his coronation robes. The abbey is being made ready. They are ordering the pageants and raising the money for the celebration of his crowning. They have sent out the invitations and summoned Parliament. Everything is being made ready. She hesitates. 'It is all rushed, of course. Who would ever have thought . . .?'

She breaks off. She has obviously promised herself that she will show no grief before me. How could she? Could his whore dare to cry before his queen for the loss of him? So she says nothing, but the tears come to her eyes and she blinks them away. And I say nothing, but the tears come into my eyes too, and I look away from her. I am not a woman to be overcome by a sentimental moment. This is his whore, I am his queen. But God knows, we both miss him. We share the grief as we once shared the joy of him.

'But you are certain?' I ask, my voice very low. 'The wardrobe is preparing his coronation robes? Everything is being made ready?'

'They have set the date for his coronation as the 25th of June and the lords of the kingdom are summoned to attend. There is no doubt,' she says. 'Sir William ordered me to tell you to be of good heart, and that he does not doubt you will see your son on the throne of England. He told me to tell you that he himself will come here on the morning to escort you to the abbey, and you shall see your son crowned. You will attend the young king's coronation as the first in his train.'

I take a breath of this hope. But I see that she may be right, that Hastings may be right, and that I am in sanctuary like a frightened hare that runs when there are no hounds, and lies low, ears flat on its back, while the reapers walk past it to another field.

'And Edward, the young Earl of Warwick, has been sent north to the household of Anne Neville, the Duke of Gloucester's wife,' she goes on.

Warwick is the boy who was orphaned by the barrel of wine. He is only eight and a frightened foolish little lad, a true son of his fool of a father George of Clarence. But his claim to the throne comes after my sons, his claim is greater than that of Duke Richard, and yet Richard is keeping him safe. 'You are sure? He has sent Warwick to his wife?'

'My Lord says that Richard fears you and your power, but he would not make war on his own nephews. All the boys are safe with him.'

'Does Hastings have news of my brother and my son Richard Grey?' I whisper.

She nods. 'The Privy Council have refused to charge your brother with treason. They say he has been a good and faithful servant. Duke Richard wanted to charge him with kidnapping the young king, but the Privy Council disagreed – they won't accept a charge. They have overruled Duke Richard, and he has accepted their opinion. My Lord thinks your brother and son will be released after the coronation, Your Grace.'

'Duke Richard will make a settlement with us?'

'My Lord says that the duke is much opposed to your family, Your Grace, and your influence. But he is loyal to the young king for King Edward's sake. He said you can be certain that the young king will be crowned.'

I nod. 'Tell him I shall be glad of that day, but I shall stay here till then. I have another son and five daughters and I would prefer to keep them safely with me. And I don't trust Duke Richard.'

'He says you have not been so trustworthy yourself.' She drops into a deep curtsey and keeps her head down as she insults me. 'He orders me to tell you that you cannot defeat Duke Richard. You will have to work with him. He orders me to tell you that it was your husband himself who made the duke lord protector, and that the Privy Council prefer his influence to yours. Excuse me, Your Grace, he commanded me to tell you that there are many who dislike your family and want to see the young king free of the influence of his many uncles, and the Rivers out of their many places. It is noticed also that you stole the royal treasure away into sanctuary with you, too, that you took the Great Seal, and that your brother the Lord Admiral Edward Woodville has taken the entire fleet to sea.'

I grit my teeth. This is to insult me and everyone of my family, especially my brother Anthony, who influences Edward more than any other, who loves him like his own, who this very day is imprisoned for him. 'You can tell Sir William that Duke Richard must release my brother without charge at once,' I snap. 'You can tell him that the Privy Council should be reminded of the rights of the Rivers family and the king's widow. I am still queen. The country has seen a queen fight for her rights before: you should all be warned. The duke has kidnapped my son and ridden into London fully armed. I will bring him to account for it when I can.'

She looks frightened. She clearly does not want to be a go-between for a career courtier and a vengeful queen. But this is where she is now called, and she will have to do her best. 'I will tell him, Your Grace,' she says. She makes another deep curtsey and then she goes to the door. 'May I express my sympathy for the loss of your husband? He was a great man. It was an honour to be allowed to love him.'

'He didn't love you,' I say with sudden spite, and I see her pale face whiten.

'No, he never loved anyone like he loved you,' she replies so sweetly that I cannot but be touched by her tenderness. There is a little smile on her face but her eyes are wet again. 'There was never any doubt in my mind but there was one queen on the throne and the same queen in his heart. He made sure that I knew that. Everyone knew that. It was only ever you for him.'

She slides the bolt and opens the little door inside the great gate. 'You too were dear to him,' I say, driven, despite myself, to be fair to her. 'I was jealous of you because I knew that you were very dear to him. He said you were his merriest whore.'

Her face lights up as if a warm flame had flared inside a lantern. 'I am glad he thought that of me, and that you are kind enough to tell me,' she says. 'I was never one for politics or place. I just loved to be with him, and if I could to make him happy.'

'Yes, very well, very well,' I say, rapidly running out of generosity. 'So God speed.'

'And God be with you, Your Grace,' she says. 'I may be asked to come again with messages for you. Will you admit me?'

'As well you as any of the others. God knows, if Hastings is going to use Edward's whores as messengers I shall admit hundreds,' I say irritably and I see her faint smile as she slips through the half-opened door and I slam it closed behind her.

# JUNE 1483

Hastings' reassurances do not delay me. I am set on war against Richard. I shall destroy him, and free my son and my brother and release the young king. I shall not wait, obedient as Hastings suggests, for Richard to crown Edward. I don't trust him, and I don't trust the Privy Council or the citizens of London, who are waiting, as turncoats, to join the winning side. I shall put us on the attack and we should take him by surprise.

'Send the message to your uncle Edward,' I say to Thomas, my younger Grey son. 'Tell him to bring in the fleet battle-ready, and we will come out of sanctuary and raise the people. The duke sleeps at Baynard's Castle with his mother. Edward must bombard the castle while we break into the Tower and get Edward our prince.'

'What if Richard means nothing but to crown him?' he asks me. He is starting to write the message in code. Our messenger is waiting in hiding, ready to ride to the fleet, who are standing by in the deep water of the Downs.

'Then Richard is dead and we crown Edward anyway,' I say. 'Perhaps we have killed a loyal friend and a York prince, but that will be ours to mourn later. Our time is now. We can't wait for him to strengthen his command of London. Half the country will still not even have heard that King Edward is dead. Let us finish Duke Richard before his rule lasts any longer.'

'I should like to recruit some of the lords,' he says.

'Do what you can,' I say indifferently. 'I have word from Lady Margaret Stanley that her husband is ours though he seems to be Richard's friend. You can ask him. But those that did not rise for us as Richard came into London can die with him, for all I care. They are traitors to me and to the memory of my husband. Those that survive this battle will be tried for treason and beheaded.'

Thomas looks up at me. 'Then you are declaring war again,' he says. 'We Rivers and our placemen, our cousins and kinsfolk and affinity against the lords of England with Duke Richard, your brother-in-law, at their head. This is York against York now. It will be a bitter struggle and hard to end once it has started. Hard to win, as well.'

'It has to be started,' I reply grimly. 'And I have to win.'

The whore Elizabeth Shore is not the only one who comes to me with whispered news. My sister Katherine, wife of the prideful Duke of Buckingham, my former ward, comes on a family visit, bringing good wine and some early raspberries from Kent.

'Your Grace, my sister,' she says to me, curtseying low.

'Sister Duchess,' I reply coolly. We married her to the Duke of Buckingham when he was an angry orphan of only nine. We won her thousands of acres of land and the greatest title in England, short of prince. We showed him that, although he was as proud as a peacock chick of his great name, greater by far than ours, still we had the power to choose his wife, and it amused me to take his ancient name and give it to my sister. Katherine was lucky to be made a duchess by my favour, while I was a queen. And now the circle of fortune goes round and round and she finds herself married not to a resentful boy but to a man of nearly thirty, who is now the best friend of the lord protector of England, and I am a widowed queen, in hiding, with my enemy in power.

She links her arm in mine as she used to do when we were girls at Grafton and we drift over to the window to look out at the sluggish water. 'They are saying you were married by witchcraft,' she says, her lips hardly moving. 'And they are finding someone to swear that Edward was married to another woman before you.'

I meet her frowning gaze. 'It's an old scandal. It doesn't trouble me.'

'Please. Listen. I may not be able to come again. My husband grows in power and importance. I think he will send me away to the country, and I cannot disobey him. Listen to me. They have Robert Stillington, the Bishop of Bath and Wells—'

'But he is our man,' I interrupt, forgetting that there is no 'us' any more.

'He *was* your man. Not any more. He was Edward's chancellor, but now he is the duke's great friend. He assures him, as he told George, Duke of Clarence, that Edward was married to Dame Eleanor Butler before he was married to you, and that she had his legitimate son.'

I turn my face away. This is the price I pay for having an incontinent husband. 'In truth, I think he promised her marriage,' I whisper. 'He may even have gone through a ceremony with her. Anthony always thought so.'

'That's not all.'

'What more?'

'They are saying that Edward the king was not even his father's son. He was a bastard foisted on his father.'

'That scandal again?'

'That again.'

'And who is serving up these cold old meats?'

'It is the Duke Richard, and my husband, talking everywhere. But worse, I think the king's mother Cecily is ready to confess in public that your husband was a bastard. I think she will do it to put her son Richard on the throne – and your son to one side. Duke Richard and my husband are claiming everywhere that your husband was a bastard, and his son too. That makes Duke Richard the next true heir.'

I nod. Of course. Of course. Then we will be banished into exile and Duke Richard becomes King Richard and his whey-faced son takes my handsome boy's place.

'And worst of all,' she whispers, 'the duke suspects you of raising your own army. He has warned the council that you plan to destroy him and all the old lords of England. And so he has sent to York for men loyal to him. He is bringing an army of northerners down on us.'

I feel my grip on her arm tighten. 'I am raising my people,' I confirm. 'I have my plans. When do the men from the north arrive?'

'He has just sent for them,' she says. 'They cannot be here for a few days yet. Perhaps a week, perhaps more. Are you ready to rise now?'

'No,' I breathe. 'Not yet.'

'I don't know what you can do from here. Had you not better come out and go before the Privy Council yourself? Do any of the lords or Privy Council come to you? Do you have a plan?'

I nod. 'Be sure we have plans. I shall get Edward released, and I shall smuggle my boy Richard away to safety at once. I am bribing the guards at the Tower to free Edward. He has good men about him. I can trust them to look the other way. My Grey son Thomas is going to escape from here. He will go to Sheriff Hutton to rescue his brother Richard Grey and his uncle Anthony, and then they will arm and come back and release us all. They will raise our people. We will win this.'

'You will get the boys away first?'

'Edward planned our escapes years ago, before they were even born. I swore I would keep the boys safe, whatever happened. Remember we came to the throne through such battles; he never thought we were safe. We were always prepared for danger. Even if Richard would not hurt them I cannot have him holding them and telling the world they are bastards. Our brother Sir Edward will bring in the fleet to attack Duke Richard, and one of the ships will take the boys to Margaret in Flanders and they will be safe there.'

She grips my elbow and her face is white. 'Dearest . . . oh Elizabeth! Dear God! You don't know?'

'What? What now?'

'Our brother Edward is lost. His fleet mutinied against him in favour of the lord protector.'

For a moment I am numb with shock. 'Edward?' I turn to her and grip her hands. 'Is he dead? Have they killed our brother Edward?'

She shakes her head. 'I don't know for sure. I don't think anyone knows. Certainly he is not proclaimed dead. He was not executed.'

'Who turned the men against him?'

'Thomas Howard.' She names the rising nobleman who has joined Richard's cause hoping for profit and place. 'He went among the fleet. They were doubtful at putting to sea anyway. They turned against the Rivers command. Our family is hated by many of the common people.'

'Lost,' I say. Still I cannot take in the enormity of our defeat. 'We have lost Edward, and lost the fleet, and lost the treasure he was carrying,' I whisper. 'I was counting on him to rescue us. He was going to come up the river and take us to safety. And the treasure would have bought us an army in Flanders and paid our supporters here. And the fleet was to bombard London and take it from the river.'

She hesitates, and then, as if my despair had brought her to a decision, she puts her hand inside her cape and brings out a scrap of thread, a corner of a kerchief. She gives it to me.

'What's this?'

'It is a scrap I cut from Duke Richard's napkin when he dined with my husband,' she says. 'He held it in his right hand, he wiped his mouth.' She lowers her voice and her eyes. She was always frightened of our mother's powers. She never wanted to learn any of our skills. 'I thought you could use it,' she says. 'I thought perhaps you might use it.' She hesitates. 'You have to stop the Duke of Gloucester. He grows in power every day. I thought you might make him sick.'

'You cut this from the Duke's napkin?' I ask incredulously. Katherine always hated any sort of conjuring; she would never even have her fortune told by the gypsies at the fair.

'It is for Anthony,' she whispers fiercely. 'I am so afraid for our brother Anthony. You will keep the boys safe, I know. You will get them away. But the duke has Anthony in his power and both my husband and the duke hate him so much. They envy him for his learning and his bravery and because he is so beloved, and they are afraid of him, and I love him so much. You have to stop the duke, Elizabeth. Truly you do. You have to save Anthony.'

I whisk it into my sleeve so that no one, not even the children, can see it. 'Leave this with me,' I say. 'Don't even think about it. You have too honest a face, Katherine. Everyone will know what I am doing if you don't put it right out of your mind.'

She gives a nervous giggle. 'I never could lie.'

'Forget everything about it.'

We walk back to the front door. 'Go with God,' I say to her. 'And pray for me and our boys.'

The smile drains from her face. 'These are dark days for us Rivers,' she says. 'I pray you keep your children safe, sister, and yourself.'

'He will be sorry that he started this,' I predict. For a moment I pause, for suddenly, like a vision, I see Richard looking as young as a lost boy, staggering in the midst of a battlefield, his great sword slack in his weakened hand. He is looking around for friends, and he has none. He is looking around for his horse, but his horse has gone. He is trying to summon his strength but he has none. The shock on his face would make anyone pity him.

The moment passes and Katherine touches my hand. 'What is it? What do you see?'

'I see that he will be sorry that he started this,' I say quietly. 'It will be the end of him and his house.'

'And us?' she asks, peering into my face as if she could see what I had seen. 'Anthony? And all of us?'

'And us too, I am afraid.'

That night when it is midnight and dark as dark, I get up from my bed and take the scrap of linen that Katherine gave me. I see the smear of food where the duke wiped his lips and I bring it to my nose and sniff at it. Meat, I think, though he is an abstemious eater and no drinker. I twist the material into a cord and I tie it round my right arm so tightly that I can feel the arm ache. I go to bed and in the morning the white flesh of my arm is blue with a bruise and my fingers are prickly with pins and needles. I can feel the arm ache and, as I untie it, I moan with the pain. I feel the weakness in my arm as I throw the cord in the fire. 'So weaken,' I say to the flame. 'Lose your strength. Let your right arm fail, let your sword arm grow weak, let your hand lose its grip. Take one breath and feel it catch in your chest. Take another and feel choked. Sicken and weary. And burn up like this.' The cord flares in the fireplace and I watch it burn away.

My brother Lionel comes to me in the early morning. 'I have had a letter from the council. They beg us to come out of sanctuary and to send your son Prince Richard to be with his brother in the royal rooms in the Tower.'

I turn to the window and look at the river as if it might bring me advice. 'I don't know,' I say. 'No. I don't want both princes in their uncle's hands.'

'There is no doubt that the coronation is going to happen,' he says. 'All the lords are in London, the robes are being made, the abbey is ready. We should come out now and take our rightful place. Hiding here we look as if we are guilty of something.'

I nibble on my lip. 'Duke Richard is one of the sons of York,' I say. 'He saw the three suns burning in the sky as they rode to victory together. You cannot think he will walk away from the chance of ruling England. You cannot think he will hand over all the power of the kingdom to a young boy.'

'I think he will rule England through your son if you are not there to prevent it,' he says bluntly. 'He will put him on the throne and have him as his puppet. He will be another Warwick, another Kingmaker. He does not want the throne for himself – he wants to be regent and lord protector. He will call himself regent and rule through your son.'

'Edward will be king from the moment he is crowned,' I say. 'We will see who he will listen to then!'

'Richard can refuse to hand over power till Edward is twenty-one,' he says. 'He can command the kingdom as regent for the next eight years. We have to be there, represented in the Privy Council, protecting our interests.'

'If I could be sure my son is safe.'

'If Richard was going to kill him, he would have done it at Stony Stratford when they arrested Anthony, and there was no one to protect him, and no witness but Buckingham,' Lionel says flatly. 'But he did not. Instead, he went down on his knee and swore an oath of loyalty to him and brought him in honour to London. It is we who have created mistrust. I am sorry, Sister: it is you. I have never argued with you in my life, you know this. But you are mistaken now.'

'Oh, easy for you to say,' I say irritably. 'I have seven children to protect, and a kingdom to rule.'

'Then rule it,' he says. 'Take up your royal rooms in the Tower and attend your son's coronation. Sit on your throne and command the duke, who is nothing more than your brother-in-law and the guardian of your son.'

I am brooding on this. Perhaps Lionel is right and I should be at the heart of the planning for the coronation, winning men over to the side of the new king, promising them favours and honours at his court. If I come out now with my beautiful children and make my court again I can rule England through my son. I should claim our place, not hide in fear. I think: I can do this. I need not go to war to win my throne. I can do this as a reigning queen, as a beloved queen. The people are mine for the taking: I can win them over. Perhaps I should come out of sanctuary into the summer sunshine, and take up my place.

There is a little tap at the door and a man's voice says, 'Confessor for the dowager queen.'

I open the grille. There is a father of the Dominican order, his hood up so his face is hidden. 'I am ordered to come to you to hear your confession,' he says.

'Enter, Father,' I say and open the door wide to him. He comes in quietly, his sandals making no noise on the flagstones. He bows and waits for the door to be closed behind him.

'I am come on the order of Bishop Morton,' he says quietly. 'If anyone asks you, I came to offer you a chance to confess, and you spoke to me of a sin of sadness and excessive grief, and I counselled you against despair. Agreed?'

'Yes, Father,' I say.

He passes me a slip of paper. 'I shall wait ten minutes and then leave,' he says. 'I am not allowed to take a reply.'

He goes to the stool by the door and sits, waiting for the time to pass. I take the note to the window for the light, and as the river gurgles beneath the window I read it. It is sealed with the crest of the Beauforts. It is from Margaret Stanley, my former lady-in-waiting. Despite being Lancaster born and bred, and mother to their heir, she and her husband Thomas Stanley have been loyal to us for the last eleven years. Perhaps she will stay loyal. Perhaps she will even take my side against Duke Richard. Her interests lie with me. She was counting on Edward to forgive her son his Lancaster blood and let him come home from his exile in Brittany. She spoke to me of a mother's love for her boy and how she would give anything to have him home again. I promised her that it would happen. She has no reason to love Duke Richard. She might well think her chances of getting her boy home are better if she stays friends with me and supports my return to power.

But she has written nothing of a conspiracy nor words of support. She has written only a few lines:

*Anne Neville is not journeying to London for the coronation. She has not ordered horses or guards for the journey. She has not been fitted for special robes for the coronation. I thought you would like to know. M S*

I hold the letter in my hand. Anne is sickly and her son is weak. She might prefer to stay at home. But Margaret, Lady Stanley has not gone to all this trouble and danger to tell me this. She wants me to know that Anne Neville is not hastening to London for the grand coronation, for there is no need for her to make haste. If she is not coming, it will be at her husband Richard's command. He knows that there will be nothing to attend. If Richard has not ordered his wife to London in time for the coronation, the most important event of the new reign, then it must be because he knows that a coronation will not take place.

I stare out at the river for a long, long time and think what this means for me and my two precious royal sons. Then I go and kneel before the friar. 'Bless me, Father,' I say, and I feel his gentle hand come down on my head.

The serving maid who goes out to buy the bread and meat every day comes home, her face white, and speaks to my daughter Elizabeth. My girl comes to me.

'Lady Mother, Lady Mother, can I speak with you?'

I am looking out of the window, brooding on the water as if I hope Melusina might rise out of the summertime sluggish flow and advise me. 'Of course, sweetheart. What is it?'

Something about her taut urgency warns me.

'I don't understand what is happening, Mother, but Jemma has come home from the market and says there is some story of a fight in the Privy Council, an arrest. A fight in the council room! And Sir William . . .' She runs out of breath.

'Sir William Hastings?' I name Edward's dearest friend, the sworn defender of my son, and my new-found ally.

'Yes, him. Mother, they are saying in the market that he is beheaded.'

I hold the stone windowsill as the room swims. 'He can't be – she must have it wrong.'

'She says that the Duke Richard found a plot against him, and arrested two great men and beheaded Sir William.'

'She must be mistaken. He is one of the greatest men in England. He cannot be beheaded without trial.'

'She says so,' she whispers. 'She says that they took him out and took off his head on a piece of lumber on Tower Green, without warning, without trial, without charge.'

My knees give way beneath me and she catches me as I fall. The room goes dark to me, and then I see her again, her head-dress knocked aside, her fair hair spilling down, my beautiful daughter looking into my face, and whispering, 'Lady Mother, Mama, speak to me. Are you all right?'

'I'm all right,' I say. My throat is dry and I find I am lying on the floor with her arm supporting me. 'I am all right, sweetheart.

But I thought I heard you say . . . I thought you said . . . I thought you said that Sir William Hastings is beheaded?'

'So Jemma said, Mother. But I didn't think you even liked him.'

I sit up, my head aching. 'Child, this is no longer a question of liking. This lord is your brother's greatest defender, the only defender who has approached me. He doesn't like me, but he would lay down his life to put your brother on the throne and keep his word to your father. If he is dead we have lost our greatest ally.'

She shakes her head in bewilderment. 'Could he have done something very wrong? Something that offended the lord protector?'

There is a light tap at the door and we all freeze. A voice calls in French, '*C'est moi*.'

'It's a woman, open the door,' I say. For a moment I had been certain it was Richard's headsman, now come for us, with Hastings' blood unwiped on the blade of his axe. Elizabeth runs to open the lantern door in the big wooden gate and the whore Elizabeth Shore slips in, a hood over her fair head, a cloak wrapped tight around her rich brocade gown. She curtseys low to me, as I am still huddled on the floor. 'You've heard then,' she says shortly.

'Hastings is not dead?'

Her eyes are filled with tears but she is succinct. 'Yes, he is. That's why I've come. He was accused of treason against Duke Richard.'

Elizabeth my daughter drops to her knees beside me and takes my icy hand in hers.

'Duke Richard accused Sir William of conspiring his death. He said that William had procured a witch to act against him. The duke said that he is out of breath and falling sick and that he is losing his strength. He said he has lost the strength in his sword arm and he bared his arm in the council chamber and showed it to Sir William from the wrist to his shoulder, and said surely he could see it was withering away. He says he is under an enchantment from his enemies.'

My eyes stay on her pale face. I don't even glance at the fireplace where the twist of linen from the duke's napkin was burned, after I tied it around my forearm, and then cursed it, to rob him of breath and strength, to make his sword arm weak as a hunchback's.

'Who does he name as the witch?'

'You,' she says. I feel Elizabeth flinch.

And then she adds, 'And me.'

'The two of us acting in concert?'

'Yes,' she says simply. 'That's why I came to warn you. If he can prove you are a witch, can he break sanctuary, and take you and your children out of here?'

I nod. He can.

And in any case, I remember the battle of Tewkesbury, when my own husband broke sanctuary with no reason or explanation, and dragged wounded men out of the abbey and butchered them in the graveyard and then went into the abbey and killed some more on the altar steps. They had to scrub the chancel floor clean of the blood, they had to resanctify the whole place, it was so fouled with death.

'He can,' I say. 'Worse has been done before.'

'I must go,' she says fearfully. 'He may be watching me. William would have wanted me to do what I can to keep your children safe, but I can do no more. I should tell you: Lord Stanley did what he could to save William. He warned him that the duke would act against him. He had a dream that they would be gored by a boar with bloody tusks. He warned William. It was just that William didn't think it would be so fast . . .' The tears are running down her cheeks now and her voice is choked. 'So unjust,' she whispers. 'And against such a good man. To have soldiers drag him from council! To take off his head without even a priest! No time to pray!'

'He was a good man,' I concede.

'Now that he is gone you have lost a protector. You are all in grave danger,' she states. 'As am I.'

She pulls the hood back over her hair and goes to the door. 'I wish you well,' she says. 'And Edward's boys. If I can serve you,

I will. But in the meantime I must not be seen coming to you. I dare not come again.'

'Wait,' I say. 'Did you say Lord Stanley remains loyal to the young King Edward?'

'Stanley, Bishop Morton, and Archbishop Rotherham are all imprisoned by order of the duke, suspected of working for you and yours. Richard thinks they have been plotting against him. The only men left free in the council now are those who will do the duke's bidding.'

'Has he run mad?' I ask incredulously. 'Has Richard run mad?'

She shakes her head. 'I think he has decided to claim the throne,' she says simply. 'D'you remember how the king used to say that Richard always did what he promised? That if Richard swore he would do something it was done – cost what it may?'

I don't like to have this woman quoting my husband to me, but I agree.

'I think Richard has made his decision, I think he has promised to himself. I think he has decided that the best thing for him, and for England, is a strong new king and not a boy of twelve. And now he has made up his mind, he will do whatever it takes to put himself on the throne. Cost what it may.'

She opens the door a crack and peers out. She picks up the basket to make it look as if she was delivering goods to us. She peeps back at me around the door. 'The king always said that Richard would stop at nothing once he had agreed a plan,' she says. 'If he stops at nothing now, you will not be safe. I hope you can make yourself safe, Your Grace, you and the children . . . you and Edward's boys.' She dips a little curtsey and whispers, 'God bless you for his sake,' and the door clicks behind her and she has gone.

I don't hesitate. It is as if the thud of axe through Hastings' neck on Tower Green is a trumpet blast which signals the start of a race. But this is a race to get my son to safety from the threat of his uncle, who is now on a path of murder. There is no doubt in my mind any more that Duke Richard will kill both my sons to make his way clear to the throne. I would not give a groat for the life of George's son, either, wherever he is housed. I saw Richard go into the room of the sleeping King Henry to kill a defenceless man because his claim to the throne was as good as Edward's. There is no doubt in my mind that Richard will follow the same logic as the three brothers did that night. A sacred and ordained king stood between their line and the throne – and they killed him. Now my boy stands between Richard and the throne. He will kill him if he can, and it may be that I cannot prevent it. But, I swear, he will not get my younger boy Richard.

I have prepared him for this moment, but when I tell him that he will have to go at once, tonight, he is startled that it has come so soon. His colour drains away from his cheeks but his bright boyish bravery makes him hold his head up and bite his little lip so as not to cry. He is only nine, but he has been raised to be a prince of the House of York. He has been raised to show courage. I kiss him on the top of his fair head and tell him to be a good boy, and remember all that he has been told to do, and when it starts to grow dark I lead him down through the crypt, down the stairs, even deeper, down into the catacomb below the building, where we have to go past the stone coffins and the vaulted rooms of the burial chambers with one lantern before us and one in his little hand. The light does not flicker. He does not tremble even when we go past the shadowy graves. He walks briskly beside me, his head up.

The way leads out to a hidden iron gate, and beyond it a stone pier extending out into the river, with a rocking rowing boat silently alongside. It is a little wherry, hired for river traffic, one of hundreds. I had hoped to send him out in the warship, commanded by my brother Edward, with men at arms sworn to protect him; but God knows where Edward is this night, and the fleet has turned against us, and will sail for Richard the duke. I have no warships at my command. We will have to make do with this. My boy has to go out with no protection but two loyal servants, and the blessing of his mother. One of Edward's friends is waiting for him at Greenwich, Sir Edward Brampton, who loved Edward. Or so I hope. I cannot know. I can be certain of nothing.

The two men are waiting silently in the boat, holding it against the current with a rope through the ring on the stone steps, and I push my boy towards them and they lift him on board and seat him in the stern. There is no time for any farewells and anyway there is nothing I can say but a prayer for his safety that catches me in the throat as if I have swallowed a dagger. The boat pushes off and I raise my hand to wave to him, and see his little white face under the big cap looking back at me.

I lock the iron gate behind me, and then go back up the stone steps, silent through the silent catacombs, and I look out from my window. His boat is pulling away into the river traffic, the two men at the oars, my boy in the stern. There is no reason for anyone to stop them. There are dozens like them, hundreds of boats criss-crossing the river, about their own business, two working men with a lad to run errands. I swing open my window but I will not call to him. I will not call him back. I just want him to be able to see me if he glances up. I want him to know that I did not let him go lightly, that I looked for him until the last, the very last moment. I want him to see me looking for him through the dusk, and know that I will look for him for the rest of my life, I will look for him till the hour of my death, I will look for him after death, and the river will whisper his name.

He does not glance up. He does as he was told. He is a good boy, a brave boy. He remembers to keep his head down and his cap pulled down on his forehead to hide his fair hair. He must remember to answer to the name of Peter, and not expect to be served on bended knee. He must forget the pageants and the royal progresses, the lions at the Tower, and the jester tumbling head over heels to make him laugh. He must forget the crowds of people cheering his name and his pretty sisters who played with him and taught him French and Latin and even a little German. He must forget the brother he adored who was born to be king. He must be like a bird, a swallow, who in winter flies beneath the waters of the rivers and freezes into stillness and silence and does not fly out again until spring comes to unlock the waters and let them flow. He must go like a dear little swallow into the river, into the keeping of his ancestress Melusina. He must trust that the river will hide him and keep him safe; for I can no longer do so.

I watch the boat from my window and at first I can see him in the stern, rocking as the little wherry moves in steady pulses, as the boatman pulls on the oars. Then the current catches it and they go faster and there are other boats, barges, fishing boats, trading ships, ferry boats, wherries, even a couple of huge logging rafts, and I can see my boy no longer and he has gone to the river and I have to trust him to Melusina and the water, and I am left without him, marooned without my last son, stranded on the river-bank.

My grown son, Thomas Grey, goes the same night. He slips out of the door dressed like a groom into the back streets of London. We need someone on the outside to hear news and raise our forces. There are hundreds of men loyal to us, and thousands who would fight against the duke. But they must be mustered and organised, and Thomas has to do this. There is no one else left who can. He is twenty-seven. I know I am sending him out to danger, perhaps to his death. 'God speed,' I say to him. He kneels to me and I put my hand on his head in blessing. 'Where will you go?'

'To the safest place in London,' he says with a rueful smile. 'A place that loved your husband and will never forgive Duke Richard for betraying him. The only honest business in London.'

'Where d'you mean?'

'The whorehouse,' he says with a grin.

And then he turns into the darkness and is gone.

Next morning, early, Elizabeth brings the little pageboy to me. He served us at Windsor, and has agreed to serve us again. Elizabeth holds him by the hand for she is a kind girl but he smells of the stables, where he has been sleeping. 'You will answer to the name of Richard, Duke of York,' I tell him. 'People will call you My Lord, and Sire. You will not correct them. You will not say a word. Just nod.'

'Yes'm,' he mumbles.

'And you will call me Lady Mother,' I say.

'Yes'm.'

'Yes, Lady Mother.'

'Yes, Lady Mother,' he repeats.

'And you will have a bath and put on clean clothes.'

His frightened little face flashes up at me. 'No! I can't bath!' he protests.

Elizabeth looks aghast. 'Anyone will know at once,' she says.

'We'll say he is ill,' I say. 'We'll say he has a cold or a sore throat. We'll tie up his jaw with a flannel and put a scarf around his mouth. We'll tell him to be silent. It's only for a few days. Just to give us time.'

She nods. 'I'll bath him,' she says.

'Get Jemma to help you,' I say. 'And one of the men will probably have to hold him in the water.'

She finds a smile, but her eyes are shadowed. 'Mother, do you really think my uncle the duke would harm his own nephew?'

'I don't know,' I say. 'And that is why I have sent my beloved royal son away from me, and my boy Thomas Grey has to go out into the darkness. I don't any longer know what the duke might do.'

The serving girl Jemma asks if she can go out on Sunday afternoon to see the Shore whore serve her penance. 'To do what?' I ask.

She dips a curtsey, her head bowed low, but she is so desperate to go that she is ready to risk offending me. 'I am sorry, ma'am, Your Grace, but she is to walk in the City in her kirtle carrying a lighted taper and everyone is going to see her. She has to do penance for sin, for being a whore. I thought if I came in early every day for the next week you might let me . . .'

'Elizabeth Shore?'

Her face bobs up. 'The notorious whore,' she recites. 'The lord protector has ordered that she do public penance for her sins of the flesh.'

'You can go and watch,' I say abruptly. One more gaze in the crowd will make no difference. I think of this young woman who Edward loved, who Hastings loved, walking barefoot in her petticoat, carrying a taper, shielding its flickering flame while people shout abuse or spit on her. Edward would not like this, and for him, if not for her, I would stop it if I could. But there is nothing I can do to protect her. Richard the duke has turned vicious and even a beautiful woman has to suffer for being beloved.

'She is punished for nothing but her looks.' My brother Lionel has been listening at the window for the appreciative murmur of the crowd as she walks around the City boundary. 'And because now Richard suspects her of hiding your brother Thomas. He raided her house but he couldn't find Thomas. She kept him safe, hidden from Gloucester's men, and then got him out of the way.'

'God bless her for that,' I say.

Lionel smiles. 'Apparently, this punishment has gone wrong for Duke Richard anyway. Nobody is speaking ill of her as she walks,' he says. 'One of the ferry-boat men shouted up at me when I was at the window. He says that the women cry shame on her shame, and the men just admire her. It's not every day that they see such a lovely woman in her petticoat. They say she looks like a naked angel, beautiful and fallen.'

I smile. 'Well, God bless her anyway, angel or whore.'

My brother the bishop smiles too. 'I think her sins were ones of love, not of malice,' he says. 'And in these hard days perhaps that is what matters the most.'

## 17 JUNE 1483

They send my kinsman, Cardinal Thomas Bourchier, and half a dozen other lords from the Privy Council to reason with me, and I greet them as a queen, draped in the royal diamonds looted from the treasury, seated on a grand chair for my throne. I hope I look queenly and dignified; in truth I feel murderous. These are the lords of my Privy Council. They have the positions that my husband gave them. He made them what they are today, and now they dare come to me and tell me what Duke Richard requires of me. Elizabeth stands behind me, and my other four daughters in a row. None of my sons or brothers are present. They don't remark that my son Thomas Grey is escaped from sanctuary and is on the loose in London, and I certainly don't draw attention to his absence.

They tell me that they have proclaimed Duke Richard protector of the realm, regent and governor of the prince, and they assure me that they are preparing for the coronation of my son Prince Edward. They want my younger son Richard to join his brother in the royal rooms in the Tower.

'The duke will be protector for only a matter of days, only till the coronation,' Thomas Bourchier explains to me, his face so earnest that I must trust him. This is a man who has spent his life trying to bring peace to this country. He crowned Edward as king and me as queen because he believed that we would bring peace to this country. I know that he is speaking from his heart. 'As soon as the young king is crowned then all the power reverts to him and you are dowager queen and mother of the king,' he says. 'Come back to your palace, Your Grace, and attend the coronation of your son. The people wonder that they don't see you, and it looks odd to the foreign ambassadors. Let us do as we all swore to the king on his deathbed – put your son on the throne and all work together leaving aside enmity. Let the royal family be housed in the royal apartments in the Tower, and let them come out in their power and their beauty for their boy's coronation.'

For a moment I am persuaded. More, I am tempted. Perhaps everything can end happily. Then I think of my brother Anthony and my son Richard Grey imprisoned together in Pontefract Castle, and I hesitate. I have to pause and think. I have to keep them safe. While I am in sanctuary, my safety and my son Richard's safety balances their imprisonment like the weights in a pair of scales. They are hostages for my good behaviour, but equally Duke Richard dare not touch them for fear of enraging me. If Richard wants to rid himself of Rivers he has to have all of us in his power. By keeping out of his reach I protect those of us he does have, as well as those who are free. I have to keep my brother Anthony safe against his enemies. I have to. This is my crusade: like the one I would not let him ride. I have to keep him safe to be the light in the world that he is.

'I cannot release Prince Richard to you,' I say, my voice filled with false regret. 'He has been so ill lately, I cannot bear anyone should care for him but me. He is not yet well, he has lost his voice, and if he were to have a relapse it could be worse than his first illness. If you want him and his brother to be together then send Edward to join us here, where I can care for them both and know that they are not in danger. I long to see my oldest son by King Edward, and know that he is safe. I pray you, send him to me, to safety. He can be crowned from here, as well as from the Tower.'

'Why, madam,' says Thomas Howard, bristling like the bully that he is. 'Can you name any reason why they should be in danger?'

I look at him for a moment. Does he really think that he is likely to trap me into confessing my enmity to the Duke Richard? 'All the rest of my family are either run away or imprisoned,' I say flatly. 'Why should I think that I and my sons are secure?'

'Now, now,' the cardinal interrupts, nodding at Howard to silence him. 'Anyone in prison will be tried before a court of their peers as they should be, and the truth of any accusation will be proved or denied. The Lords have ruled that no charge of treason can be brought against your brother Anthony, Earl Rivers. That should satisfy you that we come in good faith. You cannot imagine that I, I myself, should come to you in anything other than good faith?'

'Ah my Lord Cardinal,' I say. 'I don't doubt you.'

'Then trust me when I give you my word, my personal word, that your boy will be safe with me,' he says. 'I shall take him to his brother and no harm will come to either of them. You distrust the Duke Richard, and he suspects you – this is a sorrow to me, but you both have your reasons – but I will swear that neither the duke nor any other will harm your boys and they will be safe together, and Edward will be crowned king.'

I sigh as if I am overwhelmed by his logic. 'And if I refuse?'

He draws close to me and speaks low. 'I fear that he will break sanctuary and take you and all your family out of here,' he says very quietly. 'And all the lords think he would be right to do so. No one defends your right to be in here, Your Grace. This is a shell around you, not a castle. Let the little Prince Richard out and they will leave you here, if that is your wish. Keep him here and you will all be pulled out, like leeches from a glass jar. Or they can smash the jar.'

Elizabeth, who has been looking out of the window, leans forward and whispers, 'Lady Mother, there are hundreds of Duke Richard's barges on the river. We are surrounded.'

For a moment I do not see the cardinal's worried face. I do not see the hard expression of Thomas Howard. I do not see the half-dozen men who have come with him. I see my husband going into the sanctuary at Tewkesbury with his sword drawn, and I know that from that moment sanctuary was no longer safe. Edward destroyed his son's safety that day – and he never knew. But I know it now. And thank God I have prepared for it.

I put my handkerchief to my eyes. 'Forgive a woman's weakness,' I say. 'I cannot bear to part with him. Can I be spared this?'

The cardinal pats my hand. 'He has to come with us. I am sorry.'

I turn to Elizabeth and I whisper, 'Fetch him, fetch my little boy.'

Elizabeth leaves in silence, her head bowed.

'He has not been well,' I say to the cardinal. 'You must keep him wrapped up warm.'

'Trust me,' he says. 'He will come to no harm in my care.'

Elizabeth comes back with the changeling pageboy. He is in my Richard's clothes, a scarf tied round his throat, muffling the lower part of his face. When I hold him to me, he even smells of my own boy. I kiss his fair hair. His little-boy frame is delicate in my arms, and yet he holds himself bravely, as a prince should do. Elizabeth has taught him well. 'Go with God, my son,' I say to him. 'I shall see you again at your brother's coronation in a few days.'

'Yes, Lady Mother,' he says like a little parrot. His voice is scarcely more than a whisper but audible to them all.

I take him by the hand and I lead him to the cardinal. He has seen Richard at court, at a distance, and this boy is hidden by the jewelled cap on his head and the flannel round his throat and his jaw. 'Here is my son,' I say, my voice trembling with emotion. 'I resign him into your hands. I do here deliver him and his brother into your safe keeping.' I turn to the boy and say to him, 'Farewell, mine own sweet son, the Almighty be your protector.'

He turns his little face to me, all wrapped in the concealing scarf, and for a moment I feel a sweep of real emotion as I kiss his warm cheek. I may be sending this child into danger instead of my own, but he is still a child, and it is still danger. There are tears in my eyes when I put his little hand in the big soft palm of Cardinal Bourchier and I say to him over the little head, 'Guard this boy, my boy, please, my lord. Keep this boy safe.'

We wait as they take the boy, and file from the room. When they are gone the scent of their clothes lingers. It is the smell of the outdoors, horse sweat, cooked meats, a fresh breeze blowing over cut grass.

Elizabeth turns to me and her face is pale. 'You sent the page-boy for you think it is not safe for our boy to go to the Tower,' she observes.

'Yes,' I say.

'So you must think that our Edward is not safe in the Tower.'

'I don't know. Yes. That is my fear.'

She takes an abrupt step to the window and for a moment she reminds me of my mother, her grandmother. She has the same determination – I can see her puzzling away at the best course. For the first time I think that Elizabeth will make a woman to be reckoned with. She is not a little girl any more.

'I think you should send to my uncle and ask him for an agreement,' she says. 'You could agree that we give him the throne, and he names Edward as his heir.'

I shake my head.

'You could,' she says. 'He is Edward's uncle, a man of honour. He must want a way out of this as much as we do.'

'I will not give up Edward's throne,' I say tightly. 'If Duke Richard wants it, he will have to take it, and shame himself.'

'And what if he does that?' she asks me. 'What happens to Edward then? What happens to my sisters? What happens to me?'

'I don't know,' I say cautiously. 'We may have to fight, we may have to argue. But we don't give up. We don't surrender.'

'And that little boy,' she says, nodding to the door where the pageboy has gone, his jaw tied up with flannel so he does not speak. 'Did we take him from his father and bath him and clothe him and tell him to be silent as we sent him to his death? Is that how we fight this war, using a child as our shield? Sending a little boy to his death?'

# SUNDAY 25 JUNE 1483: CORONATION DAY

'What?' I spit at the quiet dawn sky like an angry cat whose kittens have been taken away for drowning. 'No royal barges? No booming cannon from the Tower? No wine flowing in the fountains of the City? No banging of drums, no 'prentice boys howling out the songs of their guilds? No music? No shouting? No cheering along the procession route?' I swing open the window that looks over the river and see the usual river traffic of barges and wherries and rowing boats and I say to my mother and to Melusina, 'Clearly, they don't crown him today. Is he to die instead?' I think of my boy as if I were painting his portrait. I think of the straight line of his little nose still rounded at the tip like a baby, and the plump roundness of his cheeks and the clear innocence of his eyes. I think of the curve of the back of his head that used to fit my hand when I touched him, and the straight pure line of the nape of his neck when he was bent over his books in study. He was a brave boy, a boy who had been coached by his uncle Anthony to vault into a saddle and ride at the joust. Anthony promised that he would be fearless by learning to face fear. And he was a boy who loved the country. He liked Ludlow Castle, for he could ride into the hills and see the peregrine falcons soaring high above the cliffs, and he could swim in the cold water of the river. Anthony said he had a sense of landscape: rare in the young. He was a boy with the most golden future. He was born in wartime to be a child of peace. He would have been, I don't doubt, a great Plantagenet king, and his father and I would have been proud of him.

I speak of him as if he is dead, for I have little doubt that since he is not crowned today, he will be killed in secret, just as William Hastings was dragged out and beheaded on Tower Green on a baulk of wood with the axeman hurriedly wiping his hands from his breakfast. Dear God, when I think of the nape of the neck of my boy and I think of the headsman's axe, I feel sick enough to die myself.

I don't stay at the window watching the river that keeps flowing indifferently as if my boy were not in danger of his life. I dress and pin up my hair and then I prowl about our sanctuary like one of the lionesses in the Tower. I comfort myself with plotting: we are not friendless, I am not without hope. My son Thomas Grey will be busy, I know, meeting in secret at hidden places those who can be convinced to rise for us, and there must be many in the country, in London too, who are beginning to doubt exactly what Duke Richard means by a protectorate. Margaret Stanley is clearly working for us: her husband Lord Thomas Stanley warned Hastings. My sister-in-law Duchess Margaret of York will be working for us in Burgundy. Even the French should take an interest in my danger, if only to cause trouble for Richard. There is a safe house in Flanders, where a well-paid family is greeting a little boy and teaching him to disappear into the crowd of Tournai. The duke may have the upper hand now but there are as many who will hate him, as hated us Rivers, and many more will be thinking fondly of me, now I am in danger. Most of all there will be the men who want to see Edward's son and not his brother on the throne.

I hear the rush of hurried footsteps and I turn to face new danger as my daughter Cecily comes running down the crypt and throws opens the door to my chamber. She is white with fright. 'There is something at the door,' she says. 'Something horrible at the door.'

'What is at the door?' I ask. At once, of course, I think it is the headsman.

'Something as tall as a man, but looking like Death.'

I throw a scarf over my head and I go to the door and slide open the grille. Death himself seems to be waiting for me. He is in black gaberdine with a tall hat on his head and a long white tube of a nose hiding all his face. It is a physician with the long cone of his nose mask stuffed with herbs to protect him from the airs of the plague. He turns the glittery slits of eyes on me and I feel myself shiver.

'There is none with plague in here,' I say.

'I am Dr Lewis of Caerleon, the Lady Margaret Beaufort's doctor,' he says, his voice echoing weirdly from the cone. 'She says you are suffering from woman's maladies, and would benefit from a physician.'

I open the door. 'Come in, I am not well,' I say. But as soon as the door is closed to the outside world, I challenge him. 'I am perfectly well. Why are you here?'

'The Lady Beaufort – Lady Stanley, I should say – is well too, God be praised for her. But she wanted to find a way to speak with you, and I am of her affinity, and loyal to you, Your Grace.'

I nod. 'Take off your mask.'

He takes the cone from his face and pushes back the hood from his head. He is a small dark man with a smiling, trustworthy face. He bows low. 'She wants to know if you have devised a plan to rescue the two princes from the Tower. She wants you to know both she and her husband the Lord Stanley are yours to command, and she wants you to know that the Duke of Buckingham is filled with doubt as to where the Duke Richard's ambition is leading him. She thinks the young duke is ready for turning.'

'Buckingham has done everything to put the duke where he sits now,' I say. 'Why would he change his mind on this day of their victory?'

'Lady Margaret believes that the Duke of Buckingham could

be persuaded,' he says, leaning forward to speak only into my ear. 'She thinks he is starting to have doubts as to his leader. She thinks he would be interested in other, greater rewards than those the Duke Richard can offer him, and he is a young man, not yet thirty years old, easily swayed. He is afraid that the duke plans to take the throne for himself; he is afraid for the safety of your sons. You are his sister-in-law, these are his nephews too. He is concerned for the future of the princes, his little kinsmen. Lady Margaret bids me say to you that she thinks that the servants in the Tower can be bribed, and she want to know how she can serve you in what plans you have to restore the Princes Edward and Richard to freedom.'

'It is not Richard . . .' I start to say when, like a ghost, from the door to the river, Elizabeth comes up the steps, the hem of her gown sodden.

'Elizabeth. What on earth are you doing?'

'I went down to sit by the river,' she says. Her face is strange and pale. 'It was so quiet and beautiful at first this morning and then it became more and more busy. I wondered why the river was so busy. It was almost as if the river would tell me herself.' She turns to regard the doctor. 'Who is this?'

'He is a messenger from Lady Margaret Stanley,' I say. I am looking at her wet gown, which drags behind her like a tail. 'How did you get so wet?'

'From the barges that went by,' she says. Her face is pale and hostile. 'All the barges that went down the river to Baynard Castle, where Duke Richard is holding a great court. The wash from their passing was so great that it came in over the steps. What is happening there today? Half of London is on a barge going to the duke's house, but it is supposed to be the day of my brother's coronation.'

Dr Lewis looks awkward. 'I was about to tell your royal mother,' he says hesitantly.

'The river itself is a witness,' my daughter says rudely. 'It washed over my feet as if to tell me. Anyone could guess.'

'Guess what?' I demand of them both.

'The parliament has met and declared that Duke Richard is the rightful king,' he says quietly, though his words echo in the vaulted stone hall as if he were shouting a proclamation. 'They ruled that your marriage with the king was held without the knowledge of the rightful lords, and achieved by witchcraft by your mother and yourself. And that the king was married already to another lady.'

'So you have been a whore for years and we are bastards,' Elizabeth finishes coolly. 'We are defeated and shamed. It is over, all over. Can we take Edward and Richard and go now?'

'What are you saying? I ask of her. I am as bewildered by this daughter of mine with her gown like a wet tail, like a mermaid come in from the river, as I am at the news that Richard has claimed the throne and we are cast down. 'What are you saying? What were you thinking as you sat by the river? Elizabeth, you are so strange today. Why are you like this now?'

'Because I think we are cursed,' she flings out at me. 'I think we are cursed. The river whispered a curse to me and I blame you and my father for bringing us into this world and putting us here, in the grip of ambition, and yet not holding strongly enough to your power to make it right for us.'

I snatch at her cold hands tightly, and I hold her as if I would keep her from swimming away. 'You're not cursed, daughter. You are the finest and rarest of all my children, the most beautiful, the most beloved. You know that. What curse could stick to you?'

The gaze she turns on me is darkened with horror as if she has seen her death. 'You will never surrender, you will never let us be. Your ambition will be the death of my brothers, and when they are dead you will put me on the throne. You would rather have the throne than your sons, and when they are both dead you will put me on my dead brother's throne. You love the crown more than your children.'

I shake my head to deny the power of her words. This is my little girl, this is my easy, simple child, this is my pet, my

Elizabeth. She is the very bone of my bone. She has never had a thought that I did not put in her head. 'You cannot know such a thing; it's not true. You cannot know. The river cannot tell you such a thing, and you cannot hear it, and it's not true.'

'I will take my own brother's throne,' she says as if she cannot hear me. 'And you will be glad of it, for your ambition is your curse, so the river says.'

I glance at the doctor and wonder if she has a fever. 'Elizabeth, the river cannot speak to you.'

'Of course it speaks to me, and of course I hear it!' she exclaims in impatience.

'There is no curse . . .'

She wheels around and glides across the room, her gown leaving a damp stain like a trail, and throws open the window. Dr Lewis and I follow her, fearful for a moment that she has run mad and means to jump out; but at once I am halted by a high sweet keening from the river, a longing sound, a song of mourning, a note so anguished that I put my hands over my ears to block it out and look to the doctor for an explanation. He shakes his head in bewilderment, for he hears nothing but the cheerful noise of the passing barges as they go down for the king's coronation, trumpets blaring and drums pounding. But he can see the tears in Elizabeth's eyes and sees me shrink from the open windows, blocking my ears from the haunting sounds.

'That's not for you,' I say. I am choking on my grief. 'Ah, Elizabeth, my love, that's not for you. That's Melusina's song: the song that we hear for a death in our house. That's not a warning song for you. This will be for my son Richard Grey, I can hear it. It's for my son and for my brother Anthony, my brother Anthony whom I swore I would keep safe.'

The doctor is pale with fear. 'I can hear nothing,' he says. 'Just the noise of the people calling for the new king.'

Elizabeth is at my side, her grey eyes as dark as a storm on a wave at sea. 'Your brother? What d'you mean?'

'My brother and my son are dead at the hands of Richard,

Duke of Gloucester, just as my brother John and my father were dead at the hands of George, Duke of Clarence,' I predict. 'The sons of York are murdering beasts and Richard is no better than George and they have cost me the best men of my family and broken my heart. I can hear it. I can hear this. This is what the river is singing. The river is singing a lament for my son and for my brother.'

She steps closer. She is my tender girl again, her wild fury blown away. She puts her hand on my shoulder. 'Mother . . .'

'Do you think he will stop here?' I burst out frantically. 'He has my boy, he has my royal son. If he dares to take Anthony from me, if he could bear to take Richard Grey from me, d'you think he will stop at taking Edward too? A brother and a son he has robbed from me this day. I will never forgive him. I will never forget this. He is a dead man to me. I will see him wither, I will see his sword arm fail him, I will see him turn around looking for his friends like a lost child on the battlefield, I will see him fall.'

'Mother, be still,' she whispers. 'Be still and listen to the river.'

It is the only word that can calm me. I run down the length of the room and throw open all the windows and the warm summer air breathes into the cold darkness of the crypt. The water babbles low against the banks. There is a stink of low tide and mud, but the river flows on, as if to remind me that life goes on, as if to say that Anthony has gone, my boy Richard Grey has gone, and my boy the little Prince Richard has gone downstream to strangers on a little boat. But we still might flow deep once more.

There is music coming from some of the passing barges, noblemen making merry at the accession of Duke Richard. I cannot understand how they cannot hear the singing of the river, how they do not know that a light has gone out of this world with the death of my brother Anthony and my boy . . . my boy.

'He would not want you to grieve,' she says quietly. 'Uncle Anthony loved you so much. He would not want you to grieve.'

I put my hand on hers. 'He would want me to live, and to bring you children through this danger to life,' I say. 'We will hide in sanctuary for now but I swear we will come out again to our true place. You can call this the curse of ambition if you like, but without it I would not fight. And I will fight. You will see me fight, and you will see me win.

'If we have to set sail to Flanders we will do that. If we have to snap like cornered dogs, we will do that. If we have to hide like peasants in Tournai and live on eels from the River Scheldt, we will do that. But Richard will not destroy us. No man of this earth can destroy us. We will rise up. We are the children of the goddess Melusina: we may have to ebb but surely we will flow again. And Richard will learn this. He has caught us now at a low and dry place; but by God he will see us in flood.'

I speak very bravely but once I am silent I slide into grief for my Grey son, and for my brother, my dearest brother Anthony. I think of Richard Grey as a little boy once more, sitting so high on the king's horse, holding my hand at the side of the road as we waited for the king to come by. He was my boy, he was my beautiful boy, and his father died in battle against one York brother and now he is dead at the hands of another. I remember my mother mourning her son and saying that when you have got a child through babyhood you think you are safe. But a woman is not safe. Not in this world. Not in this world where brother fights against brother and no one can ever put their sword aside, or trust in the law. I think of him as a baby in the cradle, as a toddler when he learned to walk holding on to my fingers, up and down, up and down the gallery at Grafton till my back ached from stooping, and then I think of him as the young man he was, a good man in the making.

And Anthony my brother has been my dearest and most trusted friend and advisor since we were children together. Edward was right to call him the greatest poet and the finest knight at court. Anthony, who wanted to go on pilgrimage to Jerusalem and who would have gone had I not stopped him. Richard dined with the two of them at Stony Stratford when they met on the road to London, and talked pleasantly of the England that we would all build together, Rivers and Plantagenets, of the shared heir, my boy, that we would put on the throne. Anthony was no fool but he trusted Richard – why should he not? They were kinsmen. They had been side by side in battle, brothers in arms. They had gone into exile together and returned to England in triumph. They were both uncles and guardians to my precious son.

In the morning when Anthony came downstairs to breakfast in his inn, he found the doors barred and his men ordered away. He found Richard and Henry Stafford the Duke of Buckingham armed for battle, their men standing stone-faced in the yard. And they took him away, with my boy Richard Grey, and Sir Thomas Vaughan accused of treason, though they all three were faithful servants of my boy the new king.

Anthony, in prison, awaiting his death in the morning, listens at the window for a moment, in case there is such a thing as the strong sweet song of Melusina, expecting to hear nothing, and then smiles when he hears a bell-like ringing. He shakes his head to clear the noise from his ears; but it stays, an unearthly voice that makes him, irreverently, chuckle. He never believed the legend of the girl who is half fish and half woman, the ancestor of his house; but now he finds he is comforted to hear her singing for his death. He stays at the window and leans his forehead against the cool stone. To hear her voice, high and clear, around the battlements of Pontefract Castle proves at last that his mother's gifts and his sister's gifts and her daughter's gifts are real: as they always claimed, as he only half believed. He wishes he could tell his sister that he knows this now. They may need these gifts. Their gifts may be enough to save them. Perhaps to save all the family who named themselves Rivers to honour the water-goddess who was the founder of their family. Perhaps even to save their two Plantagenet boys. If Melusina can sing for him, an unbeliever, then perhaps she can guide those who listen for her warnings. He smiles because the high clear song gives him hope that Melusina will watch over his sister and her boys, especially the boy who was in his care, the boy he loves: Edward the new King of England. And he smiles because her voice is that of his mother.

He spends the night not in praying, nor in weeping but in writing. In his last hours he is not an adventurer, nor a knight, nor even a brother or an uncle, but a poet. They bring his writings to me and I see that, at the end, at the very moment he was facing his death, and the death of all his hopes, he knew that it was all vanity. Ambition, power, even the throne itself that has cost our family so dear: at the end he knew it was all meaningless. And he did not die in bitterness at this knowledge, but smiling at the folly of man, at his own folly.

He writes:

*Somewhat musing*
*And more mourning,*
*In remembering*
*Th' unsteadfastness;*
*This world being*
*Of such wheeling,*
*Me, contrarying;*
*What may I guess?*

*With displeasure,*
*To my grievance,*
*And no surance*
*Of remedy;*
*Lo, in this trance,*
*Now in substance,*
*Such is my dance,*
*Willing to die*

*Methinks truly,*
*Bounden am I,*
*And that greatly,*

*To be content;*
*Seeing plainly*
*Fortune doth wry*
*All contrary*
*From mine intent.*

This is the last thing he does at dawn, and then they take him out and behead him on the orders of Richard, Duke of Gloucester, the new lord protector of England, who is now responsible for my safety, the safety of all my children, and especially the safety and future of my son Prince Edward, the rightful King of England.

I read Anthony's poem later, and I think that I particularly like 'Fortune doth wry/ All contrary/ From mine intent'. Fortune has gone against all us Rivers this season: he was right in that.

And I shall have to find a way to live without him.

Something has changed between me and my daughter Elizabeth. My girl, my child, my first baby, has suddenly grown up, grown away. The child who believed that I knew everything, that I commanded everything, is now a young woman who has lost her father, and doubts her mother. She thinks I am wrong to keep us in sanctuary. She blames me for the death of her uncle Anthony. She accuses me – though never saying a word – of failing to rescue her brother Edward, of sending her little brother Richard out, unprotected, into the grey silence of the evening river.

She doubts that I have secured a safe hiding place for Richard and that our plan of the changeling page will work. She knows that if I sent a false prince to keep Edward company it is because I doubt my ability to get Edward home safe. She has no hopes of the uprising that my Grey son Thomas is organising. She fears that we will never be rescued.

Ever since the morning when we heard the singing of the river, and then the afternoon when they brought us the news of Anthony and Richard Grey's death, she has no faith in my judgement. She has not repeated her belief that we are cursed but there is something about the darkness of her eyes and the pallor of her face that tells me she is hag-ridden. God knows, I have not cursed her, and I know no one who would do such a thing to such a girl of gold and silver, but it is true: she looks as if someone has put a dark thumbprint down on her and marked her out for a hard destiny.

Dr Lewis comes again and I ask him to look at her and tell me if she is well. She has almost stopped eating and she is pale. 'She needs to be free,' he says simply. 'I tell you as a physician what I hope to see soon as an ally. All your children, you yourself, Your Grace, cannot stay here. You need to be out in the good air, enjoying the summer. She is a delicate girl – she needs exercise and sunshine. She needs company. She is a young woman – she should be dancing and courting. She needs to plan her future, to dream of her betrothal, not to be cooped up here, fearing death.'

'I have an invitation from the king.' I make myself say the title, as if Richard could ever deserve it, as if the crown on his head and the oil on his breast could make him anything more than the traitor and the turncoat he is. 'The king is anxious that I take the girls to my house in the country this summer. He says the princes can be released to me there.'

'And will you go?' He is intent on my answer. He leans forward to hear.

'My boys must be released to me first. I have no guarantee of my safety or that of my girls unless my boys are returned to me, as he promised they would be.'

'Take care, Your Grace, take care. Lady Margaret fears he will play you false,' he breathes. 'She says the Duke of Buckingham thinks that he will have your boys . . .' He hesitates as if he cannot bear to say the words. 'Done to death. She says that the Duke of Buckingham is so horrified by this that he will rescue your boys for you, restore your sons to you, if you will guarantee his safety and his prosperity when you are back in power. If you will promise him your friendship, your undying friendship when you come to your own again. Lady Margaret says that she will bring him to make an alliance with you and yours. The three families: Stafford, Rivers and the House of Lancaster, against the false king.

I nod. I have been waiting for this. 'What does he want?' I ask bluntly.

'His daughter, when he has one, to marry your son, the young King Edward,' he says. 'He himself to be named as regent and lord protector till the young king is of age. He himself to have the kingdom of the north – just as Duke Richard had. If you will make him as great a duke as your husband made Duke Richard he will betray his friend and rescue your sons.'

'And what does she want?' I ask, as if I cannot guess, as if I do not know that she has spent every day of the last twelve years, ever since her son was exiled, trying to bring him safely back to England. He is the only child she has ever conceived, the only heir to her family fortune, to her dead husband's title. Everything she achieves in her life will be nothing if she cannot get her son back to England to inherit.

'She wants an agreement that her son can take his title and inherit her lands, her brother-in-law Jasper restored to his lands in Wales. She wants them both free to return to England, and she wants to betroth her son Henry Tudor to your daughter Elizabeth, and to be named as heir after your boys,' he says in a rush.

I do not pause for a moment. I have only been waiting for the terms and these are exactly what I expected. Not through foreseeing but through the commonplace sense of what I would demand if I were in Lady Margaret's strong position: married to the third greatest man in England, in alliance with the second, planning to betray the first. 'I agree,' I say. 'Tell the Duke of Buckingham and tell Lady Margaret that I agree. And tell them my price: I have to have my sons restored to me at once.'

Next morning, my brother Lionel comes to me smiling. 'There is someone to see you at the water gate,' he says. 'A fisherman. Greet him quietly, my sister. Remember that discretion is a woman's greatest gift.'

I nod and hurry to the door.

Lionel puts a hand on my arm, less a bishop, more a brother. 'Don't shriek like a girl,' he says bluntly, and lets me go.

I slip through the door and go down the stone steps that lead to the stone corridor. It is shadowy, lit only by the daylight filtering through the iron gate which opens out to the river. A little wherry is bobbing at the doorway, a small fishing net piled in the stern. A man in a filthy cape and a pulled-down hat is waiting at the doorway, but nothing can disguise his height. Forewarned by Lionel I don't cry out, and dissuaded by the stink of old fish I don't run into his arms. I just say quietly, 'Brother, my brother, I am glad with all my heart to see you.'

A flash of his dark eyes from under the heavy brim shows me my brother Richard Woodville's smiling face, villainously covered with a beard and a moustache. 'Are you all right?' I ask, rather shocked at his appearance.

'Never better,' he says jauntily.

'And you know about our brother Anthony?' I ask. 'And my son Richard Grey?'

He nods, suddenly grim. 'I heard this morning. That's partly why I came today. I am sorry, Elizabeth, I am sorry for your loss.'

'You are Earl Rivers now,' I say. 'The third Earl Rivers. You are head of the family. We seem to be getting through heads of our family rather quickly. Do you, please, hold the title a little longer.'

'I'll do what I can,' he promises. 'God knows, I inherit the title of two good men. I hope to hold it longer, but I doubt I can do better. Anyway, we are close to an uprising. Listen to me.

Richard feels himself secure with the crown on his head, and he is to go on progress to show himself to the kingdom.'

I have to stop myself spitting into the water. 'I wonder the horses have the brass neck even to walk.'

'As soon as he is out of London, his guard with him, we will storm the Tower and get Edward out. The Duke of Buckingham is with us and I trust him. He has to travel with King Richard, and the king will force Stanley go with him too – he still doubts him; but Lady Margaret will stay in London and command the Stanley men and her own affinity to join us. Already she has her men placed in the Tower.'

'Will we have enough men?'

'Near on a hundred. The new king has made Sir Robert Brackenbury the constable of the Tower. Brackenbury would never hurt a boy in his care – he is a good man. I have put new servants in the royal rooms, men who will open the doors for me when I give them the word.'

'And then?'

'We get you and the girls safely away to Flanders. Your sons, Richard and Edward, can join you,' he says. 'Have you heard from the men who took Prince Richard yet? Is he safe in hiding?'

'Not yet,' I say fretfully. 'I have been looking for a message every day. I should have heard that he is safe by now. I pray for him every hour. I should have heard by now.'

'A letter could have gone astray; it means nothing. If it had gone wrong they would have sent you news for sure. And just think: you can collect Richard from his hiding place on your way to Margaret's court. Once you are with your boys and safe again, we raise our army. Buckingham will declare for us. Lord Stanley and his whole family is promised by his wife, Margaret Beaufort. Half of Richard's other lords are ready to turn against him, according to the Duke of Buckingham. Lady Margaret's son Henry Tudor will raise arms and men in Brittany, and invade Wales.'

'When?' I breathe.

He glances behind him. The river is busy as ever with ships coming and going, little trading wherries weaving in and out of the bigger boats. 'Duke Richard—' He breaks off and grins at me. 'Forgive me, "King Richard" is to leave London at the end of July on progress. We will rescue Edward at once, and give you and him long enough to get to safety, say two days, and then, while the king is out of touch, we will rise.'

'And Edward our brother?'

'Edward is recruiting men in Devon and Cornwall. Your son Thomas is working in Kent. Buckingham will bring out the men from Dorset and Hampshire, Stanley will bring out his affinity from the Midlands, and Margaret Beaufort and her son can raise Wales in the name of the Tudors. All the men of your husband's household are determined to save his sons.'

I nibble at my finger thinking as my husband would have thought: Men, arms, money and the spread of support around the south of England. 'It is enough if we can defeat Richard before he brings in his men from the north.'

He grins at me, the Rivers' reckless grin. 'It is enough and we have everything to win and nothing to lose,' he says. 'He has taken the crown from our boy: we have nothing to fear. The worst has already happened.'

'The worst has already happened,' I repeat, and the shiver that goes down my spine I attribute to the loss of Anthony my brother, my dearest brother, and the death of my Grey son. 'The worst has already happened. There can be nothing worse than our losses already.'

Richard puts his dirty hand on mine. 'Be ready to leave whenever I send the word,' he says. 'I will tell you as soon as I have Prince Edward safe.'

'I will.'

# JULY 1483

I am waiting at the window, dressed in my travelling cape, my chest of jewels at my hand, my girls with me, ready to leave. We are silent, we have been silently waiting for more than an hour. We are straining to hear something, anything, but there is only the slap of the river against the walls and the occasional burst of music or laughter from the streets. Elizabeth beside me is tight as a lute string, white with anxiety.

Then there is a sudden crash of noise and my brother Lionel comes running into the sanctuary and slams and bolts the door behind him.

'We failed,' he says, gasping for breath. 'Our brothers are safe, your son too. They got away down the river and Richard went to earth in the Minories, but we couldn't take the White Tower.'

'Did you see my boy?' I demand.

He shakes his head. 'They had the two boys in there. I heard them shouting orders. We were so close I could hear them shouting through the door to take the boys inward, to a more secure chamber. Dear God, sister, forgive me. I was the thickness of a door away from them but we could not batter it down.'

I sit down as my knees give way beneath me and I drop the box of jewels to the floor. Elizabeth is ashen. She turns and slowly starts to take the girls' capes off, one by one, folding them up, as if it is important that they are not creased.

'My son,' I say. 'My son.'

'We got in through the water gate, and then across the first lane before they even saw us. We were starting up the steps as someone sounded the alarm, and though we sprinted up the steps to the door of the White Tower they slammed it shut. We were just seconds away from it. Thomas was firing at the locks and we threw ourselves against it but I heard the bolts slam from the inside and then they came pouring out of the guard room. Richard and I turned to face them and we fought, holding them off, while Thomas and the Stanley men tried to batter the door in, or even lift it from its hinges, but you know – it is too strong.'

'The Stanleys were there, as they promised?'

'They were, and Buckingham's men. None in their livery, of course, but they all wore a white rose. It was strange to see the white rose again. And strange to be fighting to enter a place that we own. I shouted to Edward to be of good cheer, that we would come for him, that we would not fail him. I don't know if he heard. I don't know.'

'You're hurt,' I say, suddenly noticing the cut on his forehead.

He rubs it, as if his blood were dirt. 'It is nothing. Elizabeth, I would rather have died than come back without him.'

'Don't speak of death,' I say quietly. 'Pray God he is safe tonight and was not frightened by this. Pray God they just take him to a more secure room inside the Tower and don't think to take him away.'

'And it may only be for another month,' he says to me. 'Richard said to remind you of that. Your friends are arming, King Richard is riding north with only his personal guard. Buckingham and Stanley are in his train; they will persuade him not to turn back. They will encourage him to go on to York. Jasper Tudor will bring an army from Brittany. Our next battle will come soon. When the usurper Richard is dead we will have the keys to the Tower in our hands.'

Elizabeth straightens up, her sisters' cloaks draped neatly over her arm. 'And do you trust all your new friends, Mother?' she asks coldly. 'All these new allies who have suddenly come to your side but don't succeed? All of them ready to risk their lives to restore Edward to his throne when they all ate well and drank deep at Duke Richard's coronation just a few weeks ago? I hear that Lady Margaret carried the train of the new Queen Anne, just as she used to carry yours. The new queen kissed her on both cheeks. She was honoured at the coronation. Now she calls out her men for us? Now she is our loyal ally? The Duke of Buckingham was the ward who hated you for marrying him to my aunt Katherine, and he still hates you. Are these your true allies? Or are they loyal servants of the new king set out to entrap you? For they play both parts, and they are travelling with him now, and feasting at Oxford. They weren't there in danger at the Tower, rescuing my brother.'

I look at her coldly in return. 'I cannot choose my allies,' I say. 'To save my son I would plot with the devil himself.'

She shows me the ghost of a sour smile. 'Perhaps you already have.'

# AUGUST 1483

The summer grows very hot and Lionel slips out of sanctuary and out of London to join our brothers and our allies in the rebellion that is to defeat Richard. Without him I feel very much alone. Elizabeth is quiet and distant, and I have nobody to share my fears. Downriver my son remains a prisoner in the Tower, and Jemma tells us that nobody sees him or the little changeling playing in the Tower gardens any more. They had been practising archery on the green; but nobody sees them at the butts now. Since our rescue attempt their guardians have kept them close inside, and I start to fear the danger of plague in the heat of the City and think of them in those small dark rooms.

At the end of August there is a shout from a boatman on the river and I swing open the window wide and look out. Sometimes they bring me gifts, often just a creel of fish, but this man has a ball in his hand. 'Can you catch, Your Grace?' he asks, seeing me at the window.

I smile. 'Yes, I can,' I say.

'Then catch this,' he says and tosses a white ball up to me. It comes soaring through the window over my head, and I reach up and catch it double-handed and laugh for a moment at the fun of playing again. Then I see it is a ball wrapped in white paper and I go back to the window; but the man has gone.

I unwrap it and smooth out the paper and I put my hand to my heart and then to my mouth to silence my cry as I recognise the childish round hand of my little boy Richard.

*Dearest Lady Mother,*
*Greetings and blessings* [he starts carefully]. *I am not allowed to write often, nor to tell you exactly where I am, in case the letter is stolen, except to say that I arrived safely and it is quite all right here. They are kind people and I have learned how to row a boat already and they say I am good and handy. In a little while I am to go away to school for they cannot teach me all I need to know here, but I will come back for the summer and go fishing for eels, which are very nice when you get used to them, unless I can come home to you again.*

*Give my love to my sisters and my love and duty to my brother the king, and my honour and love to you.*
*Signed,*
*Your son Richard, Duke of York.*
*Though now I am called Peter, and I remember to answer to Peter always. The woman here, who is kind to me, calls me her little Perkin and I don't mind this.*

I read the words through tears, then I mop my eyes and read them again. I smile at the thought of him being called handy, and I have to take a breath to stop myself crying out at the thought of him being called Perkin. I want to weep at him being taken away from me, so young, such a small boy; and yet he is safe, I should be glad that he is safe: the only one of my children away from the danger of being of this family in this country, in these wars, which will start again. The boy who now answers to Peter will go quietly to school, learn languages, music, and wait. If we win, he will come home as a prince of the blood, if we lose he will be the weapon they do not know we have, the boy in hiding, the prince in waiting, the nemesis of their ambitions; and my revenge. He and his, will haunt every king who comes after us, like a ghost.

'Mother Mary watch over him,' I whisper, my head in my hands, my eyes shut tight on my tears. 'Melusina, guard our boy.'

# SEPTEMBER 1483

Every day I get news of the arming and preparing of our people, not just in the counties where my brothers are active but all around the country. As the news slowly spreads that Richard has taken the crown, more and more of the common people, the small squires and market traders, and their betters: the heads of guilds and the small landlords, the greater men of the country, ask: how shall a younger brother take the inheritance of his dead brother's son? How is any man to go quietly to his Maker if such a thing can happen, unchallenged? Why should a man strive all his life to make his family great if his little brother, the runt of the litter, can step into his shoes the minute he weakens?

And there are many, at the many places we used to visit, who remember Edward as a handsome man and me as his beautiful wife, those who remember the girls in their prettiness and our strong bright little boys. Those who called us a golden family who had brought peace to England and a quiver of heirs to the throne; and these people say that it is an outrage that we should not be in our palaces with our boy on the throne.

I write to my son the little King Edward and bid him be of good cheer but my letters have started to come back without being opened. They come back untouched, the seals unbroken. I am not even spied upon. It is as if they are denying that he is even at the royal rooms in the Tower. I fret for the outbreak of the war that will free him and wish we would bring it forward, and not wait for Richard's slow vainglorious progress northward through Oxfordshire, then Gloucestershire, then to Pontefract and York. At York he crowns his son, the thin and sickly boy, as Prince of Wales. He gives my Edward's title to his son as if my boy was dead. I spend this day on my knees praying for God to give me revenge for this affront. I dare not think that it might be worse than an insult. I cannot bear to think that it might be that the title is vacant, that my son is dead.

Elizabeth comes to me at dinnertime and helps me to my feet. 'You know what your uncle has done today?' I ask her.

She turns her face away from me. 'I know,' she says steadily. 'The town crier was shouting it all around the square. I could hear him from the doorway.'

'You didn't open the door?' I demand anxiously.

She sighs. 'I didn't open the door. I never open the door.'

'Duke Richard has stolen your father's crown and now he has put his son in your brother's robes. He will die for this,' I predict.

'Haven't enough people died already?'

I take her hand and turn her towards me so she has to face me. 'We are talking about the throne of England here, your brother's birthright.'

'We are talking about the death of a family,' she says flatly. 'You have daughters too, you know. Have you thought of our birthright? We have been cooped up here like rats for all summer, while you pray all day for revenge. Your most precious son is imprisoned or dead – you don't even know which. You sent your other out into the darkness. We don't know where he is, or even if he is still alive. You thirst for the throne, but you don't even know if you have a boy to put on it.'

I gasp and step back. 'Elizabeth!'

'I wish you would send word to my uncle that you accept his rule,' she says coldly, and her hand in mine is like ice. 'I wish you would tell him that we are ready to come to terms – actually any terms that he chooses to name. I wish you would persuade him to release us to be an ordinary family, living at Grafton, far away from London, far away from plotting and treason and the threat of death. If you surrendered now, we might get my brothers back.'

'That would be for me to go right back to where I came from!' I exclaim.

'Were you not happy at Grafton with your mother and father, and with the husband who gave you Richard and Thomas?' she asks quickly, so quickly that I do not prepare my answer carefully.

'Yes,' I say unguardedly. 'Yes, I was.'

'That is all I want for myself,' she says. 'All I want for my sisters. And yet you insist on making us heirs to your misery. I want to be heir to the days before you were queen. I don't want the throne: I want to marry a man that I love, and love him freely.'

I look at her. 'Then you would deny your father, you would deny me, you would deny everything that makes you a Plantagenet, a princess of York. You might as well be Jemma the maid if you don't desire to be greater than you are, if you don't see your chances and take them.'

She looks steadily back at me. 'I would rather be Jemma the maid than you,' she says, and her voice is filled with the harsh contempt of a girl. 'Jemma can go home to her own bed at night. Jemma can refuse to work. Jemma can run away and serve another master. But you are locked to the throne of England and you have enslaved us too.'

I draw myself up. 'You may not speak to me like this,' I say to her coldly.

'I speak from my heart,' she says.

'Then tell your heart to be true but your mouth to be silent. I don't want disloyalty from my own daughter.'

'We are not an army at war! Don't speak to me of disloyalty! What will you do? Behead me for treason?'

'We are an army at war,' I say simply. 'And you will not betray me, nor your own position.'

I speak truer than I know, for we are an army on the march and that night we make our first move. The men of Kent rise first and when they hear the rallying cries Sussex rises up with them. But the Duke of Norfolk, who remains true to Richard, marches his men south from London and holds our army down. They cannot reach their comrades in the west; he blocks the only road at Guildford. One man gets through to London, hires a little boat and comes to the sanctuary water gate, under cover of mist and rain.

'Sir John,' I say through the grille. I dare not even open the gate for the screech of the iron on the wet stone, and besides, I don't know him, and trust no one.

'I have come to tender my sympathy, Your Grace,' he says awkwardly. 'And to know – my brothers and I want to know – if it is your will that we support Henry Tudor now.'

'What?' I ask. 'What d'you mean?'

'We prayed for the prince, every day we did, and lit a candle for him, and all of us at Reigate are more sorry than we can say that we are too late for him. We . . .'

'Wait,' I say urgently. 'Wait. What are you saying?'

His big face is suddenly aghast. 'Oh God spare me, don't say you did not know and I have told you like a great fool?' He wrings his hat in his hands, so the plume dips into the river water that laps at the steps. 'Oh gentle madam, I am a fool. I should have made sure . . .' He glances anxiously up the dark passage-way behind me. 'Call a lady,' he says. 'Don't you go fainting now.'

I hold the grating in clenched hands, though my head swims. 'I won't,' I promise him through dry lips. 'I don't faint. Are you saying that the young King Edward is executed?'

He shakes his head. 'Dead, is all I know. God bless your sweet face, and forgive me for being the one to tell you such dark news. Such bad news and I to bring it to you! When all we wanted to know was your wishes now.'

'Not executed?'

He shakes his head. 'Nothing public. Poor boys. We know

nothing for certain. We were just told that the princes were put to death, God bless them, and that the rebellion would go on against King Richard, who is still a usurper, but that we would put Henry Tudor on the throne as the next heir and the next best thing for the country.'

I laugh, a cracked unhappy sound. 'Margaret Beaufort's boy? Instead of mine?'

He looks around him for help, frightened by the ring of madness in my laughter. 'We didn't know. We were sworn to free the princes. We all mustered in your cause, Your Grace. So we don't know what we should do, now your princes have gone. And Thomas Howard's men are holding the road to your brother's camp, so we couldn't ask him. We thought it best that I should slip away quietly, and come to London to ask you.'

'Who told you they are dead?'

He thinks for a moment. 'It was a man from the Duke of Buckingham. He brought us some gold, and weapons for those who had none. He said we could trust his master, who had turned against the false King Richard for killing the boys. He said the duke had been the King Richard's loyal servant, thinking him the protector of the boys, but when he found out that he had killed our princes he turned against him in horror. He said that the duke knew all that the false king did and said, but he could not prevent this murder.' He looks at me warily again. 'God keep Your Grace. Should you not have a lady with you?'

'The duke's man told you all this?'

'A good man, he told us it all. And he paid for the men to have a drink to the Duke of Buckingham as well. He said that the false King Richard had ordered their deaths in secret before he left on his progress, and that, when he told the duke what he had done, the duke swore he could have no more of this murderer's reign but would defy King Richard and we should all rise up against this man who would kill boys. The duke himself would make a better king than Richard and he has a claim to the throne, and all.'

Surely I would know if my son was dead? I heard the river sing for my brother. If my son and heir, the heir to my house, the heir to the throne of England, was dead I would surely know that? Surely, my son could not be killed no more than three miles from me, and I not know it? So I don't believe it. I won't believe it until they show me his blessed body. He is not dead. I cannot believe he is dead. I will not believe he is dead until I see him in his coffin.

'Listen to me.' I draw close to the bars and speak earnestly to him. 'You go back to Kent and tell your fellows that they are to rise for the princes, for my boys are still alive. The duke is mistaken and the king has not killed them. I know this, I am their mother. Tell them also that, even if Edward was dead, his brother Richard is not with him but safely got away. He is safe in hiding and he will come back and take the throne that is his. You go back to Kent and, when the word comes for you to muster and march out, go with a proud heart for you must destroy this false King Richard and free my boys and free me.'

'And the duke?' he asks. 'And Henry Tudor?'

I make a face, and wave the thought of the two of them away. 'Loyal allies to our cause, I am sure,' I say with a certainty I no longer feel. 'You be true to me, Sir John, and I will remember you and every single one who fights for me and my sons, when I am come to my own again.'

He bows and ducks back down the stairs and steps cautiously into the rocking row-boat and then he is lost in the dark mist of the river. I wait for him to disappear and for the quiet splash of the oars to fade away and then I look down into the dark waters. 'The duke,' I whisper into the waters. 'The Duke of Buckingham is telling everyone that my sons are dead. Why would he do that? When he is sworn to rescue them? When he is sending gold and arms to the rebellion? Why would he tell them, in the very moment that he calls them out, that the princes are dead?'

I eat supper with my girls and with the few servants that have stayed with us in sanctuary but I cannot hear seven-year-old Anne's careful reading of the Bible, nor join Elizabeth in questioning them as to what they have just heard. I am as inattentive as Catherine who is only four. I can think of nothing but why there should be a rumour that my boys are dead.

I send the girls to bed early; I cannot bear to hear them playing at cards or singing a round. All night I walk up and down in my room, stepping along the one floorboard that does not creak to the window over the river, and back again the other way. Why would Richard kill my boys now, when he has accomplished all that he wanted without their deaths? He has persuaded the council to name them as bastards, he has passed an act of parliament which denies my marriage. He has named himself as the next legitimate heir and the archbishop himself has put the crown on his dark head. His sickly wife Anne is crowned as Queen of England and their son is invested as Prince of Wales. All this was achieved with me mewed up in sanctuary, and my son in prison. Richard is triumphant: why would he want us dead? Why would he need us dead now? And how should he hope to escape blame for the crime, when everyone knows the boys are in his keeping? Everyone knows he took my son Richard against my will; it could not have been more public, and the archbishop himself swore that no harm would come to him.

And it is not like Richard to ride away from work that needs doing. When he and his brothers decided that poor King Henry should die, the three of them met outside his door and went in together, their faces grim but their minds made up. These are York princes: they have no objection to wicked deeds; but they do not leave them to others, they do them first-hand. The risk of asking another to kill two innocent princes of the blood, bribing the guards, hiding the bodies, would be unbearable for Richard.

I have seen how he kills: directly, without warning, but openly, without shame. The man who beheaded Sir William Hastings on a piece of builders' timber would not wink at holding a pillow over the face of a young boy. If the thing was to be done, I would have sworn he would do it himself. At the very least he would give the order and watch that it was done.

All this is to convince me that Sir John from Reigate is mistaken and my boy Edward is still alive. But again and again as I turn at the window and glance down at the river in darkness and mist, I wonder if I am mistaken, mistaken in everything, even in my trust in Melusina. Perhaps Richard managed to find someone who would kill the boys. Perhaps Edward is dead, and perhaps I have lost the Sight, and I just don't know. Perhaps I know nothing any more.

By the early hours of the morning I cannot bear to be alone for another minute, and I send a messenger to fetch Dr Lewis to me. I tell them to wake him and get him out of bed for I am mortally ill. By the time he is admitted by the guards, my lie is becoming true, and I am running a fever from sheer agony of mind.

'Your Grace?' he asks cautiously.

I am haggard in the candlelight, my hair in a clumsy plait, my robe knotted around me. 'You have to get your servants, trusted men, into the Tower to guard my son Edward, since we cannot get him out,' I say bluntly. 'Lady Margaret must use her influence, she must use her husband's name, to ensure my sons are well guarded. They are in danger. They are in terrible danger.'

'You have news?'

'There is a rumour spreading that my boys are dead,' I say.

He shows no surprise. 'God forbid it, Your Grace; but I fear that it is more than a rumour. It is as the Duke of Buckingham warned us. He said that this false king would kill his nephews to get the throne.'

I recoil, very slightly, as if I had put out my hand and seen a snake sunning itself where I was about to touch.

'Yes,' I say, suddenly wary. 'That is what I have heard, and it was the Duke of Buckingham's man who said it.'

He crosses himself. 'God spare us.'

'But I hope that the deed is not yet done, and I hope to prevent it.'

He nods. 'Alas, I am afraid, that we may be too late, and that they are already lost to us. Your Grace, I grieve with all my heart for you.'

'I thank you for your sympathy,' I say steadily. My temples are throbbing, I cannot think. It is as if I am looking at the snake and it looks back at me.

'Please God, this uprising destroys the uncle who could do such a thing. God will be on our side against such a Herod.'

'If it *was* Richard.'

He looks at me suddenly, as if this shocks him, though he seems well able to tolerate the idea of the murder of children. 'Who else could do such a thing? Who else would benefit? Who killed Sir William Hastings, and your brother and your other son? Who is the murderer of your family and your worst enemy, Your Grace? You can suspect no one else!'

I can feel myself tremble and the tears start to come; they are burning my eyes. 'I don't know,' I say unsteadily. 'I just feel certain that my boy is not dead. I would know if he was killed. A mother would know that. Ask Lady Margaret: she would know if her Henry was dead. A mother knows. And anyway, my Richard at least is safe.'

He takes the bait and I see his response – I see the flash of a spy looking from his melting eyes. 'Oh, is he?' he asks invitingly.

I have said enough. 'They are both safe, please God,' I correct myself. 'But tell me – why are you so certain that they are dead?'

He puts his hand gently on mine. 'I did not want to grieve you. But they have not been seen since the false king left London, and the duke and Lady Margaret both believe that he had them killed before he left. There was nothing any of us could do to save them. When we besieged the Tower they were already dead.'

I pull my hand away from his comforting grasp and put it to my aching forehead. I wish I could think clearly. I remember Lionel telling me that he heard the servants shouting to take the boys deeper into the Tower. I remember him telling me that he was just the distance of the door from Edward. But why would Dr Lewis lie to me?

'Would it not have been better for our cause if the duke had kept silent?' I ask. 'My friends and family and allies are recruiting men to rescue the princes, but the duke is telling them that they are already dead. Why should my men turn out, if their prince is dead?'

'As well they should know now as later,' he says smoothly, too smoothly.

'Why?' I say. 'Why should they know now, before the battle?'

'So that everyone knows it is the false king who gave the order,' he says. 'So that Duke Richard has the blame. Your people will rise for revenge.'

I cannot think, I cannot think why this matters. I can sense a lie in here somewhere, but I cannot put my finger on it. Something is wrong, I know it.

'But who would doubt that it is King Richard who had them killed? As you say, the murderer of my kinsmen? Why would we declare our fears now, and confuse our people?'

'Nobody would doubt it,' he assures me. 'No one else but Richard would do such a thing. No one else would benefit from such a crime.'

I jump to my feet in sudden impatience, and knock the table and overturn the candlestick.

'I don't understand!'

He snatches at the candle and the flame bobs and throws a terrible shadow on his friendly face. For a moment he is as he was when I first saw him when Cecily came to tell me that Death was at the door. I gasp in fear and I step back from him as he puts the candle carefully back on the table and stands, as he should do, since I, the dowager queen, am standing.

'You can go,' I say disjointedly. 'Forgive me, I am distressed. I don't know what to think. You can leave me.'

'Shall I give you a draught to help you sleep? I am so sorry for your grief.'

'No, I will sleep now. I thank you for your company.' I take a breath. I push back the hair from my face. 'You have calmed me with your wisdom. I am at peace now.'

He looks puzzled. 'But I have said nothing.'

I shake my head. I cannot wait for him to leave. 'You have shared my worries and that is the act of a friend.'

'I shall see Lady Margaret first thing this morning and tell her of your fears. I shall ask her to put her men in the Tower to get news of your boys. If they are alive, we will find men to guard them. We will keep them safe.'

'At least Richard is safe,' I remark incautiously.

'Safer than his brother?'

I smile like a woman with a secret. 'Doctor, if you had two precious rare jewels and you feared thieves, would you put your two treasures in the same box?'

'Richard was not in the Tower?' His voice is a breath, his blue eyes staring; he is all aquiver.

I put my finger to my lips. 'Hush.'

'But two boys were killed in the bed . . .'

Were they? Oh were they? How are you so very sure of this? I keep my face as still as marble as he turns from me, and bows and goes to the door.

'Tell Lady Margaret I beg her to guard my son in the Tower as if he were her own,' I say.

He bows again and is gone.

When the children wake I tell them I am ill and I keep to my chamber. Elizabeth I turn away at the door and tell her that I need to sleep. I don't need sleep, I need to understand. I hold my head in my hands and walk up and down the room barefoot, so that they don't hear that I am pacing, racking my brains. I am alone in a world of master-conspirators. The Duke of Buckingham and Lady Margaret are working together, or perhaps they are working for themselves. They are pretending to serve me, to be allies, or perhaps they are loyal and I am wrong to mistrust them. My mind goes round and round and I pull the hair at my temples as if the pain could make me think.

I have ill-wished Richard, the tyrant; but his death can wait. He imprisoned my boys; but it is not he who is spreading the rumour that they are dead. He was holding them in prison against their will, against my will; but he was not preparing the people for their deaths. He has taken the throne and he has taken the title Prince of Wales by lies and deception. He does not need to kill them to get his own way. He is triumphant already, without murdering my son. He got all he wanted without blood on his hands, so there is no need for him to kill Edward now. Richard is safe on the throne, the council has accepted him, the lords have accepted him, he is on a royal progress in a country that greets him with joy. There is a rebellion in the making, of my making; but he thinks Howard has put it down. As far as he knows he is safe. He need only keep my boys imprisoned until I am ready to accept my defeat, as Elizabeth urges me to do.

But the Duke of Buckingham has a claim to inherit the throne that would follow that of Richard's line – but only if my sons were dead. His claim is no good unless my sons are dead. If Richard's sickly son were to die and Richard were to fall in battle and Buckingham were leading the victorious rebellion, then Buckingham could take the crown. Nobody would deny that he is the next heir – especially if everyone knew that my sons were already dead. Then Buckingham would do just as my Edward did when he claimed the crown; but there was a rival claimant in the Tower. When my Edward entered London at the head of a victorious army, he went straight away with his two brothers into the Tower of London where the true king was prisoner and they killed him, though Henry had no more strength than an innocent boy. When the Duke of Buckingham defeats Richard he will march into London and into the Tower saying he will have the truth about my boys. Then there will be a pause, long enough for people to remember the rumours and start to fear, and Buckingham will come out, tragic-faced, and say that he has found my boys dead, buried under a paving stone, or hidden in a cupboard, murdered by their wicked uncle Richard. This is the truth of the rumour that he himself started. He will say that, since they are dead, he will take the throne and there will be nobody left alive to deny him.

And Buckingham is Constable of England. He has the keys to the Tower in his hands right now.

I nibble my finger and pause at the window. So much for Buckingham. Now let me consider my great friend Lady Margaret Stanley and her son Henry Tudor. They are the heirs of the House of Lancaster; she might think it time England turned to Lancaster again. She has to ally with Buckingham and with my followers; the Tudor boy cannot bring in enough foreign recruits to defeat Richard on his own. He has lived his life in exile: this is his chance to come back to England and come back as king. She would be a fool to take such a risk as rebelling against Richard for anything less than the throne. Her new husband is an essential ally of Richard's; they are well placed in this new court. She has negotiated her son's forgiveness and safe return to England with Richard. She has been allowed to hand her lands over to her son, as his inheritance. Would she throw all this into jeopardy for the pleasure of putting my son on the throne to oblige me? Why would she? Why ever would she take such a risk? Is she not more likely to be working for her own son to claim the throne? She and Buckingham together are preparing the country to learn that my sons are dead, at Richard's hand.

Would Henry Tudor be hard enough of heart to march into the Tower declaring he is bent on rescue, strangle two boys, and come out with the dreadful news that the princes, for whom he was bravely fighting, are dead? Could he and his great friend and ally Buckingham divide up the kingdom together: Henry Tudor taking his fiefdom of Wales, Buckingham taking the north? Or if Buckingham was dead in battle, would Henry not be the uncontested heir to the throne? Would his mother send her servants into the Tower, not to save my boy, but to suffocate him as he sleeps? Could she bear to do that, saintly woman as she is? Would she countenance anything for her son, even the death of mine? I don't know. I can't know. All I can know for certain is that the duke and Lady Margaret are spreading the word, even while they are marching out to fight for the princes, that they believe the princes are already dead, and her ally lets slip that the two boys are killed in bed. The only man not preparing the world to mourn their deaths, the only man who does not benefit from their deaths, is the one that I thought was my mortal enemy: Richard of Gloucester.

It takes me all day to measure my danger, and even at dinnertime I cannot be sure of anything. The lives of my sons may depend on who I sense as my enemy and who I trust as my friend and yet I cannot be certain. My suggestion: that my son Richard at least is safe and away from the Tower should give any murderer pause; I hope I have bought some time.

In the afternoon I write to my brothers as they are raising men in the southern counties of England, to warn them of this plot that may be hatching like a snake in its egg inside our plot. I say that our enemy Richard is still our enemy; but his ill-will may be nothing to the danger posed by our allies. I send out messengers, uncertain if they will ever reach my brothers, or reach them in time. But I say clearly:

*I believe now that the safety of my sons, of myself, depends on the Duke of Buckingham and his ally Henry Tudor not reaching London. Richard is our enemy and a usurper but I believe if Buckingham and Tudor march into London in victory they will come as our killers. You must stop Buckingham's march. Whatever you do, you must get to the Tower ahead of him and ahead of Henry Tudor and save our boy.*

That night I stand at the window over the river and listen. Elizabeth opens the door of the bedroom where the girls sleep and comes to stand behind me, her young face grave.

'What is the matter now, Mother?' she says. 'Please tell me. You have been locked up all day. Have you had bad news?'

'Yes,' I say. 'Tell me, have you heard the river singing, like it did on the night that my brother Anthony, and my son Richard Grey died?'

Her eyes slide away from mine.

'Elizabeth?'

'Not like that night,' she qualifies.

'But you hear something?'

'Very faintly,' she says, 'a very soft, low singing like a lullaby, like a lament. Do you hear nothing?'

I shake my head. 'No, but I am filled with fear for Edward.'

She comes and puts her hand on mine. 'Is there new danger for my poor brother, even now?'

'I think so. I think that the Duke of Buckingham will turn on us if he wins this battle against the false King Richard. I have written to your uncles but I don't know if they can stop him. The Duke of Buckingham has a great army. He is marching along the River Severn in Wales and then he will come into England, and I don't know what I can do. I don't know what I can do from here to keep my son safe from him, to keep us all safe from him. We have to keep him from London. If I could trap him in Wales, I would.'

She looks thoughtful and goes to the window. The damp air from the river breathes into the stuffy rooms. 'I wish it would rain,' she says idly. 'It's so hot. I so wish it would rain.'

A cool breeze whispers into the room as if to answer her wish, and then the pit, pat, pit of raindrops on the leaded panes of the open window. Elizabeth swings open the window wider so that she can see the sky and the dark clouds blowing down the river valley.

I go to stand beside her. I can see the rain falling on the dark water of the river, fat drops of rain that make the first few circles, like the bubbles from a fish, and then more and more, until the silky surface of the river is pitted with falling raindrops and then the storm comes down so hard that we can see nothing but a whirl of falling water as if the very heavens are opening on England. We laugh and pull the window shut against the storm, our faces and arms running with water before we get the clasp bolted, and then we go to the other rooms, closing the windows and barring the shutters against the weather which is pouring down outside as if all my grief and worry were a storm of tears over England.

'This rain will bring a flood,' I predict, and my daughter nods in silence.

It rains all night. Elizabeth sleeps in my bed as she used to do when she was a child, and we lie in the warm and dry, and listen to the pattering of the drops. We can hear the constant wash against the windows and the splashing on the river. Then the gutters start to fill and the water from the roofs runs with a sound like fountains playing, and we fall asleep, like two water-goddesses to the sound of driving rain and rising water.

When we wake in the morning it is almost as dark as night, and it is still raining. It is high tide and Elizabeth goes down to the water gate and says the water is rising over the steps. All the craft on the river are battened down for bad weather and the few wherries that are plying for trade are rowed by men hunched against the wind with sacks over their heads, shiny with the wet. The girls spend the morning up at the windows watching the soaked boats go by. They are riding higher than usual as the river fills and starts to flood, and then the little boats are all taken in and moored or hauled up as the river goes into spate and the currents are too strong. We light a fire against the stormy day, it is as dark and wet as November, and I play cards with the girls and let them win. How I love the sound of this rain.

Elizabeth and I sleep in each other's arms, listening to the water pouring off the roof of the abbey and cascading onto the pavements. In the early hours of the morning I start to hear the dripping sound of rain leaking through the slate roof, and I get up to start the fire again and put a pot under the drips. Elizabeth opens the shutter and says that it is raining as hard as ever; it looks like it might rain all day.

The girls play at Noah's Ark and Elizabeth reads them the story from the Bible and then they prepare a pageant with their toys and roughly stuffed cushions serving as pairs of animals. The ark is my table upturned with sheets tied from leg to leg. I let them eat their dinner inside the ark and reassure them before bedtime that the great flood for Noah happened a long long time ago and God would not send another, not even to punish wickedness. This rain will do nothing but keep bad men in their houses, where they can do no harm. A flood will keep all the wicked men away from London, and we shall be safe.

Elizabeth looks at me with a little smile, and after the girls have gone to bed she takes a candle and goes down through the catacombs to look at the level of the river water.

It is running higher than it has ever done before, she says. She thinks it will flood the corridor to the steps, a rise of several feet. If it does not stop raining soon, it will come even higher. We are not at risk – it is two flights of stone stairs down to the river – but the poor people who live on the riverbanks will be packing up their few things and abandoning their homes to the water.

The next morning Jemma comes in to us with her dress hitched up, muddy to the knees. The streets are flooding in the low-lying areas and there are stories of houses being swept away and, upriver, bridges being destroyed and villages being cut off. Nobody has ever seen such rain in September and it still does not stop. Jemma says that there are no fresh foods in the market as many of the roads are washed away and the farmers cannot bring in their goods. Bread is more expensive for lack of flour and some bakers cannot get their ovens to light, for all they have is wet firewood. Jemma says she will stay the night with us – she is afraid to leave through the flooded streets.

In the morning it is still raining and the girls, at the window again, report strange sights. A drowned cow frightens Bridget as it floats by beneath the window, an overturned cart has been swept into the waters, and timbers from some building go by rolling over and over in the flood, and we hear the thud as something heavy hits the water gate steps. The water gate is a gate only to water this morning; the corridor is flooded and we can see only the very top of the ironwork and a glimpse of daylight. The river must be up by nearly ten feet, and high tide will pour water into the catacombs and wash the sleeping dead.

I don't look for a messenger from my brothers. I don't expect that anyone could get through from the West Country to London in this weather. But I don't need to hear from them to know what is happening. The rivers are up against Buckingham, the tide is running against Henry Tudor, the rain is pouring down on their armies, the waters of England have risen up to protect their prince.

## OCTOBER 1483

Richard the false king, appalled at the betrayal of his great friend and the man he had raised to be Constable of England takes only a moment to realise that the force mustered by the Duke of Buckingham is enough to defeat the royal guard twice over. He has to raise an army, commanding every able-bodied man in England to rally to his side, demanding their loyalty as their king. Mostly, they turn out for him, albeit slowly. The Duke of Norfolk has held down the rebellion in the southern counties. He is sure that London is safe, but he has no doubt that Buckingham is raising troops in Wales, and that Henry Tudor will sail from Brittany to join him there. If Henry brings in a thousand men, then the rebels and the King's army will be well matched, and nobody would bet on the outcome. If he brings in more than that, Richard will be fighting for his survival against bad odds and against an army led by Jasper Tudor, one of the greatest commanders that Lancaster has ever had.

Richard marches to Coventry and keeps Lord Stanley, Lady Margaret's husband and the stepfather of Henry Tudor, close at his side. Stanley's son Lord Strange is not to be found at home. His servants say that he has massed an enormous army of his tenants and retainers and is marching to serve his master. Richard's worry is: nobody knows who that master might be.

Richard leads his forces south from Coventry, to cut off his betraying friend Buckingham from the uprising of our forces in the southern counties. He plans that Buckingham will cross the Severn River to enter England, and find no allies but the royal army waiting grimly for him in the pouring rain.

The troops move slowly down the churning mud of the roads. Bridges are washed away and they have to march extra miles to find a crossing. The horses of the officers and the mounted guard labour chest-deep in glutinous mud; the men march with their heads down, soaked to the skin, and at night when they rest they cannot light fires, for everything is wet.

Grimly, Richard drives them on, taking a little pleasure in knowing that the man he loved and trusted above all others, Henry Stafford, Duke of Buckingham, is also pushing his way through mud, through swollen rivers, through incessant rain. This must be bad weather for recruiting rebels, Richard thinks. This must be bad weather for the young duke who is no seasoned campaigner like Richard. This must be bad weather for a man dependent on allies from overseas. Surely Buckingham cannot hope that Henry Tudor has set sail in storms such as these, and he will not be able to get word of the Rivers forces in the southern counties.

Then the king hears good news. Buckingham is not only facing the driving rain which never stops, he is constantly attacked by the Vaughans of Wales. They are chieftains in this territory and they have no love for the young duke. He had hoped they would let him rise against Richard, perhaps even support him. But they have not forgotten that it was he who took Thomas Vaughan from his master the young king and executed him. At every turn of the road there are half a dozen of them, guns primed, ready to shoot the first rank of men and ride off. At every valley there are men hidden in trees throwing rocks, firing arrows, setting a shower of spears down through the rain into Buckingham's straggling force until the men feel that the rain and the spears are the same thing and that they are fighting an enemy like water, from which there is no escape, and which drives down mercilessly and never stops.

Buckingham cannot get his messengers to ride into Wales to bring out the Welsh men loyal to the Tudors. His scouts are cut down the moment they are out of sight of the main column so his army cannot swell with hard fighting men, as Lady Margaret promised him that it would. Instead, every night, and at every stop, and even in broad daylight on the road, his men are slipping away. They are saying he is an unlucky leader and that his campaign will be washed away. Every time they line up to march they are fewer; he can see the column on the drowned road does not stretch so long. When he rides up and down, cheering the men on, promising them victory, they don't meet his eyes. They keep their heads down as if his optimistic speech and the pelting of the rain are both the same meaningless noise.

Buckingham cannot know, but he guesses that Henry Tudor, the ally he plans to betray, is also beaten by the wall of water that never stops. He is pinned in port by the same storm which is blowing Buckingham's army away. Henry Tudor has five thousand mercenaries, a massive force, an unbeatable force, paid and armed by the Duke of Brittany – enough to take England on his own. He has knights and horse and cannon and five ships, an expedition that cannot fail – except for the wind and the pouring rain. The ships toss and yaw; even inside the shelter of the harbour, they twang at the mooring ropes. The men, packed inside for the short journey across the English sea, vomit with seasickness, miserable in the hold. Henry Tudor strides like a caged lion on the dockside, looking for a break in the clouds, for the wind to change. The skies pour down on his copper head without pity. The horizon is black with more rain, the wind is onshore, always onshore, keeping his ships shuddering against the harbour walls.

Just over the sea, he knows, his destiny is being decided. If Buckingham defeats Richard without him, he knows he will have no chance at the throne. One usurper will be changed for another, and he still in exile. He has to be there at the battle and kill whoever is the victor. He knows that he must set sail at once, but he cannot set sail: the rain pours down. He can go nowhere.

Buckingham cannot know this, he knows nothing. His life has shrunk to a long march in pouring rain, and every time he looks back over his shoulder there are fewer men behind him. They are exhausted, they have not eaten hot food for days, they are stumbling in knee-deep mud, and when he says to them, 'Soon be at the crossing, the crossing to England, and dry land, thank God,' they nod but don't believe him.

Their road rounds a corner to the crossing of the Severn River, where the waters are shallow and broad enough for the army to march into England and face their enemy instead of fighting the elements. Everyone knows this crossing point – Buckingham has been promising it for miles. The riverbed is firm and stoned, hard as a road, and the water is never more than inches deep. Men have been crossing to and from Wales at this point for centuries; it is the gateway to England. There is an inn on the Wales side of the river and a little village on the England side.They are expecting that the crossing will be flooded, the river running deep. Perhaps there will even be sandbags at the doorway of the inn, but when they hear the roar of the waters they halt as one man in utter horror.

There is no crossing. There is no land that they can see. The inn in Wales is drowned; the village on the far side has disappeared altogether. There is not even a river, it is out of its banks so far that it is a lake, a watery waste. They cannot see the far side: England. They cannot even see a downstream or an upstream. This is no longer a river but an inland sea with waves and its own storms. The water has taken the land, swallowed it as if it were never there. This is not England or Wales, this is water, this is triumphant water. The water has taken everything and no man is going to challenge it.

Certainly, no one can cross it. They look in vain for familiar landmarks, the track that ran into the shallows of the river, but it is deep underwater. Someone thinks they see something in the flood and with a shudder they realise that it is the tops of trees. The river has drowned a forest: the very trees of Wales are reaching wildly for air. The world is not as it was. The armies cannot meet; the water has intervened and conquered everything. Buckingham's rebellion is over.

Buckingham does not say a word, he does not give an order. He makes a little gesture with his hand, like a surrender, a palm-raised wave: not to his men but to this flood which has destroyed him. It is as if he concedes victory to the water, to the power of water. He turns his horse's head and he rides away from the vast churning deeps of it, and his men let him go. They know it is all over. They know the rebellion is finished, defeated by the waters of England which rose as if they had been summoned by the very goddess of water.

## NOVEMBER 1483

It is dark, almost eleven o'clock. I am on my knees, praying at the foot of my bed before I sleep, when I hear a light knock on the great outside door. At once my heart leaps, at once I think of my son Edward, of my son Richard, at once I think they are come home to me. I scramble to my feet, throw a cape over my night-gown, pull the hood over my hair, and run to the door.

I can hear the streets are quiet now, though all day they have been buzzing with the return of King Richard to London, and there has been endless talk of what revenge he will take on the rebels, whether he will break sanctuary and come against me, now he has proof that I raised the country against him. He knows this, and he knows the allies that I chose: Lady Margaret and the false Duke of Buckingham.

No one can tell me if my kinsmen are safe, captured, or dead: my three beloved brothers and my Grey son Thomas, who were riding with the rebels in Hampshire and Kent. I hear every sort of rumour: that they are run away to join Henry Tudor in Brittany, that they are dead in a field, that they are executed by Richard, that they have turned their coats and joined him. I have to wait, as does everyone in the country, for reliable news.

The rains have washed away roads, destroyed bridges, cut off whole towns. News comes into London in excitable bursts, and nobody can be sure what is true. But the storm has blown itself out; the rain has stopped now. When the rivers go back into their banks I will have news of my family and their battles. I pray that they have got far away from England. In the case of defeat, the plan was to go to Edward's sister Margaret in Burgundy, find my son Richard in his hiding place, and continue the war from overseas. King Richard will grip the country with the power of a tyrant now, I am sure.

There is a repeated tap on the door and someone rattles the latch. This is no frightened runaway, not my boy. I go to the great wooden portal and slide back the porter's grille and look out. It is a man, as tall as me, his hood pulled forward to hide his face.

'Yes?' I say shortly.

'I need to see the dowager queen,' he whispers. 'A message of great importance.'

'I am the dowager queen,' I say. 'Tell me your message.'

He glances from right to left. 'Sister, let me in,' he says.

Not for a moment do I think it is one of my brothers. 'I am no sister of yours. Who do you think you are?'

He pushes back the hood and lifts the torch that he carries so I can see his handsome dark face. Not my brother, but my brother-in-law, my enemy, Richard. 'I think I am the king,' he says with wry humour.

'Well, I don't,' I say without a smile; but it makes him laugh.

'Have done,' he advises me. 'It's over. I am ordained and crowned, and your rebellion has been utterly defeated. I am king, whatever your wishes. I am alone, and unarmed. Let me in, sister Elizabeth, for all our sakes.'

Despite all that has been, I do just that. I slide the bolts on the little lantern door and open it and he slips in. I bolt it behind him. 'What d'you want?' I ask. 'I have a serving man in earshot. There is blood between you and me, Richard. You killed my brother and you killed my son. I will never forgive you for it. I have laid my curse on you for it.'

'I don't expect your forgiveness,' he says. 'I don't even want it.

You know how far your plots went against me. You would have killed me, if you had the chance. It was war between us. You know as well as I. And you have had your revenge. You know and I know what pains you have given me. You have put an enchantment on me and my chest aches and my arm fails me without warning. My sword arm,' he reminds me. 'What could be worse for me? You have cursed my sword arm. You had better pray that you never need my defence.'

I look at him closely. He is only thirty-one now; but the shadows under his eyes and the lines in his face are those of an older man. He looks haunted. I imagine he fears his arm failing him in battle. He has worked hard all his life to be as strong as his taller, thicker-muscled brothers. Now something is eating away at his power. I shrug. 'If you are ill, you should see a physician. You are like a child, blaming your own weakness on magic. Perhaps you imagine it all.'

He shakes his head. 'I didn't come to complain. I came for something else.' He pauses, looks at me. He has that frank York look, he has my husband's straight gaze. 'Tell me, do you have your son Edward safe?' he asks me.

I can feel my heart thud with pain. 'Why do you ask? You, of all people? You who took him?'

'Will you just answer? Do you have Edward and Richard safe?'

'No,' I say. I could wail like a heartbroken mother; but not in front of this man. 'Why? Why d'you ask?'

He gives a sigh and slumps down in the porter's chair, drops his head into his hands.

'You don't have them in the Tower?' I ask him. 'My boys? You don't have them locked up?'

He shakes his head.

'You have lost them? You have lost my sons?'

Silent still, he nods. 'I was praying that you had smuggled them out,' he says. 'In the name of God, tell me! If you have done so, I will not hunt them, I will not harm them. You can choose a relic for me to swear on. I will swear to leave them wherever you have sent them. I won't even ask where. Just tell me that you have them safe, so I know, I have to know. It is driving me mad not to know.'

Wordlessly, I shake my head.

He rubs his face, his eyes, as if they are gritty with lack of sleep. 'I came straight to the Tower,' he says, speaking through his fingers. 'The minute I returned to London. I was afraid. Everyone in England is saying they are dead. Lady Margaret Beaufort's people have told everyone that the princes are dead. The Duke of Buckingham turned your army into his own, fighting to win the throne for him, by telling them that the princes were dead at my hand, and that they should have their revenge on me. He told them that he would lead them to avenge the princes' deaths.'

'You didn't kill them?'

'I did not,' he says. 'Why should I? Think! Think it through. Why should I kill them? Why now? When your men attacked the Tower I had them kept closer inside. They were watched night and day – I could not have killed them then, even if I had wanted to. They had guards all the time, one of them would have known, and they would tell. I have made them bastards and dishonoured you. Your sons are no more threat to me than your brothers – beaten men.'

'You killed my brother Anthony,' I spit at him.

'He was a threat to me,' Richard replies. 'Anthony could have raised an army and knew how to command men. He was a better soldier than me. Your sons are not. Your daughters are not. They don't threaten me. I don't threaten them. I don't kill them.'

'Then where are they?' I wail. 'Where is my boy Edward?'

'I don't even know if they are dead or alive,' he says miserably. 'Nor who ordered their death or capture. I thought you might have smuggled them out. That's why I came here. If not you – then who? Did you authorise anyone to take them? Could anyone have them without your knowledge? Holding them as hostage?'

I shake my head, I cannot think. It is the gravest question I will ever face in my life, and I am stupid with grief. 'I can't think,' I say desperately.

'Try,' he says. 'You know who your allies are. Your secret friends. My hidden enemies. You know what they might do. You know what they promised you, what you plotted with them. Think.'

I put my hands to my head, and I walk a few steps up and down. Perhaps Richard is lying to me, and he has killed Edward and the poor little pageboy, and is here to throw the blame on others. But against that – as he says – he has no reason to do so, and also, why should he not admit it, and brazen it out? Who would even complain now that he has put down the rebellion against him? Why come here to me? When my husband murdered King Henry he had his body shown to the people. He gave him a fine funeral. The whole point of killing him was to tell the world that the line was ended. If Richard had killed my sons to end Edward's line, he would have announced it, now as he returned to London in victory, and given me the bodies to bury. He could say they had fallen ill. Better yet, he could say that Buckingham killed them. He could throw the blame on Buckingham, and he could give them a royal funeral and no one could do anything but mourn them.

So perhaps the Duke of Buckingham had them killed, the truth behind his rumour of their deaths? With the two boys gone, he was two steps nearer to the throne. Or would Lady Margaret have them killed, to clear the way for her son Henry Tudor? Both Tudor and Buckingham are the greatest beneficiaries from the deaths of my sons. They become the next heirs if my boys are dead. Could Lady Margaret have ordered the deaths of my sons, while claiming to be my friend? Could she have squared her holy conscience to do such a thing? Could Buckingham have killed his own nephews while swearing to set them free?

'You have searched for their bodies?' I ask, my voice very low.

'I have turned the Tower upside down, and had their servants questioned. They say that they put them to bed one night. In the morning they were gone.'

'They are your servants!' I burst out. 'They follow your commands. My sons have died while in your keeping. Do you expect me to really believe you had no hand in their deaths? Do you expect me to believe they have vanished?'

He nods. 'I want you to believe that they died or they were taken, without my order, without my knowledge, and without my consent, while I was far away preparing to fight. To fight your brothers, actually. One night.'

'Which night?' I ask.

'The night that it started to rain.'

I nod, thinking of the soft voice that sang a lullaby to Elizabeth, so quiet that I could not even hear it. 'Oh, that night.'

He hesitates. 'Do you believe me, that I am innocent of their deaths?'

I face him, the man that my husband loved: his brother. The man who fought beside my husband for my family and my sons. The man who killed my brother and my Grey son. The man who may have killed my royal son Edward. 'No,' I say coldly. 'I don't believe you. I don't trust you. But I am not certain. I am horribly uncertain of everything.'

He nods, as if to accept an unjust judgement. 'It's like that for me,' he remarks, almost as an aside. 'I don't know anything, I don't trust anyone. We have killed certainty in these cousins' wars and all that is left is mistrust.'

'So what will you do?' I ask.

'I'll do nothing, and say nothing,' he decides, his voice is bleak and weary. 'No one will dare to ask me directly, though they will all suspect me. I shall say nothing and let people think what they will. I don't know what has happened to your boys; but nobody will ever believe that. If I had them alive I would produce them and prove my innocence. If I found their bodies I would show them and blame it on Buckingham. But I don't have them, alive or dead, and so I cannot defend myself. Everyone will think that

I have killed two boys in my care, in cold blood, for no good reason. They will call me a monster.' He pauses. 'Whatever else I do in my life, this will cast a crooked shadow. All that everyone will ever remember of me is this crime.' He shakes his head. 'And I didn't do it, and I don't know who did it, and I don't even know if it was done.'

He pauses. 'What will *you* do?' he asks as it occurs to him.

'I?'

'You were here in sanctuary so that your girls should be safe when you believed that their brothers were in danger from me,' he reminds me. 'That worst thing has now happened. Their brothers are now gone: what will you do with your girls, with yourself? There is no point in staying in sanctuary now – you are no longer the royal family with an heir who might make a claim. You are the mother of nothing but girls.'

As he says this, the loss of Edward suddenly hits me, and I give a moan, and take the pain in my belly, like the pangs of his birth all over again. I drop to my knees on the stone floor and I bend over my pain. I can hear myself groaning, and I can feel myself rocking.

He does not rush to comfort me, or even to raise me up. He stays seated in his chair, his dark head leaning on his hand, watching me as I keen like a peasant woman over the death of her firstborn son. He says nothing to deny my grief nor staunch it. He lets me cry. He sits beside me for a long long time and he lets me cry.

After a while, I take the hem of my cloak and I rub my wet face and then I sit back on my heels and look at him.

'I am sorry for your loss,' he says formally as if I were not kneeling on a stone floor with my hair falling down and my face wet with tears. 'It was not of my ordering, nor of my doing. I took the throne without harming either one of them. I would not have harmed them after. They were Edward's sons. I loved them for him. And God knows, I loved him.'

'I know that, at any rate,' I say, as formal as he.

He gets to his feet. 'Will you leave sanctuary now?' he asks. 'You have nothing to gain by staying here.'

'I have nothing,' I agree with him. 'Nothing.'

'I will make an agreement between you and me,' he says. 'I will promise the safety and good treatment of your girls if you come out. The older ones can come to court. I shall treat them as my nieces, honourably. You can come with them. I shall see them married to good men, with your approval.'

'I shall go home,' I say. 'And take them with me.'

He shakes his head. 'I am sorry, I can't allow that. I will have your girls at court, and you can live at Heytesbury in the care of Sir John Nesfield for a while. I am sorry, but I cannot trust you among your tenants and affinity.' He hesitates. 'I cannot have you where you might raise men against me. I cannot allow you to be where you would find men to plot with. It is not that I am suspicious of you, you understand: it is that I cannot trust anybody. I never trust anybody, anywhere.'

There is a footstep behind him, and he whirls around and draws his dagger to hold before him, ready to strike. I scramble up and put my hand on his right arm and push it easily down: he is terribly weak. I remember the curse I have laid on him. 'Put up,' I say. 'It will be one of the girls.'

He steps back and Elizabeth comes out of the shadows to my side. She is in her nightgown with a cape thrown over it and her hair in a plait under her nightcap. She is as tall as me now. She stands beside me and regards her uncle gravely. 'Your Grace,' she says with the smallest of curtseys.

He hardly bows to her; he is staring at her in amazement. 'You are grown, Elizabeth,' he hesitates. 'You are the Princess Elizabeth? I would hardly have known you. I last saw you when you were a girl and here you are . . . you.'

I glance at her, and to my amazement I see that the colour is rising in her cheeks. She is blushing under his bewildered look. She puts her hand to her hair, as if she wishes she were dressed and not barefoot like a child.

'Go to your room,' I say abruptly to her.

She curtseys and turns, obedient at once, but she pauses at the door. 'Is it about Edward?' she asks. 'Is my brother safe?'

Richard looks to me to see if she can be told the truth. I turn to her. 'Go to your room. I will tell you later.'

Richard rises to his feet. 'Princess Elizabeth,' he says quietly.

Again she stops though she has been told to leave, and she turns to him. 'Yes, Your Grace?'

'I am sorry to tell you that your brothers are missing; but I want you to know that it is no fault of mine. They are gone from their rooms in the Tower and nobody can tell me if they are alive or dead. I came here to your mother tonight in case she had smuggled them away.'

The quick glance she throws towards me would tell him nothing. I know she is thinking that at least our boy Richard is safely away in Flanders, but she is expressionless.

'My brothers are missing?' she repeats, wonderingly.

'They are likely dead,' I say, pain making my voice harsh.

'You don't know where they are?' she asks the king.

'I wish to God that I did,' he says. 'Without knowing where they are or if they are safe, everyone will think they are dead and blame me.'

'They were in your keeping,' I remind him. 'And why would anyone take them as hostages without telling? At the very least, you have let my boy die while you were fighting to keep the throne which was his by right.'

He nods as if to accept that much of the blame and turns to go. Elizabeth and I watch in silence as he unbolts the door.

'I won't forgive this wrong done to me and my house,' I warn him. 'Whoever it was that killed my boys, I shall put a curse on their house that they will have no firstborn son to inherit. Whoever took my son will lose his son. He will spend his life longing for an heir. He will bury his firstborn and long for him, for I cannot even bury mine.'

He shrugs his shoulders. 'Curse him, whoever did it,' he says indifferently. 'Blight his house. For he has cost me my reputation and my peace.'

'We two will curse him,' Elizabeth says, standing beside me, her arm around my waist. 'He will pay for taking our boy. He will regret this loss that he has dealt to us. He will be sorry for this terrible cruelty. He will suffer remorse. Even if we never know who did this.'

'Oh, but we will know him,' I chime in like a coven's chorus. 'We will know him by the death of his children. When his son and heir dies, we shall know him then. We shall know that the curse we lay on him now is working, all down the years, generation after generation, until his line dies out. When he puts his own son in the grave it will be our curse that buries him. And then we shall know who it was who took our boy, and he will know that our curse has taken from him what he took from us. When he has only girls to inherit, we will know him then.'

He steps through the doorway and looks back at the two of us, a wry smile twisting his mouth. 'Do you not know yet that there is only one thing worse than not getting your wish?' he asks. 'As I have done? I wished to be king and now I am king and it has brought me no joy at all. Elizabeth, has your mother not warned you to take care what you wish for?'

'She has warned me,' she says steadily. 'And since you took my father's throne, and took my uncle and my beloved brothers, I have learned to wish for nothing.'

'Then she would do well to warn you against the working of your curse.' He turns to me with a bitter smile. 'D'you not remember the wind that you whistled up to destroy Warwick, which blew him away from Calais so his daughter lost her baby at sea? That was a weapon for us that no one else could have summoned. But d'you not remember that the storm went on too long and nearly drowned your husband and all of us that were with him?'

I nod.

'Your curses last too long and strike at the wrong people,' he says. 'Maybe one day you will wish that my right arm was strong enough to defend you. Maybe one day you will regret the death of someone's son and heir, even if they were guilty, even if your curse runs true.'

The revenge of Richard the king falls heavily on the lords and leaders of the rebellion; he forgives the lesser men for having been misled. He discovers that Margaret Beaufort, the wife of his ally, Lord Stanley, was the mistress of the plot and the go-between for her son and the Duke of Buckingham, and he banishes her to her husband's house and orders her to be kept close. Her allies – Bishop Morton and Dr Lewis – escape out of the country. My son Thomas Grey has got clean away and is at the court of Henry Tudor in Brittany. It is a court of young men, hopeful rebels, filled with ambition and desire.

King Richard complains of my son Thomas Grey as a rebel and an adulterer, as if treason and love were both alike crimes. He charges him with treason and puts a price on his head. Thomas writes to me from Brittany and tells me that, if Henry Tudor could have landed, the rebellion would have gone our way for sure. Their fleet was scattered by the storm that Elizabeth and I called down on Buckingham's head. The young man who said he was coming to save us was nearly drowned. Thomas has no doubt that Henry Tudor can raise an army great enough to defeat even a York prince. He tells me that Henry will come again to England, as soon as the winter storms have died down, and that this time he will win.

*And put himself on the throne*, I write to my son. *There is no longer any pretence that he is fighting for the inheritance of my boys.*

My son replies: 'No, Henry Tudor fights for nobody but himself, and probably always did and always will. But the Prince, as he calls himself, will bring the crown to the House of York, for he will marry Elizabeth, and make her Queen of England, and their son will be King of England.

'Your son should have been King of England,' Thomas writes. 'But your daughter still could be queen. Am I to tell Henry that Elizabeth will marry him if he defeats Richard? It would bring all of our kinship and affinity to his side, and I cannot see what future you and my half-sisters have while the usurper Richard is on the throne, and while you are hiding in sanctuary.

I write back:

*Tell him, I am still as good as the word that I gave to his mother, Lady Margaret. Elizabeth will be his wife when he defeats Richard and takes the throne of England. Let York and Lancaster be as one and let the wars be over.*

I pause, and add a note.

*Ask him if his mother knows what happened to my boy Edward.*

# DECEMBER 1483

I wait till the turning of the year, the darkest night of the year, and I wait for the darkest hour, the hour between midnight and one, then I take a candle and throw a warm cape over my winter gown and tap on Elizabeth's door. 'I am going now,' I say. 'Do you want to come?'

She is ready. She has her candle and her cape with the hood pulled forward over her bright hair. 'Yes, of course. This is my loss too,' she says. 'I want revenge too. Those who killed my brother have put me a step closer to the throne, a step further away from the life I might have made for myself, and into the heart of danger. I don't thank them for that, either. And my brother was alone and unguarded, taken away from us. It would have to be someone made of stone to kill our prince and that poor little page-boy. Whoever it was has earned a curse. I will curse him.'

'It will be on his son,' I warn her, 'and his son after him. It will end their line.'

Her eyes shine green in the candlelight like a cat's eyes. 'So might it be,' she says, as her grandmother Jacquetta would say when she was cursing or blessing.

I lead the way and we go through the silent crypt, down the stone stairs to the catacombs, and then down again, another flight of cold stone stairs, icy damp underfoot, until we hear the lapping of the river at the water gate.

Elizabeth unlocks the iron door and together we pull it open. The river is high, at the level of a winter flood, dark and glassy, moving swiftly by us in the darkness of the night. But it is nothing to the storm that Elizabeth and I called up to keep Buckingham and Henry Tudor out of London. If I had only known that someone was coming for my son that night, I would have taken a boat on that flood and gone to him. I would have gone on the deep waters to save him.

'How shall we do this?' Elizabeth is shivering from the cold and from fear.

'We do nothing,' I say. 'We just tell Melusina. She is our ancestor, she is our guide, she will feel the loss of our son and heir as we do. She will seek out those who took him, and she will take their son in return.'

I unfold a piece of paper from my pocket and give it to Elizabeth. 'Read it aloud,' I say. I hold the two candles for her as she reads it to the swiftly moving waters.

'Know this, that our son Edward was in the Tower of London held prisoner most wrongly by his uncle Richard, now called king. Know this, that we gave him a companion, a poor boy, to pass for our second son Richard but got him away safe to Flanders, where you guard him on the River Scheldt. Know this, that someone either came and took our son Edward, or killed him where he slept; but, Melusina! we cannot find him, and we have not been given his body. We cannot know his killers, and we cannot bring them to justice nor, if our boy still lives, find him and bring him home to us.' Her voice quavers for a moment and I have to dig my nails into the palms of my hands to stop myself from crying.

'Know this: that there is no justice to be had for the wrong that someone has done to us, so we come to you, our Lady Mother, and we put into your dark depths this curse: that whoever took our firstborn son from us, that you take his firstborn son from him. Our boy was taken when he was not yet a man, not yet king – though he was born to be both. So take his murderer's son while he is yet a boy, before he is a man, before he comes to his estate. And then take his grandson too, and when you take him, we will know by his death that this is the working of our curse and this is payment for the loss of our son.'

She finishes reading and her eyes are filled with tears. 'Fold it like a paper boat,' I say.

Readily she takes the paper and makes a perfect miniature vessel; the girls have been making paper fleets ever since we were first entrapped here beside the river. I hold out the candle. 'Light it,' I whisper, and she holds the folded paper boat into the flame of the candle so the prow catches fire. 'Send it into the river,' I say and she takes the flaming boat and puts it gently on the water.

It bobs, the flame flickers as the wind blows it, but then it flares up. The swift current of the water takes it and it turns and swirls away. For a moment we see it, flame on reflected flame, the curse and the mirror of the curse, paired together on the dark flood, and then they are whirled away by the rush of the river and we are looking into blackness, and Melusina has heard our words and taken our curse into her watery kingdom.

'It's done,' I say and turn away from the river and hold the water gate open for her.

'That's all?' she asks as if she had expected me to sail down the river in a cockleshell.

'That's all. That's all I can do, now that I am queen of nothing, with missing sons. All I can do now is ill-wishing. But God knows, I do that.'

## CHRISTMAS 1483

I make merry for my girls. I send out Jemma to buy them new brocade and we sew new dresses, and they wear the last diamonds from the royal Treasury on their heads as crowns for Christmas day. The defeated county of Kent sends us a handsome capon, wine and bread for our Christmas feast. We are our own carollers, we are our own mummers, we are our own wassailers. When finally I put the girls to bed they are happy, as if they had forgotten the York court at Christmas when every ambassador said he had never seen a richer court, and their father was King of England and their mother the most beautiful queen the country had ever seen.

Elizabeth my daughter sits late with me before the fire, cracking nuts and throwing the shells into the red embers so they flare and spit.

'Your uncle Thomas Grey writes to me that Henry Tudor was going to declare himself King of England and your betrothed in Rennes cathedral today. I should congratulate you,' I say.

She turns and gives me her merry smile. 'I am a much married woman,' she says. 'I was betrothed to Warwick's nephew, and then to the heir of France, d'you remember? And you and Father called me La Dauphine, and I took extra lessons in French and thought myself very great. I was meant to be Queen of France, I was certain of it, and yet now look at me! So I think I shall wait till Henry Tudor has landed, fought his battle, crowned himself king and asked me himself before I count myself a betrothed woman.'

'Still, it is time you were married,' I say almost to myself, thinking of her rising blush when her uncle Richard said that she had grown so much he hardly knew her.

'Nothing can happen while we are in here,' she says.

'Henry Tudor is untested.' I am thinking aloud. 'He has spent his life running away from our spies, he has never turned and fought. The only battle he ever saw was under the command of his guardian William Herbert, and then he fought for us! When he lands in England with you as his declared bride then everyone who loves us will turn out for him. Everyone else will turn out for him for hatred of Richard, even though they hardly know Henry. Everyone who has been deprived of their places by the northerners that Richard brought in will turn out for him. The rebellion has left a sour taste for too many people. Richard won that battle but he has lost the trust of the people. He promises justice and freedom but since the rebellion he puts in northern lords and he rules with his friends. Nobody will forgive him that. Your betrothed will have thousands of recruits, and he will come with an army from Brittany. But it will all depend on whether he is as brave in battle as Richard. Richard is battle-hardened. He fought all over England when he was a boy, under the command of your father. Henry is new to the field.'

'If he wins, and if he honours his promise, then I will be Queen of England. I told you I would be Queen of England one day. I always knew it. It is my fate. But it was never my ambition.'

'I know,' I say gently. 'But if it is your destiny you will have to do your duty. You will be a good queen, I know. And I will be there with you.'

'I wanted to marry a man that I loved, as you did Father,' she says. 'I wanted to marry a man for love, not a stranger on the word of his mother and mine.'

'You were born a princess, and I was not,' I remind her. 'And even so, I had to take my first husband on the say-so of my father. It was only when I was widowed that I could choose for myself. You will have to outlive Henry Tudor and then you can do as you please.'

She giggles and her face lights up at the thought of it.

'Your grandmother married her husband's young squire the moment she was widowed,' I remind her. 'Or think of King Henry's mother, who married a Tudor nobody in secret. At least when I was a widow I had the sense to fall in love with the King of England.'

She shrugs. 'You are ambitious. I am not. You would never fall in love with someone who was not wealthy or great. But I don't want to be Queen of England. I don't want my poor brother's throne. I have seen the price that one pays for a crown. Father never stopped fighting from the day he won it, and here we are – trapped in little better than prison – because you still hope we can gain the throne. You will have the throne even if it means I have to marry a runaway Lancastrian.'

I shake my head. 'When Richard sends me his proposals we will come out,' I say. 'I promise you. It is time. You won't have another Christmas in hiding, I promise you, Elizabeth.'

'We don't have to come out to glory, you know,' she says plaintively. 'We could just go to a pleasant house, and be an ordinary family.'

'All right,' I say, as if I think we can ever be an ordinary family. We are Plantagenets. How could we be ordinary?

# JANUARY 1484

I hear from my son Thomas Grey, in a letter which comes to me travel-stained from Henry Tudor's ragamuffin court in Brittany, dated Christmas day 1483.

*As he promised, he swore to his betrothal to your daughter Elizabeth in the cathedral in Rennes. He also claimed the title of King of England and was acclaimed king by all of us. He received our homage and oaths of loyalty, mine among the others. I heard one man ask him how he could claim to be heir, when the young King Edward might be living for all we know. He said something interesting . . . he said that he had certain proof that the young King Edward is dead, and that his heart is sore for it, and that we should have revenge on his murderer – the usurper Richard. I asked him what proof he had, and reminded him of your pain without a son to bury, nor any knowledge of him; and he said that he knew for a fact that Richard's men had killed your boys. He said they had pressed them under their bedding as they slept, and then buried them under the stair in the Tower.*

*I took him to one side and said that at the very least we could place servants or suborn those who are there and order them to find the bodies if he would only tell me where they are, which stair in the Tower. I said that if we found the bodies as his invasion of England began, we could accuse Richard of murder, and the whole country would be on our side. 'Which stair?' I asked. 'Where are the bodies? Who told you of the murder?'*

*Lady Mother, I lack your skills of seeing into the dark hearts of men; but there was something about him that I couldn't like. He looked away, and said it was no good, he had thought of it already, but a priest had lifted their bodies and taken them away in a chest to give them a christian burial, and buried them in the deepest waters of the river, never to be found. I asked him the name of the priest but he did not know it. I asked him how the priest knew where they were buried and why he put them in the river instead of taking the bodies to you. I asked him if it was to be a christian burial then why put them in the water? I asked him which part of the river and he said he did not know. I asked him who told him all this, and he said it was his mother Lady Margaret, and that he would trust her with his life. It will be just as she has told him, he knows this for a fact.*

*I don't know what you make of this.*

*It stinks to me.*

I take Thomas's letter and put it into the flames of the fire that burns in the hall. I take up a pen to reply to him, trim the nib, nibble the feather at the top, and then write.

*I agree. Henry Tudor and his allies must have had a hand in the death of my son. How else would he know they were dead and how it was done? Richard is to release us this month. Get away from the Tudor pretender and come home. Richard will pardon you and we can be together. Whatever vows Henry takes in church and however many men show him homage, Elizabeth will never marry the murderer of her brothers, and if he is indeed the killer then he carries my curse to his son and his grandson. No Tudor boy will live to manhood if Henry had a hand in the death of my son.*

The end of the twelve days of Christmas and the return of the Parliament to London brings me the unwelcome news that Parliament has obliged King Richard and ruled that my marriage was invalid, that my children are bastards and that I myself am a whore. Richard had declared this before, and no one had argued with him. Now it is law and the Parliament, like so many moppets, nods it through.

I don't make any objection to the Parliament, and I don't command any friends of mine to object for us. It is the first step in freeing us from our hiding place that has become our prison. It is the first step in turning us into what Elizabeth calls 'ordinary people'. If the law of the land says that I am nothing more than the widow of Sir Richard Grey, and the former king's former lover, if the law of the land says that my children are merely girls born out of wedlock, then we are of little value alive or dead, imprisoned or free. It does not matter to anyone where we are, or what we are doing. This on its own sets us free.

More importantly, I think, but I do not say, not even to Elizabeth, that once we are living in a private house quietly my boy Richard might be able to join us. As we are stripped of our royalty my son might be with me again. When he is no longer a prince, I might get him back. He has been Peter, a boy living with a poor family in Tournai. He could be Peter, a visitor to my house at Grafton, my favourite pageboy, my constant companion, my heart, my joy.

# MARCH 1484

I receive a message from Lady Margaret. I had been wondering when I would hear again from this my dearest friend and ally. The storming of the Tower which she planned failed miserably. Her son tells the world that my sons are dead, and says that his mother alone knows the details of their death and burial. The rebellion which she masterminded ended in defeat and my suspicions. Still her husband is high in favour with King Richard, though her part in the rebellion is well known. For sure, she is an unreliable friend and a doubtful ally. She seems to know everything, she seems to do nothing, and she is never punished.

She explains she has not been able to write, and that she cannot visit me herself, for she is cruelly imprisoned by her husband Lord Stanley, who was Richard's true friend, standing by him in the recent uprising. It turns out now that Stanley's son Lord Strange raised a small army in support of King Richard; and that all the whispers that he was marching to support Henry Tudor were mistaken. His loyalty was never in doubt. But there were enough men to testify that Lady Margaret's agents had gone back and forth to Brittany to summon her son Henry Tudor to claim the throne for himself. There were spies who could confirm that her great counsellor and friend Bishop Morton persuaded the Duke of Buckingham to turn against his lord Richard. And there were even men who could swear that she had made a pact with me, that my daughter should marry her son, and the proof of that was Christmas day in Rennes cathedral when Henry Tudor declared that he would be Elizabeth's husband and swore that he would be King of England; and all his entourage, my son Thomas Grey among them, knelt and swore fealty to him as King of England.

I imagine that Margaret Beaufort's husband Stanley must have had to talk fast and persuasively to convince his anxious monarch that, though his wife is a rebel and a plotter, he himself had never for a moment thought of the advantages that might come to him if his stepson took the throne. But he seems to have done it. Stanley *Sans Changer* remains in favour with the usurper, and Margaret his wife is banished to her own house, forbidden her usual servants, banned from writing or sending messages to anyone – especially her son – and robbed of her lands and wealth and inheritance. But they are all given to her husband on the condition that he keeps her under control.

For a powerful woman she does not seem much disheartened by her husband taking all her wealth and all her lands into his own hands, and imprisoning her in her house, swearing that she shall never write another letter and never stir another plot. She is clearly right not to be too disheartened, for here she is, writing to me and plotting again. From this I think I can assume that Stanley *Sans Changer* is faithfully and loyally following his own best interests as perhaps he has always done – promising fealty to the king on one hand, letting his wife plot with rebels on the other.

*Your Grace, dear sister – for so I should call you who is mother to the girl who will be my daughter, and who will be mother to my son,* she starts. She is flowery in style and emotional in life. There is a smudge on the letter as if she has overflowed with tears of joy at the thought of the wedding of our children. I look at it with distaste. Even if I did not suspect her of the wickedest of betrayals, I would not warm to this.

*I am much concerned to hear from my son that your son Thomas Grey thought to leave his court and had to be persuaded to return to them. Your Grace, dear sister, what can be the matter with your boy? Can you assure him that the interests of your family and mine are the same and that he is a beloved companion to my son Henry? Please, I beg of you, command him as a loving mother to endure the troubles that they have in exile to make certain of the rewards when they triumph. If he has heard anything, or fears anything, he should speak to my son Henry Tudor, who can put his mind at rest. The world is full of gossips and Thomas would not want to appear a turncoat or a faint-heart now.*

*I hear nothing, locked away as I am, but I understand that the tyrant Richard is planning to have your older girls at his court. I do beg you not to allow them to go. Henry would not like his betrothed to be at the court of his enemy, exposed to every temptation, and I know you as a mother would feel such revulsion to have your daughter in the hands of the man who murdered your two sons. Think of putting your girls in the power of the man who murdered their brothers! They themselves must be unable to bear the sight of him. Better to stay in sanctuary than force them to kiss his hand and live under the command of his wife. I know you will feel this as I do: it is impossible.*

*For your own sake at least, command your girls to stay with you quietly in the country if Richard will release them, or peacefully in sanctuary if he will not, until that Happy Day when Elizabeth shall be queen of her own court and my beloved daughter as well as yours.*

*Your truest friend in all the world, imprisoned just as you are,*
*Lady Margaret Stanley*

I take the letter to my Elizabeth and watch her smile broaden until she laughs outright. 'Oh my God, what a crone!' she exclaims.

'Elizabeth! This is your mother-in-law to be!'

'Yes, on that Happy Day. Why does she not want us to go to court? Why do we have to be protected from temptation?'

I take back the letter and reread it. 'Richard will know that you are betrothed to Henry Tudor. Tudor announced it so that everybody knows. Richard knows that will put the Rivers affinity on Tudor's side. The House of York follows you now. You are our only heir. It would be in his interest to take all you girls to court and marry you well within his own family and friends. That way Tudor is isolated once more, and you York heiresses are all married to commoners. The last thing Lady Margaret wants is you dancing off with some handsome lord, leaving her Henry looking like a fool, without his bride and without your supporters.'

She shrugs. 'As long as we get out of here, I am happy to live with you in the country, Lady Mother.'

'I know,' I say. 'But Richard wants you older girls at court where people can see you are safe in his keeping. You and Cecily and Anne shall go, and Bridget and Catherine will stay with me. He will want people to know that I allowed you be with him, that I consider you safe in his care. And I would rather you were out in the world than cooped up at home.'

'Why?' she asks, turning her grey gaze on me. 'Tell me. I don't like the sound of this. You will be plotting something, Lady Mother, and I don't want to be in the centre of plots any more.'

'You are the heir to the House of York,' I say simply. 'You will always be at the centre of plots.'

'But where will you go? Why won't you come to court with us?'

I shake my head. 'I couldn't bear to see that skinny stick Anne Neville in my place, wearing my gowns cut down to her size with my jewels around her scrawny neck. I couldn't curtsey to her as Queen of England. I couldn't do it, Elizabeth, not to save my life. And Richard will never be a king to me. I have seen a true king and loved him. I have been a true queen. These are mere imposters to me – I cannot bear them.

'I am to be put in the charge of John Nesfield who has guarded us here. I will live at his manor of Heytesbury and I think it will suit me very well. You can go to court and you girls can get a little court training. It is time you were away from your mother and out in the world.'

She comes to me like a little girl, and kisses me. 'I shall like it better than being a prisoner,' she says. 'Though it will be so strange to be away from you. I have never been away from you in all my life.' Then she pauses. 'But will you not be lonely? Won't you miss us too much?'

I shake my head and draw her close to whisper, 'I won't be lonely, for I hope that Richard will come home. I hope to see my boy again.'

'And Edward?' she asks.

I meet her hopeful gaze without evasion. 'Elizabeth, I think he must be dead, for I cannot see who would have taken him and not told us. I think Buckingham and Henry Tudor must have had both of the boys killed, not knowing that we had Richard safely hidden, thinking to open their way to the throne and put the blame on King Richard. If Edward is alive, then pray God he will find his way to me. And there will always be a candle in the window to light his way home, and my door will never be locked, in case one day it is his hand on the latch.'

Her eyes are filled with tears. 'But you don't expect him any more?'

'I don't expect him,' I say.

## APRIL 1484

My new home of Heytesbury is in a pretty part of the country, Wiltshire, in the open rolling countryside of Salisbury Plain. John Nesfield is an easy guardian. He sees the benefits of being at the side of the king; he doesn't really want to play nursemaid over me. Once he was assured of my safety and judged that I would not attempt to run away, he took himself off to the king at Sheriff Hutton, where Richard has established his great court in the north. He is making a palace fit to match Greenwich among the people of the north who respect him and love his wife, the last Neville.

Nesfield orders that I am to run his house as I please and very quickly I have the furniture and things around me that I request from the royal palaces. I have a proper nursery and a schoolroom for the girls. I am growing my favourite fruits in the gardens, and I have bought some good horses for the stables.

After so many months in sanctuary I wake every morning with a sense of utter delight that I can open the door and walk out into the air. It is a warm spring and to hear the birds singing, to order a horse from the stables and ride out is a joy so intense that I feel reborn. I set duck's eggs under the hens and watch the ducklings hatch and waddle about the yard. I laugh when I see them take to the duck pond with the hens scolding on the bank, fearful of water. I watch the young foals in the paddock and talk with the master of horse as to which might make a good riding horse and which should be broke to the cart. I go out in the fields with the shepherd and see the new lambs. I talk with the cowman about the little calves and when they should be weaned from their mothers. I become again what I was once before, an English country lady with her mind on the land.

The younger girls go half mad in their release from confinement. Every day I catch them doing something forbidden: swimming in the swift deep river, climbing the haystacks and ruining the hay, up in the apple trees breaking off the blossom, running into the field with the bull and dashing to the gate, screaming when he lifts his big head and looks at them. They cannot be punished for such an overflow of joy. They are like calves released into the field for the first time in their lives. They have to kick up their heels and run about, and don't know what to do to express their amazement at the height of the sky and the wideness of the world. They are eating twice what they ate in sanctuary. They hang around the kitchen and badger the cook for scraps, and the dairymaids delight in giving them fresh-churned butter to eat on hot bread. They have become light-hearted children again, no longer prisoners, afraid of the very light.

I am in the stable yard, dismounting after a morning ride, when I am surprised to see Nesfield himself ride up to the main door of the house and, seeing my horse, he turns to come round to the yard and gets off his hunter, throwing the reins to a groom. From the very way he dismounts, heavily and with his shoulders bowed, I know that something bad has happened. My hand goes out to my horse's neck and I take a handful of thick mane for comfort.

'What is it, Sir John? You look very grave.'

'I thought I should come and tell you the news,' he says shortly.

'Elizabeth? Not my Elizabeth?'

'She is safe and well,' he assures me. 'It is the king's son, Edward, God keep him, God bless him. God take him to his heavenly throne.'

I feel a pulse in my temple hammer like a warning. 'He is dead?'

'He was always frail,' Nesfield says brokenly. 'He was never a strong boy. But at the investiture he looked so well we called him Prince of Wales and thought he was certain to inherit—' He breaks off, remembering that I too had a son who was Prince of Wales and seemed certain to inherit. 'I am sorry,' he said. 'I did not mean . . . anyway, the king has announced mourning for the court. I thought you should know at once.'

I nod gravely, but my mind is racing. Is this a death from Melusina? Is this a working of the curse? Is this the proof that I said we would see – that the son and heir of the murderer of my son and heir would die, and thus I would know him? Is this her sign to me that Richard is the killer of my son?

'I will send the king and Queen Anne my sympathy,' I say and turn to go to the house.

'He has no heir,' John Nesfield repeats as if he cannot believe the gravity of the news he has brought me. 'All this, all that he has done, his defence of the kingdom, his . . . his acceptance of his throne, all this that he has done, all the fighting . . . and now he has no heir to follow him.'

'Yes,' I agree, my words like frozen stones. 'He did all this for nothing, and he has lost his son and his line will die out.'

I hear from my daughter Elizabeth that the court falls into mourning as if it was an open grave, and none of them can bear to live without their prince. Richard will not hear laughter or music, they have to creep about with their eyes on the ground and there are no games or sports, though the weather is getting warmer and they are in the very heart of greening England, the hills and the dales all around them are teeming with game. Richard is inconsolable. His twelve-year marriage to Anne Neville gave him only one child, and now he has lost him. It cannot be possible that they will have another at this late stage and, even if they do, a baby in the cradle is no guarantee of a Prince of Wales in this savage England that we Yorks have made. Who knows better than Richard that a boy must be fully grown and strong enough to fight for his rights, to fight for his life, if he is to be King of England?

He names as his heir Edward the son of his brother, George of Clarence, the only York boy known to be left in the world; but in a few months I hear a rumour that he is to be disinherited. This comes as no surprise to me. Richard has realised that the boy is too weak to hold the throne, as we all knew. George, Duke of Clarence had a fatal mixture of vanity and ambition and outright madness: no son of his could be a king. He was a sweet smiling baby but slow of wit, poor child. Anyone who wants the throne of England will have to be fast as a snake and wise as a serpent. He will have to be a boy born to be a prince, reared in a court. He will have to be a boy accustomed to danger, raised to be brave. George's poor half-wit boy could never do it. But if not him, then who? For Richard must name an heir and leave an heir and the House of York is now nothing but girls, for all that Richard knows. Only I know for sure that there is a prince, like one in a fairy tale, waiting in Tournai, living like a poor boy, studying his books and music, learning languages, watched over at a distance by his aunt. A flower of York, growing strong in foreign soil and biding his time. And now he is the only heir to the York throne, and if his uncle knew he was alive perhaps he would name him as his heir.

I write to Elizabeth.

*I hear the news from court and I am troubled by one thing – do you think that the death of Richard's son is Melusina's sign to us that Richard is the murderer of our boys? You see him daily – do you think he knows it is our curse which is his destruction? Does he look like a man who has brought this grief on his own family? Or do you think that this death was just chance, and it was another man who killed our boy, and it will be his son who must die for our revenge?*

## JANUARY, 1485

I am waiting for my girls to come home from court on a frosty afternoon in the middle of January. I expected them in time for dinner and I am striding up and down on my doorstep, blowing on my gloved fingers to keep my hands warm as the sun sets, red as a Lancaster rose, over the hills to the west. I hear hoofbeats and I look down the lane and there they come, a great guard for my three girls, almost a royal guard, and the three bobbing heads and rippling dresses in the middle. In a moment their horses are pulled up and they have tumbled off and I am kissing bright cheeks and cold noses quite indiscriminately and holding their hands and exclaiming at how tall they have grown and how all equally beautiful they are.

They romp into the hall and fall on their dinner as if they are starving and I watch them as they eat. Elizabeth has never been in better looks. She bloomed, once out of sanctuary and out of fear, as I knew she would. The colour is high in her cheeks, her eyes sparkle, and her clothes! I take another disbelieving look at her clothes: the embroidery and the brocade, the insetting of precious stones. These are gowns as good as I wore when I was queen. 'Good God, Elizabeth,' I say. 'Where do you get your gowns from? This is as fine as anything I had when I was Queen of England.'

Her eyes fly to mine and her smile dies on her face. Cecily

gives an abrupt snort of laughter. Elizabeth rounds on her. 'You can shut your mouth. We agreed.'

'Elizabeth!'

'Mother, you don't know what she has been like. She is not fit to be maid-in-waiting to a queen. All she does is gossip.'

'Now girls, I sent you to court to learn elegance, not to quarrel like fishwives.'

'Ask her if she's been learning elegance!' Cecily whispers loudly. 'Ask Elizabeth how elegant she is.'

'I certainly shall, when we are talking and you two are in bed,' I say firmly. 'And that will be early if you cannot speak politely one to another.' I turn from her to Anne. 'Now, Anne.' My little Anne looks up at me. 'Have you been studying your books? And have you been working at your music?'

'Yes, Lady Mother,' Anne says obediently. 'But we were all given a holiday at Christmastide, and I went to court at Westminster with all the others.'

'We had suckling pig here,' Bridget tells her older sisters solemnly. 'And Catherine ate so much marchpane she was sick in the night.'

Elizabeth laughs, and that anxious look has gone from her. 'I have missed you little monsters,' she says tenderly. 'After dinner I shall play, and you can dance, if you like.'

'Or we can play at cards,' Cecily offers. 'The court is allowed cards again.'

'Has the king recovered from his grief?' I ask her. 'And Queen Anne?'

Cecily shoots a triumphant look at her sister Elizabeth, who blushes deep red. 'Oh, he has recovered,' Cecily says, her voice quivering with laughter. 'He seems much recovered. We are all quite amazed. Don't you think, Elizabeth?'

My patience, which never lasts very long with female spite, even when it is my own daughter's, is exhausted at this point. 'Now that is enough,' I say. 'Elizabeth, come to my privy chamber now, the rest of you can eat your dinner, and you Cecily can ponder on the proverb that one good word is worth a dozen bad ones.'

I rise from the table and sweep from the room. I can feel Elizabeth's reluctance as she follows me and when we get to my room she shuts the door and I say simply to her, 'My daughter, what is all this about?'

For a second only she looks as if she would resist and then she quivers like a doe at bay and says, 'I have so wanted your advice, but I could not write to you. I had to wait till I saw you. I meant to wait till after dinner. I have not deceived you, Lady Mother . . .'

I sit down and gesture that she may sit beside me. 'It is my uncle Richard,' she says softly. 'He is – oh Lady Mother – he is everything to me.'

I find I am sitting very still. Only my hands have moved and I am gripping them together to keep myself silent.

'He was so kind to me when we first came to court, then he went out of his way to make sure that I was happy with my duties as a maid-in-waiting. The queen is very kind, a very easy mistress to serve, but he would seek me out and ask me how I was doing.' She breaks off. 'He asked me if I missed you and told me you would be welcome at court any time, and the court would honour you. He would speak of my father,' she says. 'He would remark how proud my father would be of me if he could see me now. He would say that I am like him in some ways. Oh Mother, he is such a fine man, I can't believe that he . . . that he . . .'

'That he?' I echo her, my voice a little thread of an echo.

'That he cares for me.'

'Does he?' I feel icy, as if wintry waters are running down my spine. 'Does he care for you?'

She nods eagerly. 'He never loved the queen,' she says. 'He felt obliged to marry her to save her from his brother George, Duke of Clarence.' She glances at me. 'You would remember. You were there, weren't you? They were going to trap her and send her to a nunnery. George was going to steal her inheritance.'

I nod. I don't remember it quite like that; but I can see this makes a better story for an impressionable girl.

'He knew that if George took her as his ward then he would take her fortune. She was anxious to be married and he thought it was the best thing that he could do. He married her to secure her inheritance and for her own safety, and to put her mind at ease.'

'Really,' I say. My recollection is that George had one Neville heiress and Richard snapped up the other and they quarrelled like stray dogs over the inheritance. But I see that Richard has told my daughter the more chivalrous version of the story.

'Queen Anne is not well.' Elizabeth bows her head to whisper. 'She cannot have another child, he is certain of it. He has asked the doctors and they are sure she will not conceive. He has to have an heir for England. He asked me if I thought it possible that one of our boys had got away safely.'

My mind suddenly sharpens like a sword throwing sparks on a whetstone. 'And what did you say?'

She smiles up at me. 'I would trust him with the truth, I would trust him with anything; but I knew you would want me to lie,' she says sweetly. 'I said we knew nothing but what he had told us. And he said again that it had broken his heart but he did not know where our boys are. He said if he knew now, he would make them his heirs. Mother, think of it. He said that. He said that if he knew where our boys were, he would rescue them and make them his heirs.'

Oh would he? I think. But what guarantee do I have that he does not send an assassin? 'That's good,' I say steadily. 'But even so, you must not tell him about Richard. I cannot trust him yet, even if you can.'

'I do!' she exclaims. 'I do trust him. I would trust him with my life itself – I have never known such a man.'

I pause. Pointless to remind her that she has known no men. Most of her life she has been a princess kept like a statue of porcelain in a box of gold. She came of age as a prisoner, living with her mother and her sisters. The only men she ever saw were priests and servants. She has had no preparation for an attractive man working on her emotions, seducing her, urging her to love.

'How far has this gone?' I ask bluntly. 'How far has this gone between the two of you?'

She turns her head away. 'It's complicated,' she says. 'And I feel so sorry for Queen Anne.'

I nod. My girl's pity for Queen Anne will not stop her from taking her husband is my guess. After all, she is my daughter. And nothing stopped me when I named my heart's desire.

'How far has this gone?' I ask her again. 'From Cecily, I take it that there is gossip.'

She flushes. 'Cecily doesn't know anything. She sees what everyone sees, and she is jealous of me getting all the attention. She sees the queen favouring me, and lending me her gowns and her jewels. Treating me as a daughter and telling me to dance with Richard, urging him to walk with me, to ride with me when she is too ill to go out. Truly, Mother, it is the queen herself who commands me to go and keep him company. She says that no one can divert him and cheer him as I do, and so the court says that she favours me overmuch. That he favours me overmuch. That I am nothing more than a maid-in-waiting but I am treated as . . .'

'As what?'

She bows her head to whisper. 'The first lady at court.'

'Because of your gowns?'

She nods. 'They are the queen's own gowns; she has mine made to her pattern. She likes us to dress the same.'

'It is she who dresses you like this?'

Elizabeth nods. She has no idea that this fills me with unease. 'You mean she has gowns for you made from her own material? To her own style?'

My girl hesitates. 'And, of course, she does not look well in them.' She says no more but I think of Anne Neville, grief-stricken, weary, ill, side by side with this blooming girl.

'And you are first into the room behind her? You have precedence?'

'No one speaks of the law which made us bastards. Everyone calls me princess. And when the queen does not dine, and often she does not, then I go into dinner as the first lady and I sit beside the king.'

'So, it is Queen Anne who puts you into his company, even into her own place, and the world sees this. Not Richard? Then what happens?'

'He says that he loves me,' she says quietly. She is trying to be modest but her pride and her joy blaze in her eyes. 'He says that I am the first love of his life and will be the last.'

I rise from my chair and go to the window and pull back the thick curtain so I can look out at the bright cold stars over the dark land of the Wiltshire down. I think I know what Richard is doing, and I don't for one minute think that he has fallen in love with my daughter, nor that the queen is making gowns for her out of love.

Richard is playing a hard game with my daughter as pawn, to dishonour her, and me, and to make a fool of Henry Tudor, who has vowed to make her his wife. Tudor will hear – as quickly as his mother's spies can take ship – that his bride to be is in love with his enemy and is known throughout the court as his mistress while his wife looks on smiling. Richard would do this to damage Henry Tudor even though he dishonours his own niece. Queen Anne would be compliant rather than stand up to Richard. Both Neville girls were boot-scrapers to their men: Anne has been an obedient servant from the first day of her marriage. And besides, she cannot refuse him. He is King of England without a male heir and she is barren. She will be praying that he does not put her aside. She has no power at all: no son and heir, no baby in the cradle, no chance of conception, she has no cards to play at all. She is a barren woman with no fortune of her own – she is fit for nothing but the nunnery or the grave. She has to smile and obey; protests will get her nowhere. Even helping in the destruction of my daughter's reputation will probably earn Anne nothing more than an honourable annulment.

'Has he told you to break off your betrothal to Henry Tudor?' I ask her.

'No! It's nothing to do with that!'

'Oh,' I nod. 'But you can see that this will be a tremendous humiliation for Henry Tudor when the news gets out.'

'I would never marry him anyway,' she bursts out. 'I hate him. I believe it was he who sent the men to kill our boys. He would have come to London and taken the throne. We knew that. That's why we called down the rain. But now . . . but now . . .'

'Now what?'

'Richard says that he will put Anne Neville aside and marry me,' she breathes. Her face is alight with joy. 'He says that he will make me his queen and my son will sit on my father's throne. We will make a dynasty of the House of York and the white rose will be the flower of England for ever.' She hesitates. 'I know you cannot trust him, Lady Mother, but this is the man I love. Can you not love him for my sake?'

I think that this is the oldest, hardest question between a mother and her daughter. Can I love him for your sake?

No. This is the man who envied my husband, who killed my brother and my son Richard Grey, who seized my son Edward's throne and who exposed him to danger, if nothing worse. But I need not answer the truth to this my most truthful child. I need not be open with this most transparent child. She has fallen in love with my enemy and she wants a happy ending.

I open my arms to her. 'All I ever wanted was your happiness,' I lie. 'If he loves you and will be true to you, and you love him, then I want nothing more.'

She comes into my arms and she lays her head on my shoulder. But she is no fool, my daughter. She lifts her head and smiles at me. 'And I shall be Queen of England,' she says. 'At least that will please you.'

My daughters stay with me for nearly a month and we live the life of an ordinary family, as Elizabeth once wanted. In the second week it snows and we find Nesfield's sleigh and harness up one of the carthorses and make an expedition to one of the neighbours, and then find the snow has melted and we have to stay the night. The next day we have to trudge home in the mud and the slush as they cannot lend us horses and we take turns to ride bareback on our own big horse. It takes us the best part of the day to get home and we laugh and sing all the way.

In the middle of the second week there is a messenger from court and he brings a letter for me, and one for Elizabeth. I call her to my private chamber, away from the girls, who have invaded the kitchen and are making marchpane sweetmeats for dinner, and we open our letters at either end of the writing table.

Mine is from the king.

*I imagine Elizabeth will have spoken with you about the great love I bear her, and I wanted to tell you of my plans. I intend that my wife shall admit she is past the years of childbearing and take residence in Bermondsey Abbey and release me from my vows. I will seek the proper dispensations and then marry your daughter and she will be Queen of England. You will take the title of My Lady, the Queen's Mother and I will restore to you the palaces of Sheen and Greenwich on our wedding day, with your royal pension. Your daughters will live with you and at court, and you shall have the arranging of their marriages. They will be recognised as sisters to the Queen of England and of the royal family of York.*

*If either of your sons has been in hiding and you know of his whereabouts, then you may now send for him in safety. I will make him my heir until Elizabeth gives birth to my son.*

*I will marry Elizabeth for love, but I am sure you can see that this is the resolution of all our difficulties. I hope for your approval but I will proceed anyway. I remain your loving kinsman.*

*RR*

I read the letter through twice and I find a grim smile at his dishonest phrasing. 'Resolution of all our difficulties' is, I think, a smooth way of describing a blood vendetta which has taken my brother and my Grey son, and which led me to foment rebellion against him and curse his sword arm. But Richard is a York – they take victory as their due – and these proposals are good for me and mine. If my son Richard can come home in safety and be a prince once more at the court of his sister, then I will have achieved everything that I swore to regain, and my brother and my son will not have died in vain.

I glance down the table at Elizabeth. She is rosy with blushes and her eyes are filled with luminous tears. 'He proposes marriage?' I ask her.

'He swears that he loves me. He says he is missing me. He wants me back at court. He asks you to come with me. He wants everyone to know that I will be his wife. He says that Queen Anne is ready to retire.'

I nod. 'I won't go while she is there,' I say. 'And you may go back to court but you are to behave with more discretion. Even if the queen tells you to walk with him you are to take a companion. And you are not to sit in her place.'

She is about to interrupt but I raise my hand. 'Truly, Elizabeth, I don't want you being named as his mistress, especially if you hope to be his wife.'

'But I love him,' she says simply, as if that is all that matters.

I look at her and I know my face is hard. 'You can love him,' I say. 'But if you want him to marry you and make you his queen you will have more to do than simply loving.'

She holds his letter to her heart. 'He loves me.'

'He may do, but he will not marry you if there is a whisper of gossip against you. Nobody gets to be Queen of England by being lovable. You will have to play your cards right.'

She takes a breath. She is no fool, my daughter, and she is a York through and through. 'Tell me what I have to do,' she says.

# FEBRUARY 1485

I bid my daughters farewell on a dark day in February and watch their guard trot off through the mist which swirls around us for all of the day. They are out of sight in moments, as if they had disappeared into cloud, into water, and the thud of the hoofbeats is muffled and then silenced.

The house seems very empty without the older girls. And in missing them, I find my thoughts and my prayers go to my boys, my dead baby George, my lost boy Edward, and my absent boy Richard. I have heard nothing of Edward since he went into the Tower, and nothing of Richard since that first letter when he told me he was doing well and answering to the name Peter.

Despite my own caution, despite my own fears, I start to hope. I start to think that if King Richard marries Elizabeth and makes her his queen I will be welcomed at court again, I will take up my place as My Lady, the Queen's Mother. I will make sure that Richard is trustworthy, and then I will send for my son.

If Richard is true to his word and names him as his heir then we will be restored: my son in the place he was born to, my daughter as Queen of England. It will not have come out as Edward and I thought it would when we had a Prince of Wales and a Duke of York and we thought, like young fools, that we would live for ever. But it will have come out well enough. If Elizabeth can marry for love and be Queen of England, if my son can be king, after Richard, then it will have come out well enough.

When I am at court, and in my power, I shall set men to find the body of my son, whether it is under the convenient stair – as Henry Tudor assures us – or buried in the river, as he corrects himself, whether it has been left in some dark lumber room, or is hidden on holy ground in the chapel. I shall find his body, and trace his killers. I shall know what took place: whether he was kidnapped and died by accident in the struggle, whether he was taken away and died of ill health, whether he was murdered in the Tower and buried there, as Henry Tudor is so very certain. I shall learn of his end, and bury him with honour, and order masses for his soul to be said for ever.

# MARCH 1485

Elizabeth writes to me briefly of the queen's worsening health. She says no more – she need say no more – we both realise that if the queen dies there will be no need for an annulment or the settlement of Queen Anne in an abbey; she will be out of the way in the easiest and most convenient way possible. The queen is afflicted with sorrows, she weeps for hours without cause, and the king does not come near her. My daughter records this as the queen's loyal maid-in-waiting and does not tell me if she slips from the sick-chamber to walk with the king in the gardens, if the buttercups in the hedgerow and the daisies on the lawn remind her and him that life is fleeting and joyful, just as they remind the queen that it is fleeting and sad.

Then one morning in the middle of March I awake to a sky unnaturally dark, to a sun quite obscured by a circle of darkness. The hens won't come out of their house, the ducks put their heads under their wings and squat on the banks of the river. I take my two little girls outside and we wander uneasily, looking at the horses in the field who lie down and then lumber up again, as if they don't know whether it is night or day.

'Is it an omen?' asks Bridget, who of all of my children seeks to see the will of God in everything.

'It is a movement of the heavens,' I say. 'I have seen it happen with the moon before, but never with the sun. It will pass.'

'Does it mean an omen for the House of York?' Catherine echoes. 'Like the three suns at Towton?'

'I don't know,' I say. 'But I don't think any of us are in danger. Would you feel it in your heart, if your sister was in trouble?'

Bridget looks thoughtful for a moment then, prosaic child, she shakes her head. 'Only if God spoke to me very loud,' she says. 'Only if He shouted and the priest said it was Him.'

'Then I think we have nothing to fear,' I say. I have no sense of foreboding, though the darkened sun makes the world around us eerie and unfamiliar.

Indeed, it is not for three days that John Nesfield comes riding to Heytesbury with a black standard before him and the news that the queen, after a long illness, is dead. He comes to tell me but he makes sure to spread the news throughout the country, and Richard's other servants will be doing the same. They will all emphasise that there has been a long illness, and the queen has at last gone to her reward in heaven, mourned by a devoted and loving husband.

'Of course, some say she was poisoned,' Cook says cheerfully to me. 'That's what they're saying in Salisbury market, anyway. The carrier told me.'

'How ridiculous! Who would poison the queen?' I ask.

'They say it was the king himself,' the Cook says, putting her head to one side and looking wise as if she knows great secrets of the court.

'Murder his wife?' I ask. 'They think he would murder his wife of a dozen years? All of a sudden?'

The Cook shakes her head. 'They don't have a good word to say of him in Salisbury,' she remarks. 'They liked him well enough at first and they thought he would bring justice and fair wages for the common man, but since he puts northern lords over everything – well, there's nothing they would not say against him.'

'You can tell them that the queen was always frail, and that she never recovered from the loss of her son,' I say firmly.

The Cook beams at me. 'And am I to say nothing about who he might take as his next queen?'

I am silent. I had not realised that gossip had gone so far. 'And nothing about that,' I say flatly.

I have been waiting for this letter ever since they brought me the news that Queen Anne was dead and the world was saying that Richard would marry my daughter. It comes, tearstained as always, from the hand of Lady Margaret.

*To Lady Elizabeth Grey*
*Your Ladyship,*

*It has come to my notice that your daughter Elizabeth, the declared bastard of the late King Edward, has sinned against God and her own vows and dishonoured herself with her uncle the usurper Richard, a process so wrong and unnatural that the very angels hide their gaze. Accordingly I have advised my son Henry Tudor, rightful King of England, that he should not bestow his hand in marriage on such a girl alike dishonoured by act of parliament and by her own behaviour, and I have arranged for him to marry a young lady of birth far superior and of behaviour far more christian.*

*I am sorry for you that in your widowhood and your humiliation you should have to bow your head under yet another sorrow, the shame of your daughter, and I assure you that I shall think of you in my prayers when I mention the foolish and the vain of this world.*

*I remain your friend in Christ,*
*To whom I pray for you in your old age that you may learn true wisdom and womanly dignity,*
*Lady Margaret Stanley*

I laugh at the pomposity of the woman, but as my laughter drains away I feel cold, a shiver of cold, a foreboding. Lady Margaret has spent her life waiting for the throne that I called my own. I have every reason to think that her son Henry Tudor will also go on waiting for the throne of England, calling himself king, drawing to him the outcasts, the rebels, the disaffected: men who cannot live in England. He will go on haunting the York throne until he is dead, and it may be better that he should be brought to battle and killed sooner rather than later.

Richard, especially with my daughter at his side, can face down any criticism and should certainly win any battle against any force that Henry could bring. But the cold prickling of the nape of my neck tells me otherwise. I pick up the letter again and I feel the iron conviction of this Lancaster heiress. This is a woman whose belly is filled with pride. She has been eating nothing but her own ambition for nearly thirty years. I would do well to be wary of her now that she has decided that I am so powerless she need not pretend friendship any more.

I wonder who she intends for Henry's wife now? I guess she will be casting about for an heiress, maybe the Herbert girl, but nobody but my daughter can bring the love of England and the loyalty of the York House to the Tudor claimant. Lady Margaret may vent her spite but it does not matter. If Henry wants to rule England he will have to ally with York; they will have to deal with us one way or another. I take up my pen.

*Dear Lady Stanley,*

*I am sorry indeed to read that you have been listening to such slander and gossip and that this should cause you to doubt the good faith and honour of my daughter Elizabeth, which is, as it has always been, above question. I have no doubt that sombre reflection on your part, and on his, will remind you and your son that England has no other York heiress of her importance.*

*She is beloved of her uncle as she was beloved of her aunt, as she should be; but only the whispers of the gutter would suggest any impropriety.*

*I thank you for your prayers, of course. I will assume that the betrothal stands for its many manifest advantages; unless you seriously wish to withdraw, which I think so unlikely that I send you my best wishes and my thanks for your prayers, which I know are especially welcome to God coming from such a humble and worthy heart.*
*Elizabeth R*

I sign 'Elizabeth R', which I never do these days; but as I fold the paper and drip wax and stamp it with my seal I find I am smiling at my arrogance. 'Elizabeth Regina,' I say to the parchment. 'And I shall be My Lady, the Queen's Mother while you are still Lady Stanley with a son dead on the battlefield. Elizabeth R. So take that,' I say to the letter. 'You old gargoyle.'

## APRIL 1485

*Mother, you must come to court*, Elizabeth writes to me in a letter smudged in haste, folded twice and double-sealed.

*It is all going terribly wrong. His Grace the king thinks he must go to London and tell the lords that he will not marry me, that he has never had any intention of marrying me, in order to scotch the rumours that he poisoned the poor queen. Wicked people are saying that he was determined to marry me and would not wait for her death or agreement, and now he thinks he has to announce that he is nothing to me but my uncle.*

*I have told him that there is no need for such a declaration, that we could wait in silence for the gossip to die down but he listens only to Richard Ratcliffe and William Catesby, and they swear that the north will turn against him if he insults the memory of his wife, a Neville of Northumberland.*

*Worse, he says that for my reputation I have to go away from court, but he won't allow me to come to you. He is sending me to visit Lady Margaret and Lord Thomas Stanley of all terrible people. He says that Lord Thomas is one of the few men that he can trust to keep me safe, whatever happens; and no one can doubt that my reputation is perfect if Lady Margaret takes me into her house.*

*Mother, you have to stop this. I cannot stay with them: I shall be tormented by Lady Margaret, who must think I have betrayed my betrothal to her son, and who is bound to hate me for her son's sake. You must write to Richard, or even come to court yourself, and tell him that we will be happy, that all will be well, that all we have to do is to wait out this time of gossip and rumour and we can marry in the end. He has no advisors that he can trust, he has no Privy Council who would tell him the truth. He is dependent on these men that they call the Rat and the Cat and they fear that I will influence him against them, for revenge for what they did to our kin.*

*Mother I love him. He is my only joy in this world. I am his in heart and in thoughts and in body and all. You said to me that it would take more than love for me to become Queen of England: you have to tell me what to do. I cannot go to live with the Stanleys. What am I to do now?*

In truth, I don't know what she is to do, poor little girl of mine. She is in love with a man whose survival depends on him being able to command the loyalty of England and, if he were to tell England that he hopes to marry his niece before his wife is cold in the ground, he will have donated the whole of the north to Henry Tudor, in a moment. They won't take kindly to an insult to Anne Neville, quick or dead, and the north is where Richard has always drawn his strength. He will not dare to offend the men of Yorkshire or Cumbria, Durham or Northumberland. He cannot even risk it, not while Henry Tudor recruits men and raises his army and waits only for the spring tides.

I tell the messenger to get some food, to sleep the night and be ready to take my reply in the morning, and then I walk by the river and listen to the quiet sound of the water over the white stones. I hope that Melusina will speak to me, or that I will find a twist of thread with a ring shaped like a crown trailing in the water; but I have to come home without any message, and I have to write to Elizabeth with nothing to guide me but my years at court, and my own sense of what Richard can dare.

*Daughter,*

*I know how distressed you are – I hear it in every line. Be brave. This season will tell us everything, and everything will be changed by this summer. Go to the Stanleys and do your best to please them both. Lady Margaret is a pious and determined woman; you could not ask for a guardian more likely to scotch scandal. Her reputation will render you as spotless as a virgin, and that is how you must appear – whatever happens next.*

*If you can like her, if you can endear yourself to her all the better. It is a trick I never managed; but at the very least live pleasantly with her, for you will not be with her for long.*

*Richard is putting you in a safe place, far from scandal, far from danger, until Henry Tudor makes his challenge for the throne and the battle is over. When this happens, and Richard wins, as I think he must, he will be able to fetch you from the Stanleys' house with honour, and marry you as part of the celebrations of victory.*

*Dearest daughter, I don't expect you to enjoy a visit to the Stanleys but they are the best family in England for you to show that you acknowledge your betrothal to Henry Tudor and that you are living chastely. When the battle is over and Henry Tudor is dead then nobody can say a word against you, and the disapproval of the north can be faced down. In the meantime, let Lady Margaret think that you are happy in your promise to Henry Tudor, and that you are hopeful of his victory.*

*This will not be an easy time for you, but Richard has to be free to summon his men and fight his battle. As men have to fight, women have to wait and plan. This is your time for waiting and planning and you must be constant and discreet. Honesty matters so much less.*

*My love and blessing to you,*
*Your Mother*

Something wakes me early, at dawn. I sniff at the air as if I were a hare sitting up on my hind legs in a meadow. Something is happening, I know it. Even here, inland in Wiltshire, I can smell that the wind has changed, almost I can smell the salt from the sea. The wind is coming from the south, due south; it is a wind for an invasion, an onshore wind, and somehow I know, as clearly as if I could see them, the crates of weapons being loaded to the deck, the men striding down the gangplanks and jumping to the boats, the standards furled and propped in the prow, the men-at-arms mustering on the dock. I know that Henry has his force, his ships at the dockside, his captains plotting a course: he is ready to sail.

I wish I could know where he will land. But I doubt that he knows himself. They will untie fore and aft, they will throw the lines on board, they will raise the sails and the half-dozen ships will nose their way out of shelter of the port. As they get to the sea the sails will billow, the sheets crack and the boats rise and fall on the choppy waves, but then they will steer as best they can. They might head for the south coast – rebels always get a good welcome in Cornwall or Kent – or they might head for Wales, where the name of Tudor can bring out thousands. The wind will catch them and take them and they will have to hope for the best, and when they see land, calculate where they have arrived, and then beat up the coast to find their safest haven.

Richard is no fool – he knew this would come as soon as the winter storms died down. He is in his great castle at Nottingham, at the centre of England, calling out his reserves, naming his lords, prepared for the challenge that he knew would come this year, as it would have come last year but for the rain that Elizabeth and I blew up to keep Buckingham from London and away from my boy.

This year, Henry comes with a following wind: the battle has to be met. The Tudor boy is of the House of Lancaster and this is the final battle in the cousins' war. There is no doubt in my mind that York will win, as York mostly does. Warwick has gone – even his daughters Anne and Isabel are dead – there is no great Lancaster general left. There is only Jasper Tudor and

Margaret Beaufort's boy against Richard in his power with all the levies of England. Both Richard and Henry are without heirs. Both know that they themselves are their only cause. Both know that the war will be ended with the death of the other. I have seen many battles in my time as a wife and a widow in England, but never one as clear-cut as this. I predict a short and brutal battle and a dead man at the end of it and the crown of England, and the hand of my daughter, to the winner.

And I expect to see Margaret Beaufort don black to mourn the death of her son.

Her sorrow will be the start of a new life for me and mine. At last, I think I can send for my son Richard. I think it is time.

I have been waiting to set this part of my plan in motion for two years, ever since I had to send my boy away. I write to Sir Edward Brampton, loyal Yorkist, great merchant, man of the world and sometime pirate. Certainly a man who is not afraid of a little risk and who relishes an adventure.

He arrives on the very day that Cook is gabbling the news that Henry Tudor has landed. Tudor's ships were blown ashore to Milford Haven and he is marching through Wales recruiting men to his standard. Richard is levying men and marching out of Nottingham. The country is at war once more, and anything could happen.

'Troubled times again,' Sir Edward says to me urbanely. I meet him far from the house, on the banks of the river, where a willow copse shields us from the passing track. Sir Edward's horse and mine crop the short grass companionably as we stand, both of us looking for the flicker of brown trout in the clear water. I am right to keep us out of sight: Sir Edward is a striking man, richly dressed, black-haired. He has always been a favourite of mine, a godson of Edward my husband who sponsored his baptism out of Jewry. He always loved Edward for being his godfather; and I would trust him with my life, or with something more precious than life itself. I trusted him when he commanded the ship to take Richard away, and I trust him now, when I hope he will bring him back.

'Times that I think might be to the good of me and mine,' I observe.

'I am at your service,' he says. 'And the country is so distracted by the summoning of the levies that I think I might do anything for you, unobserved.'

'I know,' I smile at him. 'I don't forget that you served me once before, when you took a boy on board your ship to Flanders.'

'What can I do for you this time?'

'You can go the town of Tournai, in Flanders,' I say. 'To the St Jean Bridge. The man who keeps the water gate there is called Jehan Werbecque.'

He nods, committing the name to his memory. 'And what will I find there?' he asks, his voice very low.

I can hardly speak the secret that I have held in silence for so long. 'You will find my son,' I say. 'My son Richard. You will find him and bring him to me.'

His grave face lifts to me, his brown eyes shining. 'It is safe for him to return? He will be restored to his father's throne?' he asks me. 'You have made an agreement with King Richard and Edward's boy will be king in his turn?'

'God willing,' I say. 'Yes.'

*Melusina, the woman who could not forget her element of water, left her sons with her husband, went away with her daughters. The boys grew to be men, dukes of Burgundy, rulers of Christendom. The girls inherited their mother's Sight and her knowledge of things unknown. She never saw her husband again, she never ceased to miss him; but at the hour of his death, he heard her singing for him. He knew then, as she knew always, that it does not matter if a wife is half fish, if a husband is all mortal. If there is love enough, then nothing – not nature, not even death itself – can come between two who love each other.*

It is midnight, the time we agreed, and I hear the quiet knock at the kitchen door and go down with my candle shielded by my hand to open the door. The fire casts a warm glow over the kitchen, the servers are asleep in the straw in the corners of the room. The dog lifts his head as I go by, but no one else sees me.

The night is warm, it is still, the candle does not flicker as I open the door and pause to see a big man and a boy, an eleven-year-old boy, on the doorstep.

'Come in,' I say quietly. I lead them into the house, up the wooden stairs to my privy chamber, where the lamps are lit and the fire is burning brightly and there is wine poured, waiting in the glasses.

Then I turn, and put down my candle with trembling hands, and look at the boy that Sir Edward Brampton has brought to me. 'Is it you? Is it really you?' I whisper.

He has grown, his head comes up to my shoulder, but I would know him anywhere for his hair, bronze like his father's, and his eyes, hazel. He has his familiar crooked smile and a boyish way of hanging his head. When I reach for him he comes into my arms as if he were still my little boy, my second son, my longed-for boy, who was born into peace and plenty and always thought the world an easy place.

I sniff at him as if I were a mother cat finding a lost kitten. His skin smells the same. His hair is scented with someone else's pomade, and his clothes are salty-smelling from the voyage but the skin of his neck and behind his ears has the smell of my boy, my baby. I would have known him anywhere for my boy.

'My boy,' I say and I can feel my heart heave with love for him. 'My boy,' I say again. 'My Richard.'

He puts his arms around my waist and hugs me tightly. 'I have been on ships, I have been all over, I can speak three languages,' he says, muffled, his face against my shoulder.

'My boy.'

'It's not so bad now. It was strange at first. I have learned music and rhetoric. I can play the lute quite well. I have written a song for you.'

'My boy.'

'They call me Piers. That's Peter in English. They call me Perkin as a nickname.' He pulls back from me and looks into my face. 'What will you call me?'

I shake my head, I cannot speak.

'Your Lady Mother will call you Piers for the time being,' Sir Edward rules from the fireplace, where he is warming himself. 'You are not restored to your own yet. You have to keep your Tournai name for now.'

He nods. I see that his identity has become like a coat to him; he has learned to put it on or off. I think of the man who made me send this little prince into exile and made him hide in a boatman's house, and sent him to school as a scholarship boy, and I think that I will never forgive him, whoever he may be. My curse is on him, and his firstborn sons will die, and I will have no remorse.

'I will leave you two,' Sir Edward says tactfully.

He takes himself off to his room and I sit in my chair by the fire and my boy pulls up a footstool and sits beside me, sometimes leaning back against my legs so that I can stroke his hair, sometimes turning around to explain something to me. We talk of his absence, of what he has learned while he has been away from me. His life has not been that of a royal prince but he has been given a good education – trust to Edward's sister Margaret for that. She sent money to the monks as a scholarship for a poor boy; she specified that he must be taught Latin and law, history and the rules of governance. She had him taught geography and the boundaries of the known world, and – remembering my brother Anthony – she had him taught arithmetic and Arabic learning, and the philosophy of the Ancients.

'And when I am older, Her Grace Lady Margaret says that I will come back to England and take up my father's throne,' my boy says to me. 'She says that men have waited longer and with worse chances than me. She says look at Henry Tudor thinking he has a chance now, Henry Tudor who had to run away from England when he was younger than me, and now comes back with an army!'

'He has had a lifetime in exile. Pray God, you will not.'

'Are we going to see the battle?' he asks eagerly.

I smile. 'No, a battlefield is no place for a boy. But when Richard wins and marches to London we will join him and your sisters.'

'And I can come home then? Do I come back to court? And be with you for always?'

'Yes,' I say. 'Yes. We will be together again, as we should be.'

I reach out and stroke his fringe of fair hair from his eyes. He sighs and puts his head on my lap. For a moment we are very still. I can hear the old house creaking around us as it settles for the night, and somewhere out in the darkness an owl is calling.

'And what of my brother Edward?' he asks very quietly. 'I have always hoped you had him in hiding, somewhere else.'

'Has Lady Margaret said nothing? Sir Edward?'

'They say that we don't know, that we cannot be sure. I thought that you would know.'

'I am afraid he is dead,' I say gently. 'Murdered by men in the pay of the Duke of Buckingham and Henry Tudor. I am afraid your brother is lost to us.'

'When I am grown I will avenge him,' he says proudly, a York prince in every way.

I put my hand gently on his head. 'When you are grown and if you are king you can live in peace,' I say. 'I will have taken vengeance. It is not for you. It is finished. I have masses said for his soul.'

'But not for mine!' he says with his cheeky boyish grin.

'Yes, for yours, for I have to keep up a pretence just as you do, I have to pretend that you are lost to me as he is, but when I pray for you at least I know that you are alive and safe and will come home. And besides, it will do you no harm to have the good women of Bermondsey Abbey praying for you.'

'They can pray to bring me safely home again then,' he says.

'They do,' I say. 'We all do. I have prayed for you three times a day since you went, and I think of you every hour.'

He leans his head against my knees and I run my fingers through his blond hair. At the back, behind his ears, it is curly; I can wind the curls around my fingers like golden rings. It is only when he gives a little snore like a puppy that I realise we have sat for hours and he is fast asleep. It is only when I feel the weight of his warm head against my knees that I realise he is truly home, a prince come to his kingdom; and that, when battle is met and won, the white rose of York will bloom once more in the green hedgerows of England.

# BIBLIOGRAPHY

Baldwin, David, *Elizabeth Woodville: Mother of the Princes in the Tower,* Sutton Publishing, 2002

Baldwin, David, *The Lost Prince: The Survival of Richard of York,* Sutton Publishing, 2007

Castor, Helen, *Blood & Roses: The Paston family and the Wars of the Roses,* Faber and Faber, 2004

Cheetham, Anthony, *The Life and Times of Richard III,* Weidenfield & Nicolson, 1972

Chrimes, S. B., *Henry VII,* Harvard Monarchs Series, Eyre Methuen, 1972

Chrimes, S. B., *Lancastrians, Yorkists, and Henry VII,* Macmillan, London, 1964

Cooper, Charles Henry, *Memoir of Margaret: Countess of Richmond and Derby,* Cambridge University Press, 1874

Crosland, Margaret, *The Mysterious Mistress: The Life & Legend of Jane Shore,* Sutton Publishing, 2006

Fields, Bertram, *Royal Blood: King Richard III and the Mystery of The Princes,* Regan Books, 1998

Gairdner, James, 'Did Henry VII Murder the Princes?', *English Historical Review*: VI, 1891

Goodman, Anthony, *The Wars of the Roses: Military Activity and English Society, 1452–97,* Routledge & Kegan Paul, 1981

Goodman, Anthony, *The Wars of the Roses: The Soldiers' Experience,* Tempus, 2006.

Hammond, P. W., and Sutton, Anne F., *Richard III: The Road to Bosworth Field,* Constable, 1985

Harvey, Nancy Lenz, *Elizabeth of York: Tudor Queen,* Arthur Baker, 1973

Hicks, Michael, *Anne Neville: Queen to Richard III,* Tempus, 2007

Hicks, Michael, *Richard III,* Tempus, 2003

Hicks, Michael, *The Prince in the Tower: The Short Life & Mysterious Disappearance of Edward V,* Tempus, 2007

Jones, Michael K., and Underwood, Malcolm G., *The King's Mother; Margaret Beaufort: Countess of Richmond and Derby,* Cambridge University Press, 1992

Kendall, Paul Murray, *Richard the Third,* Norton and Company, 1975

MacGibbon, David, *Elizabeth Woodville 1437–1492: Her Life and Times,* Arthur Baker, 1938

Mancini, D., Cato, A., Armstrong, C.A.J., *The Usurpation of Richard the Third: Dominicus Mancinus Ad Angelum Catonem De Occupatione Regni Anglie per Ricardum Tercium Libellus,* Clarendon, 1969

Markham, Clements, R., 'Richard III: A Doubtful Verdict Reviewed', *English Historical Review: VI,* 1891

Neillands, Robin, *The Wars of the Roses,* Cassell, 1992

Plowden, Alison, *The House of Tudor,* Weidenfield & Nicolson, 1976

Pollard, A. J., *Richard III and the Princes in the Tower,* Sutton Publishing, 2002

Prestwich, Michael, *Plantaganet England 125–1360,* Clarendon, 2005

Reed, Conyers, *The Tudor: Personalities & Practical Politics in 16th Century England,* Oxford University Press, 1936

Ross, Charles, *Edward IV,* Harvard Monarchs Series, Eyre Methuen, 1974

Ross, Charles, *Richard III,* Harvard Monarchs Series, Eyre Methuen, 1981

Seward, Desmond, *A Brief History of The Hundred Years War,* Constable and Company, 1973

Seward, Desmond, *Richard III: England: Black Legend,* Country Life Books, 1983

Simon, Linda, *Of Virtue Rare: Margaret Beaufort: Matriarch of the House of Tudor,* Houghton Mifflin Company, 1982

St Aubyn, Giles, *The Year of Three Kings 1483,* Collins, 1983

Thomas, Keith, *Religion and the Decline of Magic,* Weidenfeld & Nicolson, 1971

Weir, Alison, *Lancaster & York: The Wars of the Roses,* Jonathan Cape, 1995

Weir, Alison, *The Princes in the Tower,* Bodley Head, 1992

Willamson, Audrey, *The Mystery of the Princes,* Sutton Publishing, 1978

Williams, Neville, *The Life and Times of Henry VII,* Weidenfeld & Nicolson, 1973

Wilson-Smith, Timothy, *Joan of Arc: Maid, Myth and History,* Sutton Publishing, 2006

Wroe, Ann, *Perkin: A Story of Deception,* Cape, 2003

# AUTHOR'S NOTE

This new novel, the first of a series about the Plantagenets, came from my discovery of one of the most interesting and thought-provoking queens of England: Elizabeth Woodville. Most of the story that I tell here is fact not fiction – she lived a life far beyond even my imagination! She was indeed the famously beautiful descendant of the Dukes of Burgundy, who cherished the tradition that they were descended from Melusina, the water goddess. When I discovered this fact I realised that in Elizabeth Woodville, a rather disregarded and disliked queen, I would be able to re-write the story of a queen of England who was also the descendant of a goddess and the daughter of a woman tried and found guilty of witchcraft.

Given my own interest in the medieval view of magic, of what it tells us about women's power, and of the prejudice that powerful women meet, I knew this was going to be rich terrain for me as a researcher and writer – and so it has been.

We know that Elizabeth first met Edward with a request for financial help, and that she married him in secret, but their meeting on the road as she stood under an oak tree (which is still growing at Grafton Regis, Northamptonshire, today) is a popular legend and may or may not be true. Her drawing of his dagger to save herself from rape was a contemporary rumour; we don't know it was historical fact. But much of her life with Edward was well-recorded, and I have drawn on the histories and based my novel on the facts wherever they exist. Of course, sometimes I have to choose from rival and contradictory versions, and sometimes I have to fill in the gaps of history with explanation or accounts of my own making.

There is more fiction in this novel than in my previous ones, since we are further back in time than the Tudors, and the record is more patchy. Also, this was a country at war and many decisions were taken on the spot, leaving no documentary record. Some of the most important decisions were secret plots and often I have had to deduce from the surviving evidence the reasons for particular actions, or even what took place. For example, we have no reliable evidence as to the so-called 'Buckingham Plot', but we know that Lady Margaret Stanley, her son Henry Tudor, Elizabeth Woodville, and the Duke of Buckingham were the main leaders of the rebellion against Richard. Clearly, they all had very different reasons for the risks they took. We have some evidence of the go-betweens, and some idea of the plans, but the exact strategy and command structure of the plot was secret and remains so. I looked at the surviving evidence and the consequences of the plot and I suggest here how it may have been put together. The supernatural element of the real-life rain storm is, of course, fiction, and was a joy to imagine.

Equally, we don't know even now (after hundreds of theories) exactly what happened to the princes in the Tower. I speculate that Elizabeth Woodville would have prepared a safe haven for her second son, Prince Richard, after her first son, Prince Edward, was taken from her. I genuinely doubt that she would have sent her second son into the hands of the man she suspected of imprisoning the first. The provocative suggestion, by many serious historians, that Prince Richard might have survived, led me to speculate that she might not have sent him to the tower at all, but used a changeling to take his place. But I have to warn the reader that there is no hard evidence for this.

Again, there is no definitive evidence as to how the boys met their deaths, if they did; nor who gave the order, and of course, there are still no bodies positively identified as those of the princes. I suggest that King Richard would not have murdered the boys, as there was little to gain and much to lose for him; and I don't believe that Elizabeth Woodville would have put her daughters in his care if she had thought him the murderer of her sons. It seems also that she recalled her son Thomas Grey from the court of Henry Tudor, which perhaps indicates that she was disenchanted with the Tudor claim, and allying with Richard. All this remains a genuine mystery and I merely add my suggestion to the many others proposed by historians, some of which you can find in the books listed in the Bibliography.

I am indebted to the scholar Professor David Baldwin, author of *Elizabeth Woodville: Mother of the Princes in the Tower*, both for his clear and understanding portrayal of the queen in his book, and for his advice on this novel, and I am grateful also to the many historians and enthusiasts whose studies are based on their love for this period, which I now share, and I hope you do too.

More information about the research and writing of this book can be found on my website, PhilippaGregory.com, where there are also details of seminars on this book which I give on tour in the UK , US and worldwide, and as regular webcasts.